Praise for Richard S. Wheeler

"Skye is one of the most memorable
figures in Western fiction since
Max Brand's Destry."

—*Tulsa World*

"Wheeler's Westerns just keep
getting better and better."

—*Publishers Weekly*

"Pages strong as sun-hardened adobe."

—*Kirkus Reviews* on *The Deliverance*

"Wheeler is a master storyteller whose many
tales of the Westward Movement . . . weave fact,
fiction, and folklore into pure entertainment."

—*Library Journal*

BY RICHARD S. WHEELER
FROM TOM DOHERTY ASSOCIATES

Aftershocks

Anything Goes

Badlands

The Buffalo Commons

Cashbox

Eclipse

The Exile

The Fields of Eden

Fool's Coach

Goldfield

Masterson

Montana Hitch

An Obituary for Major Reno

The Richest Hill on Earth

Second Lives

Sierra

Snowbound

Sun Mountain: A
    Comstock Novel

Where the River Runs

Skye's West

Sun River

Bannack

The Far Tribes

Yellowstone

Bitterroot

Sundance

Wind River

Santa Fe

Rendezvous

Dark Passage

Going Home

Downriver

The Deliverance

The Fire Arrow

The Canyon of Bones

Virgin River

North Star

The Owl Hunt

The First Dance

Sam Flint

Flint's Gift

Flint's Truth

Flint's Honor

The Deliverance

· AND ·

The Fire Arrow

RICHARD S.
WHEELER

A TOM DOHERTY ASSOCIATES BOOK · NEW YORK

This is a work of fiction. All of the characters, organizations, and events portrayed in these novels are either products of the author's imagination or are used fictitiously.

THE DELIVERANCE AND THE FIRE ARROW

The Deliverance copyright © 2003 by Richard S. Wheeler

The Fire Arrow copyright © 2006 by Richard S. Wheeler

A Forge Book
Published by Tom Doherty Associates
120 Broadway
New York, NY 10271

www.tor-forge.com

Forge® is a registered trademark of Macmillan Publishing Group, LLC.

ISBN 978-1-250-16565-7

Our books may be purchased in bulk for promotional, educational, or business use. Please contact your local bookseller or the Macmillan Corporate and Premium Sales Department at 1-800-221-7945, extension 5442, or by email at MacmillanSpecialMarkets@macmillan.com.

First Edition: July 2019

Printed in the United States of America

0 9 8 7 6 5 4 3 2 1

CONTENTS

THE DELIVERANCE
1

THE FIRE ARROW
317

The Deliverance

For Jean Sandberg, who suggested it.

1

With the quickening of the grass, the Cheyenne woman came once again to Bent's Fort. Barnaby Skye saw her from a great distance, a small, blue-blanketed woman crouched in her usual spot just outside the massive gate where she could watch every mortal who entered or left. He knew her sad story; everyone in the post did.

He had been out hunting, along with his Crow wife he had named Victoria, and now they were returning at sundown with a groaning wagonload of buffalo meat, butchered and wrapped in the hide against the year's first green flies.

He rode his shaggy, winter-haired buckskin down the slight grade and out upon the velvet-grassed bottoms of the Arkansas River, which severed the plains and two nations as well. He hoped to escape the sharp March wind that reddened and chafed his flesh, but he knew it would harry him clear to the post and even into his rooms.

William Bent's great adobe post lorded over a riverside pasture on the Mountain Branch of the Santa Fe Trail, just within United States territory, a lonely outpost hundreds of miles from settlements; a haven and refuge for weary travelers; a source of white men's magic for the Indians.

Victoria drove the mule team that was hauling the remains

of two skinny cow buffalo. Poor doings. This hard day's toil would supply the post with meat for barely a day, but the buffalo were scarce and had wintered down to bones and hide.

The Cheyenne woman saw them coming but didn't move; it was only when strangers arrived, a Missouri wagon train, or St. Louis teamsters, or Santa Fe muleteers, or a band of Kiowas or Utes or Arapahos or Jicarillas riding in for some trading, that she stirred. Thus it had been ever since Skye arrived in the fall of 1838; thus it was now in the spring of 1841.

Her name was Standing Alone. He wondered whether the winter in Black Dog's camp had been good to her; whether her copper flesh had withered prematurely, or her jet hair had grayed, or whether her stocky Cheyenne body had begun to shrink with her sorrow. She wasn't old; perhaps upper twenties, early thirties, but her ordeal had added twenty years, and she peered at the world from eyes that had seen centuries of torment.

She would soon be given some of this very meat. William Bent himself saw to it. Once each day, Archibald the cook took a wooden bowl full of scraps through the creaking cottonwood gate, and handed her whatever was that day's fare. She would eat swiftly, nod her thanks, and settle again at her post, to continue her vigil. Some said she was there because she never got over the tragedy and was obsessed. Others said that she was there because she had received those instructions in a sacred vision. Injun hoodoo, they called it. There was also the possibility that she was mad. Her husband, Cloud Watcher, respected her desires, and brought her each spring, and left her there to watch for the missing ones.

No one ever touched her; not even the cruel Comanches when they came to trade. They despised the Cheyenne and murdered them on sight, but not Standing Alone; no blood flowed below the towering tan adobe ramparts of Bent's Fort.

Indeed, even these mortal enemies of her people called her Grandmother, this vigiling woman, and passed gently by.

Skye paused to let Victoria draw up beside him. She sat on the hard wagon seat, hunched against the wind, her wiry frame fierce against the weather and weariness, ready to subdue the mutinous mules with great oaths and swift lashes of her whip. Upon her rite of passage into womanhood she had been named Many Quill Woman, of the Otter Clan, of the Kicked-in-the-Belly band of Mountain Crows, and now she was a long way from home, and a white man's woman.

The earth had softened under the winter's wetness, and made hard work for the mules. But Victoria spoke mule language even better than English, understood mule wiles and extortions, and knew how to compel these beasts of burden to her small, iron will. She had mastered all the oaths of white men, employed them enthusiastically, and the mules listened respectfully to her music.

"She's there," he said. "Never so early as this."

"Something's different," Victoria said.

Skye felt it, too.

The biting wind harried them toward the post. No one was out in the fields; not on such a cruel day. Bent's Fort rose amazingly out of nothing; a tawny apparition, made of cottonwood logs and golden mud, its round bastions promising protection, and its towering walls promising respite from nature. It was a laird's castle, the seat of empire, the work of hard-willed men who had found fortune in the wilderness of the southern plains. The Bents of Missouri had built it out of nothing but iron hearts and a vision of empire.

Skye rode ahead, eager now to escape the wind and warm his chilled body before a cottonwood blaze in one of the massive fireplaces within. He reached the gate, expecting to pass through the portcullis into the great yard within. But this time, Standing Alone rose suddenly, her blue blanket wrapped about her, and blocked his way, her black eyes surveying him boldly.

"Grandmother," he said politely. "How are you?"

She could not understand a word, nor could he fathom the Cheyenne tongue, so he could not translate the torrent of words pouring from her. He turned helplessly to Victoria, who had stopped the mules just behind, but he could see no comprehension in Victoria's face.

"Dammit, I don't know what the hell she's spouting," she said.

He lifted his battered beaver hat, and settled it again. It stayed aboard his head no matter how treacherous the wind, but just how was a secret that only Skye knew. The hat was his hallmark. Anyone within a mile could recognize Barnaby Skye by his black beaver hat. Anyone closer up might recognize him by his small bleached-blue eyes, deep-set in a ruddy face occasionally shaved; a formidable hogback of a nose, much battered and pulped by fisticuffs and hard use; great slabs of bristly jowl that hung to either side, giving him the look of a bulldog; and the stocky, short body and seaman's roll to his gait that was familiar to men anywhere in the mountains or the plains.

Standing Alone had recognized him from afar, and this time she wanted something.

"Can you make out what she wants?" he asked Victoria.

"Something awful damn bad," Victoria replied. She didn't like Cheyennes, ancient and bitter enemies of her Crow people.

Skye released his looped rein, wondering whether his unruly buckskin would behave, and hand-signaled to the woman.

"What say?" his hands asked.

She responded at once, her hands flashing. "Talk to you."

"I will later."

She nodded.

He would have to find William Bent or Kit Carson to translate. It was certainly odd.

He lifted his black hat to her once again, and settled it on the shaggy brown hair that reached his shoulders and helped keep his neck and ears warm in the winter. The hair was showing its first streaks of gray, which had shocked him. How could he be getting gray when he was still young? But he knew. His had been the hardest and most brutal of lives.

"Cheyenne killer bastards," Victoria said.

Around the fort, Victoria was celebrated as the most advanced cusser in all the Indian nations. She had honed her skills by listening to profane mountain men, and not even the fort's legendary chief trader, Goddam Murray, could match her.

But Skye never cursed at all. He touched the flanks of his horse with his winter moccasins, and steered toward the kitchen. The cooks would be glad to add this meat to the larder even if it was fit for nothing more than stew.

He steered his buckskin hard left, toward an alley that led to the corrals. Victoria steered her wagon across the yard, stopping at the far corner before the kitchen and cook's quarters. Skye swiftly unsaddled, turned the horse loose, and hurried to help her. No one else was going to pitch in. The cooks were busy, or pretended to be, and besides, dragging hunks of meat wrapped in bloody hide was beneath them.

Wordlessly, Skye opened the wagon gate, rolled a massive quarter of meat to the ground, and dragged it into the hot kitchen, where cooks were preparing a supper for the fifty mouths they were expected to feed twice a day. Skye yanked and tugged, pulling the meat past cursing cooks, until he reached a cool locker area to the rear. He and Victoria repeated the process, winning only curses from the harried cooks. That happened often. He often arrived while a meal was in the making, so they waved bloody butcher knives at him and snarled.

By the time he and Victoria had finished, they were both even grimier than before. Skye touched her arm, and she smiled gratefully. She would scrape the gore off of her arms and hands and face, and somehow make herself clean.

Skye clambered onto the wagon seat and turned the mules, only to discover the post's bourgeois, Alexander Barclay, observing him.

"Two cows, poor doings," Skye said.

"Buffalo aplenty here."

Skye repressed his anger. It had been hard enough to come up even with that. Barclay, like himself, was an Englishman, but there the resemblance ended. Barclay knew all about Skye, the deserter from the Royal Navy who had jumped ship at Fort Vancouver and become a mountain man. His obdurate disapproval of Skye stood between them, and had made life at Bent's Fort grim at times, and never joyous.

Skye, not wishing to talk further, hawed the mules, and steered the wagon around to the rear of the post and into the spacious corrals there. He was bone tired but he compelled himself to remove the harness, hang it up on its pegs, rub down and grain the mules, and check their feet for hoof cracks and stone bruises.

By the time he had finished, the gong had sounded. But he headed for his apartment, a cubicle partitioned off from the hunters' quarters, to clean himself. Victoria was there, freshened and ready to eat. She was one of few women on the post, and the only pureblooded Indian, and that made for uneasy circumstances. Some of the engagés resented her; others eyed her intently, their designs plain in their gazes. Skye suspected she had fought several off with the glint of her skinning knife, and had chosen not to tell him about it.

He sighed. Bent's Fort had given them security, comfort, a modest wage, and a refuge from weather. But Victoria was too much alone among so many white men, and Skye knew she was enduring life rather than enjoying it. He wasn't faring much better. But the beaver trade was plumb belly-up and a man had few places to turn.

They exited their quarters, passed through the empty dormitory and into the yard, where they encountered Lucas Goddam Murray, the chief trader.

"Say, mate," said Skye, falling in with the trader, "you mind translating for a minute?"

"Planned to eat."

"Standing Alone wants to talk with me."

"Cold meat." He glared. "Well, the day's been ruined enough, so I guess I can translate for the Cheyenne and eat cold stew."

"I'm obliged," Skye said. He steered Lucas and Victoria toward the great cottonwood gate, to see what the savage woman wanted.

2

The chief trader veered resolutely toward the gates, stepped under the portcullis, and stopped without. The Cheyenne woman stirred at the sight of him. Skye and Victoria followed.

"Grandmother," Murray said, using the Cheyenne word of greatest respect. "Grandmother, we will talk in the trading room."

He held out his big white hand to her, and she stood gracefully, peering into his face, then into Skye's, and finally into Victoria's. She nodded, drew her blue blanket about her as if it were a queen's ermine, and walked toward the trading store, the place where Murray and his squinty black-clad traders pulled the proffered robes and other peltries onto the worn counter, examined each one, offered a miserable price, and bartered the pelts for white men's wonders on the rough shelves.

This was Murray's lair; he even knew where the dust was thickest. The Skyes followed.

Standing Alone seemed much younger when she stood; erect and slim, and not so worn. The transformation was startling, and did not escape Skye and his woman.

"I am here to tell them what you say to me," Murray said

in her tongue, wanting to get it over with. He looked at her impatiently, wanting food in his belly.

She nodded, touched his wrist, and turned toward the Skyes. "All of my people know this man," she said. "All of my people know this woman too," she said.

Goddam Murray translated hastily, hoping that Standing Alone wouldn't sink into the redskin oratory that could consume hours.

"I say this: For four winters I have waited for my boy and my girl to return here to the place I last saw them and they last saw me. I have waited upon the westwind and the eastwind. I have waited upon the southwind and the northwind. But the winds have not brought my son and my daughter back to me. Now the four winds have passed, and I have not seen my children. They are far away."

He turned to the Skyes. "She's waited four years for her children, and they haven't come."

Standing Alone had a sweet, melancholy voice, and he listened closely as she continued. "I say this: Now I will go look for my children. In a vision I saw this man and woman leading me. They will know where to go and who to talk to."

Murray turned to the Skyes. "She wants to hire you to find her children. She'll go with you."

Skye looked nonplussed. Victoria muttered something that Goddam Murray thought was a curse. The Crow and Cheyenne weren't bosom friends.

"I have brought them a present," Standing Alone said. "This comes from my people. It is a sacred bundle, with great powers. This I give to Mister Skye to wear."

She pulled open her blanket and lifted a small medicine bundle, no larger than the palm of her hand, from her bosom, and passed the cord over her neck, stirring her silken jet hair.

"Medicine bundle's for you, Skye. That's her gift for taking her."

"Me? Me?"

Such a sacred gift could not be refused and Skye accepted it reluctantly, cupping his brown hand to receive the leather-bound packet. He could not ask what was in it, nor its powers, nor how to honor it.

Victoria lifted the bundle, examined it with a keen eye, and slipped the thong over Skye's neck. It hung over his bear-claw necklace.

"Thank her, mate."

Murray did: "Mister Skye is honored to receive the sacred gift of the Cheyenne."

"I say this: Tell the man I am ready to go whenever he is ready to go. We will find my children."

"She's ready when you're ready, Skye. You'll find her wayward ones."

Skye lifted his black beaver and settled it on his stringy hair. "I can't say as I'm ready to go, mate."

"You've got the bundle on your chest, Skye."

"I'll find some excuse. Is that it? That's what Standing Alone wanted to say?"

The Cheyenne woman seemed to understand, and nodded. That was it. Go with her. Find her children. Take the sacred bundle and wear it.

Murray thought to pour oil on those turbulent waters. "Grandmother, our hunter may not wish to go to find your children and he will want to talk to his woman about this."

The Cheyenne nodded.

"I can't do this. Tell her," said Skye.

"Wait. We'll talk," Victoria said.

"Go? With what? A bundle of pebbles and bird bones wrapped in leather?"

"You are blind, dammit, Skye. She's paid you honor."

"It's not an honor I want."

The Cheyenne woman waited for a translation, so Murray provided it. "They are thinking about it."

"They are disagreeing."

"Yes, Grandmother."

"I say this: It is honor enough, the sacred bundle. It was given to me by Strong Runner, a keeper of the arrows."

Big medicine, Murray thought.

Skye looked desperate. "I will talk with her in the morning. Will you translate?"

Murray nodded. "If I'm not in the store, Wagner knows the tongue."

"Grandmother, we will take you back to your place, and soon the cooks will bring you your bowl."

"Thank you, Grandfather Murray," she said. She turned to the Skyes, peered into each of their faces, touched each one on the hand, touched the bundle on Skye's chest, and pulled her blue blanket about her.

Murray escorted her out the door and through the gates, and then returned to the silent yard.

"You satisfied, Skye?"

Skye lifted his beaver and settled it. "It's Mister Skye, mate."

Murray laughed. The man in charge, Barclay, had ridiculed Skye's pretensions from the moment the renegade had applied at the post for a position. The seaman off the docks of East London had taken on airs, and the post's chief factor had seen through them and made light of Skye's peculiar manner. The mockery had spread through the post, and for two years no one had honored Skye's request that he be addressed as "Mister." But Skye never stopped requesting that he be addressed as he wished.

"In the new world, I will be Mister, not Subject," he had said, amiably, when anyone asked.

"Tell me again how she chose me," Skye said.

Goddam Murray shrugged. "Indian hoodoo."

"I will think about it."

"Don't."

Murray pushed the great doors closed, sealing out the

savage world and its savage inhabitants, including Standing Alone. He dropped a heavy bar, which fell in its iron slot with a slap.

"Skye, that was four years ago. That Ute band doesn't even have the same chief. The trail's colder than the bottom layer of hell. You could spend the rest of your goddamn life going from rancho to hacienda and never find them."

"I'll think about it."

"Did you hear me?"

Murray was annoyed that the Limey even was taking the request seriously. The supper was probably over, and he'd be picking at cold meat.

Skye didn't answer. He was peering at the heavens, as if some secret of the universe was about to be unveiled. Murray left them there in the shadowed yard and hastened to the kitchens, peeved at the world. Maybe they should evict Standing Alone. Get rid of her. Tell her to go sit in the bulrushes, but stay a mile from the post. That would do it. The old bat. Costing the post a meal every day, and for what? Because they all felt sorry for her?

He spat.

Her story was simple, and old, and known to everyone on the southern plains, Indian and white, Mexican and Yank. Over four years earlier, in the spring of 1837, Standing Alone's Cheyenne band, led by Black Dog, had come to trade with William Bent, their white brother and protector of their people. They had set up their lodges north of the post in a grassy flat and spent their time lazily dickering away the fine, winter-haired buffalo pelts and dressed robes for all the plunder on Bent's shelves.

Then one day, a band of Utes rode in to trade; the two tribes weren't friends but Bent imposed peace everywhere in the vicinity of his great adobe fortress, so the Utes camped well to the west, leaving a no-man's-land strip between the tribes. Even so, they got along. Stocky Ute warriors gambled against taller Cheyenne warriors, playing the stick game. The women shyly visited, their nimble fingers making words. The boys swiftly organized war games against each other. The girls traded dolls.

Each of those breezy spring days, Standing Alone plucked up some good fox or wolf or buffalo skins and wandered happily into the trading room to see what marvels she might have: blue beads, awls, sharp steel knives, jingle bells, keen hatchets, bolts of gingham or flannel, needles and thread, sugar by the pound . . .

On this day, the last that the Ute band intended to stay at the post, she had brought her nine-year-old son, Grasshopper, and her twelve-year-old daughter, Little Moon, to the gates.

Wait, she had said. They would each receive a surprise from their mother. And into the trading store she went to begin the process of turning peltries into little gifts for her children. And even as she whiled away the time, the Utes finished their trading and left.

Standing Alone could not find her children when she left the post but that didn't disturb her. They had probably gotten weary of waiting and had gone back to the camp. Hours later, they still were missing. Night fell, and they had not returned. It was only then that she realized, with a chilling wail heard through her village and in every corner of the hushed post, that the Utes, famous stealers of children and slave traders, had stolen her son and stolen her daughter and were long gone.

3

Irritably, Skye sawed at a haunch of buffalo and added some boiled maize to his trencher. His mood matched that of the cooks, who were cleaning up when he and Victoria wandered in. Victoria sawed a huge piece of buffalo and scorned the vegetable.

Skye sat down at a vacant trestle table and Victoria joined him. The last of the engages were mopping up their food. The post's officers, including Murray, ate separately.

"That is big damn medicine," Victoria said, eyeing the bundle.

Skye didn't answer. It was nothing but a leather pouch with feathers and pebbles and God knows what else in it. He was feeling trapped. He knew what he had to do. At dawn, he would find Standing Alone and return the thing. If she thought a leather pouch with some totems inside of it committed him to anything, she was mistaken.

He had no intention of going out to hunt for those children, long gone and probably dead. Northern Mexico was full of Indian slaves, many of them sold to hacendados by the Utes, who made the traffic of human flesh a good business. They abducted children of working age from neighboring tribes and peddled them in Taos for cash. The docile children made good field hands, doomed to hoe and weed

and scythe and harvest until they died at a young age from
sheer exhaustion. Some ended up in the mines, hauling
heavy baskets of ore, fed just enough to keep them going,
until they, too, died at a young age, their bones twisted and
backs curved.

Mexican officials averted their eyes; the church also
looked elsewhere, upon heavenly vistas. There was wealth
in the slave traffic; cheap stoop labor for the haciendas,
mines, and plantations. And the wily Utes, in their mountain lair, were the principal suppliers of human flesh.

Skye pondered all that as he masticated tough and stringy
buffalo, which the cooks had scarcely bothered to subdue
with fire. Meals for engaged men, hunters, laborers, and
others like himself, tended to be perfunctory at best. Men
up the ladder ate better here and at any other large western
post. Skye remembered the officers and clerks' meals he had
seen, or eaten, at Fort Vancouver, run by the Hudson Bay
Company, and Fort Union, the great outpost of American
Fur. This was no different.

No, he wouldn't go. Not that this post offered him anything but subsistence. He hadn't advanced and didn't expect
to, not with Barclay the chief factor. Skye's formidable reputation as a mountaineer mattered little here. His recent
experience as a brigade leader counted for naught. His
youthful history, however, counted for all too much. But the
post offered company, security, food, and comfort. Many
were the winter days when he cherished being behind its
thick walls, beside a crackling fire. Here he slept in a bunk,
defied weather, enjoyed the safety, and got a regular pittance
for his troubles. When the beaver trade faded he didn't know
what he would do. Bent had given him his answer.

No, he wouldn't leave. Not for some wild-goose chase.
Not to track two children lost four years ago, first by heading into the dangerous warrens of the Utes to find out where
the children went, and then probably wandering around, illegally, in Mexico, hunting two slaves. And if he did find

one or both, getting them out would be still another problem. Hacendados commanded small merciless armies.

He couldn't even buy the children's freedom; he had scarcely ten dollars to his name. The rest had gone to sustain himself, clothe Victoria, and gradually replenish his outfit. But most had gone for aguardiente, Taos Lightning.

When the Utes had fled Bent's Fort with the Cheyenne children, William Bent had swiftly organized a pursuit; he and his best men tracked the band for days, only to be defeated by veils of rain and the wily maneuvers of the warrior Utes. He didn't stop there; William Bent would do anything to help his wife's people. He had written Governor Armijo of New Mexico, asking that the children be returned. He had posted rewards. The Cheyenne themselves had sallied into Ute fastnesses, all to no avail.

And then Standing Alone began her vigil, and had stood her watches at the gate long before Skye had first set eyes on the post. He had never known a summer season without the sight of her huddled beside the gate.

What had changed her mind now? He knew the answer to that, at least. She had dreamed it; her spirit guide had ordained it. Her husband had understood, and brought her there in the spring, and returned for her when the geese flew south.

Victoria was glaring at him. "You gotta go," she said.

"For what? I need money."

"Because of the bundle."

"I'll return it."

"You are dumb."

There were moments when Skye sunk deep into himself, especially when Victoria was needling him, as she was now. He picked stringy buffalo out of his teeth and let her gusts of importuning sail past him.

He halfway wanted to go; the idea of finding the children and restoring them to their mother appealed to him. The idea of righting a wrong, wreaking trouble on the damnable Utes, stealing them from some heartless and cruel hacendado, delighted him. But most of all, that face of Standing Alone, the suffering in it, the hope in it, the trust and dream, all worked on his heart.

But all the practical considerations warred against such a quixotic adventure. Money, food, security, clothing, weapons, horses. Why throw all that away?

Murray was right: don't even think about it.

"I'm going upstairs," Skye said, sullenly.

Upstairs at Bent's Fort was the billiard room and saloon. It had started as Bent's offices, and had evolved into a place for the men at the post to congregate. Amazingly, it had a billiard table dragged out the trail from St. Louis, more than half a thousand miles away. William Bent's saloon probably soaked up most of the monthly salaries of the post's men; for a little Taos Lightning, a brandy made of agave leaves, he got his wages back.

"You'll get drunk, dammit. You got to be ready to go," she said.

He laughed. Soon she would follow him, and together they would drink up half a month's wage and forget about Standing Alone.

This evening, in a velvety twilight, as cool air eddied into the second-story saloon, Skye found few men. It was the middle of the week and the middle of the month. But one of those present was William Bent himself, lounging at a table with Goddam.

"Skye," Bent said, "let me see that bundle."

"You've been talking to Murray."

"You'd be crazy to go, Skye."

"Mister Skye, mate."

Bent laughed. The man was actually younger than Skye, but the sheer force of his personality, and his lordship over this amazing castle in the wilds, made him seem ten years older.

Bent drew an oil lamp close and studied the bundle

pending from Skye's neck. He turned to Murray. "That's it. I know that one."

"What is it?" Skye asked.

"Owl Woman's talked about it," Bent said. "That's the bundle worn by Strong Runner, keeper of one of the sacred arrows. He was wearing it when he led the famous attack on the Pawnees, who'd stolen the arrow. For my wife's people, that's quite a piece of merchandise."

Bent talked like that. A sacred item became merchandise.

"I'm giving it back when the gate opens."

Bent smiled. "I would too. That thing obligates you to lead the whole Cheyenne nation. When Strong Runner died, that bundle went to his senior wife, and then it was hung in a special lodge, and after that . . . I'm not sure. Say, Skye, fetch a dram and sit here. I don't want you to go on that wild-goose chase, and I'll list the reasons why."

Skye nodded, headed for the bar, where a clerk delivered a dram drawn from a cask and made a notation. Skye knew he was in for more than his next payday would yield; a position the Bents wanted to keep him in.

Bent sipped, felt the fiery stuff lava down his throat, and settled down beside Bent and Murray. The aguardiente felt just fine, and he sipped again.

"Skye, first of all, Standing Alone's crazy. You know that. Secondly, you haven't a chance of finding that boy and girl. They're probably a few provinces down, in Sinaloa or Sonora or Chihuahua. The Utes probably traded them off in Taos, but there are half a dozen slavers there who carry the flesh south, deep into Mexico."

"Why'd she pick me?"

Bent shrugged. "Hoodoo."

"Why not one of her own?"

"A Cheyenne can't do it. He'd be butchered trying to talk to Utes or dealing with Mexicans. It has to be a white man. She elected you. Carson tells me you had something of a reputation up north. That's why."

"Why now?"

"More hoodoo. They do everything in fours. Sacred number. She waited four years. Her brats didn't show up. Skye, amigo, that trail's so cold and those children are so dead you'll waste a year of your life. And besides, you're a good hunter and we need you here."

"What happens when I return the bundle?"

Bent sighed, obviously searching for words. "That's one of the most revered bundles the Cheyenne have. Might be an insult to return it. But make no mistake, she picked you. She got that bundle from her elders or chiefs, and gave it to you. It's flattering, Skye. That's honor. That's a passport, too. You show that to any Cheyenne and you'll get help."

"What's in it?"

"Who knows? Strong Runner's totems. It's not what's in it, it's what happened. He got the stolen sacred arrow back from the Pawnees, wearing that thing around his dusky neck."

Skye sipped, feeling the heat build in his belly. The damned bundle somehow seized him and he knew what he was going to do, and William Bent wouldn't like it, and everyone at the post, save for Victoria, would consider him a lunatic. She would just grin.

But William Bent had the last word: "Skye, don't do it. I mean it."

4

Skye tossed in his robes that night. He was remembering things he desperately wanted to forget; those years of virtual slavery in the Royal Navy, powerless to live his own life or choose his destiny. He had been pressed into the navy at the age of thirteen, lifted right off the cobbled streets of East London by a press gang. He never saw his family again. He never felt the sweetness of liberty until he jumped ship at Fort Vancouver.

But most of all, he remembered the cruelty. He remembered being tied to the deck gratings and lashed with a cat-o'-nine-tails until his back ran with his own blood. He remembered being brutally beaten by boatswains. He remembered being robbed of porridge by older seamen; being reduced to a starving bundle of muscles subdued to the will of 'tween-decks tyrants and captains.

He wallowed in his bunk, remembering the brutal punishment every time he protested, the despair, the hopelessness of ever living his own life, the prison of the forecastle, the desolation that he meant no more to others than useful muscle and bone.

He remembered how they took away even his pittance as punishment for imagined infractions, so he was not only a slave, but without a pence to his name.

Many was the night, lying in his hammock in the fore-castle, that he would gladly have jumped overboard and given himself to the sea but for some glimmering sense that he was not alone; somewhere, God hovered, offering hope. And yet it hadn't all been bad. He remembered the dolphins sporting in the green sea, the strange tropical shores, the seamen's hornpipes and rough humor, their pride in their skills. He remembered the breathtaking views of the end-less gray seas from the crow's nest as it swayed to the tides. But all that was part of a life not chosen or desired.

Out of that seven-year ordeal was born in him a loathing of slavery that ran so deep and fierce that he despised every form of it, from the indenture of pressed seamen in the na-vies of the world, to the wage peonage and perpetual debt that bound a man to his creditor, to convict labor, to the ob-scene slavery of black men that stained and tarnished the American South. In every case, people were being used; hu-man beings were forcibly denied their right to live their own lives. In every case, the oppressed lived in hopeless-ness and sorrow.

And so he thrashed in his bunk until Victoria slipped over to him in the darkness and placed a small, cool hand on his forehead.

"It is a bad night," she said.

Skye came fully awake at once, and all the dark phan-tasms slithered away. He clasped that small hand and held it.

"Bad dreams," he said.

"Dreams? You were asleep?"

"Memories, then. When I was a sailor."

She had heard of all these horrors. "Aiee, it is bad to think of that."

"Can't help it."

He felt her hands on him, comforting him, sending mes-sages of love and grace to him.

"No master commands you," she said.

"I'm not so sure."

"Only in your thoughts."

"You want to go after those children? Go on the wild-goose chase?"

"What is this, a wild-goose chase?"

"A foolish quest. A futile effort."

"If it makes you think such bad memories, maybe we shouldn't."

"If I go, it's because of those memories. If those children are still alive, they're probably slaves in Mexico. That's what the Utes do. Sell them into slavery. They would be down there somewhere, being ruined, hopeless, denied happiness, used and used and used and used until they die."

"Let's go, Skye." Her voice was urgent.

He pulled her to him until her head nestled into the hollow of his shoulder. He liked that; liked sharing life with her.

"You opposed to slavery so much? Your people got slaves."

"It's for her. Standing Alone."

She pitied the woman even if she was Cheyenne. He did too, but not so much. She was free to do what she wanted. It was the two captive children whose fate stirred him.

"We have different reasons," he said.

"Not so different."

"It's a stupid thing to do. No money in it."

"Skye, you are so damned dumb."

He laughed. She always did that to him when he was being buffalo-witted. "I'll talk to Bent in the morning. We've got problems from the get-go."

"Like what?"

"We can't even talk to Standing Alone. Except in signs. How's she going to tell us anything? We need someone with us who knows Cheyenne."

"I don't want anyone with us. Just me, you, and her."

"That's just one thing. I'm in debt to Bent. We've been sipping a lot of Taos Lightning. How can I get out of that?"

"We just go!"

"I am a man of honor."

"Well, who says he is, eh? He charges too damn much."

"There's a few more problems than that. If we find her children, how do we free them?"

She grunted. He knew she had no reply.

"I don't have any money," he added.

"We got to steal them children, then."

He didn't reply to that. He knew what the odds were.

And so they spent the night snugged together but in the morning Skye felt exhausted. He splashed himself with water and called that his toilet, and headed into the quiet yard just as Goddam Murray was opening the front gates.

As always, Standing Alone huddled against the mud walls, greeting the day.

Skye stepped outside into the golden hush. The Cheyenne woman saw him, and stood slowly. She was waiting for an answer, and her gaze enveloped him, missing nothing.

He had to think of the signs. The finger language was so poor it never sufficed. But finally, he signaled her: Grandmother, I will go. Soon. Not today. Much to do first.

Standing Alone nodded and touched him with her hand. He felt a strange power flowing from that gentle touch, from the tips of her fingers upon his wrist. There were things about life he never would grasp, and one of them was this strange touch that sent something deep into his heart, something that was more than gratitude or encouragement; something that bonded him to this Cheyenne woman.

He felt mesmerized by the force of it and then shied away from her, fearful of this strange force.

"Soon, Grandmother. I must talk to Bent. Quit this place and get my horses and all. Then we'll go."

It was English, but she nodded. Odd how meanings sometimes conveyed, even if words failed.

She stood solemnly in that gold dawn light, the level rays of the sun strong on her face, her features once again young.

He knew she was barely thirty and yet all those years at the gate she had been an old woman.

He left her there, and hunted down Bent but failed to find him. He looked for Barclay, intending to give notice. It was too early. The post didn't stir until midmorning.

He crossed the quiet yard again, and then up the stairs to the hunters' rooms. He would need to look at his outfit. He would need powder and balls and caps at the least. The out-fitting worried him. He owed the company. Many a night he had squandered his future pay in that billiards parlor and saloon.

He found Victoria in their room, packing up gear.

"We going?"

"Soon as we can."

"You ain't got much powder."

"That's going to be tricky."

He left Victoria to the packing and headed for the pens to round up his three horses. Two of these he saddled. The third would carry a pack. Someone of them would be walking.

That done, he headed for the store and there at last he found Bent.

"Mr. Bent, I'm resigning."

"No you're not. You owe the company three months of back wages."

"I'll write you an IOU."

"No you won't. You're going to stay here and hunt. If it's Standing Alone, forget it. I told you, leave her alone."

"I've told her I'm going."

Bent was growing angry. "Well I'll tell her otherwise. You will not duck out on me."

Skye sighed. "What I owe is just about the price of a horse. I'll give you a bill of sale."

"The hell you will, Skye." Bent loomed over him, beetle-browed and tough.

"All right, what are your terms?" Skye asked.

"Terms? Terms? There are none. You'll go hunting today as usual and you'll give me your word you'll return this evening. Your wife stays here. Your outfit stays here."

"You didn't hear me, Bent. I've quit. You'll get a horse for what I owe. I'm going to do something that will make the Cheyenne happy. If you pen me up, they are not going to be happy."

He glared at Bent, ready to pound the man if it came to that. No one, no one on earth, would imprison him again if he could help it.

Bent retreated. "Your funeral," he said.

"I need powder and ball and some other stuff."

"Your problem, not mine." He turned to the chief trader. "Murray, he's got no credit. Don't give him any."

"My word is my credit."

Bent laughed. "Don't come back," he said.

5

Two young hunters, Tom Boggs and Lyle Lilburn, braced Skye while he was packing his duffel in the plaza.

"We hear you're leaving us, Mister Skye," Boggs said.

"Word gets around fast."

"You going to help that crazy Cheyenne woman?"

Skye nodded.

"That's a fine thing to do," Boggs said.

That wasn't what Skye had expected. He supposed they would all echo William Bent, and greet his decision with a horselaugh, or consider it a self-imposed death sentence.

Goddam Murray and the clerks had been talking, and it took only about two minutes for gossip to work through Bent's Fort.

"You're doing it for nothing, too," Lyle said.

"No, I'm being paid," Skye replied.

"Yeah, with that." Lilburn pointed at the Cheyenne medicine bundle. "That don't buy DuPont."

Skye shrugged. "It's just something I want to do. That's pay enough."

Boggs shook his head. "You're likely going to get yourself killed, if not by a pack of mean Utes, then by some ornery greasers. You're walking into the devil's own lair."

Skye nodded. There was no point in denying it.

"You're doing it to help Standing Alone?"

Skye straightened, lifted his top hat and settled it. "I suppose I am."

"You *suppose* you are!"

"Maybe help those children, then."

Lilburn grinned. "Now that sounds more like the Skye I know. Help those young 'uns escape from ten years of stoop labor and an early death. That wouldn't have something to do with your sailor past, would it?"

Skye grinned.

Boggs eyed the heap of goods. "You outfitted proper?"

Skye evaded that. These boys were relatives by marriage to the Bents.

"No, you ain't," Boggs said, relentlessly. "I heard they wouldn't even spare you powder."

"I've enough," Skye replied, tightly.

"It's bad enough you going off on this grouse hunt, like you're after the Holy Grail, but it's worse you going off half fixed."

"I can live like an Indian," Skye said.

"Indians don't live like Indians anymore; they get stuff from us. How long since you seen a stone arrowhead?"

Lilburn lifted Skye's powderhorn and shook it. "Thought so," he said. "A man going off into Ute country without spare powder is a man gonna push up flowers. Skye, you just stay right here."

"I'm busy, mate."

But Lilburn ran up the stairs and into the dormitory where the trappers and hunters bunked. Skye could hear him up there, and moments later half a dozen of his comrades and rowdies burst out the door, clattered down the stairs, and surrounded Skye. There was something afoot, and it made Skye uncomfortable.

Then Will Gibbs thrust a powderhorn at him. "This here's for you, Mister Skye. I got me another. It's full of DuPont."

He hung the horn over Skye's neck, and patted Skye's arm.

"What a thing, helping that savage," he said.

Johnny Case was next. "I got a spare bullet mold, fifty caliber like yours, and here's a few pigs." He dropped the one-pound lead bars into Skye's duffel, and added the mold. "This'll let you throw something that stings."

"I think maybe we'd better get us a proper pen and paper so I can record what I owe," Skye said.

"You don't owe nothing," Boggs said. "Not one in a thousand would do it. Risk his life like this for nothing."

"It's not for nothing," Skye said, uncomfortably.

"I seen that woman there at the gate all this time, and I feel bad for her, but you're the one who's doing something about it."

"She chose me, mate."

"So I heard, but you said yes."

Skye felt itchy. He wasn't used to anything like this. He saw Victoria watching quietly, approval in her face. The crowd grew, until most of the engaged men in Bent's Fort crowded the plaza around Skye. And one by one, they brought him sustenance.

"Mister Skye," said Walt Gillis, "this here's cowhide shoe leather; real sole leather, tougher than any buffler hide you'll ever find. You'll need it."

Skye accepted it gratefully. He and Victoria and Standing Alone would be walking because they did not have enough horses.

One by one they brought him valuable things: from the clerks in the store, some trading items, including the prized blue beads the tribes loved so much. From the cooks, some jerky, tallow, cornmeal, sugar, flour, salt, and tea. From the engages, spare flints and steels, a spare blanket, soap, half a candlestick, a canvas poncho, thong.

Skye watched the pile grow, wondering whether he could fit it all on his two remaining horses, wondering what he had done to earn this sudden outpouring of honor and esteem.

Now a silent crowd stood around him in the plaza. Skye saw Victoria standing proudly by; and there at the gate was Standing Alone herself, oddly isolated, as if this blanket squaw had no connection to the portentous events unfolding a few yards away.

Above, on the broad deck of the galleries, stood those in command: William Bent himself, his posture dour and his face furrowed. Beside him the chief factor, Alexander Barclay, exuding disapproval as only the English can disapprove. And the excitable Goddam Murray, rising up and down on his toes like a tottering barrel. The entire post had come to see the Skyes off.

The heap of offerings exceeded what his horses could carry. And offerings they were, as if a church's collection plate had passed through this motley crowd of bearded men, and they had spilled their very substance into it. They were honoring him. He had never been so honored. These were a bold race of men, whose imaginations were fired by this quest for the Holy Grail, two imprisoned children; or more likely, the news of their deaths. Not for money was Skye setting out into dangerous lands, nor for fame, but only to help a woman whose presence had haunted the post for years.

Skye scarcely knew what to say, so he pulled off his top hat and bowed his head.

When he lifted his gaze again, he discovered Bent racing down the stairs, and that spelled trouble. He'd get out just as fast as he could.

Bent pushed through the silent crowd until he reached Skye.

"I'll lend you the horse," he said. "You'll need it."

Skye nodded. "I do need it."

"And another. You need another."

"Mr. Bent, I can't assure you that I'll ever—"

Bent wasn't listening. "Get that horse, and the dun pack mule, rigged up."

The stable man, Voller Campbell, leaped to the command.

"It's yours. Skye, I can steer you a little, if you're so determined to commit suicide. The Ute band you want isn't the Mouache who live around here. Those were maybe Weeminuche or Capotes. We think Capotes, from the San Luis Valley. We don't know. We looked hard, offered bribes and rewards. They're trouble, the Utes. Treacherous buzzards. I don't have to tell you what you're facing. You know the Utes. Dangerous and unpredictable. All smiles and murder. Likely to sell these women into slavery if they can."

Bent offered his hand, and Skye found the grip strong and affectionate. "I will remember this," Skye said.

"We'll remember you."

The stable man brought the bay horse Skye had turned over to Bent to pay debts, and a mule, each rigged with a packsaddle.

Then, while Skye hastily wrapped and balanced his loads among the animals, Standing Alone slowly walked to the heart of the plaza, her gaze soft upon them all. She had seen the hunters and trappers, and finally the whole post, contribute something to this venture, and now she passed through them, touching each, mumbling something in her own tongue that Skye knew was a thanksgiving. She paused long before Bent; he understood the woman's Cheyenne, and nodded.

Then the moment came.

Skye nodded to Victoria, who grabbed the halter rope of one horse.

"Thank you all," he said. "With all these things, we'll succeed."

"It'll take more than things, Mister Skye," William Bent said. "My wife's people will remember."

Skye nodded. Nothing more needed saying. He beckoned to Standing Alone, who took up a halter rope, and he col-

lected the other two, and they made their way out the gate
and into the morning.

It seemed oddly silent. No breeze hummed through grass.
No crows gossiped. No sounds emerged from the great yellow fort. He led his bride, and Standing Alone, along the
river trail west, scarcely knowing where to go.

They reached a point where cottonwoods and a slope
threatened to conceal Bent's Fort, and paused to look back.
Skye had an odd, hollow feeling as he stared at that solemn
walled city, a strange island of safety and comfort in a wild
land. Something about the place tugged him back even if
he had not had the happiest sojourn there.

He turned to Standing Alone, whose gaze was sharp upon
the silent white man's castle. But then she smiled, first at
Victoria and then at Skye. Her few possessions had been
heaped upon the old mule so she could walk beside them
unburdened. But it was her face that caught his eye.

She had come alive. The woman who had huddled at the
gate, awaiting her loved ones, had seemed ancient, but this
majestic woman standing proudly beside Skye and Victoria had shed thirty years overnight, and her strong-boned
face was alive with hope.

6

S traight toward the Utes. Skye didn't quite know what his hurry was. And yet he chafed at every delay, as if the children had been abducted four days ago instead of four years ago. But he knew why he hurried. Less for the Cheyenne woman's sake than for theirs.

Walking pained him. His ungainly gait, comfortable on the rolling teak deck of a man-o'-war, served him ill on land. The women walked easily, each leading horses, but he felt the hard clay hammer his feet and calves with every step.

The Taos Trail took him where he wanted to go, straight up the Arkansas River. Mexico lay on one side; the United States of America on the other. He belonged to neither and probably would always be a man without a country, a friend of suffering people whoever they might be. For he had suffered, and knew how much any small kindness meant.

The river coursed through rolling plains, short-grass country, dry all summer but verdant now with spring rains. At least the weather was bearable. Later on, this blistered and blistering land would be impassible from midafternoon until dusk, and one would be wise to shade up until the worst of the day had passed.

Even so, the walking sweated him. He paused frequently and always with the same salutation:

"You ladies will wish to rest," he said, his courtliness concealing other motives.

But Victoria only laughed as she watched him collapse into grass, undo his laced-up bullhide moccasins, and massage his white feet. She was more careful than he, scanning the distant vistas and studying the hilltops before she settled herself.

Skye splashed river water on his face, and sometimes threw it down his shirt to cool off. But the heavy mountain rifle was always at his side, and even during his ablutions he was aware of everything: the gossip of the crows, the sudden silences, the flight of hawks, and subtle alterations of nature.

He knew he was virtually helpless, alone with two women. The Comanches would make quick sport of all three and so would the Jicarilla Apaches. The Utes themselves could go either direction depending on their mood. But his octagon-barreled rifle spoke with authority, especially when pointed casually at a headman.

He chose his campsites carefully, sometimes half a mile off the trail, and in a hollow where they could scratch up a cook fire and not be seen. He didn't want to meet anyone, not even friendly traders.

During those first days, he quietly studied Standing Alone. She was a mystery to him. Questions teemed in his mind but he could not converse with her, and the finger signs were crude and unhelpful. What had impelled her to huddle through four travel seasons at the gate of Bent's Fort waiting for children who would never return? Why couldn't she simply surrender, grieve, and go on living? What did her tribe, her husband, her clan and parents think of this strange conduct?

She had built a small wickiup downriver from the fort, and had repaired to that place many evenings to cleanse herself and do her toilet. The hut was known to all the tribes trading at the fort, and was sacrosanct. No one disturbed one item within it. But always, when daylight stirred and travelers arrived or departed, she could be found at her self-appointed post, wrapped in her blue blanket, watching them with a keen and searching eye.

Sometimes she had cried out and leapt to her feet, run toward some youth or girl who looked like her own, only to wither back into inert sorrow. Most of the men at the post had seen her do that; they could only shake their heads. Some wondered whether she was mad, but Skye had never seen any suggestion of it. He had seen a determined mother, waiting for her children.

But Victoria was making progress with the woman, and somehow they were conversing in simple terms. Standing Alone had absorbed many English words over those years, and while she could not put them together she had acquired some understanding. With fingers, a few words in common, much pointing, and sheer guesswork they were starting to talk.

"Skye, dammit, you know she's got a younger daughter?" Victoria asked, one late hour in the dark.

"Daughter? Where?"

"In her band. Aunts take care of her, like mothers."

"What do her relatives think of her?"

Victoria shrugged. "It's her way. She has chosen a way, and they got no more say in it."

"But her husband—"

"Dog Soldier." She spat it out. The hated Dog Soldiers of the Cheyenne were deadly, lived for war, and bullied others.

"Why are there no more children?"

"She wears the rope."

That was a cord worn between the legs and around the thighs by Cheyenne women to announce and protect their virginity if they were unmarried girls, or to signal their wish to avoid mating, if married. Men usually honored it when girls were wearing it; husbands sometimes did not. Skye knew of no other tribe with a tradition like that.

"For four years?"

Victoria nodded. "Me, you never get me to wear some rope," she snapped.

Skye responded with an arm around her shoulders and she nestled into his chest. "What does her man think about that?"

"He don't question her medicine. She got it from somewhere, and she live by it. He got other wives now. Pretty lucky, eh? There's something else she don't tell me. She's big stuff in that band. She got big powers. She can make a bird fall out of the sky. Maybe someday she will say what her medicine is."

"If we find her children are dead, then what?"

Victoria sighed. "How the hell should I know. I'm some dumb Absaroka, not some beautiful Cheyenne saint that blinks her eyes and talks you into getting her children for her."

Skye sensed something in that; maybe envy. Was Victoria envious of the grieving mother, Standing Alone, who had somehow gotten a white man to hunt for her lost children?

"Don't," he said, roughly.

She turned silent, and the moment passed.

Standing Alone always unrolled her robes a little distant from them, as much to preserve her own privacy as to give them theirs. She was as solitary as her name.

She had been an able and willing travel companion, wordlessly helping Victoria with everything from building a fire to butchering an antelope. She knew her way around horses even though Victoria sniffed at that for a while. Crows considered themselves the best horsemen of the North, and no mere Cheyenne woman could possibly possess the fund of horse-knowing that Victoria possessed. But Skye knew differently. This Cheyenne woman knew horses from the hooves up, and understood their natures, too. And she handled the balky mule in a ruthless way that revealed deep familiarity with the most obstreperous of four-foots.

The enigma of Standing Alone remained on his mind as he took the women farther and farther west. What had led her to pick an obscure white man to find her children? What did she expect if she found one or both? The children would scarcely recognize her now. What manner of medicine had she bestowed on him? Sometimes her gaze was miles away from anywhere; as if she had a world into which no other mortal was permitted. *Madness?*

They traveled twelve or fifteen miles each day along the river, mostly in utter solitude. A few sharp showers were all that marred the exodus, but mostly they trudged through long silences keeping their thoughts to themselves. The world was vast. In the southern and western distances, snowy mountains lifted from horizons, but a day's travel scarcely brought them any closer.

Skye himself was holding up the progress. The women and packhorses could have walked twenty miles easily, but Skye's legs and feet rebelled, and he needed to pause for rest every little while, rub his feet and doctor his blisters, while the women grinned.

They pierced, at last, into a sunny flat where Fountain Creek tumbled into the Arkansas. It had always been a favorite trading place among the tribes; a place that looked eastward over the plains, but backed against isolated ranges of the Rockies. And it was here that they discovered in the distance a crude cottonwood log trading post, brand-new, with a few bearded white men lounging in the shade of its broad veranda. Who were they? Small-time traders and renegades, doing a lively business with the surrounding tribes, including the Utes?

Skye stood at some distance, assessing the quiet, sunlit place, which had no name that he knew of, though he knew that traders and Indians had rendezvoused there. Such places could bring swift and brutal grief to a man, and even worse to a woman. Victoria and Standing Alone pulled up beside him to study this new phenomenon, a white men's building where there had not been one only weeks before by all accounts of travelers.

"I'll go in; you wait," he said to Victoria.

"Alone? Hell no," she said, drawing her bow and quiver from the back of a horse.

"Easy pickings for them," he said, eyeing the pack horses, the mule, and the women.

Victoria glared, and he knew he had offended her. Victoria would never be easy pickings for anyone.

They walked slowly in, across a barren flat denuded of grass by livestock, and knew that they were being watched. But Skye saw no steel poking from shuttered windows. And the three white men on the rude veranda made no move.

They proceeded through afternoon sunlight toward the porch, but saw no sign of activity from the lounging men shaded up there.

"Hello the fort," Skye cried.

"Well, are you all coming in or pickin' a fight?" someone yelled back.

"Coming in," Skye yelled.

He nodded to the women and walked forward, and saw no sign of trouble. One of the men on the veranda did bestir himself, and stood up.

"You looking to trade?" he asked.

"Might be. Looking for some information, too."

"We got both, and they all got a price," the gent said.

Skye looked him over: rail thin, black bearded, squinty, and probably a man with a past, judging by the wariness he showed. These men were armed with horse pistols and had a military bearing, though they wore no uniform. They also were barbered and clean, with trimmed beards, a great rarity in the wilds.

He had reached the veranda, studying them all, and decided there would be no trouble. Not at least for a while.

"I'm Mister Skye," he said. "My wife, Victoria, and our friend Standing Alone. Maybe you could tell us how to find the Utes."

The man laughed. "You all don't need to do that; the Utes will find you."

"And separate you from them delicious horses and wimmin," added another of the loungers.

"And likely sell the whole lot of you down deep in old Mexico, Sah," added still another, a rotund gent with a goatee, muttonchops, a wide straw planter's hat, and a sweatstained white shirt.

"Skye, is it?" said the thin one. "I know the moniker. Working for Bent?"

A sudden wariness stretched through the shaded veranda. Skye understood it. These were the opposition; small-time traders wanting to horn in on William Bent's empire.

"Quit 'em," said Skye. "Good people, but I'm on my own."

That's when the big-lipped hairy monkey swung down from the rafters, jumped on the fat one's shoulder, and started chattering.

7

Victoria shrieked.

"Aiee!" she cried, and whipped behind her horses.

Never had she seen such a thing. It sat there, grinning at her, picking its nose, a Little Person crouched on the sweating fat man, its tail curling lazily around his neck.

A person from the other world. A person long gone, come back to this world to haunt her. Truly, she was seeing the dead. It was a perfect Little Person, with wide-set, bright eyes, little hands that picked at its reddish-gray fur, long skinny limbs, and that strange hairy tail that had wrapped itself around log rafters to enable it to float in the sky.

She covered her eyes with her hands, and furtively squinted at it through her fingers.

Standing Alone had retreated behind her horses too, punched backward by an invisible hand, and now looked as if she were preparing for her own death. Or maybe, yes! She was seeing her own dead son come back from the other side. Never had Victoria seen such a haunted look upon a woman's face.

Skye grinned. "Where'd you get him?"

The fat man chucked his hand under the bewhiskered chin of the little monkey and scratched. "Panama," he said.

She did not know this place, Panama, but it must be a vast distance away, and in some other world.

"First one I've seen on this continent," Skye said.

"He's my helper," the fat man said. "Can't get along without him. He fetches wood, entertains the savages, and can even make war."

Aiee! A real Little Person. The Absaroka had always known about the Little People, the secret ones who could help them or cause them big trouble, purely on whim. She had never seen one of the Little People but now she was staring at the very first.

"Saw a lot of 'em when I was in the navy," Skye said.

"Along the coast of Africa and Asia. They hardly let me off the ships, but still I saw a few. Rhesus, gibbons, apes, lots of 'em. Never expected to see one here. This one's South American, then."

"Spider," said the fat man. "Central America. Some have more hair."

Victoria listened carefully, her hand on her skinning knife. If this Little Person came too close, she would dispatch it.

Skye lifted his battered topper. "I didn't catch your name, sir," he said, offering a hand. But it was the Little Person who took it and shook it cheerfully. Aiee! Her man was a friend of this Little Person. Maybe she should flee to her people before worse happened.

"I'm called the Colonel," the man said.

"Colonel?"

"Call me that; it'll do. The Colonel, Sah, rules all things including Shine. That's the name of this business associate of mine, Shine."

"The monkey's called Shine?"

"No other. I first named him Cayenne, after the robust pepper, but no one called him that. He became Shine, but he's no less spicy. He's uncommonly smart. Wiggle your finger and call him."

Skye lifted his thick hand and wiggled a finger. The monkey gathered itself and leaped gracefully, settling on Skye's shoulder. It reached for Skye's black top hat and stole it, turning it around in its little hands, then biting the rim and spitting.

"Guess it tastes bad," the Colonel said.

Victoria squinted at this apparition. Never in all her years with Skye did she suspect him of truckling to such evil. Maybe she should nock an arrow and kill that thing.

"Colonel, this is my wife, Victoria, and yonder is our friend Standing Alone of the Cheyenne People," Skye said.

The fat man stared right at Victoria, much to her horror, and didn't even avert his bright blue eyes. He doffed his fine straw Panama, and settled it.

"It's my great pleasure, and indeed an honor," he said. She nodded curtly.

"Mister Skye," she said, "we go now."

Skye studied her. The Little Person on his shoulder grinned and patted Skye and tugged Skye's earlobe.

"Victoria, this is a monkey from South America. There are many types. This type lives in the trees. His long tail is like a spare hand or arm. They are friendly little fellows and often mimic mortals."

The thing leered at her.

She had nothing to say to that. Plainly he had a Little Person on his shoulder, and this was an evil unspeakable. But she saw Standing Alone eyeing the monkey with curiosity. Aiee, what would a stupid Cheyenne woman know about Little People? She felt a flood of scorn for such an ignorant tribe.

Skye saw he had made no dent in Victoria's fears, so he turned to the Colonel.

"Shine is your servant, I gather?"

"He is, Sah. I need one because of my girth. I weigh twenty stone, as you can see, and I would not trade an ounce of it. Twice I have been pierced by arrows, but my avoirdupois is my shield, and neither arrow reached my vitals. It's the perfect means of survival in Indian country."

Victoria was fascinated. She had never seen anyone so fat. How could he even bend over, or lift himself off the ground, or dress himself?

The Little Person dropped off of Skye and bounded to the top of Victoria's packhorse, chattering cheerfully as it began undoing the pack.

"Aiee! Stop him!" she cried, reaching for her skinning knife.

"Shine, conduct yourself in a gentlemanly manner," the Colonel said sternly.

The Little Person rested on his haunches atop the horse, sucking his odd-shaped right thumb. Victoria loosed her knife just in case. But Standing Alone was grinning.

"I will answer your questions before you ask them, Mister Skye. You, by the way, are known to us all as a brave-hearted man of the wilds. I am, Sah, a trader by profession, owner of Childress and McIntyre, Outfitters—we're from the Republic of Texas—and my current project is to supply the Utes with whatever they desire from my stores, while I in turn rake in valuable robes, hides, peltries, and leathers, which in turn I sell here and there or ship downriver."

"The Utes?" Skye asked. "Here?"

"These gents take care of our store. I travel by myself, preferring the open road."

"Alone, in Ute country?"

"Sah, I am never alone with Shine at my side. I have a cart rigged with a seat and storage for my merchandise. We are welcomed everywhere, and my friends the Utes will come from great distances to befriend Shine."

The Little Person held out a hand to Victoria, who shrank from it.

"You . . . Lakota!" she cried, hoping to offend the beast. She would never touch such an abomination. It would destroy her medicine. Let him hold his paw out forever; nothing would alter the stony resolution of her heart.

Shine grinned, sighed, and jumped straight at Victoria.

"Aieee!" she howled, contorting herself in such a way that the Little Person could gain no purchase on her, and landed in the grass.

Standing Alone smirked.

Victoria was angry. She tried to kick the Little Person but it scampered toward Skye and with one bound landed on Skye's shoulder, where it turned and chattered meanly at Victoria, and ended up spitting and clacking its teeth.

"I go back to Yellowstone River now," Victoria said. "Absaroka country."

Skye started laughing. Her man, laughing at her. Nothing like this had ever befouled their marriage.

"Madam will come to enjoy Shine; nary a soul does he fail to win to his bosom," the Colonel said.

That was pretty fancy talk. Sometimes Skye talked like that, instead of like the trappers and mountain men.

"As it happens, Mister Skye, Shine is my manservant. If I say build a fire, he gathers the wood for me, lays up the sticks, ignites some kindling with a flint and striker, fetches a kettle, and prepares my repast."

This time Skye was silent, but plainly he was wondering whether there was a scintilla of truth in it. The Little Person was playing with Skye's medicine pouch, the very one given him by Standing Alone. Victoria recoiled at the very sight of it.

"He is also my counselor, Mister Skye. If something goes amiss, I listen to the monkey."

"And what if he's wrong, Colonel?"

"The monkey accepts blame without cavil."

Skye laughed. "One more question, Colonel. How do the tribes respond to Shine?"

Victoria listened closely. If the scheming, forked-tongue

Utes liked that thing, then it would be clear that they are even more evil than she imagined.

"They enjoy him," the Colonel said. "Shine is my passport. When fat Colonel Childress and Shine the spider monkey show up, they welcome us with a feast, and Shine entertains them deep into the night. They call him The Thief, because he pilfers anything he can put his hands on. He jumps from shoulder to shoulder, pats them all for anything he can extract, and then races off to a tree, chittering and chattering and laughing."

Victoria squinted at Shine, having learned of some new reasons to despise the monkey.

Standing Alone studied the monkey silently, and the men, no doubt comprehending very little, and Victoria thought the woman was fortunate to be so ignorant of such an evil, ill-mannered animal.

Then Shine glided off his perch atop the packhorse, and landed at Victoria's feet, hugging her high moccasins.

"See, madam, he likes you," the Colonel said.

"Aiee! I am attacked!"

The monkey scurried off while the men laughed. Let them laugh! They would suffer if they knew this thing was a Little Person, bent on making trouble. Victoria smoothed her skirts and calmed her ruffled composure.

"Mister Skye, let us go," she said.

But her man shook his head gently. "I was thinking maybe the Colonel and his monkey might be the perfect passport to the Utes and the Mexicans," he said softly. He turned to the fat man. "Your name is Childress, sir?"

"Jean Lafitte Childress, of Galveston Bay, Republic of Texas. I come from a long line of privateers and soldiers of fortune."

"I hear London in your voice."

"London? London? No, but I did spend a year at a seminary in Canterbury before choosing a vocation as a privateer."

"What brings you here, then?"

"I am seeking my fortune, Sah."

"This is not your usual line of work," Skye said. Victoria heard the skepticism in his voice.

The Colonel sighed. "I am the black sheep of my family, Mr. Skye. I might have enjoyed a perfectly respectable career flying the Jolly Roger, but the sea terrifies me, death curdles my blood, my nature is gentle and romantic, and I have had to make a living on my own terms, much to the despair of my family."

Skye laughed. Victoria wondered what was so damned funny.

"Perhaps you're the man we want to talk to, Colonel Childress. Ah, where does the title come from?"

"To confess my private intentions, Sah: it is my purpose to detach a vast portion of this wild land from Mexico and set up an empire from here to the Pacific, the empire of Childress, devoted to the nurture of the humble, the weak, the needful, the oppressed, and of course to advance my own fortune. My men share my ideals, and call me 'Colonel' as a courtesy."

Skye laughed softly, and again Victoria wondered what the hell she was missing.

"A filibuster," Skye said.

The Colonel looked pained. "You make it sound so crass, sir. In fact, I am at the service of large and noble ideals."

"In that case, perhaps you could help us. We're looking for a gentleman who knows the Utes and can talk their tongue, as well as the Mexicans and can talk Spanish. Your reward would be exactly nothing in terms of wealth, but deep satisfaction in other respects."

The Colonel turned serious. "Mister Skye, Sah, your purposes are unknown to me and my partners. You may think me excessively cautious, but I assure you, there is calculation in all that I do, and further, Shine is an important reason I am harvesting furs from the Utes as no one has ever done before. I must know every detail of your intentions, and then I will judge."

Skye didn't reply for a while. He gazed at these ruffians, at the fat man and his monkey, and at Standing Alone.

"Our purposes are nothing but charity," he said. "There's not a peso in it. Let us put up our horses, pay you for some feed for man and beast, and then I'll tell you a story. And I'd like to hear yours, Colonel Childress."

8

Skye and the women cared for their horses and the mule, splashed water bucketed from a shallow well over themselves, and settled on the veranda in time for a quiet twilight visit. The man who called himself Colonel Childress always enjoyed that time of day at this arid place not far from where the Arkansas River erupted from the mountains. The place cooled swiftly except in midsummer, and the air was so dry that his armpits chafed.

The Colonel knew of Skye; so did the Colonel's colleagues. No man of the western borders was ignorant of this legend of the mountains. The Colonel also knew about the Cheyenne woman, and that excited his curiosity more than anything else. Why was the storied Standing Alone with Skye and Victoria Skye?

Well, there would be an answer soon enough—if Skye was willing to tell the whole story.

"Tell us about your post, Colonel," Skye said, after completing his ablutions.

"Why, Sah, we're six in all, out of the Texas Republic but we trade in Taos and sometimes Fort William, up on Laramie's River. We've two Mex boys also, from the ranchos down below, and they herd and do our chores."

"That's a goodly number."

"Dangerous land, Mister Skye; not for greenhorns and fools. But the post has loopholes and a small tower, and we can defend."

Skye turned toward the others. "Gentlemen, I am Mister Skye, and whom do I address?"

The Colonel caught the glances, and nodded. One by one, his militia proffered a name. Crowsnest Jones, Horace, Spade, and Deuce. Men with ugly scars, squinty eyes, and a loose-limbed quickness that made them deadly. Men with long knives, dragoon pistols, and rifles standing nearby.

"Men of the borders?" Skye asked blandly.

"Every one a Texan and a water man. We're a seafaring nation, Sah. Texas is. Most of them have walked a teak deck and climbed rigging. Not men to tangle with."

"I would not think of it," Skye said. "I always want to know who I am with. Especially when I may have business to transact."

"Business," the Colonel said, sardonically. "Business or charity?"

Skye stared at the Colonel with a gaze so intense that the Colonel was taken aback.

Crowsnest Jones, his skinny cook, hustled around inside the hot building, putting some corn tortillas on a trencher for the guests. He added some cold chorizo and beans, and brought the platter out. The guests could build their own meals from that. Crowsnest Jones was a sailor once, a soldier now. The surname probably had not been Jones until recently. His shirt covered a Louisiana convict brand. All of the Colonel's men had been handpicked for the reconnaissance.

Shine stole a tortilla and some beans, and retreated with one graceful leap to the log vigas, where it ate and slurped and licked its little fingers.

Victoria Skye hissed at him. But Standing Alone laughed, and looked to be ready to toss more tortillas at the bandit.

Skye finished eating, belched luxuriously, and settled back against the log wall.

"Victoria and I are assisting our friend here, Standing Alone of the Cheyennes," he said. "If you haven't heard of her, I'll tell her story."

He waited, but not a man responded.

"We are looking for her children," he said.

Sheer amazement flooded through Childress.

The astonishment was palpable. No one said a word. The Colonel thought that such a quest was the most quixotic venture he had ever heard of, and he had heard of plenty of foolish things. But he was smitten by the whole idea, because he was a born Don Quixote. And for other, more profound reasons. His interest quickened, and he began to see possibilities in this.

"Good luck," he said.

"We're going to find that boy and girl and return them to their mother, and to their people. Wherever they are, we'll find them. Some thread will lead the way. If they're alive, down in the Mexican silver mines or hoeing the fields or herding the cattle, we'll find them. I'm hoping you might help us deal with the Utes who stole them and probably sold them—to someone, somewhere."

"My dear Mister Skye, Sah. A most admirable enterprise, but we can't help. We're not in the brat business." He laughed. "Maybe we should be. Steal flesh and peddle it. Beats trading for buffalo robes."

"How long have you been open for business here?"

"A week. But we've been in this country for some while, scouting and trading from our wagons. We decided on this place, got out the axes, and began laying up logs a fortnight ago."

"I thought so. New logs. No one at Bent's Fort knows of this post. Any band show up here yet?"

"No. They'll find us. We're open for business. Mister

Skye, Sah, what you'll do is head straight into Mexico. There's slave markets in every town. Taos first, then the city of the Sacred Faith, and then the duke of Albuquerque's town, and on down the royal road clear to the City of Mexico or beyond. You have an entire walled and private nation to search, and you no doubt can devote a lifetime to the task. Some hacendado down there has the brats, if they're still alive. Not the Utes."

"Why not the Utes, mate?"

"Because stolen children are commodities to them; they even sell their own. A working-age brat is worth a horse, and Utes lack horses because they're a mountain tribe. Sometimes they keep a little nit a few months, looking for a place to peddle him. But not four years. There are two choices: the children are dead or the children are alive in Mexico trapped in slavery."

Skye nodded.

Shine leaped from viga to viga, using his prehensile tail to swing through the air, until he landed on Skye's bench, and then he sprang gracefully to Skye's shoulder and stole his battered black hat.

"Hey!" roared Skye, as the top hat sailed toward Victoria, who caught it.

But Shine wasn't done. He plucked the medicine bundle from Skye's chest, lifted the thong over Skye's head, and ran off with it.

Standing Alone leaped to her feat, stricken, and cried out.

The thieving monkey whirled the sacred bundle around and around merrily, and then sprang toward the Colonel and lowered the thong over the Colonel's head. Childress stared at the small leather packet that contained some redskin's totems, stared at the delicately dyed leather full of symbols that meant something to those people.

Standing Alone trilled like a wounded bird, and staggered toward the Colonel, stared at the bundle as it rested on a new bosom, and wailed.

"Grandmother," he said in his rudimentary Cheyenne, "what is this?"

She squeezed her eyes shut and shook her head, as if this sight were too much for mortal eyes.

"Grandmother?"

"I will say this: Whoever wears the sacred bundle must help me find my children. I gave the sacred bundle to Mister Skye, and now it is no longer upon his breast." She began a strange chant, dolorous and sad, like a death song the Colonel once had heard sung by an ancient Aztec. But something melodic and haunting about her song told him she was singing about life at its very roots, not death.

He fingered the bundle and found it light, and yet oh, so heavy.

"What did she say, mate?" Skye asked.

"It seems you were the one to find the boy and the girl, Sah," the Colonel said. "My monkey has upset her universe. The sacred bundle obligates whoever wears it."

But the Cheyenne woman tugged at his sleeve.

"Grandfather," she whispered, "now you have worn the bundle, and now you must help me find my children, for that is the meaning of this. It is your fate."

"She says, Mister Skye, that now I'm committed to her cause, because I have worn the bundle."

Skye held out a hand, wanting the bundle back, but Childress was in no hurry to return it.

Maybe there was merit in it. Childress had always lent himself to any good cause, and maybe he could lend himself to this one, and serve several good causes at once. Maybe this would be a way to serve President Mirabeau Buonaparte Lamar. Maybe . . . it would offer concealment for his other designs, the original ones, worked out long ago in another land.

He weighed the risks. The things he had told Skye about himself were true enough, but there was so much more to it. He was indeed engaged in a filibuster but not on his own behalf. He was serving Lamar's great vision of a Republic of Texas stretching from sea to sea. He had come here with a few picked members of the Texas militia to reconnoiter northern New Mexico in advance of the army that was even then being marshaled in Texas. The whole of this province was being held by scarcely a hundred armed Mexicans, and was there for the plucking. Ah! What an enterprise! But of this Skye knew nothing. Childress believed in smoke as the best way to conceal true purpose.

Thus did Colonel Childress sit on that veranda pondering this sudden turn of events. And the more he pondered them, the more opportunity he saw.

"Mister Skye, Sah, I do believe I greatly favor your cause. What a noble heart you have, gallantly assisting this lovely princess of the Cheyennes. My own jaded heart is soft and tendah toward any urchin trapped by the greed of cruel masters. If you should desire my company whilst you roam northern Mexico in pursuit of mercy and grace and communion with saints, Sah, I think I might join you. I am not a bad companion of the road. Perhaps I can even contribute a bit to your enterprise, for I have an able tongue, and a sturdy cart, and the assistance of the little pirate and thief Shine, who has talents you cannot fathom, all of which will become manifest as we ransack Mexico, each in our own fashion."

Skye was staring again. "Colonel, the bundle, please," he said, holding out his hand. The mountaineer meant business.

9

The bundle," said Skye, holding out his hand. But Childress was not surrendering it. The monkey jumped to the trader's shoulder and scolded Skye.

"The bundle," Skye repeated.

Childress did not lift the thong over his head.

"Make your Little Person give the sacred medicine bag back," Victoria snapped. "It is Skye's."

Childress addressed her, inflating himself in his chair.

"Ah! If it were a mere thing of material value, gold, rubies, aphrodisia, rupees, Grecian statuary, anything of that miserable sort, I would remove the dead weight from my neck at once, for I have no patience with mere wealth. But this is purely a mystical gift and it was intended that I should receive it so that I might be empowered by the Spirits. Thus it represents my destiny, my incubus, which my discerning monkey at once recognizes."

He scratched the simian's jaw.

"The bundle," said Skye.

Childress addressed Victoria. "Shine didn't steal it; he merely bestowed it, and now I am committed to your noble cause, without reservation or cavil. Someday, when this is over, I will return it to your esteemed husband . . ." He peered at her. "But let us ask the woman whose will and intention matters most to us."

He turned to Standing Alone, who stood transfixed, understanding little of this, and spoke to her in her tongue, his fingers lifting the sacred bundle even as he spoke to her.

Standing Alone replied in the simplest manner: she approached the fat colonel, lifted the bundle from his possession, and gently gave it to Skye. He felt its mysterious power as it lay in his hand, and then he lifted his hat and settled the medicine bundle upon his chest, where it belonged. That made things right. The Cheyenne woman nodded.

But Standing Alone was not through. She was talking in her tongue to Childress, and pointing at the monkey.

"She says, Sah, that I must come with you. The monkey is very wise. I am at your service, Sah."

Skye saw how it would be. He had gotten in with a daft adventurer, a self-confessed privateer and soldier of fortune, alleged Texan, and only God knew what else. Those gents on the veranda were not traders. Skye had spent years among Indian traders, and none of them resembled this phalanx of cutthroats. Colonel, indeed! Buccaneer, fraud, mountebank, confidence man, these were the correct titles. Skye had made mistakes in his life, but this would not be one of them.

"Colonel, tell our friend Standing Alone that we respect her wisdom, and we are honored that she asked us to look for her children. But we're going on our way now, without your help."

"Skye—"

Standing Alone somehow fathomed what Skye was saying. She probably grasped plenty of English after all those seasons at the gate of Bent's Fort, though she didn't speak it.

She did not hesitate, but rushed to Skye, a tall, proud woman who each day seemed younger than the previous day, and gently pressed her hands over his.

"All come," she said, and then spoke in her own tongue to Childress.

The Colonel translated. "She wants me to help you to find the Utes and look for her children in the nation across the river; she means the Mexicans, Sah. The monkey has told her that I must come with you on this great quest for justice and liberty and reunion. I accepted with pleasure."

Craziness. The woman had never seen a monkey before, so the monkey was a new god.

Skye had rarely felt such misgivings. He felt trapped. Here he was, committed to Standing Alone, being pulled and tugged by a Cheyenne tribal medicine bundle and a thieving monkey named Shine and a fat trader who sounded more like a pirate, and probably was one.

He turned to Victoria.

"Big medicine," she said. "Little Person gives the fat man the medicine bundle. Skye, we go get them damned Cheyenne Dog Soldier children, and he comes with us." Victoria gestured toward Childress. "You and me and Standing Alone and the fat man and the Little Person."

Monkey or not, Victoria wanted Childress along. Skye gawked at her. Suddenly he laughed, the miraculous, booming Skye laugh that shook the mountains and shivered the grasses, and settled his mind and lifted his heart.

"All right, we will."

All those hard-eyed scoundrels on the porch stared. He wondered whether the warrants for their arrest numbered in the twenties, fifties, or hundreds. They weren't border men; they were men a thousand miles beyond the borders, and for good reason.

Skye eyed the fat man. "How are you going to travel?" he asked. "Not by horse, that's certain."

"I have a cart and a dray."

"We need more horses."

"I'll arrange it. What will you offer?"

"I need the loan of them."

"I will do it."

"At dawn, then, Colonel?"

"I sleep late," he said.

"We'll be ready whenever you are."

"Our accommodations leave something to be desired, but you are welcome." He waved toward the gloomy chamber.

Skye had already peered into the rectangular dirt-floored room stacked with trade goods but redolent of sweat and viler odors. This outfit had yet to erect bunks or build an outhouse, and were simply making their beds among the spiders and snakes.

"Think we'll camp down by the river, Colonel."

"As you wish, Sah."

He led his silent women down to a flat near the water where they could bathe. The sky didn't threaten, and they could unroll their robes on soft dry silt that would shape to their bodies.

Standing Alone retreated to her own space thirty or forty yards distant, as usual, leaving Skye and Victoria alone under the bright canopy of stars. A chill breeze swept out of the western mountains, and by dawn Skye would be pulling his robes tight around him.

He could hear the water lapping. Far off, a coyote barked. He listened closely. Not all coyote sounds were coyotes.

Victoria huddled close this time, which was not like her.

"Skye, that thing you call monkey. I know what it is," she whispered.

"It's just a critter from far south."

"No! It is a Little Person!"

Skye sat up. "What is that?"

"Only my people know them. A few Absaroka have seen them. But that is one. Aiee! I never thought I would see one."

Skye waited intently. If Victoria didn't want to say more, nothing could persuade her to.

"Sometimes they are friends and help us. Sometimes one

of our warriors or hunters is in trouble, and a Little Person helps him. He brings a lost horse, or brings wood to splint a broken leg, or finds water. They live in caves and hidden places. This man the Colonel, he does not know this, but I know."

"Then we have a helper," Skye said.

"Ha! Skye, you don't know nothing. The Little People are tricksters too, like the coyote, making everyone miserable. Maybe this Little Person makes us miserable. They steal, too, and that is how I know. This Little Person, he would steal everything we got and hide it if he could." She paused. "Don't you trust no Little Person."

"The Colonel obviously does."

Victoria laughed sardonically. "Look at him. Fat man run by a Little Person like a gelded horse hitched to a wagon and he don't even know it."

Skye didn't reply. Sometimes silence was best. He squeezed her hand. It wasn't the monkey he was worried about; it was the erratic and strange Colonel from Galveston Bay who could put them all into a parcel of trouble. But when he thought of those missing Cheyenne children, and the ever-blooming Standing Alone, who was so filled with hope now, he didn't have any regrets.

10

To Skye's discerning eye, the Colonel's equipage was as bizarre as the man. His men loaded a scarlet enameled cart with trade items and then backed a huge draft horse between the hardwood shafts and hitched it.

"A Clydesdale," Childress said. "Brown or black, blaze nose, stockings, and a spray of hair around the fetlocks."

"I wouldn't know one from another," Skye replied.

"Came out with traders, but draft animals don't do on the Santa Fe Trail; trader sold his six-hitch in Santa Fe, and I bought a pair."

"And the cart?"

"Best carriage for overland travel. Goes where wagons can't."

This one was fitted with a bench, though most carts had no seating at all; their drivers walked beside the horse or mule.

Most startling of all was a familiar insignia enameled on the side of the cart. It was a Jolly Roger, white skull and crossbones on a black field. It gave Skye the chills. All his years in the navy, he had heard forecastle stories about the outlaws of the sea.

"I'm an old, watersoaked pirate," the Colonel explained. "Hard to get rid of old habits."

"So it seems."

"Some take the Jolly Roger for a pirate's death's head, but they're wrong," he said. "It is a signal that quarter will be given if there is no resistance. That's my motto. I give the redskins quarter if they don't resist."

"Who would resist, and why, Colonel?"

The fat man smiled and let the question hang. When all was ready, he slapped the lines over the back of the draft horse. From the shade of the veranda, his ruffians watched lazily. He had given them no instructions; not even a time when he expected to return. Skye could not even discern which of them was in charge.

Skye had a thousand doubts, but after all, this fat entrepreneur was going only to hunt down some Utes, and do some translating.

They departed in a cloud of dust, the Colonel and his cart leading, followed by the Skyes and Standing Alone, all mounted now on sturdy nags, and trailing the packhorses. The little monkey sat calmly on the Clydesdale's withers, but occasionally bounded back to perch on the Colonel's shoulder.

They crossed the frothing Arkansas River at a hard-rock ford and headed into Mexico along a dusty trail, through arid slopes and building heat. Skye often rode beside the Colonel, wanting to talk to the man as well as observe him. The trader was so bizarre and unpredictable that Skye felt an urgent need to fathom the man and foresee trouble.

"Where are we going?" Skye asked.

"San Luis valley. That's home to one band of Utes, the Capotes. Pestiferous lot. They should be boiled in oil. Probably the child thieves you're after."

"Bright red wagon with a Jolly Roger. You want to be seen."

"I never hide. It says the Fat Trader is coming. The trader can be seen twenty miles away."

"What do the Utes see in the Jolly Roger?"

"They see their own death if they harm me. That is what it tells them."

"You told them that?"

"Their own shamans did, after studying the device."

"That's what you intended?"

The Colonel grinned from under his straw Panama. "We are safe, and you can thank my hard calculation, my understanding of savages, the bright red cart, the monkey, and the ensign, which I had painted onto my cart in Santa Fe by a devout and grandfatherly monk who relished the task. I told him I was a Lafitte by marriage and I could cut his heart out if he refused, and he told me he would have the priest perform an exorcism after he had finished the artwork."

The trader was already sweating. Skye imagined that by the time the midday heat built, Childress's flowing clothes would be soaked. He sat upon the red bench, his flesh bobbing with every lurch, growing stains under his armpits.

"Did you cut his heart out?"

"Only in my dreams, Skye."

Skye eyed the monkey, who leered insolently. Shine was calculating evil. Skye's gray horse laid its ears back and pitched slightly. The horse had been unruly from the start, and didn't like walking beside the cart, didn't like that monkey, and probably had it in for the Clydesdale as well. Skye had learned to deal gently with horseflesh, so he did nothing. The horse would settle down eventually. The reddish-gray monkey clacked teeth and tugged its ear.

"What happens when we meet other bands? Apaches, Paiutes? Comanches?"

"I am known, Sah, in this region quite as well as you are known among the border fraternity."

"Indians roam, Childress."

"And so do reputations, Mister Skye."

They toiled southwest through the cool spring morning, passing into rougher and higher country. The gray sagebrush gave way to juniper, and ahead Skye could see slopes dotted with piñon pine. The well-used trail took them through long gulches, some of which showed signs of running snowmelt not long before.

The Sangre de Cristo pass lay ahead, and if the grade was no worse than this, the Clydesdale might yet pull that mountain of flesh and loaded cart over the top and down the other side. Skye watched the hardwood shafts closely, saw them flex at every pothole and bump, and wondered what Childress would do if one snapped.

As the sun neared Zenith, Childress pointed to an island of bright green ahead.

"A pool. We'll refresh. I always stop there."

Skye discovered a pool, all right, far below the trail, in a narrow gulch. Cattails surrounded it; birds flitted close to it, and numerous narrow animal trails descended to it.

"We'll rest the nags," Childress said.

Skye nodded and dismounted, ready to help Childress unhook the harness from the shafts, but the fat man shooed him off. Laboriously, he clambered to earth and sighed. He lumbered forward, released the harness, and handed the lines to Shine.

"Water," Childress commanded.

Shine sprang forward and led the draft horse out of the shafts and down the steep path to the pond.

Skye stared. The fifteen-hundred-pound draft horse placidly followed the monkey to water, shambling down the steep slope while the little monkey tugged him onward, chittering at the horse.

"Sonofabitch," Victoria snarled. "Little Person."

To her this was further proof that the thing Skye called monkey was one of the tribe of small people known only to the Absaroka. But Skye just shook his head.

Shine led the Clydesdale not only to water, but also to succulent grasses that lay just below the pond, and there the giant horse munched contentedly while the monkey hung on to the lines.

Standing Alone laughed, enchanted with the sight.

"I am beginning to see the utility of that little rascal," Skye said to Childress.

"You've seen only the beginning. He's a phenomenon. And I've been training him for six years."

In due course, without any instruction from Childress, the monkey led the gentle draft horse upslope, and backed him between the shafts, and Childress hooked up.

Skye thought surely a man so enormous would want to chow down, but Childress seemed content as he stepped into the creaking cart and settled himself on the red seat. Shine handed him the lines.

The women had completed their ablutions and the cavalcade started down the trail once again. This time Shine nestled in Childress's lap and went to sleep.

The day passed uneventfully except for a chafing wind. They encountered no one, but that was the usual in these wilds. Twilight caught them well upslope, in scattered piñon woods, with plenty of parks to graze the horses. A rivulet splashed its way toward the dusty plains far below.

"We shall halt here in this demiparadise," Childress announced. "Here we shall be provisioned, the horses succored, and all of us hydrated."

Judging from the sopping black stains on Childress's clothing, Skye supposed he needed hydrating worst of all.

Once again the monkey turned itself into manservant for the gargantuan trader. Little Shine led the huge draft horse to the runnel, let it drink, and brought it back for Childress to halter. The giant horse drifted off, snapping at good grasses with each step, belching and farting in horse heaven.

"You gonna picket him?" Skye asked.

The response was a withering stare.

Skye's women prepared a camp and set off to gather deadwood, but Shine had already beat them to it, and was heaping it at the feet of his master.

Skye wasn't sure who was master; monkey or man, but it

made no difference. They each had a high order of intelligence, but so did many madmen.

Skye knew he would sleep well that night. He was saddle sore and weary, but the sweet smell of piñon pine floated through the evening breezes; the air was fresh and gentle; the clouds promised no rain but a good sunset, and all in all, they were off to a hopeful start. The only unhappy person in the party was Victoria, who was locked in mortal terror of Shine.

11

our days later they reached the summit of Sangre de Cristo pass, a grassy plateau, and there ran smack into Utes. A dozen warriors, brightly dressed with all their war honors on display, raced their fleet mounts straight toward the red cart, whooping ever closer.

Skye slipped his rifle from its beaded sheath, checked to see whether a cap was on the nipple, and waited for whatever came.

"It's the Capotes," Childress proclaimed as the advance guard hurried forth and surrounded Skye and his women. He lifted his broad-brimmed straw hat and waved them on, with a gallant and cavalier swoop.

All but two or three of these bronze, lean, bare-chested warriors were young and ready for anything. But Skye saw no nocked bows, and their war clubs hung from saddles. He slipped the rifle back into its nest. Shine fairly bounced and somersaulted on the back of the draft horse, chittering and yammering at the Utes, who pointed and laughed. They were all familiar with the monkey. Shine, not the trader, was the cynosure.

Skye saw Victoria ease back on her horse. Her skirts were hiked high, baring slim brown legs. Standing Alone rode in the same fashion, but she was not relaxed and her gaze was somber and piercing as she looked over these rawboned warriors. Something malign rose from within the Cheyenne woman.

Childress immediately plunged into intense talk with a graying warrior, probably a subchief, and for once Skye regretted having a translator present because there was no finger talk he could read. The crafty Utes spoke a Shoshonean tongue, similar to that of the Comanches and Shoshones, and Skye wished he might understand.

The likelihood of trouble seemed remote, but with these Utes one could not know. He saw no easy escape. The open plateau offered no concealment, no help. He would have to wait and see how things went.

At last Childress turned to his fellow travelers.

"They're heading out to the plains on a big spring buffalo hunt. They're hungry. Whole band's following, every last one. Back a way is Chief Tamuche and the rest of them."

Skye nodded. "What have you told them?"

"I'm trading; you're with me. That's all."

"Do they know what we're about?"

"No."

"Would they recognize Standing Alone?"

Childress shrugged. "This woman, Skye, looks two decades younger than the one huddled at the gate of Bent's Fort. I saw her there last summer."

"Please tell Standing Alone all this."

Childress switched to the Cheyenne tongue, which he spoke hesitantly, and Standing Alone absorbed his news without a flicker of emotion. Several of the warriors listened intently, barely controlling their restless horses, and Skye suspected that some of them understood Cheyenne, and maybe English.

Skye didn't like it. He lifted his hands to draw attention to them, and addressed the older one who bore the scars of war upon his torso, Skye's fingers and palms and wrists and elbows spelled out messages.

Friend, peace, who are you?

The warrior pointed at himself. "Degadito," he said aloud. Chief, friend, buffalo hunter. You trade? Hungry. Who are you?

Skye replied. Maybe, few things. Looking for lost people.

Ah, looking for people. The subchieftain nodded.

Skye made the sign for the heavens, and pointed at himself.

"Ah! Skye!" the headman said. The name was obviously known. Skye marveled that his name was so well known from tribe to tribe and band to band. The warrior studied him, examined Victoria, and then gazed at the beautiful Cheyenne woman, registering curiosity in his face.

The rest of the village rounded a copse of pine, and rode majestically forward. Now other warriors and headmen raced ahead, the red cart galvanizing them all. Soon Childress's wagon was surrounded, ten deep, and Shine put on a show, swinging gayly from horse to cart to the ground, where he shook hands with squealing children. Soon the women were crowding close, wanting to see Shine. He obliged them by tugging at skirts and grinning broadly.

Skye saw the value of the monkey who entertained these Utes but was looking for other things: children who looked Cheyenne, or any other color or race or breed, and there were plenty of them to consider. The Utes seemed even more varied in racial composition than most tribes, and Skye thought he saw Hispanic and other European blood in the younger ones. The men were lean; the women stocky.

Standing Alone, too, was studying the Utes from the back of her horse. Here was an entire village on the road, the lodges loaded onto travois, households bundled onto the backs of burros and mules and horses, and even a few oxen. There was no place to hide a child.

The Ute women were smiling, poking fingers at the monkey, and obviously having a grand time, while Childress continued a conversation with the Utes. But Standing Alone was sliding off her horse. She handed the rein to Victoria, who was muttering things, and then Standing Alone walked slowly through the throng, her piercing gaze resting on each young man and woman, missing not one young person. Her back was arched and she walked proudly, as if to say that she was a Cheyenne woman and not afraid. Once she cried out, only to turn away after staring at a girl.

All this suited Skye fine; Standing Alone could examine the entire band without making her purpose known. In a settled village, with lodges erected and life within them hidden, it would be much harder.

Victoria edged her shaggy horse closer to Skye. "We damn well got big luck this time," she said. "They don't know her. We don't have to say."

Skye nodded, lifted his top hat, and settled it.

Tamuche had dismounted and sent a boy to summon them; he wanted to be introduced. Childress did the honors, hastening across the flat with Shine riding his shoulder. Skye and his women followed. Tamuche stood on his tiptoes, erect; wiry, intense, dark as mahogany. Some black chin whiskers curled around his jaw, his eyes glowed like agates, and his demeanor was a studied indifference, a theatrical yawn. Tamuche plainly considered it beneath him to be impressed. The chief and headmen and shamans looked Skye over, nodded, and talked among themselves. Eventually, they turned to Childress.

"We'll have a fiesta," the Colonel said. "They want to trade with me and have a big Bear Dance in your honor. They got them a gander at that grizzly bear-claw necklace around your neck, Sah, and think that's big medicine. There's a spring around the bend, and that's where they'll break out the champagne and caviar."

"I'm agreeable," Skye said.

"They're inclined toward anything bearish, Mister Skye. They have an affinity for bears, and think of themselves as bear people. Their Bear Dance is mighty medicine. So you're being highly honored. They look upon you as a good omen; a bear-claw man like you, can only mean a good hunt."

"Sonofabitch," said Victoria.

"Your wife expresses herself poignantly, Mister Skye. I am at a loss when it comes to matching her elocution."

Victoria laughed. Skye could read her mind. If she was lucky, she might even get some hooch this dance night under the stars.

Childress continued: "I'll tell them about our new store and hand out a few trinkets; I'll remind them they'll be passing it en route to the buffalo grounds. And I'll probably sell some iron arrow points, and some powder, perhaps, but not a dozen of them have muskets. This outfit's low on food, too."

That all seemed just fine to Skye. He wanted to observe the Utes; watch them trade, study their physiognomy, and maybe learn how to approach them about the children—and stay out of trouble.

The Utes retreated to the small spring that dribbled icy water into a green pool with no outlet, while Childress drove his red rig there. Soon the squaws had some fires lit and the warriors were watering the ponies at the small spring. When Shine led the big draft horse to the spring, the warriors parted at once to observe this amazing thing, twenty pounds of monkey leading fifteen hundred pounds of horse.

No meat. The Utes didn't have any, which was why they were en route to buffalo country. The squaws stood about, waiting for some provisions from the traders, but Skye had none to spare and Childress wasn't carrying much. It was going to be a hungry night.

The Utes had a small herd, heavily guarded by the boys, and Skye looked them over carefully, unsure of what a Cheyenne boy would look like. But Standing Alone had already done that, walking imperiously among the laughing and joking Utes, her face a mask but her will and determination springing from every step.

The fat trader opened his store with a majestic flourish and gymnastic entertainment from Shine, who plucked up awls and blue beads and arrowheads and flasks of powder and held them up, clacking and dancing before the studious Utes. Soon the cart contained some heavy buffalo robes and a few glistening beaver pelts, and the Indians were busy ogling their ribbons and beads.

Some cooking smells drifted on the breeze, along with piñon pine smoke, the sweetest aroma Skye had ever smelled, and in time he realized they were boiling a few dogs. He would gladly have rolled up in his blankets by then, but the night's festivities were just beginning. Chief Tamuche invited the Colonel's party to sit beside him, smoke the pipe as twilight thickened, and then see the great Dance of the Bears.

The dogs vanished down Ute gullets, and Skye saw Childress watching. But the Colonel asked for nothing, and contented himself with some tea, which he brewed in a small kettle all by himself. That in itself seemed to be a mystery: a fat man who didn't need food. Shine had no trouble at all stealing a meal. In time, Tamuche's wives presented Skye and his women with a half a dozen fat roasted lizards, glistening and yellow, with black collars, on a slab of bark. Some piñon nuts, Ute emergency food, completed the repast. Skye ate. He had learned to eat when he could and what he could, because the natural world provided nothing else. The whole meal consisted of a few smoky, stringy bites, and some starchy nuts.

Victoria laughed. She preferred the cuisine of the plains tribes.

The Bear Dance began in the velvet quiet of the evening, softly at first, each portion of it varying from the next. Skye listened to the metronomic drumming, the low gutterals, the honoring of all bears, the pantomimic capture and killing of a bear, the portioning of its spirit to the bear dancers, and then he nodded.

He awakened with a start as silence enveloped the encampment. A chill spring wind cut through the uplands, scattering orange sparks. Skye worried about his horses, which were being herded with all the rest. He worried about the Utes' famous propensity to lift whatever they could lift. The women were slipping into their blankets. Childress was snoring under his cart. Skye had never found raw ground comfortable to sleep on, and knew that few mountaineers did either, though they bragged about their toughness. This ground was hard as stone and he could not shape it. The night would be long and wakeful. But all things considered, maybe that was good, not bad.

But it was Standing Alone who filled his mind that night. Among these Utes, she was a different and forbidding woman.

12

S kye awakened at the earliest gray light of dawn thinking something was wrong. But nothing seemed wrong.
The Utes slept. Childress's red cart, perched on its
wheels and its shafts, still sheltered the trader. The draft
horse grazed nearby, its halter rope trailing. No one stirred.
No cook fires burned. None of these people had erected a
lodge, but lay on the cold ground, grouped as families or
clans.

He felt about for his rifle and powderhorn, and found
them beside his robes. Victoria's quiver and bow lay beside
her. Standing Alone's few things, captured in a parfleche,
lay at her blankets. The Skye provisions, heaped where they
had been lifted off the horses, had not been touched. Nothing stolen. It was not going to storm. No hostile warriors
were filtering through the slumbering encampment. There
were fewer dogs this morning than last night, and those that
survived the cookpots were not roaming. Nothing was
wrong.

He turned and found Victoria staring at him silently.

"What?" he muttered.

"I don't know, dammit," she replied.

They began a systematic search as they often had done
when they sensed danger. Stare at each twenty degrees of

the compass, wait for movement, wait for whatever it was they were waiting for.

Skye ran his hands over the stubble of his jaws, and down his chest, finding the bear-claw necklace, a treasure any Ute warrior would have coveted. He picked up his short-barreled mountain rifle, which felt sweet and heavy in his chapped hands. There was nothing to shoot at.

The light improved perceptibly, and the first hints of color began to tint the grayness. Skye could not shake the feeling that something was amiss. The one thing he could not see from where he lay was the horse herd. But no alarm had sounded and he had no reason to suppose that this Capote band had lost their four-foots to marauders.

Then, as the light quickened, Victoria pointed. On a distant knoll, ghostly in the murk, stood Standing Alone, her arms stretched upward, her back arched, her fingers reaching for something that lay in the beyond.

"Praying, big damn bad medicine, makes the world ache," Victoria whispered.

Skye nodded. He could not fathom this mystery. The woman's morning prayer was infecting this place, making him jumpy, as if she had called down pox and plague upon these Utes and demons were cursing the land under him.

"Maybe she wants these here damn Utes to get scabs, starve, sicken, and die," Victoria muttered.

Whatever it was, the Cheyenne woman had wrought an uncanny malaise upon this place, and it resonated in his bones.

He stood; Victoria did, too. It felt good to escape the cast-iron hardpan that had formed his bed. His body ached as it often did when sleeping in the wilds. Life lived in nature was no lark: bitter cold, fierce heat, mosquitos, horseflies, hornets, hunger, thirst, bad water, rain, hail, snow, frozen toes, chafing wind, and solid rock for a bed.

The Utes would probably not sleep late into the morning;

they would leave for the plains in a rush to find buffalo for their bellies, their sleeping robes, their lodges, their war shields. Buffalo weren't easy to find and were hard to kill. Butchering them was brutal work. Tanning their hides was just as toilsome.

He glanced around sharply, still ill at ease, stretching the ache out of his muscles. Now he could see the horses scattered on a grassy slope just beyond. They looked unattended, but he knew Ute boys had been entrusted with the task of keeping them close and chasing off predators.

The camp stirred. An old man padded to the edge of camp and made water. A woman stood, wrapped a blanket about herself, and walked toward some brush. Off in the distance, Standing Alone finished her incantations and walked slowly toward the encampment. Skye sensed a strange force radiating from her.

There was indeed one unaccounted for, and that was Shine. Where was the little pirate? A dread crept through Skye. He could think of scores of reasons why these people might want to kidnap Childress's monkey, maybe even to worship a creature that so resembled human beings. Whoever possessed Shine would possess great medicine. Worried, Skye edged toward the trader's cart looking for the spider monkey, and found him curled up under it, next to his master. Or was the monkey the master? The monkey was safe with Childress, and Skye felt sheepish about his strange foreboding.

By the time the sun's orange light was lancing the treetops, the Utes were up and preparing to move. Skye saw no cookfires this morning. There was little to do at this impromptu camp but load the travois and packhorses and start. One by one, the men headed into the herd and caught horses for the women. They were good horsemen and able to drop a braided leather loop over a horse's neck without stirring the herd. They had probably learned equestrian skills from the Spanish.

Skye and Victoria caught their horses, bridled them, and led them back to the encampment.

He found Childress up and brewing tea at a tiny fire, the only one in the camp. Shine had vanished.

"How are you and the monkey this morning, Colonel?"

"We're fine; Shine's hungry. He's fetching himself a meal."

"And you?"

"I live on my padding, Sah. It is a great asset at times, on the road."

"You know the Utes. Would this be a good time to ask about the missing children?"

"There is never a good time for that, Mister Skye," Childress said, pouring steaming tea from a tin pot into a battered cup.

"Would you ask Tamuche?"

Childress turned silent and stared at the ground. Finally, he nodded. "It is a great and just and noble cause we pursue, my friend Mister Skye. I'll commence a powwow with the devil."

"How would you approach the chief?"

"You brought something to give him?"

"Blue beads, a few tools and knives."

"He might prefer food. This band is down to pine nuts."

"I have a little."

"There's no time like the present, Mister Skye."

The heavy man rose nimbly to his feet while Skye extracted some gifts from his meager supplies: beads, a knife, a pound of sugar in a cotton sack. Most Indians loved sugar and he suspected Tamuche would too.

They walked to the chief's bedground and stood at the edge, awaiting an invitation. The wiry man was watching his wives toil.

Eventually the chief nodded, and Childress began a colloquy with him in the Ute tongue, finally turning to Skye.

"He says not now; no talk. They are going to find buffalo. Their stomachs are empty. They are in a hurry."

"Tell him I have a gift if he would answer some questions about missing children. A pound of sugar. A knife."

This was conveyed to Tamuche, who shook his head.

"They cannot delay," Childress said.

Skye set the gifts before Tamuche and added an awl to the knife and sugar sack and skein of beads. "A pound of sugar, an awl, a knife, and a string of blue beads for his women. Very quickly. A few questions. All for some knowledge he might possess."

Tamuche replied with a question: About what?

"About two Cheyenne children, a boy and a girl, who disappeared from Bent's Fort four winters ago. Their mother is with us. We want to find them."

Tamuche listened and fell into silence. Skye noticed that two headmen had gathered also and were monitoring this exchange. He saw no change of expression among the Utes, yet something had changed.

Childress spoke, and there was a vast silence, broken only by the soughing of the zephyrs through pine boughs.

Tamuche spoke sharply, and Skye thought all was lost, but Childress conveyed an unexpected message. "We will smoke," he said.

That was good news. The great ritual of negotiation would begin. So time didn't matter. Reaching the buffalo didn't either. A smoke could last half a day.

A brief word to one of his wives brought Tamuche a long-stemmed pipe with a red pipestone bowl, an alien pipe for this country, along with a beaded leather pouch of loose tobacco. He signaled that all should be seated.

A Ute boy appeared with a glowing coal from Childress's fire, borne on a green leaf. Tamuche accepted the coal, used it to fire the pipe, then offered the smoke to the four winds, and passed it in the small circle. By now, a dozen Ute headmen had gathered around and stood watching. The camp itself was largely ready to travel. Time had stopped; this was ritual, and no white man's clock governed it.

But at last, after the pipe had circled the seated Utes and white men, Tamuche began with a question, translated by Childress.

"Is the Cheyenne woman with you the one we hear of, who huddles at the gate and awaits her children? We have heard of this woman. We admire her, and believe she is following her own bright pathway, and all the Utes talk well of her."

Childress answered without waiting for Skye, saying yes, this is the very woman. Indeed, Standing Alone was standing apart, outside the circle, a strange bleak aura separating her from other mortals.

"But she is young; the one we know of is very old."

"It is the same woman, Standing Alone, of the Cheyenne. She has washed her hair, put on a new dress, and wears spirit moccasins that take her where she must go. And so her years fall away. Her spirit helpers have told her the time has come to go find her children, and now she has enlisted us." All this Childress explained, this time fingering the sacred medicine bundle.

"Ah!" exclaimed Tamuche, studying the bundle. "Why does this Cheyenne woman think I might know such a thing? The Utes are accused of many bad things. Many lies! We have many enemies, and they tell lies about us. We are nothing but a poor band of mountain people who cannot find enough food and must get horses and food any way we can."

When this was translated, Skye thought it amounted to an admission that the Utes did indeed traffic in children.

In any case, Childress was earnestly conversing and all Skye could do was sit there and wait, and interpret the occasional gestures that accompanied their talk.

"He says the gifts are not enough."

"Tell him maybe his information isn't enough."

Tamuche's face registered nothing upon hearing that. He was a master of diplomacy in his own way, Skye thought.

"Enough of this, he says. He will go to the buffalo lands now and kill the hairy ones and fill their empty bellies. He says, Have we not been good hosts, fed you from our poor stores? Have we not given you enough? We go in peace. You have not given us enough, but we will accept it anyway."

Skye nodded, but Tamuche was talking again.

"He says, go to the Weeminuche and talk to White Coyote," Childress said.

A thread of something.

Skye nodded. "We thank the chief of the Utes, and wish him great success."

Within minutes, the Utes headed east, and Skye and his women, Childress and his monkey, and all their horses and equipment headed west, down the long grade into the San Luis valley.

13

The farther Skye pierced into Mexico, the more he felt its brooding silences. For days after they had descended into the San Luis Valley, Skye and his entourage had progressed southward through a moody and austere land. Scarcely a breeze stirred the air. The skies were a transparent indigo that he had never before seen in all his wanderings, and he found this heaven utterly strange and marvelous, as if God had fashioned a different firmament for a different nation.

But most of all, Skye felt the fearsome silence. Mexico was a land of such deep silences that the slightest noise was startling, like a lamentation in heaven. They rode their docile mounts along a dry trail toward the village of San Luis, northernmost of Nuevo Mexico's settlements, or so Childress said.

So transparent was the air that Skye was sure he could see peaks a hundred miles distant, brooding and mysterious, harboring secrets. Crystal air, deep silences, and forbidding ranches in hidden havens.

Where would the children be? This country was so vast that a glance could sweep hundreds of square miles and yield nothing. Yet it was an illusion. They had passed hidden valleys verdant with foliage, which were invisible from the plain. Ranchos could be tucked into any of them. How would they search? Who would guide them? The sheer grandeur of the country they were slowly penetrating humbled Skye.

Somewhere off to the west the Rio Grande tumbled through a gorge, according to Childress, and in various places its bottoms were farmed and settled. Yet none of that was visible from the trail to Taos. They saw only vast and mysterious reaches of the earth's surface, endless flats, distant mountains rising in air so clear they seemed sharp-edged and near.

They reached a watered basin filled with thick grasses that didn't bend to any wind, and beheld skinny longhorned cattle there, some of them herded by children.

"Approaching San Luis," Childress said from his seat on the cart. "Nothing here. Half a dozen adobe jacals, and a defense tower. You won't find the missing ones. These peasants couldn't afford to buy a slave, much less feed and clothe one."

"We'll look anyway," Skye said, determined to miss nothing. "Where'd you learn about Mexican slavery?"

"Mister Skye, you'll spend a lifetime looking for the Cheyenne children, and get nowhere doing it that way. What you want is information. We'll get that in Taos, if it is to be gotten anywhere, Sah. We'll buy it or steal it, but we'll fetch it some fashion or other, and thereby find the string that will lead us to the children."

Skye knew it was so, and yet wanted to ride to every rancho for a look. Childress's strange enthusiasm piqued him.

They reached San Luis late in the afternoon of another quiet day, and their arrival drew everyone in the village into a rude plaza. They knew this trader and his monkey, and jabbered about him, with bright smiles. Skye rode through clay streets between brown buildings while a small crowd followed the horses and cart. Skye could scarcely see a difference between these dark, wiry people and the Indians, except for the dress. Older women wore black rebozos; younger ones wore lighter cottons, and most of the men wore only pantalones. All were barefoot.

Childress began to banter with them in Spanish, and again Skye could fathom none of it.

"I'm going to look at that tower," the Colonel said, sliding off his cart. "Always interested in blood and death." Several young men eagerly escorted him to the two-story adobe structure.

The monkey stayed on the cart, entertaining the Mexicans, who laughed at him much as the Utes had. Shine shook hands, pilfered anything he could, and chittered at them.

Skye watched the trader vanish into the shadowed interior of the tower, curious as to why the man chose to see that rather than to trade. But maybe these people had no coin, nothing to trade. Still, they would have grains, and that would be worth some dickering. The travelers had fed themselves almost entirely on the few provisions Skye had brought along.

As usual, Standing Alone was surveying the young people in the village, and finding no sign of her own.

When the Colonel returned, he pulled back the canvas covering his wares, and set a few out. The women crowded about, but the men held back.

"Won't sell a dime's worth," Childress said. "They've nothing to trade."

"We could use some wheat or maize," Skye said.

"Well, I won't trade for that. Mister Skye, that tower's never been used. Built to defend against Utes and Apaches, but it never was put to a test. There's only two escopetas in town anyway. That's blunderbuses, if you don't know the word. And no powder for the lot. All the tower's good for is to store grains."

Skye dismounted, dug into his packs, and found a couple of knives he had been given for trade.

"Tell 'em I'll trade knives for grain," he said.

"But, Sah, why?"

"Because we're about starved."

A few minutes later, Skye had surrendered two knives but had a sack of rough-ground flour that Skye knew would have sand and bits of husk in it. He'd eaten plenty in his day.

They trotted out of San Luis in midafternoon heat, but suddenly Childress seemed to be in a hurry and snapped a whip over his Clydesdale.

"You learn something there?" Skye asked.

"Only that there's nothing here. These are all peasants, Skye, with their kitchen gardens and a few kine. We won't find any big ranches, the kind that might use Indian herders, until we approach Taos."

"Did you ask about workers or slaves?"

"Sah, the only thing I inquired about was that tower."

Skye puzzled that, and could not explain the man's interest in defenses.

"Trust me, Skye, when we approach a great ranch, you will find me a bloodhound on a trail. I do so yearn, Sah, yearn to find those little red gnats."

Skye stared.

"I'm a sucker for any good cause, Mistah Skye. Wherever there's injustice, cruelty, lives ruined, death, and misery, there's old Childress trying to make things right."

That afternoon they struck an icy creek that tumbled out of the Sangre de Cristos, hurrying toward the Rio Grande off to the west somewhere. Beside it was a faint road. They paused where these merry waters laughed their way west, and refreshed themselves and their horses.

Skye thought that the Clydesdale was looking gaunt, and perhaps they should all recruit for a day on the lush grasses that grew along the banks.

"Behold the trace, my English friend," said Childress. "I take it that we're near a hacienda, and we can begin our quest for the Holy Grail hereabouts."

"Where's the ranch?"

"Oh, I take it that one or two leagues will suffice."

"One or two leagues!"

"Sah, you are in country so large that it dwarfs the Republic of Texas, God spare me for saying it."

"I thought you were aiming to get information first."

"My dear Mistah Skye, here we are; a road leads westward to someplace that might harbor vile slavery and cruel servitude. As for me, I will not only search for the lost tribe of Israel there, but also reconnoiter."

"Reconnoiter?"

"A filibuster, my dear Sah, needs a map of the territory and its armed men burnt into his gray matter."

Skye laughed. "Your purposes grow clearer with every mile, Emperor. All right. We will use one another. I'm cover for you and your schemes, and you're my translator and guide in old Mexico. I'm beginning to understand the Jolly Roger painted upon the sides of your bloodred cart."

Childress grinned. "You are a man to reckon with, Sah. Let us examine this rancho, if such it be."

The Colonel took it upon himself to explain this to Standing Alone, who brightened. At last, she would be going to a place where her children might be snared.

They turned westward along the two-rut trail that paralleled the creek, and soon found themselves in a broad, grassy valley that could only be paradise for cattle.

Even Victoria brightened. Skye had never seen her so dour, so distrustful, and judging from her glare at the spider monkey, she probably had slaughtered him a hundred times in her mind.

Shine himself sensed that they were piercing toward some nearby objective, and began doing handsprings on the sweated brown back of the patient Clydesdale. The brook babbled, relieving at last the oppressive silence Skye had felt ever since he entered Mexico.

Thus they continued, under an azure sky, until near sundown they beheld an adobe settlement, a rural fortress situated on a vast meadow that was sheltered by a long arid bluff to the north. This place, too, had an earthen tower high enough to command the surrounding fields. A great black bell hung on a frame above it; a bell that might be heard for miles.

"Well done," Childress said. "See that brass poking out of the tower? A field piece. Stuff it with grape and see the carnage."

"What might threaten them, Colonel?"

"Utes and Comanches and Jicarillas," the Colonel replied. "Every one of them capable of slaughtering the occupants, ravishing their women, and roasting the males over a fire until they are cooked alive."

By then their imminent arrival had attracted attention, and assorted Mexicans, mostly male, flooded out of the placita, and stood waiting.

"Oh, one thing, Skye," the Colonel said. "These hacendados play God. If they don't like us, they can bind us up and ship us to Mexico City for a decade in a dungeon."

"For what?"

"For anything, Sah. For trespassing, for trading without permission, for breathing, for being Protestant, for failure to pay import duties. Or for warring upon the Republic of Mexico."

"Thanks for the warning," Skye said.

14

The patron of this great hacienda was not the sort of man Skye expected to see. He stood quietly at the tower awaiting his guests, intelligent eyes shelved under a pale dome of forehead that surrendered reluctantly to kinked coppery hair. He was accoutered in a fine frock coat of royal blue velvet with white knee breeches. At his arm was a raven-haired beauty in white cotton.

The hacendado's gaze took in everything there was to see about Skye's party, resting on the red cart with its strange insignia, then upon the trader in his broad-rimmed Panama and open white shirt, and then upon Skye, and finally, briefly, the Indian women.

"Gentlemen?" he said, in English.

"At your service, Sah," Childress said, with a sweep of his Panama. "Traders. Perhaps we can supply your necessaries?"

"Americans?"

"I am a Texan, Jean Lafitte Childress of Galveston Bay."

"A rebel."

"Why, Sah, Lone Star Texan and proud of it, and if I give offense, it's because I mean to. You'll not find a more loyal Texan than the gent you see before you. We defended certain sacred and holy rights promised all Texans by the Republic of Mexico and wantonly abandoned by that scoundrel Santa Anna. If we distress you, we shall depart at once. With whom do we speak?"

The hacendado nodded, and then focused on Skye. "And you, sir?"

"I am Mister Skye, London born but a man without a country."

"Are you from Australia, then, or Van Dieman's Land?"

"No, sir, seven years in the Royal Navy."

"Ah, a surprise! And what do you do?"

"I am in the fur trade."

"And why are you without a country?"

"That is my choice, sir."

"And why are you here in Mexico?"

"I am looking for two young Indians we believe are in northern Mexico."

"And who are these?" the man asked, waving languidly at the two women.

"One is Victoria, my wife, of the Crow people, and the other is Standing Alone, of the Cheyenne people."

"And why are you stopping here, so far off the Taos Camino?"

Childress replied: "To trade, Sah. We have a small but select number of items for your consideration."

"Have you the permiso from Santa Fe?"

"We're en route, to obtain just such a license."

"Then it is very indiscreet of you to offer merchandise in a nation where you have no right to do business."

This man with the blue velvet frock coat exuded some strange force of will that was belied by his soft attire. Skye sensed that a word from the man could decide their fate. There was the slightest pause, while the master of this fortified rancho, almost a village, came to some conclusions.

"You will forgive me if I prefer to do business here rather

than within," he said. "I don't know that I've ever seen a conveyance with a skull and crossbones enameled on the side of it; pray thee, what means it?"

Childress's response astonished Skye. "I'm a privateer, Sah, once employed by the Republic of Texas to prey on Mexican shipping. Now I prey on Mexicans in another fashion. The Jolly Roger is my whimsy, and the mark of my passage. I shall extract the highest possible price for anything I part with, having piracy in my bones."

The response plainly nonplussed the hacendado.

Shine leaped and chittered and danced on the back of the Clydesdale. The gathered peons, sun-stained and worn, stared at the little creature.

The hacendado laughed gently. "I like candor. You're probably here for some other reason. Admit to one sin to hide a larger one."

This time it was Childress's turn to laugh. The monkey chittered and jumped to the ground. Children squealed.

"I am Gabor Rakoczi," the master of the place said, "and this is my wife, Maria Elena Salvador y Rakoczi. I have never had the pleasure of commerce with self-confessed pirates before."

"You speak English fluently, Mister Rakoczi," Skye said.

"Three years at Cambridge does that, doesn't it? I speak the Spanish better. Love does that. Anyone who serves the Hapsburgs, as I did for years, would know Spanish." He smiled at his wife. "Mrs. Rakoczi is well advanced with Hungarian, which is the language of domesticity in the home." He paused. "Well, are you going to display your wares or is there some other purpose for which you honor us with your sterling company?"

Again, Skye sensed the iron willfulness of the man who ruled over this empire in the wilderness.

Childress hastened off his seat on the red cart and drew back his canvas. His wares suddenly looked to be few and poor.

Rakoczi dismissed them at a glance. "It is not even a good show, Mister Childress." He grinned, displaying even white teeth. "And that brings us to purposes. What does a handful of tinker's items conceal? A filibuster, perhaps? What a word! A coinage of Washington, District of Columbia, I think. Are you examining northern Mexico as a plum to be plucked? Are you here to assess my strength? Ah, I will show you if you wish. Behold the tower. There's a six-pounder in it, and plenty of grapeshot and ball, and my muchachos are experienced cannoneers. Arms? I can put thirty men into the field on horse, all with good Prague steel in hand. Lances, pikes, muskets. We are a cavalry troop, in case you wonder. Good Spanish Barb stock I brought up from Vera Cruz, Toledo sabres, pikes and pistolas. Say, would you sell me your Clydesdale there? I saw them in England and thought them dumb and docile, just like the English. Yes, a sturdy animal, useful here, but not a thrifty eater. We would have to fatten him. He's rather gaunted, wouldn't you say? I'll give you a piratical offer for it, or maybe just take it from you if you protest too much at the few pesos in my palm."

Skye stared at this hacendado who was toying with them before the gates of his rural fortress, and enjoying every moment of it. The man could do anything he threatened to do.

Childress laughed politely.

"The monkey's a good touch," Rakoczi said. "Yes! See how he entertains while you conduct your reconnaissance. Your insignia's a fine touch, too. It starts conversations all by itself. Yes, and how much information you can fetch in a hurry, with a monkey and a crossbones." He turned suddenly to Skye. "Now tell me about these Indians you seek."

Skye scarcely knew how to approach this man, but candor had always served him best. "Two Cheyenne children were abducted by the Utes four years ago and sold here in Mexico, as far as we know. This is their mother. We hope to free them."

"Sold? Sold? Free them, Skye? You are suggesting they are not free?"

"It's Mister Skye, mate."

"Mister Skye, is it?" Rakoczi's teeth were showing again. "This is the Mexican Republic, and there's not a soul here who is held in bondage, unlike the American South, or the misnamed and alleged Republic of Texas."

Skye ignored him. "We're prepared to purchase the two Indian children. They'd be almost adult now, about sixteen and thirteen."

"Purchase, Mister Skye? Are you suggesting that mortals are bought and sold here? Are you telling me that you're talking about slavery?"

"Peonage, Señor Rakoczi. Binding laborers to the land with debt. Indenture. Do you have peons?"

Rakoczi laughed softly. "Slavery! I have never heard of it. I shall tell the bishop of Durango. The church would be distressed. Come, let us talk to these slaves."

He drifted toward a young couple who stood nearby. "I shall translate the Spanish, and Mr. Childress can correct me if he detects the slightest flaw in my translation, yes? I take it you speak Spanish, yes?"

He didn't wait for a response, but questioned the couple intently, while Childress listened.

"They say, Mister Skye, that they are glad to work for me, and are proud to be under the protection of so great a master as the owner of the Hacienda de Las Delicias, which is very like heaven to them, and the master is very like a saint who will sit at the right hand of God."

Skye nodded.

Standing Alone was sitting her horse, restlessly studying the fifty or sixty people clustered there.

"Are there any Indians here?" Skye asked, abruptly.

"We always employ some, Mister Skye."

"If any of them are the children of this woman, we wish to reunite them with their mother, who grieves for them."

"They drift in, and who knows, sir. Some are domestics, and some are herders. Shall we seek them out?"

Skye thought he might do just that. "They are free to leave, then?"

"Oh, it might not be quite that simple. Perhaps they owe something. Often they have to be equipped with clothing, and tools, and of course we add their room and board."

Skye nodded.

"But come in, my English friend, and see. Tell the Cheyenne woman she is free to examine my whole placita."

Childress translated.

"And if the Cheyennes are hers, sir, and wish to leave your employ, then what?"

"I am a Christian gentleman, the nephew of a cardinal bishop of Hungary, Mister Skye, and you will find me utterly opposed to your effort to surrender them to their heathen mother when I can provide them with all the civilizing virtues, as well as the True Faith, all of which is to their benefit.

"Shall I send a young man on the brink of accepting Our Lord back to the pagan life from which he came? Never. It would be a sin. But such as you describe aren't here; let her look among us." He glanced at the low sun. "Come to vespers and see for yourself. And freshen yourselves with us for the night. You are guests here at the estancia of Don Gabor. I've never entertained a pirate before, nor a monkey, nor a rebel Texan, nor men who drown beavers for a living, and I look forward to it. Maria Elena is eager to welcome such exotic company, men of callings beyond her experience. She will be especially interested in pirates."

He beckoned them to enter the placita, which they did. But Skye wondered whether they would freely leave it.

15

The adobe chapel filled slowly at sundown, while Standing Alone posted herself at its rough-planked door to observe every soul who entered there. The man who called himself Childress had advised her to examine those who came, and assured her that everyone in the hacienda would be present because the master required it. He could scarcely fathom what it was like to search in such a fashion for a lost daughter or son. She stood at the portal, resolute and silent, her gaze flicking from one to another of the Mexicans.

He stood beside her, ready to assist. One by one the peons drifted in, their faces shy and meek and sun-stained, their cottons virtually rags of faded blue and soiled white. Most were barefoot. The women looked weathered from work in the fields, bent from scrubbing clothing in the sun, worn from herding.

The narrow earthen chapel exuded gloom, save for a single candle upon a waxed hardwood altar. The men and women of Las Delicias settled silently on cottonwood benches to thank God for this day. A baby whimpered, but Childress felt himself wrapped in a peaceful and solemn celebration of a good day. He remembered his other mission, and counted sixty-two souls, datum to file away against the conquest of northern Mexico by Lamar's army.

Standing Alone saw no one who resembled her daughter or son, and when the crowd had settled she and Childress and Shine sat down at the very rear, beside Skye and Victoria.

Don Gabor Rakoczi, attired in black, recited the vespers rite in Latin, and at certain ringing of an altar bell his flock responded by rote. The air was so still that the candle never guttered, and not even the mumbling of the congregation shook the flame.

Both Victoria and Standing Alone beheld all this with unalloyed curiosity, and Childress wondered what, exactly, was passing through their minds. Here was the white men's God. The trader had a more commercial view of things, and eyed the carved and enameled wood bultos, and the gilded altar crucifix, and found no worth in them. Shine liked the occasional summons of the bell in Rakoczi's sure hand, and bounced happily on the bench. Childress supposed that the monkey knew about as much of what was being said in Latin as Don Gabor's flock.

This evening rite concluded swiftly, and the peons filed out, their gaze quick and curious upon the strangers and the monkey. The smell of mesquite woodsmoke hovered in the air.

"We will summon you," Rakoczi said, while escorting his wife toward their rambling adobe house. She looked particularly striking this twilit moment, with a mother-of-pearl comb pinning her raven tresses back from her aquiline face. She lifted the black mantilla from her head as she and her husband traced their way across the placita.

That proved to be the last time the Colonel saw her. He whiled away the hour by settling himself in the barren adobe room adjacent to the stables where he had been posted by a whipcord-thin aged servant. Next to it was another, with the Skyes and Standing Alone in it.

A bell clanged sourly, and at that time, the venerable servant collected the guests and took them to a dining commons, with two trestle tables in it. There they were served rice and beans and some beef stew by silent bronze Indian women; later the women fed themselves at a separate bench. There was no sign of the master of the Hacienda de Las Delicias or his lady.

The majordomo arrived just when the Colonel was wondering what might happen next, and escorted the women back to their quarters. The men proceeded to the great house, where Don Gabor, now attired in a burgundy silk smoking jacket, led them into a shadowed parlor, lit by a pair of candles, and furnished mission-style, with upright chairs that would put backbone into the most slovenly posture.

"Gentlemen," he said, offering each a cigarro. "A little smoke and talk. I am curious about you. And you are curious about me and life in Mexico. I mean to inform you." He poured ruby wine into cut-glass goblets and handed one to Skye and the Colonel.

"But first a toast." He lifted his glass. "To Mexico, forever, glorious and untrammeled, and to our Holy Faith."

The don's gaze had settled upon Childress.

"Hear, hear," the Colonel said.

Skye nodded and sipped. Skye looked odd without his battered top hat. He had washed himself, and slicked his hair, and scraped his face, so that he seemed almost civilized. But not entirely. Not ever civilized in any true sense of the word, yet not a ruffian either. The man was unlike any other.

"You have seen," Don Gabor continued, "that we maintain a certain gentility here, even in a place as remote from the heart of Mexico as this. We are a bastion of the border and the Faith; indeed, that was how this grant of a hundred square leagues came to me; anyone willing to anchor the north for the republic and the church might receive the land.

So here I am, among pieces of furniture and linens and china and glass and books and arms brought by ox-team from the Sea of Cortez, or up the Rio Grande. Do you approve, Mister Childress, or do you think all this should fall to, say, the United States?"

"Sah, my esteem for your nation and its industries and arts is boundless."

Rakoczi cocked a brow and grinned, baring those white teeth again. He turned to Skye. "And you, sir. I understand you were with the Royal Navy, but I am not clear about the rest."

Skye settled into a stiff-backed chair that was plainly tormenting him. "I deserted, sir."

The candid response caught Rakoczi by surprise. "Really?"

"I was pressed into the navy off the streets of East End, when I was a boy of twelve. That was the last I saw of my mother and father and sisters. My father had an import and export business and I was much around the Thames docks. They made me a powder monkey.

"The harder I struggled to escape this—this involuntary servitude—the harder it went for me. Seven years, sir, was I held aboard ships of war, the hulls my prisons, rarely seeing land, my pittance fined away or stolen from me, my gruel stolen by older and harder men until I learned to defend myself, with the only thing I had, my fists and my rage. I came to love the sea, but I loved liberty more. I gained my freedom at Fort Vancouver in 'twenty-three, penetrated into the mountains, and have been a man without a country ever since."

"Many good men are grateful to serve the crown."

"I might have gladly, if I had not been kidnapped bodily. English are subjects, sir, not citizens, and subjects are still at the disposal of the throne in spite of the Magna Carta. I prefer the new world, and a republic, where a man is a citizen rather than a subject."

Rakoczi listened intently. The Colonel was amused. At last, he had an inkling of what inspired Skye.

"So we have a self-confessed privateer and a self-confessed deserter for guests," the don said, fires building in his eyes. "And no man of honor."

Bear baiting, the Colonel thought.

Smoothly, Rakoczi refilled Skye's wineglass, and Skye downed the wine in one gulp. His face had darkened and he was about to explode, but Childress interrupted.

"Sah, I am no man of honor whatsoever, and find the very word repugnant," Childress said, cheerfully. "I come from a long line of brigands."

Skye had turned red. Obviously, the border ruffian didn't know what the smooth-talking don was up to. If the powerful lord of this estate could provoke an explosion, they would all be shipped to Mexico City in chains.

Somehow, Skye subsided. "Until you know what servitude is, sir, until you know endless months and years when your life is not your own, until you know what it is to be summoned only to obey, until you know a time when you cannot dream or hope, until you know what it is to walk the earth as a free man, you know nothing of my circumstance or of honor."

Skye was eloquent, Childress had to admit that of him.

The hacendado didn't seem very impressed, though. He chuckled politely. "I'm sure every prisoner in every jail thinks quite the same way, Skye."

"Mister Skye, sir. *Mister.*"

"Yes, yes, of course, forgive me my lack of delicacy." The hacendado was toying with Skye. He filled the glass again.

Skye downed the entire glass of wine, and rocked gently in his torture-backed chair. "There are various species of slavery, sir, but they all involve the capture of another mortal and ownership of his services. In the American South is a terrible form of it, in which a mortal is pure property, the same as a cow or a dog; in which a slave has no rights, can be tortured or even killed for any infraction.

"The Indians of the plains have a gentle form of it. They acquire slaves mostly in war raids, and these are usually women and children, and often they become members of the tribe in time, and marry into it. . . . And then there's your country's system of slavery, sir, called peonage."

Skye was heated now by wine and anger, and the more Skye's face reddened, the more the don was amused. But he shouldn't be, Childress thought. Skye was a brawler, and the don would find his teeth stuffed down his throat before he knew what hit him.

"We have no slavery in Mexico, Skye. The peons are Mexican citizens, with rights guaranteed by the constitution. We take care of them because they can't take care of themselves. These walls offer protection against the savages. My fields offer them employment. My wealth supplies them with all they need, even when they are old or sick and have no economic value to me. The church would condemn us if we treated them badly. We have an excellent system, humane and productive. Did even one of my peons voice one word of sorrow? Would one leave, even if he could?"

"Slaves," Skye said, his voice half strangled with his own heat. "The Indians are slaves. I know their story. They live short and brutal lives in the mines, where they starve on gruel and suffer exhaustion and injury and disease, and not much better lives in the fields, where they hoe until they drop. They last five years or ten and then they die, all used up. They aren't paid and they aren't free, and if they try to escape, they are whipped to death. But we'll find two of them—if they live."

Rakoczi finally realized the sort of man he was dealing with, and moved quickly backward.

"I think, my friend Skye, it's time for us to retire," Childress said, fearing mayhem and City of Mexico dungeons. "We'll leave honor to our host."

Slowly, almost as if he were returning from another planet, Skye quieted.

Don Gabor Rakoczi, whose hand had been in a desk drawer, slowly withdrew it. A ball would not even have slowed down Barnaby Skye. At last Colonel Childress knew, as epiphany, the sort of man he traveled with.

16

Far to the west, a half dozen riders were tracking Skye's little caravan, ghosts lost in haze. He saw and noted them, though no one else did. He would have missed them but for the sheer beauty of Mexico, the etched blue ridges, the blinding sun-bleached flats, the mysterious brooding silence, all under a cobalt heaven such as Skye had never before seen. He had never penetrated a land of such aching beauty and mystery, and felt this strange sweetness of the countryside in his bones.

The riders were not angling closer, but neither did they depart. They were stalking.

Skye kept an eye on them, and an eye on natural defenses, but there wasn't much he could do. His mind was on other matters. Colonel Childress's conduct at the Hacienda de Las Delicias had all but clamped irons on their ankles and chains on their legs. The man had made a great point of announcing he was a rebel and a pirate and a scoundrel. And all this he had proclaimed to an autocrat of the wilderness who had the men and arms to throw Childress and Skye into an eternal hell. Just why the hacendado had seen them off the following morning with a white-toothed smile and a languid wave of his arm was more than Skye could understand. But they were free and had been for two silent days.

Skye intended to do something about it before he and his wife and Standing Alone were enmeshed in even greater peril. Just what, he wasn't sure. He had spent the quiet hours of travel pondering it.

This silent morning, he had made up his mind: he and the crazy Childress were about to part company. The only question was whether to wait until they reached Taos, or whether it would be right now, period.

Victoria, who knew his moods, had fathomed what he was thinking. "He's no damn good," she had said, out of the blue.

Childress rolled along in his carmine cart with the Jolly Roger emblazoned on its flanks, his draft horse clopping its way to Santa Fe, his face shaded by his straw planter's hat, and his gaze restless, his attention flicking from person to person.

All that day the riders far off to the west tracked them, but never approached. Skye guessed they would attempt something at night if they were not friendly, and as the day waned he began looking for a place to fort up, maybe even a dry camp.

Late that soft spring day they struck a creek burbling out of the Sangre de Cristos, and a much-used campsite. The creek rolled out of a canyon half a mile east, and Skye decided to retreat there.

He pointed.

"Camp in there tonight," he said.

"But Mister Skye, Sah, that's a piece, and there's no road."

"In there."

Victoria nodded, and steered her horse and packhorses eastward. Standing Alone followed. Childress looked like he might not, but surrendered with an angry shrug and steered his cart overland.

A while later they were unpacking in a secluded flat hidden from the great plain they had been traversing.

"At least the grass is good," Childress muttered, as he

slipped to earth and unharnessed the Clydesdale. For a fat man, he was nimble.

It was a good place. The grass rose lush and tender. The fragrance of piñon pine drifted across the creek-carved hollow, a demiparadise of live oak, juniper, and pines. Skye thought they could risk a cook fire, but not after dark. He hadn't seen the stalkers for some while but he was ready for them, and this was a place with a narrow mouth that could be watched.

The monkey watered the Clydesdale, and then, as usual, began gathering dry wood, upon Childress's command. But the monkey and his master would have to go, Skye thought.

They had nothing but parched corn to eat, so the women started water heating. With a little salt, the mush wasn't bad, and it put energy into a man. In Taos, they would replenish.

Skye scarcely knew how to do what he had to do, but he was a man and he would do it, and that would end his alliance with this bizarre fool from Texas.

He waited until they had all scooped the mush into their mouths, including Shine, whose portion was tenderly dished out by Childress. While the women were scouring the blackened cookpot, Skye studied the canyon where the creek burst out of the foothills. He saw nothing in the violet twilight.

"Mr. Childress," he said harshly. "In Taos we'll go our separate ways."

The fat Texan looked surprised. He lifted his fine planter's hat, and pursed his lips. "It's a mistake," he said.

"No, it's what I want. It's necessary. Sorry."

Childress sighed. "I feared it would come to this, and I know why you're doing it."

"Then I don't have to say any more."

Childress laughed softly. "No, but I will. You're a man of honor, pursuing an honorable cause that rests heavily upon you. You've allied yourself with a privateer and God only knows what else." He was enjoying himself. "Scoundrel, reckless fool who endangered the whole party at Las Delicias calling himself a rebel and adventurer and privateer and pirate. Yes, Sah, and a man who's got the Jolly Roger painted on his cart for good measure." He chuckled softly, enjoying himself. "I knew it would come to this, Sah."

"Then that's how it'll be."

"I trust you'll pay me for my horses."

"Take them. We'll walk if we have to."

"Over a thousand miles of northern Mexico."

"Yes, ten thousand miles if that's what it takes."

The Colonel sighed. "Admire your determination, Skye."

"It's—"

"Yes, yes, yes, and with good reason. You'd make a fine Texan, Sah."

"We've had company all day," Skye said.

The trader's gaze steadied on Skye.

"That's why we're here. Good concealment, and we can defend."

"Who?"

"Half dozen riders far west, tracking us."

"Rakoczi's?"

"Don't know."

"Utes, Apaches, Federales, Rakoczi."

Skye nodded.

"My friend Skye, you're a man of honor, and you make uneasy alliance with a man like me. I know that. But I beg to advise you that the problem isn't me, it's you. The Mexicans enjoy a scoundrel, in particular, a fat scoundrel with a spider monkey. I'm the sideshow, Sah. I'm your diversion, and you proceed unmolested."

He lowered his voice almost to a whisper. "It would not be like that if you proceed without me. They fear an earnest man pursuing a good cause. It upsets them. Don Gabor Rakoczi, for instance. You he baited, me he ignored. You he drove to the brink, not me. And it was a deliberate act, I assure you. I know the Mexicans. Their entire way of life rests on the backs of peons, cheap labor, slaves in all but name, indebted and forced to stay on the land for protection. In a trice, they could turn you into a peon, my friend."

"No, they couldn't. Because no one will ever take my liberty from me again."

It was the way he said it that made Childress blanch. A breeze tucked sparks into the sky. Skye motioned to Victoria, who brought a leather camp bucket and doused the fire. It hissed, and sour smoke stained the air. But then the velvet purple twilight settled over their camp. Standing Alone headed downstream, toward some brush. She was largely left out of these conversations because of the barriers of tongue and tradition.

Skye wasn't done.

"Colonel, who are you?" he asked. "And why are you here?"

"A filibuster, Skye, a man looking for pots of gold at the end of rainbows."

"Neither of us will leave this camp until you tell me the entire truth."

"Why, Sah, what more is there to say?"

"There's plenty more."

"You've gone sour on me, I'm afraid. Can't be helped. Some men don't take to society."

"You didn't answer my question. This outfit doesn't move until you do. And that goes for you and your cart."

"I've responded to the best of my ability, and I'm sorely tested and offended, Mister Skye."

"We're not moving."

"I'm exactly what I say I am."

"And what else?"

"Sah, if you could only know how much I am a sucker for good causes. Your quest to free two hapless Cheyenne touched my very heart, my core, my soul, the center of my bosom. You have the whole of me there. Give me a great cause, liberty, justice, honor, the relief of oppression—save for religion, Sah, I don't get fired up for the Faith, but all else, I am a guerrilla and a reformer, ready to walk beside you to the southern tip of Mexico to find these children and restore them to their blessed mother. I'd have run the guillotine in France. I'd be dumping tea into Boston Harbor. I'd have fired one of those shots heard round the world at Concord. I'd be following Simón Bolívar across South America, holding his flag. And that, Sah, is how I swear and uphold the holy and unpolluted truth, my conscience, my heart, so help me God."

Skye grinned. "Guess we'll just stay here until you're ready to level with us," he said.

The fat man peered off into the gloom, fidgeted, leaned forward, and whispered: "I'm doing advance reconnaissance for President Mirabeau Buonaparte Lamar. He has it in his thick head, affixed somewhere just behind his receding forehead, that the Republic of Texas ought to reach to the Western Sea, and he set me onto it like a fat dawg sniffing trees. And you, poor old Skye, are an unwitting conspirator."

Skye hiccuped, fell to the grasses laughing, roared like a lunatic grizzly, and Victoria wanted to know what was so damned funny; all white men were crazy.

17

The chittering of the monkey awakened Skye but it was already too late. Above him, as he peered into the gray predawn, were half a dozen skeletal faces. These materialized into Indians standing over him, one with a nocked bow but the others were simply watching. Skye felt for his rifle and found that it was gone.

He scarcely dared move. Victoria was stirring beside him, and then he heard her soft cussing in the quietness.

"We've been had," said Childress from under his cart.

Very carefully, Skye sat up. The Indians let him. They wore loincloths and little else. Some had shirts, many wore a red bandanna or headband that pinned their black straight hair, most had light moccasins. Skye didn't have the faintest idea who they might be or what they intended to do.

"Jicarilla Apaches," Childress muttered. "Not tame, no Sah."

The monkey leaped about, mesmerizing the Apaches.

Off in the gloom, Skye saw a dozen others collecting the horses. They had been hobbled except for the Clydesdale, which had grazed freely, as usual, dragging a halter rope with him. Maybe this was only a horse raid. Maybe he would live a few more minutes. Maybe not.

Slowly Skye lifted his hands, showing that they contained no weapon, and then signed, Friend.

An older Apache laughed.

That was a good joke. Skye eyed the steel arrowhead aimed straight at his chest and subsided into utter quietness. But his gaze searched restlessly for anything, any clue as to what might happen, any means of escape. He saw nothing. These could be his last moments, then. He helped Victoria sit up and held her hand.

The monkey mesmerized the Apaches. They tried to grab the little creature but he was much too agile for them. A young warrior raised his bow but an older one stayed him with a guttural bark.

Some of the Apaches began opening the packs and extracted various items: cookpots, knives, a powderhorn, spare clothes. Others gathered around the red cart, yanked the canvas off, and plunged into the heaps of trade items and robes and pelts in it.

"Bloody thieves. I'll flay the hide off your backs," Childress proclaimed from under the cart, rising up in wrath. A foot on his chest flattened him. One young warrior discovered the skeins of blue beads, and exclaimed. He held one up and howled. In moments, the beads were parceled out, along with awls, flints and steels, knives, ladles, cookpots, sacks of sugar, jugs of molasses, bolts of calico, bed ticking, and two pairs of four-point blankets.

Skye observed Standing Alone, imprisoned between two of the Jicarillas and not resisting. She looked grimly at Skye and the trader, but said nothing. She looked disheveled.

Skye dared to hope. This was a looting party, but maybe not a murderous one—at least so far. But he knew the reputation of all Apaches and knew how lucky he would be to see the sun set on this day, or a sunrise tomorrow. He did not know whether these were the ones who had ridden parallel all the previous day, but it seemed likely.

The Apaches seemed to be looking for spirits. They

opened the molasses and sampled it. But as far as Skye knew, Childress wasn't carrying any ardent spirits, and that was a stroke of luck. They'd all die, and fast, once the Apaches began working on some Indian whiskey.

It was not yet dawn. He adjudged their number at thirty. They had the horses in hand, bridled and saddled, except for the Clydesdale. Shine, ever helpful, snatched the halter rope of the big animal, and led it to the rest of the horses, while the Apaches watched, amazed. Then with one graceful bound, Shine leaped up to the Clydesdale's neck; halter rope in hand, and sat there over the mane, chattering and babbling.

Most of these Apaches were on foot. Maybe they had a horse-holder down the creek somewhere, or maybe not. The Apaches wouldn't have many horses. These would be enormously valuable to them.

"I think if we're quiet, they might leave us," Skye said softly to Victoria.

The older Apache, probably a war leader, kicked him and waved his knife. The meaning was not lost on Skye.

Skye made the sign for water, but the chieftain just stared. So far, they hadn't even let Skye or Victoria stand up, and Childress was a captive under his cart.

As the day quickened, one of the younger Apaches discovered the skull and crossbones enameled on Childress's cart, and drew the rest to it. This occasioned much talk among them. They fingered it, examined the identical insignia on the other side, and studied Childress.

Skye tried a finger message: "Big man makes death."

The chieftain muttered something, and some of the warriors prodded Childress to his feet. They marveled at his girth, poking fingers into him to see what all that fat felt like. The Texan fetched his straw hat, stood quietly while they absorbed his stature, and then he launched into a soft, conversational, almost delicate address:

"I've thrown better men than you to the sharks," he said

blandly. "I've strung up your kind by your thumbs and delivered a hundred lashes, and I'll do the same to you. Let me have that whip, the one you have in hand there, you miserable cur, and I'll flail your skin right off your back and take your nose off and snap your eyes out for good measure, and while you're poking arrows into me I'll cut your chief over there to pieces and feed him to the wolves. Then I'll pull out your arrows and stuff them down your gullets, you bloody buggers."

All this Childress delivered with such aplomb that Skye marveled. Had the privateer no fear? Skye's own fear caught the spittle in his throat and silenced him and set his heart to racing, but here was the fat man blaspheming everything about the Apaches. The mad Texan was about to get them all massacred.

"You miserable dogs, you curs who sniff your own vomit, give me that whip and I'll show you a thing or two," he said, never raising his voice, and yet the power of his words reached every one of the Jicarillas.

Childress walked slowly with his hand outstretched toward the Apache boy with the whip in hand, and surprisingly, the boy surrendered it. Childress plucked it up, and suddenly the whip turned into a live, whirring thing, rattle-snaking here and there, snapping and popping, while the Apaches stood spellbound.

"Put everything back in that cart or I'll cut your heart out," he said, never raising his voice. But he did point at the cart, and at the loot the warriors had lifted. Some of it now adorned them.

Skye had never seen anything like it. Not in all his years in the Royal Navy, or all his years in the mountains, had he seen a man as vulnerable as Childress rake a hostile crowd with sheer force of will. The stern commands issued out of him with the precision of a metronome, and the plaited whip whirred and cracked, but no one moved.

It was not enough. The chieftain said something.

Half a dozen warriors circled Childress just outside of whip range, then rushed in and subdued him. Only one felt the lash. At another wave of the hand, other warriors caught Skye and Victoria and Standing Alone, and began stripping away their clothing, relentlessly, methodically, until they had it all.

Victoria snarled but she was helpless against such brute force, and so was Standing Alone. Childress had been reduced to the buff, and then it was Skye's turn. By the time the Apaches were done, Skye's party didn't own a stitch of clothing except for Childress's hat. For some reason, they awarded him his hat, which perched on his head majestically, as he stood in huge white array. His gargantuan white belly and piano legs rose like a mountain under his Panama.

Skye could not even describe his feelings, standing there before them all with every last shred yanked off of him, and now adorning the Apaches. The chieftain had commandeered his black top hat along with his rifle, powderhorn, and knives. A subchief had his bear-claw necklace. But they did not take his medicine bundle. Victoria cringed and covered herself, but Standing Alone seemed resigned to her fate, and stood calmly, her slim beauty astonishing. Then, with innate Cheyenne modesty, she turned her back upon them, and stood quietly, all the more galvanizing for having turned her back to them.

At a word from the chieftain, the Apaches swiftly loaded their booty onto the backs of the horses and their own backs, and vanished as silently as they had come, padding out of the secluded bottoms. Skye watched his horses head downriver, along with the Clydesdale with the monkey riding the mane.

Dawn had scarcely penetrated this canyon on the west slope of the Sangre de Cristos. Skye watched the Apaches vanish around a bend in the creek, and waited a moment more for surprises, but nothing else happened. He felt helpless, more so than ever in his life because he was naked.

He turned, wanting to inventory what was left, and found that nothing was left. Only the cart, and the useless harness for the Clydesdale, which was lying beyond the cart. The cart was empty. Every bit of merchandise and every pelt was gone. The canvas that covered it was gone.

The Colonel approached. His Panama stayed proudly atop his vast acreage of flesh.

"We've walked the plank, and now we're bobbing in the sea," said Childress. "A plague on their bloody bodies. Where's Shine?"

"He rode the Clydesdale."

Something vital seemed to bleed from the Colonel. "Lost him, too, then."

"The Clydesdale was last; he can't keep up with those lighter horses."

"Then the Apaches'll kill him. They won't let him return here."

"You got any ideas?"

The Colonel brightened. "I will perform my ablutions and then we can sit down under the cart and wait. None of us can walk more than a hundred yards in this cactus."

Skye thought it would be a long wait.

18

Nothing for food. Nothing to keep the sun from frying them or the wind from chafing them or the chill of night from numbing them. Nothing for their feet. Nothing to hunt with, or to defend themselves with.

Skye well knew what the odds were. The Colonel was right: they had walked the plank and now bobbed in the empty ocean. It was only a matter of time. Yet he had been in tight corners before and he was not a man to surrender.

"Let's look around," he said to Victoria.

She nodded. Slowly they patrolled the area looking for anything useful. A forgotten knife, edible roots, a rag. The others were doing the same. But the Jicarillas had been thorough, and had left nothing.

"We'll find someone on the Taos road," Skye said.

"That's a half mile of cactus, Skye," the Colonel said.

"I'll get you there without stepping on one cactus," Skye replied.

He motioned to Victoria to bring along Standing Alone.

"Let her walk behind us," he said, respecting her needs.

"Skye, I'm staying right here under the cart," Childress said. "I've water and shade, and I'll wait for help."

"Colonel, you'll have water and some shade with me. We'll walk the creek."

"I'm staying."

The Colonel sat down under his cart.

The man was determined not to move, so Skye didn't argue. "We'll send help if we can," he said.

"Skye, Sah—good to know you."

"And you, Colonel." He turned to the women. "All right, then. The sooner we reach the Taos road, the better chance we have."

He stepped into the creek and found the water numbing, the rocks slippery, and the footing treacherous. He lurched forward, tumbled, and landed splat in the icewater.

He roared, bolted to his feet, and began shivering. But there wasn't so much as a rag to dry himself.

Victoria laughed.

He turned to roar at her, but she just stood there up to her calves in water, grinning at him.

They started down the creek, one miserable step at a time, often in rocks, sometimes in sand, occasionally in muck. Skye stubbed his toes and wondered whether this was any better than walking the faint trail beside the creek. He wanted sunshine but there wasn't any; the sun lay low behind the towering Sangre de Cristos in the east.

Still . . . they walked, step by step by step, for a half hour before Skye called a halt. His feet were numb and bruised. Instantly Standing Alone turned her back to them. He sat down and rubbed his legs, which had turned blue. Victoria was cold, too, and working on her slim brown legs.

Then they started again, hiking down the river, plunging into hidden holes, teetering along until Skye's feet gave out and they rested again, this time beside sedges.

That's when Standing Alone began waving frantically, uttering sharp cries, pointing.

They looked.

The Clydesdale was progressing toward them. No Apache was driving it.

"Bloody horse," Skye said.

"Monkeee," Standing Alone said.

She was right. Shine was patiently leading the horse by its halter rope.

Victoria scowled. "Little Person," she snapped.

Skye stepped to land, stubbed his toe, but eventually reached the horse. The women followed.

The monkey chittered, danced, and leaped up on the back of the big brown horse.

"We've been rescued. Don't know how he did it," Skye said. "You ladies ride it back, harness him to the cart, put the Colonel in, and return. I'll wait."

Victoria grinned malevolently. She helped Standing Alone clamber onto that big animal, and Skye helped her, and then he watched the Clydesdale trot smartly upstream.

Skye sat in the bullrushes, wanting some clothing and some moccasins and feeling vulnerable. Hunger caught him, too. They had eaten nothing. The sun was burning in, and he lowered himself into the shade of the bankside brush, fighting off insects. Adam and Eve, he thought, could not have enjoyed Eden.

It took an hour, but Skye barely noticed. His feet still hurt. But at last, midday, he heard the clopping of the draft horse, stood, and beheld the horse and red cart approaching swiftly, driven by that great white whale, Colonel Childress, still wearing his Panama. Shine had resumed his usual perch on the Clydesdale.

"Sorry, Skye, I'm out of fig leafs," Childress said as he pulled up.

The women, both of them sprawled in the bed of the cart, grinned at him. With what little dignity he could muster, Skye clambered in, and immediately the Colonel snapped the lines over the croup of the draft horse and took off at a swift trot.

"Colonel, how far to Taos?" Skye asked.

"I reckon forty or fifty miles—three days."

"We'll be burnt. Maybe we should travel at night."

"Well, aren't you the modest one. Once you're in the drink, Skye, you have to swim for the nearest shore."

"Maybe we should pull up some grasses to cover ourselves."

"Skye, you're naked as Adam. Enjoy it. Admire the scenery. What you need is a good Mexican cigarro."

"Are there any villages closer?"

"Maybe some ranchos."

"What'll we tell people?"

"Why, Skye, that we're a pack of libertines and lechers en route to scandalize the pueblo."

"What is this word, lecher?" Victoria asked, anticipation in her voice.

Skye grunted. It was all he could do to sit naked in a bouncing cart with two bouncing naked women, both beautiful.

Victoria was enjoying it. Standing Alone mostly turned her back, but once she flashed her warm, knowing smile at Skye. Then, unaccountably, the two Indian women began giggling.

"Look for food," Skye grumbled.

They reached the Taos Camino and paused there for one last drink from the creek before turning south. The sun had climbed well into the firmament and soon would be scorching their flesh.

Skye, disturbed by his proximity to the women, offered to drive the cart, but the Colonel declined, perhaps for the same reason. The trail traversed an empty waste, and they saw nothing. Thirst built again in Skye, along with hunger and the sensation that the sun was going to destroy him.

"We'd better hole up if you can find shade," he said.

"Mister Skye, Sah, tell me where that might be."

Skye examined a bright arid plain devoid of trees. But there was brush, and an occasional arroyo.

"Find an arroyo, Colonel. We'll perish in this sun, if we

haven't already." At least the two white men would, he thought.

"The sooner we reach succor, the sooner we will be preserved, Sah. The shore is still beyond sight, but we'll make landfall soon."

There was no stopping the man. Beyond the turning wheels of the cart lay white clay, dust, small waxy plants that could endure in such a climate, rock, and boundless blue skies.

Skye turned himself on the cart bed, figuring to roast all sides evenly, but he knew he would be in trouble by nightfall.

Skye's world reduced to the walls of the cart, and he closed his eyes. There was little he could do. The heat built, sucking moisture out of him. His stomach rumbled. He felt the first pangs of dehydration; a dry mouth, a fearsome thirst.

"You all right?" he asked Victoria.

"Damn hot," she said.

The women were doing better than he was. He closed his eyes against the midday glare.

Some while later, the Colonel whooped.

"Succor, assistance, help," he bawled, and the passengers peered out to see a carreta coming their way, far ahead, with three people walking beside it.

Skye squinted at the apparition. It was a rude cart with stakes holding a tottering load of crooked firewood on it, drawn by a gaunt burro. Three young men in peasant cottons and sandals walked beside it, axes over their shoulders. They were so swart they could have been Indians themselves.

"Ah, amigos!" bawled Colonel Childress, waving a white arm at them as the parties closed.

They stared.

The Colonel rattled on in Spanish, and all Skye fathomed

was that he was talking about the Jicarilla Apaches. The young men's gaze roved between Childress, huge and white and naked, and the occupants of the cart, resting at last on the women. They gaped, unable to look elsewhere. Standing Alone turned from their stare.

"Agua, agua," Childress was saying.

The young men conferred and then produced a goatskin water bag that had been hanging from the back of their cart, which they handed to Childress, who lifted it and ran a trickle down his gullet while Skye watched enviously, afraid the fat man would drink it all. But Childress took only a swallow and handed it to Skye, who handed it to the women. There was enough for them all to get a few swallows. Childress handed it to the monkey, who drank expertly while the woodcutters stared dumbfounded.

But they had no food and no clothing to spare; not even a rag. Childress talked with them while Skye and the women waited.

At last the Colonel turned to his passengers. "Arroyo Hondo, a village, is an hour or two ahead. We are saved!"

Just barely, Skye thought.

19

Arroyo Hondo lay before them, a scatter of adobes nestled in a steep-walled canyon cut by a creek. The man styled Jean Lafitte Childress saw his salvation, but knew it would come only at the price of his mortification. He sat nakedly upon the cart, with a cargo of naked people. It would not be easy.

He spotted an adobe church or chapel, and two hundred yards behind it, through trees, a black-clad crowd that plainly was burying someone. Probably most of this rural village was there.

"We're close," he said to those huddled miserably behind him. "A long plunge downslope first."

He steered his Clydesdale down a steep incline, trusting the heavy horse to brake the cart, and when the land leveled he found himself among cultivated fields. And coming toward him was a bent old woman in black, supporting herself with a staff.

He wished he had encountered a male, but there was no help for it. He slid his Panama off and onto his lap, not that it would help much.

She tottered forward, paused at the amazing sight of the red cart driven by a naked man, and waited.

"Señora," he began in Spanish, "we have been waylaid by the Apaches, and they took everything from us, even our clothes."

"Yes, it is true," she replied. "Dios! I have never seen a man in such condition in sunlight."

"We need help, señora. Por favor, could you find something for us to wear?"

She peered up at him, shaking her head. "Señor, finding something for you is a task beyond my poor ability. The amount of fabric! It would take a month to weave it and another to sew it. And what of the others?"

She hobbled slowly toward the rear of the cart, paused, peered in at the cringing occupants, who presented their backs to her. "Yes, they need covering also. The pale man looks burnt. The women endure the sun. It has been a long time since I have seen such nakedness."

"You are our salvation, señora!"

"I wish I were thirty years younger," she said. "I would have a body like those women. Then I would attract the smiles of men. I have not been smiled upon for longer than I can remember, now that my paps are withered. Ah, to be young and smooth!"

"We are all suffering from the sun, señora."

She leaned on her staff, pondering. "Let us go to the church, and there will I find something for you. But you cannot let that monkey in. It would be a sacrilege."

"The church! Where that crowd is burying someone?"

She nodded. "They are burying Manuel, my son-in-law."

"Your son-in-law? Why aren't you there?"

"Because he is my son-in-law."

The last place Childress wanted to drive was the church.

"But that crowd—"

"Naked man, that crowd has only begun to bury him and they are on the other side and will not see you. He was a prominent man, so they will take their time hating him and wishing perdition upon him. They want to make sure he is good and buried, so that his bones will not escape and haunt us."

"Ah . . . What will we find there? A sheet? Altar linen? I don't think—"

"Come," she said, and hastened toward the long adobe edifice, rapping her staff on the clay. Colonel Childress followed, grateful that the adobe walls and trees hid the graveyard beyond, and the reproachful eyes of that crowd.

At last they pulled up before the dark doors.

"I'm not going in there, mate," Skye said slowly, peering over the top of the cart.

"Me neither, Skye, but she says it's the place to get help."

She paused at the hand-sawed plank door. "I have the honor of sweeping this holy place each day," she said. "I know everything. Come with me."

The women peered out of the cart but didn't move. Childress felt glued to his bench. Finally Skye eased to the ground, and crabbed his way toward the door, hunched over with whatever modesty he could summon. He had found courage that eluded the colonel of the militia of the Republic of Texas.

Childress sighed, lowered himself to earth, and followed, his mind swarming with disasters and shame.

They watched the old woman enter, curtsey, then trot along the shadowed wall of the nave toward the sacristy, pass a bulto in its niche, and vanish around a corner.

"I can't go in there, Skye. Not without a stitch."

Skye grunted, plunged into the gloom, and knelt suddenly at the back of the nave.

Childress could scarcely imagine such an act.

"Forgive us this trespass, Lord, and we thank you for our salvation," Skye said. "We mean no affront to you. We are desperate, and you have promised to help the naked and the poor."

Skye was speaking for both, and Childress was comforted.

The privateer knew suddenly that Skye had inner resources that were quite beyond his own. Skye stood, with quiet dignity, and walked through cool shade, no longer crouching in desperate modesty. The chapel was a simple place, with pine benches. No candle flickered. A small dark cross stood upon the altar.

The old woman in black beckoned from the door of the sacristy, so Skye and Childress padded there. Not even Skye's desperate prayer made it right to be naked in such a place.

The woman headed straight toward a closet where robes hung.

"See, señor," she said. "He is a Franciscan who is the priest here, and fat like you." She squinted at him, and pulled a brown-dyed woolen habit from the closet. "Though I doubt that his parts equal yours, but with a priest, who cares?"

It was a generous one, a monk's attire, with a hood and a soft white rope at the waist.

Childress had a fit of conscience. "Is this right, señora?"

She sniffed. "Would you prefer to offend little girls?"

That did it. He pulled the brown habit over him and knotted the rope at the waist. The presence of that cloth over him was as comforting as a keg of rum, he thought. She gave another to Skye, who gratefully slipped it on and sighed. It was a little long for Skye, and trailed in the dust.

"I have never appreciated what clothing means," Skye said. "It is more than warmth and protection. It is dignity and safety. It keeps us from offending."

Childress turned to the woman. "We cannot pay. We have nothing. The Jicarillas left us in a wilderness to perish. Is there something for the women?"

He eyed the embroidered vestments, chasubles and surplices, albs and stoles, but she shook her head. "Those belong to God," she said. "God forbid that I surrender them. But these that you wear belong to our padre, and I will confess this to him."

He hunted for sandals, and she saw his intent.

"The feet of Franciscans are bare," she said. "It is a mortification of the flesh."

Childress wanted to get out of there before the burial crowd broke up. "Señora, let us find something for our women."

She nodded, led them through the nave and into the sunlight. Standing Alone and Victoria stared at the brown-robed men.

The old woman walked to the rear of the cart and clambered in. "I will show you, señores," she said.

Childress steered the horse away from the little church and followed the woman's instructions. They headed down a lane, and finally stopped at a flower-decked patio enclosed by a low adobe wall. Even in this raw frontier place, these people had fashioned serenity and beauty.

"A few things of my daughter will suffice," she said, sliding off the red cart. The women followed her shyly, while Childress and Skye settled themselves in the courtyard.

"Do you realize, Brother Skye, that I was more famished for cloth over my carcass than for food?" he said.

"Brother Childress, that will pass," Skye replied. "I am ready to eat lizards again."

"Do you suppose we can find a begging bowl? If I beg in my bastard Spanish and you keep silent, we might be taken for a pair of mendicant monks."

"With concubines," Skye said.

"And a red cart with a Jolly Roger upon it."

"Are your bare feet fit for walking, Brother Childress?"

"Alas, we will have to master the ways of this country."

The monkey had fled the back of the nag, and was swinging through a peach tree.

"There is nothing there, Shine. It is much too early and they are green," Childress said.

The monkey chittered and swung toward a string of red chiles. He bit into the end of one chile, spat out the vile contents, and scolded the monks.

When the women emerged into that courtyard, each wore a simple shift of unbleached linen, modest and plain. The dresses fit loosely, and the women looked pleased to be shielded once again. The covering would suffice. The women, too, had been transformed from crouching creatures to dignified persons.

The old woman appeared, this time with two round loaves of bread. "Take this, my friends. It is warm still," she said, thrusting the loaves toward Childress.

Bread never tasted so fine.

"Señora, to whom shall we give thanks for this?" Childress asked, wanting a name.

"I was christened Milagro," she said.

20

Skye marveled. That very morning they had found themselves naked and bereft, a deadly circumstance that should have destroyed them all. But they did not perish. He could thank a monkey for that, and this old woman whose name, he gathered, was Milagro.

He looked at his brown habit and smiled; and Brother Childress was even more the fat monk. The women sat quietly, masticating chunks of fresh bread. The monkey was swinging everywhere, his tail wrapped around branches as he explored this little green courtyard of the most gracious house and garden in Arroyo Hondo.

The old woman sat on a split-log bench, watching them, her eyes bright. The monkey vanished inside the building, and when it emerged it carried something that looked like an earthen jug.

Skye leaped up. The monkey was stealing something and Skye would not abuse this woman's kindness by letting that happen. But when Skye approached, it swung upward and sat on an eave, scolding Skye and waving the crockery jug.

The old woman laughed.

He turned to Childress. "Tell her I will get it, whatever it is. We'll not be stealing this old woman's food."

The old woman nodded and said something.

"It's molasses," Childress said. "Very precious, the only molasses in Arroyo Hondo."

The monkey dodged Skye's every effort until Skye began shouting at it. And then Shine leaped meekly to Skye's feet and left the jug there. Skye carried it to the woman, who nodded and set it in her lap.

"Ask her how far it is to Taos," he said.

Childress queried the woman, and learned that Taos could be reached in a day if one left at dawn and the weather was dry and the horse didn't go lame.

"We should go," Skye said, restlessly. He really didn't want that funeral party to return and discover him in a monk's habit and his women wearing someone's dresses with nothing under them. There could be trouble.

Childress caught his urgency, and thanked Milagro profusely, and listened to her lengthy reply, whispered in a throaty, soft voice, punctuated with small smiles, and finally a giggle and a euphoric grin.

"What was that?" Skye asked.

Childress flashed one of his buccaneer smiles. "I told her I could not repay her, for we have nothing, and she said she was already repaid. I said, yes, you're repaid by God, and by our gratitude. She said that wasn't it at all. She'll get another sort of payment from it.

"She said that when the family and neighbors return, she will tell them that she saw a red cart drawn by a huge horse with a monkey on its mane, and everyone in the cart was naked, and a skull and crossbones was painted on its side, and so she took the naked ones to the chapel.

"She says she will recite that with relish to young and old and that the family will stare at her as if she is daft, and pat her on the shoulder and tell her that she's getting old and seeing things and listening to the devil, and saying things she has invented, and maybe she should say her beads more often.

"She says they would rather believe that Jesus Christ

Himself had visited her than believe a red cart with naked people in it had arrived in Arroyo Hondo. And then she would giggle and laugh, and they would never know the truth, and she would have her secret the rest of her days, and it is an old lady's joke."

Skye laughed. He saw the old woman grinning primly, a finger at her mouth, anticipating the big joke she would play on her family, and how they would all think she was a loco old lady, and that was just fine with her.

They drove off with clothing covering their bodies, fed and comforted. At the last moment, Shine leaped aboard the Clydesdale, unhappy to abandon such a paradise. Skye sat on the bench beside Childress as the horse dragged the cart up the long grade and out upon the open plains once again.

"Now we're monks," Childress said. "Maybe that's best."

"No, mate, we're not monks and if we pretend, we'll be found out."

"I don't know how we can get into worse trouble than we're in, Skye. We haven't so much as a knife or a cookpot, no money, food, shelter, horses, boots or sandals, and I'm the only one who speaks the language. At least, as monks, we could beg a meal."

"We could always hire out."

"I've never worked a day in my life, Skye. I take what I want, but that requires an evil heart, a cutlass, some grapeshot, a few pistols, a dirk, and assorted instruments of terror. I'm not fitted out to be a monk or a laboring man. I've been a buccaneer for as long as I can remember, and it's a family tradition. Skye, there isn't a thing in my Galveston digs that I purchased. I take great pride in it. Everything's stolen."

"We can work."

"Work! You can; I won't."

"First thing is to get to Taos and keep ourselves and the horse fed," Skye said, not wanting an argument just then. "We have two Cheyenne children to find."

"You still thinking about that?"

"I've never stopped thinking about it."

"With nothing but the clothing on our backs, and that borrowed? And not an ounce of food?"

"Yes," Skye said.

Victoria, who was listening, laughed. "When he sets his mind to something, it gets done," she said. "That's how he gets drunk."

Dusk found them in an open flat. The mountains to the east caught the setting sun and glowed gold. They were far from water, and would have to make a dry camp. But Taos was not far away. At least there was bunch grass for the horse, and the last of the bread. They found a shallow arroyo that offered some protection from the rattling wind, and settled there in the twilight. Skye divided the bread, reserving a piece for Shine, who snatched it happily. He eyed the skies, worried about the clouds building up in the east over the great black mountains.

He and Victoria settled against the warm slope. They were without blankets, and Victoria's thin linen dress would not ward off the chill. He put an arm over her shoulder and drew her into his coarse brown robe. Childress vanished into the juniper brush for a while, while Standing Alone chose solitude. For her, a modest Cheyenne woman, the dress she wore meant everything, and especially an end to her suffering and the endless violations of her person by other eyes. The monkey was steering the Clydesdale from place to place, sometimes tugging on the lines when the horse lingered.

"You glad you came?" Victoria asked.

"Yes."

"You think we'll get out of here?"

"We're in trouble."

"I don't know much about these Mexicans. But that Milagro, I like her. She helped us."

"Yes, she did. But from now on, we're going to depend

on the Mexicans for everything—food, shelter, warmth, clothing, sandals, and . . . liberty. I hear they don't take kindly to strangers."

"What is liberty?"

The question startled Skye. Victoria had never known anything but liberty, subject only to the traditions of her people.

"The children we're looking for don't have it. They can't live their life as they choose. They're slaves. We may not have it if we run into trouble. I think we'll be all right."

"Some Apache has your rifle."

"That's one of the ways I'm feeling naked. But there's this about it. Now we're no threat to anyone. No alcalde— that's a mayor, sort of—of any town here is going to worry about us."

He wasn't sure he believed that, especially with Childress obviously collecting military information. For all he knew, the Mexicans might have an exact understanding of Colonel Childress and his mission. But he wanted to hearten her.

Standing Alone approached, and after some hesitation, settled down beside Victoria in the lee of the arroyo.

"She says it's cold and this is better," Victoria said.

The women conversed softly, often using their hands, and Skye listened patiently, understanding very little of it.

"She says the old woman was kind, and the Mexicans are good people," Victoria said. "Food and clothing for us all. The old woman shared what she had. She likes Mexico. Standing Alone thinks maybe her children are comfortable here."

Skye had no answer for that. If her son had been taken to the mines in the south, he had been subjected to a life of unremitting toil. He would be fed barely enough to keep life in him, and he would be naked, because the masters spared their slave labor nothing beyond what kept body and soul together.

"Yes," Skye said, "tell her the Mexicans are good people,

most of them. They have a beautiful spirit. They would help anyone in trouble. They have a great faith that teaches them good things, but sometimes they ignore the teaching of their church. Sometimes they treat their own people badly and sometimes they treat Indians badly too."

Victoria did, and Standing Alone absorbed that bleakly.

"If her son was sent to the mines where they dig the metal, he is suffering and in danger. If he's working on a plantation, hoeing and weeding, or herding cattle, he would be better off. If her daughter's working in a household, she may be well off. But they aren't free. They are either peons, held to the land by perpetual debt, or slaves."

Victoria translated as best she could, and listened to the reply.

"Then they are savages, she says. The Cheyenne would never do such a thing. We must hurry, before it is too late."

Skye pressed Victoria's hand in the dusk. "We will, and it may take months," he said. "But there will be a way."

21

They rode into Taos so starved that Skye barely saw the bold beauty around him. Even the monkey had turned cross with an empty stomach, and clacked angrily. But in the midst of Skye's suffering he beheld an adobe town snugged close to piñon-clad foothills under a bold blue heaven. Here were more earthen dwellings, wizened old women in black, warm-fleshed men in faded unbleached cottons, some wearing peaked hats of straw.

But he barely saw them. His stomach howled; a dizziness possessed him. The women were enduring their famine better than he, and even Colonel Childress was weathering the terrible hunger better than Skye. But Childress could somehow live on his fat, while Skye grew fainter with each passing hour as the horse and cart clopped slowly into the village.

Taos amazed him. Bursts of green, the leaves of towering cottonwoods, startled the pervasive earthen tones. Water spilled here and there, its sources unknown to him. The town looked somnolent, but when they reached the plaza and were caught in the middle of commerce, he knew that Taos was a lively place. Maybe someone could spare him a crust of bread.

Not only hunger was tormenting him. He was appalled

to be wearing the habit of a Franciscan, and didn't want to be taken for one. Even worse was Childress, wearing the holy robes that concealed his vast torso, but also his broad-brimmed planter's hat. This duplicitous dress concealed a pirate and opportunist, who even then was examining assets with a grasping gaze.

They had argued all the way into town. Skye wanted to head straight for the alcalde, or whoever was in authority, and explain their circumstances. Skye hated false pretenses and deception. They would surely be found out soon enough; he couldn't even speak Spanish, and knew nothing of the rites and customs of the Franciscans, and it would go badly for them to be exposed as impostors. But Childress had forcefully argued that the Mexicans were likely to throw them into jail if they told the truth; they never believed a story, even of hardship and loss, and their impulse was to throw irons on anyone arousing their suspicions.

Slowly, the red cart negotiated the narrow alleys leading into the plaza, and then Childress drove around the perimeter of that heart of the city, his huge horse attracting a crowd. The monkey soon added to the mass of people pacing beside the cart, pointing to the skull and crossbones, and shouting questions at Childress, who smiled, lifted his Panama, and proceeded to show off. Victoria and Standing Alone gazed at this lively village from the bed, whispering to each other.

They passed a vendor of some sort of Mexican treats, and that was when Shine abandoned the mane of the Clydesdale and leaped toward the vendor, his heart set on pilferage.

People shouted, and then laughed. The monkey won himself some morsel Skye couldn't identify, covered with a thin dough and contained in husks of corn. Shine returned to his perch on the horse in one bound, and began peeling off the husks and nipping at whatever lay within. Skye envied the little rascal.

"Shine's got a tamale. Here we are, Brother Skye. Food

and succor everywhere. Just let Brother Childress collect some food."

Skye nodded sourly. He was too dizzy with hunger to resist. The women watched from the bed of the red cart, even as strangers gathered around it, pointing to the emblem on the side, and to the giant Clydesdale and the monkey. Shine soon abandoned his perch and was looting everyone in sight of food, springing hither and yon, sometimes even to the vigas, the projecting beams, of the buildings, where he chattered. The people of Taos gladly fed the little fellow, laughing at his thievery.

They certainly were curious about this strange assemblage in a bright red cart, and whispered among themselves. Children studied them shyly, and then giggled at the monkey, who sat masticating his loot and scolding the crowd.

"Ah, amigos, amigas," Childress said, standing in his seat, sweeping that grand hat off his head. "Socorro, por favor. Donativos, help some poor brothers in distress, foster the faith, feed the hungry, share your food with those in holy servitude to God."

No one moved. No one believes him, Skye thought.

But then the monkey began some gymnastic whirls, ending in the theft of a sweet from the vendor, accompanied by shouts and bawling, and suddenly the crowd laughed and dug into their purses for a coin or a bit of grubby paper. Childress passed his hat, which collected not only some coin, but also the corn husk-wrapped things Childress called tamales. The Colonel was not shy about thrusting his Panama toward anyone who looked like he might have a coin, and occasionally a brown hand would snake out and drop something into the hat, whether from charity or because of Shine, who was a born showman, Skye could not know.

"Mil gracias, a thousand thanks for serving God and the brothers and sisters," Childress cried. "You have fed two humble brothers, and their, ah, helpers." He turned to Skye. "The women. What'll I say?"

Skye hadn't any idea.

"Ah, succor for the concubines," Childress roared in English.

Skye, already faint from hunger, suddenly got a lot fainter.

His eye was upon various burly Mexican males standing quietly about who did not seem so amused and whose gazes were not friendly. The law? Store keeps? Politicians? Powerful ranchers? Skye could not know. He was in a foreign nation, broke, hungry, dizzy, and in bizarre company.

But Childress was not idle. Nimbly, he handed a corn-wrapped tamale to the women, and another to Skye, who didn't bother to be polite. He wolfed the food, and found it filling.

"Ah, Brother Skye, a delectable repast, a faith offering from the humble to the exalted brothers of Saint Francis," Childress said. "You see? In Mexico, religion gets you everywhere. Now, Brother Skye, make the sign of the cross."

"I will not commit sacrilege," Skye replied. "We're impostors, that's what, not friars."

Childress beamed, faced the cheerful multitude, and made an elaborate sign for all to see.

"There now. I've turned us both into holy men, Skye. Consider me a master of the revels."

Skye's stomach howled for more, but Childress had distributed every scrap of food that had fallen into his hat. There remained in the Panama some sort of specie, both paper and silver, and Skye eyed it eagerly. His scruples had all but vanished in the face of rank desperation, and he even felt a glow of thanksgiving. The pirate and his little simian had put a little food in his belly.

"Where do they hide the slaves?" Victoria whispered. "I don't see none."

Skye didn't either, and wondered whether these smiling people had been maligned by Yanks and Texans with avarice in their craniums. Many of the spectators in that clay plaza looked as though they might be part-Indian, but that was the essence of Mexico, that admixture of bloods. Standing Alone slowly unfolded, slipped off the end of the cart, the thin covering of her dress barely concealing her form, and catching fevered glances from warm-eyed males, and then began quietly walking through this cheerful multitude. Skye knew she was looking. She would never stop looking for the boy and the girl ripped from her so suddenly, long ago.

A frowning rail-thin Anglo man in a black suit approached from the door of a mercantile, and stood staring.

"Who are you? You're no more friars than I'm a Chinaman," he said in English. "If you're trying to pull the wool over the eyes of these people, you're making fools of yourselves. You're already in trouble."

"I am Barnaby Skye, and this is Mr. Childress, a trader," Skye said before Childress could stop him.

"And what brings you here in monks' habits? With two Indian women, the first Clydesdale ever seen here, a monkey, and a red cart?"

"We can discuss that later, in private. With whom do I speak?"

Skye's old English reserve and correctness was asserting itself. Childress glared. It was apparent to everyone watching the exchange that Skye was speaking English to this merchant. Childress's game was up.

The merchant curtly motioned Skye off the cart. Skye slid to earth, feeling the weight of that unfamiliar habit slow him.

"William Larrimer," the man said in a low voice that didn't carry more than a yard. "Merchant here. Now tell me what you're doing, and be fast about it. Your time is running out."

Skye glanced at Childress, who was studiously ignoring all this.

"He's a trader. I'm with the two Indian women. We're looking for the children of one. We think they're here, in trouble."

"What? Say that again? No, don't. Godalmighty. Why are you wearing disguises that any half-baked idiot can see through?"

Skye choked back his temper. "We had trouble with the Jicarillas thirty or forty miles north of here. They left us with nothing but the cart. Naked. Not a stitch of clothing, not a scrap of food, not a riding horse or saddle, not a knife or weapon or a pot. Childress's horse escaped, and that saved our lives. We got the habits in Arroyo Hondo."

"Let me get this straight. Childress is a trader with a monkey, a red cart, and a goddamned Clydesdale and you're along for the ride."

Skye nodded.

The man's skepticism oozed out of his corded face and fired his sapphire eyes. "This doesn't add up. Now I want the truth, Skye, and fast, because if you're not telling it true, you'll endanger every Yank trading here. Childress knows better than to wander in here and trade without a license from Santa Fe. Especially in some damned Franciscan habit. This isn't the United States. What did you say his company is?"

"Childress and McIntyre. They've put up a store north of here, on the Yank side of the Arkansas."

"Where's he from?"

"Galveston Bay, he says."

"A Texan?" Larrimer's face turned hard.

Skye nodded.

"One damned mess," the merchant said. "You're trouble and you'll be lucky to walk away."

22

Skye watched an odd-looking priest start across the plaza with a lumbering gait.

"You're too late," Larrimer said. "That's the Calf."

"The what?"

"Padre Martinez. His head, see it? They call him the Calf. He hates Yanks."

"I'm not a Yank."

"Lot of good that'll do you. I shouldn't even be seen with you."

"Mr. Larrimer, we're destitute and we need help. Anything you can do—"

"What you've done, Skye, if that's your name, is start trouble for every citizen of the United States living here."

Colonel Childress, who had been bantering with the people of Taos, paused as he watched the ponderous progress of the priest, who parted the frightened peons as if he were Moses.

"Why does he worry you?" Skye asked Larrimer.

"He's more powerful than the alcalde, and an alcalde is not just a mayor; he's police chief and judge, too. The Calf's agitating to put all us heathen out of the territory, or march us off to the City of Mexico. The Calf's a law unto himself. Not even the governor rules this priest."

The Calf was indeed a strange-looking priest, his huge walleyed head perched heavily on a stocky frame covered with a dusty black cassock.

At last the priest stopped before them, as the crowd fell back. He peered at each man from bright and penetrating brown eyes, then the cart, monkey, and Indian women, and finally at Larrimer.

"Que pasa?" he asked Larrimer.

But Childress replied in a burst of Spanish that Skye couldn't follow. The fat privateer gesticulated grandly, foam at the lips, pointed at his empty cart and the two women, at himself, and at Skye.

"What's he saying?" Skye whispered.

"That you're a pair of Franciscans from St. Louis that got robbed by the Jicarillas."

Skye barely contained his rage. This was worse trouble because it was a lie, and preposterous.

The Calf peered, skeptically, as if nearsighted, wetting his lips and pondering. He turned to Larrimer, and said something.

"I'm translating. Who are you; what are you doing here?"

Skye was damned if he would lie. "I'm a man without a country, Barnaby Skye, and I'm helping this grieving Cheyenne woman find her son and daughter. We think they were brought here by the Utes. We came to obtain their liberty."

"Are you a friar?" Larrimer translated.

"No, I am in the fur trade, working for Bent, St. Vrain. We were left without clothing, or a weapon or a pot thirty miles north by marauding Jicarillas. A merciful woman in Arroyo Hondo lent us these garments, fed us, and sent us on our way. She took us to the church there, put these habits over our nakedness, and urged us to leave swiftly."

"A likely story. Where are you from?" Larrimer translated.

"London."

"Where's the fat one from?"

"He says Galveston Bay."

"Tejas! Who owns that monkey?"

Skye gestured toward Childress.

"What is his name? The Texas one. What is he doing here?"

"Jean Lafitte Childress. He started with a wagon of trading goods. We lost them all to the Apaches, and our horses except for this. We came with him, with our own horses and gear."

The Calf stared at the Clydesdale. "The great horse looks like the Calf," he said, and Larrimer translated. "Why are these symbols of piracy and death painted on the side of this cart?"

Skye shook his head. There were facets of Childress that were beyond fathoming.

"He wants to know who she is," Larrimer said, pointing at Victoria.

"She is my Crow wife, Victoria."

The Calf laughed heartily. "Concubina," he said.

Skye didn't need the translation. "Wife," he said, heat building in him.

The Calf chuckled nastily, and spoke again.

"You will be of great interest to the authorities," Larrimer translated. "One says he's a monk from St. Louis. The other says he's a man from London looking for Cheyenne children. Monks with two sluts, a bloodred wagon, and a monkey." He beckoned. Skye thought the priest's finger was an inch in diameter.

"Do we have to go with him?"

"Skye, if you don't, you're likely to get yourself killed. See that?"

On the periphery of this crowd stood three young men bearing lances. Skye thought all of Taos had collected there, twenty deep. These were no longer warm and friendly faces.

"What's going to happen to us?"

"I don't second-guess Mexican officials. But the last few illegal traders or . . . filibusters, is that it, Skye? . . . got sent off to Mexico City in chains, and the few that survived the long walk in irons are still there and won't be leaving there. Not unless they leave feet first."

All this Colonel Childress absorbed angrily, glaring at Skye as if his truth-telling were a criminal act in its own right. Skye didn't care. Childress's lies had gotten them into this.

Skye saw that they had little choice. He nodded to Larrimer. Did he see some pity in the man's corded face? Then the huge, ominous crowd began to seethe along, carrying Skye, Childress, Victoria, and Standing Alone with it. Shine leaped up to Childress's thick shoulder, and even he looked subdued and afraid. Someone was leading away the Clydesdale and the wagon, and Skye doubted he would ever see the rig again.

Skye glanced at Standing Alone, who bore all this with her innate dignity, enduring the stares, keeping her thoughts private. Victoria, always the observant one, was studying the clothing and weapons of these people, looking at faces one by one, as she was harried along with the throng. Where were they going? Did this earthen village have a jail?

They were escorted across the dusty plaza and through an alley to a massive building with walls as blank as the future, and there pushed through the thick doors and into the sharp coolness within. Skye had no inkling of the purpose of this structure; only that it contained chairs of rawhide, benches, and a beehive fireplace in a corner. The sole window could swiftly be shuttered; the heavy slab-wood door could be barred. As a jail it would do just fine. The women in their thin shifts would soon be chilled in such a place.

This was some private residence. The massive door creaked shut behind them, and Skye felt the claustrophobia he had experienced deep in the bowels of men-o'-war. The room wasn't large. Skye headed for the high window, and could see one of the men with a lance standing beside it.

"Skye, why didn't you keep your trap shut?" Childress asked. "I could've talked my way out of it."

"Lied your way out of it," Skye retorted.

The monkey abandoned the Colonel's shoulders and explored the room with swift bounds, hunting food but settling at last in the patch of sun on the sill of the high window.

"Skye, get this straight. I'm a privateer. I will do what I will do."

There was no sense arguing with the man. Skye turned his back on him and looked to see how Victoria and Standing Alone were faring. The Cheyenne woman had settled into a chair.

"Victoria, tell her we came here without the permission of the governor—the chief. I'll get her out some way, but I don't know when or how."

Childress started laughing. "That's what they all think before they walk the plank."

Skye boiled. He started toward that fat pirate, but the door opened again, shooting bright sunlight into the room and half blinding him. Shine started chittering.

This time a hawkish black-bearded man appeared and surveyed them all with imperious eyes. Four soldiers backed him, this time armed with broadswords.

"I am prefect, Juan Andres Archuleta. I make a, a . . . disposition of your case," he said. "I speak little English."

"We're hungry," Skye said.

"That is of no consequence. We are much entertained by your party, but we have learned many lessons from our past."

He nodded, and two of the guards caught the women by the arm and escorted them out. The last view Skye got of Victoria, she was being dragged into the sunlight but she was looking back to him, and her eyes told him of love, and desperation and determination. Standing Alone didn't require dragging. She walked willingly, but paused at the bright door frame, looked back at Skye with sorrow. Then they were gone.

"We'll deal with your concubines separately."

"My wife is not a concubine!" Skye snapped.

"She is what I choose to call her, a puta."

Skye lurched at him, only to be constrained by Childress, who clamped an arm over him. The grip was hard. Bright steel blades gleamed just ahead of him.

"Very gallant, Americano."

"I'm not an American. And that was my wife."

"Si, si, you have to say that. You're a man without a nation, and therefore, all the easier for us to deal with." He turned to Childress. "A Tejano rebel. A privateer. Maybe a spy. Maybe doing some little task for el Presidente Lamar."

"I'm an ordinary privateer, señor, at the service of whoever has the biggest purse. And when no one has a purse, I engage in my own violations of the laws of the sea."

Archuleta contemplated that. "Ah! I am glad to have your . . . *confesión* before witnesses, and that of your friend Skye," he said. "That is all I need."

23

Standing Alone found herself in a chill adobe room along with Victoria Skye. A guard with a lance and lust had taken them to this place east of the plaza.

Through a small window she could see the dark mountains, the fierce blue of the sky, and the buildings of the village. Outside was freedom, a place to walk unimpeded across sunny fields. Never had she been without her freedom. This place called Mexico had a strange way of welcoming people, putting them in earthen boxes.

She had come a great distance. She had long since ceased to grieve her boy and girl, who were like the dead now, phantoms, fading spirits in her mind. This quest had become something else, and she didn't know exactly what. If her children still lived—and she sensed that one of them did— she would find them and give them as a gift to the People, who needed understanding of where their flesh and blood were taken, and how they were used, for the loss of a child was a loss to the whole People.

This was new to the Cheyenne, this slavery, this using of children. Somehow she knew, and it was spirit-knowledge, that if she brought her children, or surviving child, back to the People, then the Cheyenne would triumph over the Ute thieves, and over these strange Mexicans who lived inside buildings of mud.

She knew, too, that if she could find and free her son, Grasshopper, he would become a great leader of the Cheyenne, a tower of strength for his people. She burned to free him, not just for herself and her clan, but for the People themselves. He would take a new name and leave the boy's name behind. Out of his captivity and suffering would come a man of such strength and spirit and holiness that his blessings would last for generations.

All this she had been given in four visions and dreams; all this she kept to herself, locking it in her bosom until the time might come to reveal it. This was her secret as well as her passion, and she would willingly die to fulfill the things she had seen in her dreams.

For years she had sat quietly at the gate of Bent's Fort, listening to Americans and Mexicans. It was the Mexicans she studied the most because they might reveal the whereabouts of her children. Gradually, during those four years, she learned to fathom the words spoken by these people though she never uttered a single one. But there were many words still unknown to her. They had called her a concubina, which she had never heard, but she knew what a puta was, and because they said that of her she despised them right down to the marrow of her bones.

At least she despised the men. The old woman who had succored them and given her the shift she now wore she did not despise. She knew how thin was the loose-woven cloth, how revealing it was in sunlight, the shadows of her body always visible, and she had not missed the stares that pierced right through that thin shroud to her bosom and belly.

The Mexican women wore several layers and thus armored themselves from the stares of men. But she and Victoria had only the thinnest cover of this loose fabric they called linen. For this had the holy man, the Calf, stared at them both and the look in his eyes was unmistakable.

They were prisoners for the moment, but she did not intend to remain one. Neither did Victoria. They were not sheep to be herded by shepherds. They were women of the People, not Mexican women, and women of the People knew the arts of war. Victoria Skye was merely an Absaroka dog, and without the powers any Cheyenne woman possessed, but it didn't matter. They would help each other. She had not come this far, looking for her children, to surrender.

She peered about her: this was a small storeroom. In the dim brown light she saw coarse sacks of beans, some dried red fruits strung on a cord and hanging. A closed door stained the color of the sky led to some other part of the building.

Then that door opened, and a voluptuous full-breasted Mexican woman appeared, looked them over, smiled, and closed the door again. This woman looked to be not more than twenty winters.

"We could go out that door," Victoria said in the polyglot tongue they had evolved, half signs, half words.

Standing Alone shook her head. She had learned patience. "Let's eat," Victoria said. There was food if only they could prepare it. "I will even eat what these people eat."

They converged on the sacks and earthen jugs, looking for something to wolf down. But they found nothing like that. Grains in great crocks, oils in jars, beans in sacks. The thought of food made her salivate, and then ache for something, anything to assuage her hunger.

But she was a woman of the People and sternly contained herself. Her captors would not know of her desperation. She drew herself proudly, and stood still, while Victoria hunted relentlessly for anything she could eat, poking a hard bean into her mouth and trying, without luck, to masticate it.

"I will find a way to take some of this to Skye," Victoria said, hunting for a cloth or a sack or a pouch she might conceal on her person. "I will help my man."

Standing Alone was not sure Victoria would ever see her man again. But they both hunted, and finally settled on tearing a piece of burlap out of a sack, using their teeth for the want of a knife. They realized that every scoop and ladle had been removed; there was no iron to turn into a weapon.

That's when the door of the storeroom swung open on its leather hinges, creaking noisily. The walleyed holy man, Father Martinez, peered into the gloom, and motioned them out into a kitchen room with a beehive fireplace, tables, and benches to sit upon. The pretty young woman hovered behind him. The scent of meat stewing in a pot hung over the fire dizzied Standing Alone.

"Come, come," he said in Spanish, motioning them out of the cramped dark storage room. "Do you understand my tongue?"

Standing Alone did not acknowledge that she understood him perfectly well. He stared a moment, his gaze roving over her.

"The sluts don't understand," he said to his young companion. "Very well, Juanita, I'll show them things more ancient than words."

The young woman laughed, baring an even row of white teeth that contrasted to her lush brown lips. Standing Alone looked closely at this woman and thought she might be pregnant. Was this holy man the sire? She had heard that the priests of these people never embraced a woman, but here was this young one living so familiarly with him.

"I will see what they understand," he said, surveying them with some amusement.

What a strange man he was, with his huge head shaped by its bones into the face of a calf, with malice in his eyes and a certain slyness visible because he did not guard his spirit.

He turned to his captives.

"Is it that you speak Spanish?" he asked.

Standing Alone wondered whether to respond. Maybe it was best not to admit to it. But maybe it was better to find out what was in store. She nodded, slowly.

"Ah! It is good, bien. You have been the sluts of these Texas spies I caught, and that is a grave offense, and worthy of death. But I will spare you. A good, obedient savage, willing to work and sew and cook, willing to hoe the fields, weed, harvest, do whatever is required, can redeem her life."

Standing Alone nodded. Soon she would translate for Victoria, but not yet.

"Ah, I see you understand. Now, first, to prepare you for your new life, I will baptize you, for this is required of all who live in Mexico. This will seal you in your new faith, and you will become Christians and your souls will be saved."

Saved from what? She would find out. And she would find out what this baptism meant, too.

She nodded, and searched her mind for the words she needed to ask a question. "What of the hombres?" she asked, not able to summon more words.

The priest laughed. "The men? They will be taken to Santa Fe to plead before our governor. He will decide whether to execute them or send them to the City of Mexico to be tried."

"Why?" she asked.

"Don't trouble your head about it. They are gone. You will never see them again."

He reached for a small bowl, which had the emblem of a cross upon it.

"Ah, what is your name, woman?"

"Call me what you will."

"And her name?"

"That is for her to say."

"No, it is for me to say, for the name your people gave you is gone, and you will receive a new one from the church and the civilized world, so that you can partake of the gifts of God. You will be Maria, and she will be Juana. It is so, yes?"

She fumbled for words. "So it is you name us." Victoria asked what was being said. Swiftly, with the fingers and hands, and with their patois, she explained.

"Sonofabitch," Victoria said.

Standing Alone wished she might know what that meant. The Crow woman said it all the time. It was some holy invocation of the speakers of English.

The priest, meanwhile, lifted a lid from the vessel in his hands, and summoned them to him. He gestured that they should kneel before him. Standing Alone and Victoria both understood, and both refused.

"You must bow before God," said the Calf.

Standing Alone stared.

The priest pushed her downward, but she refused to kneel.

"It will go hard for you, then, concubina," he said, and she registered the word she did not understand.

The priest's woman watched, her gaze somber for a change.

Then this padre, Martinez, she remembered, decided it didn't matter: he dipped his fingers into that water and pressed his moist fingers upon her head, firmly, until she felt wetness. "I baptize you in the name of the Father, the Son, and the Holy Ghost," he said in his tongue.

He performed the same rite upon Victoria.

"Now you will know what sin is," he said.

Standing Alone did not feel any different, but wondered whether she was cursed or blessed.

24

Skye's fury exceeded even his hunger. He paced his adobe prison, brimming with bitterness. There were guards outside, each armed with a lance and two with swords. They would be taking him somewhere, probably Santa Fe, for some purpose. Maybe it wouldn't end there: he had heard talk of being taken to the City of Mexico, there to rot in some dank prison.

He glared at Childress, who sat quietly. Skye wished he had never met the man. He should have seen through the fat trader, if that is what he was, instead of making common cause with him. Childress had not hesitated to lie to the Mexicans and that got them into grave trouble.

It would have been hard enough to win a sympathetic ear just telling the truth; but Childress had attempted to fob the pair of them off as monks, which had won him a horselaugh and a spell in prison, if not something much worse.

Skye rued the day he had stumbled upon the man and his phony trading company and his bloodred cart and draft horse and monkey, all guaranteed to call attention to the man. And if that weren't enough, Childress had painted piratical emblems on his cart and boasted of his years as a privateer. Any sensible man would have kept silent about his nefarious life.

He slowed his pacing and paused before the Texan, who was still bulging out of his monk's habit.

"Get one thing straight, Childress. We're through. If we get out of here, we're going our separate ways. You understand?"

"I do, but I don't suppose Shine does."

"And that goes double for the monkey."

"Skye, we work well together."

"No man who lies to anyone works well with me."

"I salute a man of honor," Childress said. "I myself impose no constraints on my conduct. I do what's necessary."

"And get us into trouble," Skye snapped.

"Yes, a pity, isn't it? Here you are, stuck with Jean Lafitte Childress, born without a scruple. I've sent innocents off a plank into the briny sea, robbed merchant ships, pillaged coastal towns, beheaded assorted women and children . . ."

Skye didn't know what to make of the imbecile. He only knew that if and when he got free, he would go in the opposite direction of wherever Childress and his damned monkey, if he still had his monkey, were heading.

If he hadn't hooked up with the flamboyant fool he and Standing Alone and Victoria would have arrived in Taos without disturbing anyone and would have been perfectly free to make inquiries about the children. They probably would have had their horses and packs, too. That cart had attracted the attention of the Jicarillas, and that was the beginning of their downfall.

Skye paced, the only defense he had against the howling of his empty stomach. It had been the better part of two days since he had eaten. Childress didn't seem to mind; he dined on his own fat. But Skye knew if he didn't get fed soon, he would take on those guards if he had to and head for the plaza and the markets he saw there. He would eat.

The door creaked open, and this time a sturdy raven-haired man with vast mustachios entered, flanked by guards.

The man surveyed his prisoners, obviously enjoying himself.

"Juan Andres Archuleta, prefect of the northern province," he said.

So he spoke a little English.

"I'm hungry. Haven't eaten."

Archuleta turned to Skye, studying him blandly, and then smiled. "Monks are succored on spiritual food," he said. "You eat the Bread of Life."

Skye forced himself not to do what he was about to do, which was to land on the man and throttle him.

"I am not a monk. And I haven't eaten today and most of yesterday."

"A pity." Archuleta looked the prisoners over, and yawned. "You will proceed at dawn toward Santa Fe. It is a matter for our gobernador, Armijo. Si, he will settle your fate. He enjoys such proceedings. He's very fond of foreigners. If he finds you guilty, he will give you a quick and merciful death against the wall."

"What are we charged with?"

Archuleta shrugged. "Just now, nothing, Brother Skye. There is nothing against you. But there is much testimony, which I have written down and will send along to Santa Fe."

"I am not a monk."

"So you keep saying. A pity, for if you were, I might set you free. Your *boca grande* puts you farther and farther into the trouble, no?"

"I am here with my wife and our friend, a Cheyenne woman, to find her children."

Archuleta yawned. "Si, si, a pity, Reverend Brother Skye. How cold is the rule of justice, and how it crushes the unfortunate. But your sweet piety, it will you see you through, a martyr of the Holy Faith. Maybe they will canonize you someday, and make you a saint."

"Where is my wife?" he said.

"Your wife? You are married, Brother?"

"Where is she? And our friend?"

"You'll be pleased to know she is with our padre, Martinez, si?"

"And what is she doing there?"

Archuleta smiled softly. "Ah! I am told she has received the baptism. Soon she will be a daughter of the faith."

Baptism? Victoria? She who lived within the soul of her people?

"You imprison not only bodies, but souls, señor," he said. "You capture souls for Christ at the point of a lance. Do you think the Lord would approve?"

Archuleta smiled, obviously amused at the thought. "We leave at dawn," he said.

With that, he withdrew. The door creaked shut. Skye heard the thud of a bar locking it. He knew he would spend the hungriest night of his life unless succor arrived. At least there was an olla of water available to the prisoners.

He drank of the cup, bitterly.

He did not sleep that night. There was no bed, but that was not what caught him in fits of wakefulness. Neither was it his hunger, which bit cruelly at him. It was an ancient anguish. Other mortals now controlled his destiny by force of arms; the food and water and clothing he needed depended not on his efforts, but on their whim.

He felt at one with all the world's most helpless people, those whose fate, whose tomorrows were unknown to them. He felt at one with those Indian children, abducted years earlier, whose fate was not their own; deprived of hope, of caring, of love, of comfort, but simply bodies to be used by masters and then discarded.

On the floor in the far corner, Childress lay curled up on his side, apparently asleep, and far less concerned by this twist of the noose of life than Skye was. Skye stared, knowing he had learned a lesson: never again would he willingly ally himself with anyone he didn't trust.

He would never trust anyone who deliberately called attention to himself with bizarre stories, or conduct. He would never trust anyone with a loose mouth and a lack of ordinary honesty. For the rest of his days, if he escaped this hell, he would let caution govern him.

He didn't know where the monkey was; it could easily leap to the high window and out. Skye amended his views: never trust a man with a monkey. He peered around in the gloom, trying to see the little simian by whatever light was given him by the stars, but he saw nothing. Maybe the guard had run his lance through the little monster, a prospect that did not displease Skye. A chill settled upon the already cold room, but Skye had little to cover himself, so he pressed his body into another corner and waited for dawn.

The stars sailed through their orbits, and Skye sat rigidly, his heart with Victoria, his mind unsettled. And then he heard a scrambling up on the sill above, and felt the faint rush of movement. The monkey had returned to the master. It sprang over to Childress, who muttered something, and then back to Skye, and chittered softly. There in his hands was some object, but Skye could not make it out at first. Then his nostrils did, and he felt himself holding a chunk of bread. Half a loaf of bread.

He felt its springy hardness in his hands, and smelled the yeasty aroma. He sighed, grateful for this mercy, but ashamed of his harsh thoughts. Only minutes earlier he was entertaining the hope that a lancer had run the monkey through. It was another lesson, he thought, bitterly.

He tried to pet Shine, but the monkey seemed a blur of motion, and Skye saw the shadow up on the sill once again.

"Well, thanks anyway," he muttered.

"You can have mine," Childress said.

Skye refused to reply, even if the offer was kind.

He ate slowly, savoring the moist and textured bread, the humblest but greatest of blessings. He could have eaten two loaves, but this would do. A spider monkey with an uncanny way of being helpful had rescued him, at least for the moment.

A few merchant seamen had monkeys, kept as mementos of some tropical port. Some merchant ships had monkeys aboard, mostly for amusement. But they were the rarest of domestic animals and served no useful purpose. He wondered where Childress had found this one, and how Childress had trained him to be so useful.

Skye settled himself against a cold wall, and tried to think: How would he escape both the Mexicans, and the flamboyant Childress, alleged privateer and trader, and rescue the women?

But no answer came to him.

25

The prefect, Archuleta, entered, flanked by two soldiers. Jean Lafitte Childress eyed them from the floor, where he had curled in his monk's habit, staving off the sharp chill. Skye sat against an earthen wall watching, his gaze sharp in the soft dawn light. The monkey leaped for the high window and sat there studying the intruders.

The prefect pointed at Childress, and then beckoned him.

Slowly, his bones aching from cold, Childress stood and walked through the door, followed by the soldiers and the man who would decide his fate.

"Buenos dias, amigos," Childress said expansively. "I respect your persons, but your hospitality leaves something to be desired."

They marched him into the plaza, hushed now as the villagers of Taos slumbered into the dawn. The sweet smoke of piñon pine drifted from chimneys. Where were they taking him?

They left the plaza, turned up an alley, scattered two cats, and the prefect opened a door of a substantial building. Childress could see that its interior was better furnished than most in this rude town; massive mission-style chairs and a settee filled a room. A small fire wavered in a beehive fireplace.

The prefect waved Childress to a chair. "Sit yourself," he said in Spanish.

A hefty woman with her hair in a tight black bun immediately brought a steaming cup of coffee.

"Ah! Nurture for the body! Perhaps I will soon enjoy the famous hospitality of the Mexicans," he said, hopefully.

But the prefect said nothing, drew up a straight-backed dining chair directly opposite Childress, and sat in it.

"Who are you?" he asked abruptly.

"You have my name, sir."

"What are you doing here?"

"I am engaged in the pursuit of empire, Sah."

"What the Americanos call a filibuster?"

Childress stared, scornfully. "They lack imagination. My purpose is much more noble, Señor Archuleta. I am going to sever the northern reaches of Mexico from the mother country and found my own nation, the Republic of Childress."

Archuleta smiled slightly. "Yesterday you were a monk. The day before, you were a trader operating as Childress and McIntyre. The day before that, so to speak, you were a Texas privateer preying on Mejico!"

"I am all that and more, Sah."

"Now let me see, señor. A monk in a Franciscan habit with a monkey, a red cart, a draft horse, and the ensigns of piracy on the side of your cart. Two beautiful savages accompanied you, indecently attired. You entertained us with a fine story: the Apaches took everything, except of course your horse and cart and harness. So you drove to Arroyo Hondo stark naked, baking in the sun, where you wished to be succored. And an elderly woman came to your assistance, si?"

"Ah, señor, it is all true, as true as the gospel."

Archuleta laughed softly. "Tejas, you are from Tejas," he said.

"Indeed, sir, sired in the bosom of piracy, Galveston, the home of the most black-hearted of all mariners."

"And what are you going to do next?"

The question surprised Childress. "Why, Sah, outfit myself on credit, recruit an army of peons and mestizos and indios to overthrow Mexico, and establish my capital up on the Rio Arkansas."

Archuleta smiled. "A noble enterprise, señor. A large task for a man of great girth. What else have you done?"

"Sah, I have sent Mexican women and children off the plank and into the sea; I have plundered Mexican galleons and barques. I have run the Jolly Roger up my masts and flown it from the pinnacle. I have financed wars and excursions against Mexico, widowed Mexican women, orphaned children, stolen casks of gold doubloons, driven men mad, schemed against Santa Anna . . ."

Archuleta yawned. "The missioner up at Arroyo Hondo wants his cassocks back. I've gone to great expense, from the public purse, to put raiment on you. I shall have to levy a tax to pay for all the cloth. I regret that it's rather like a tent; at least it covers your vast white belly. There. Shirt, pantalones, sandals, and you already have a Panama."

He gestured toward some clothing hanging on a peg.

"I will shed this disguise, Sah, and encase myself in your rags. They look to be utterly beneath my standards. Clothing makes the man. You have dressed an emperor like a peon."

Archuleta lifted a blue-veined hand. "Not yet. Not until you tell me about Skye, if that is his name. Everything. Leave out nothing. Your life depends on it."

"Skye? Why, amigo, there's the meat you want. I never beheld the man until a few weeks ago, when he rode in with his concubines. I questioned him closely, of course. Amigo, I can tell you, in all privacy, that he is a Protestant revolutionary, intending to overthrow all that is sacred in Mexico and turn it over to Puritans."

"Ah! It is so?"

"He is such a Calvinist that he does not touch his savage women; they are servants, there to comfort him only, and help him in his designs to transform Mexico."

"Why should I believe this, señor?"

"Have you seen him laugh?"

Archuleta nodded. "He is a serious man."

"Beware Skye. He confessed things to me, as we came along the trail. He is a burning man. He is a man brimming with wild ideas. He is a man to ignite gunpowder. He is a man to hand out pamphlets, recruit armies, sow discontent. Sah, beware the smoldering revolutionary, who outwardly seems calm, but inwardly is a raving wolf."

Archuleta nodded. "A likely story. Why should I believe you, when everything you have told me is absurd?"

"Ask him. He never lies, which is most unfortunate. He could go far if he knew how to invent."

"I have. He says he is looking for the children of one of his savage women. That is his story. How do you make that to be a crime against Mejico?"

"Ah! Wake up, amigo. He will enter each estancia, each hacienda, looking for the children, or so he says. And he will be actually collecting information: how many hombres, how well is the place fortified? Dios! His story is perfect for his purposes. . . . Ah, what are you going to do with him?"

Archuleta exhaled slowly. "Send him away."

"And his women?"

Archuleta smiled. "They have already been taken care of."

"How?"

"Labor is scarce; they will be valuable."

"They are slaves, then?"

"No, we have no slaves in Mejico. They will be taught the faith, and employed in the province."

"By whom?"

"Padre Martinez is looking into it. Perhaps he will keep one, give one to his brothers."

"Will they be free to return to their people?"

"*Basta.* Put on those clothes. Leave the habit. I will return it to the church, as a favor."

Archuleta slipped outside, and Childress found himself alone. He cast his glance about, looking for useful items such as a knife or spoon or bit of food or flint and steel, but he found little of immediate value in the room.

He lifted the heavy brown robe over his head, and sorted out the clothing left for him: a pair of cotton drawers, a great shirt of unbleached muslin, and some baggy pantalones of heavy material that he thought might be duckcloth or canvas.

There were two pairs of leather sandals, large and smaller. The large ones were too large, but were the only choice. He settled his Panama on his majestic locks, and looked once again rather like himself.

When at last Archuleta reappeared, he motioned Childress out the door and into the sunny alley. And there was his shining red cart, hitched to the Clydesdale, and Shine perched upon the Clydesdale's back, licking his fingers.

"You are free. I have no reason to hold you, señor."

"But I have given you a dozen."

"Indeed. They were entertaining."

"How shall I make my way? I haven't a peso."

"You have a monkey."

"Ah, yes, Shine. But he is a thief. You would set a thief loose among your people?"

"It is an entertainment, señor. They give him whatever he wants. And so you will fill your belly."

"This is disappointing. I thought I would at least have the honor of facing the firing squad before the wall. Mexico has shed the blood of thousands, si?"

"I cannot give you that great honor, Señor Childress, even if you should find it fitting and glorious."

"And what of Skye?"

Archuleta shook his head. "Do not pity him, señor."

"Ah, the wall, then?"

"He will have a chance to confess, first. But that is a trifle. Maybe I will send him down to Santa Fe, so that his fate will be well known and a lesson to the army of Tejas."

"Ah! Most fitting, señor. He has no country and is alone."

Archuleta smiled.

26

The helplessness that engulfed Skye that morning was familiar. He had spent a large part of his life unable to shape his own destiny or choose his fate or seek his own happiness. He spent a bad night, famished, his only sustenance the bread he had miraculously received, his body aching from being propped against an earthen wall through the endless dark, and his senses offended by the foul odor rising from a pit in a corner where many before him had relieved themselves.

But there was a certain solace in familiarity. Through all the terrible years as a slave boy on a frigate, he had waited for his chance and eventually fashioned it at Fort Vancouver. The odds here were even worse. He possessed nothing, not even the monk's cowl that clothed his body. His feet were naked in a land of cactus. He didn't know the tongue, had no weapons, could not even ask directions. He could not explain himself, seek help, seek comfort, seek to free Victoria and Standing Alone. And yet he would watch and wait and look for his opportunity. Someone, somewhere, would help him. These were a cheerful and generous people; someone would help.

When Childress returned, accompanied by the prefect,

Archuleta, and two soldiers, the Texan had startling news:
the Galveston privateer was being freed.

"They're letting me go, soon as I translate for them."

"You free? No charges?"

"Free as a lark, and they're giving me my horse and rig,
too."

"And me?"

"Sorry, Skye."

Skye stared first at Archuleta, and then at Childress, waiting for reasons. Why not himself? What had he done?

Archuleta began whispering in sibilant Spanish, and
Childress translated.

"You're a Texas spy, he says, and they're keeping you,
sending you down to Santa Fe. Your fate will be decided
by the governor, Armijo."

"Fate?"

"They shot a couple of Texans poking around there, collecting information for Lamar, pretending to be traders.
There's a Texas army crawling west, Skye. Over three hundred armed men, determined to expand Texas at least to the
Rio Grande, if not more. Naturally, the Mexicans are a little
jumpy."

Skye absorbed that bleakly. "Why are you free?"

Childress didn't reply, shrugged, smiled blandly. Archuleta started in again, this time in harsh tones.

"He says you're spying for Texas, and he has a witness to
prove it, and if you confess it might go easier for you. You
know the fate of spies in time of war."

"Witness?"

"Archuleta says he wants the entire story; what Lamar is
paying you, what your purposes are, who you report to, how
many Texans are coming, where they will come, who leads
them, how they are equipped, and how long you have been
snooping in Mexico."

Skye stared warily at Childress, suspicion mounting up
like lava in a volcano.

"He says you are a self-confessed man without a country, so there is no help for you, no international rules to observe. You are alone. You do not claim Texas. You do not claim the United States. So you are without hope. You will be entitled to a priest before the end. But if you talk, and give them intelligence, you might be kept alive . . . They are not opposed to mercy, for the truly repentant."

"Mercy?"

"A quick death rather than a slow one; firing squad rather than noose."

Skye stared at Childress, suddenly knowing where Archuleta got all this. The fat man had betrayed him to save his own miserable hide. There was no sense in talking further; not one word, that could be twisted or ignored. He doubted that one word he might say would be accurately conveyed to the prefect.

Archuleta continued to cajole him: talk, and there would be a good meal, beans and some brandy. Talk and he would have sandals, and see some daylight.

But Skye had nothing to say. He would not lie, would not invent stories, would not alter the story he had already given Archuleta and Father Martinez. Archuleta badgered him, but Skye's mouth was sealed. He stared at Childress, the fat man who had called himself a friend, who was now dressed in pantalones and a shirt and sandals, and whose Panama covered his head. The fat man who had betrayed him for a few rags and some food and a chance to save his hide.

Eventually, Childress stopped translating altogether. Skye's silence rebuffed them. Archuleta shrugged, glared at Skye, and herded Childress out the door. Skye was suddenly alone, never so alone, and suddenly without much hope. He raised himself on his toes and could just see out the high window to the enameled red cart, hitched to the Clydesdale, awaiting the Judas from Galveston Bay.

Archuleta and Childress shook hands; the prefect bowed slightly. Skye's erstwhile partner clambered up and drove away in the bright sun, beneath the bold blue of the heavens, heading for the plaza. The monkey would no doubt feed him there, entertaining the Taos people, stealing whatever Childress needed to keep body and soul together.

Skye exhaled slowly, feeling that foreboding and sinister knowledge that his life was swiftly draining away. He had felt it before, this special loneliness. But this time he was not alone; he had Victoria to think of, and Standing Alone.

He had no idea what had happened to his women, but he knew they were not free, that they had been forcibly baptized into a faith they didn't understand, and that the padre, Martinez, had commandeered them. He hoped desperately that they might be free; that Victoria would somehow learn of his whereabouts, slip along this narrow alley, letting him know she was there and seeking means to free him. But the alley was silent.

He had to do something. He might not be able to save himself, but perhaps he could save her. Did they want information about Texas? He had none, but maybe he could conjure up some, if it would save his beloved woman and their Cheyenne friend. The thought stabbed him; he never lied. He had always been a man of honor, whose word was true. But now he was tempted. If the prefect would free those two and start them back to Bent's Fort, he could conjure up whole armies of Texans, enough Texans to satisfy every civil and military officer of the Republic of Mexico. And die for it.

But he loathed that very idea. He would sacrifice himself to save her; that was the nature of love. There had to be a way. Yet he could think of none. He scarcely even knew how to begin. There was no option except to wait, look for chances, and strike hard and fast if he could.

He cased the plain room, which made do for a jail, with its high windows with iron bars planted in them. Given time, he could escape, even if he had to claw apart the adobe with his fingernails. There was nothing. An empty box. A bench of clay to sit or lie upon. An earthen olla and earthen cup. He could crack that over the head of a soldier, maybe.

They still had not fed him.

A while later the door creaked open again, and this time the merchant, Larrimer, entered, with the prefect and two soldiers. One soldier brought a bowl of stew to Skye, who wolfed it down. It was not enough.

"Mr. Skye, there are rules to this engagement," Larrimer said. "Any question you ask, I must translate exactly and wait until Señor Archuleta decides whether I should answer."

Skye nodded. Larrimer looked worried.

"I myself am suspect, Mr. Skye. Every foreigner is, especially those who speak English."

Skye nodded. "Why am I held?"

Larrimer translated and Archuleta answered: "You are a spy for Texas."

"Who says?"

"Childress the trader has told everything."

"Childress! Is that how he freed himself?"

"Archuleta believes the information given him is accurate."

"It's a pack of lies!"

"Careful, Mr. Skye."

"Where is my wife?"

"You have no wife."

"Where?"

"She is under the loving care of Padre Martinez. And the other squaw."

"Is she a prisoner?"

"She is being succored, so that she might become a woman of the faith."

"What will come of me?"

This time, Archuleta spoke at length, while Larrimer nodded.

"The prefect says that soon you will be paraded naked

three times around the plaza, so all who see you can revile you and spit upon you, who invade our homeland. Then you will be put in chains, and will walk with a squad of soldiers to Santa Fe, where you will be subject to a trial. Governor Armijo has taken to holding trials for Texans and provocateurs just like General Santa Anna's trials. You will reach into an earthen jar where there are many beans, half white and half black. If you draw out a black bean, you, ah, stand at the wall while the snare drums rattle. If you draw a white bean, your life is spared, but not your liberty. You will be in Mexico all the rest of your days."

Skye sagged into the wall.

The prefect had one further instruction.

"You will please to pull off that habit of the Franciscan, which so fraudulently covers you."

Skye could not bring himself to do it, or to face what was to come, so he stared.

But the sharp scrape of a sword pulled from its scabbard changed his mind, and moments later he stood naked.

27

His camouflage had never failed him. The world saw a giant gaudy grandee telling impossible stories, calling attention to himself in every possible way, and dismissed him as a man demented.

And so it was this time: he had spun stories, each more improbable than the one before, some of them even true, and he and his monkey and bloodred cart had caught the eye of everyone, and soon these people had taken the measure of him and dismissed him, just as he intended.

The man called Childress settled in the sunny plaza, and soon enough a crowd collected around him to watch Shine, who was even then swinging from the vigas, dropping to the clay, pilfering everything in sight, much to the delight of grinning children and smiling adults and nervous mothers. Shine was an accomplished thief and considered theft to be his mission in life.

He sprang toward the cart of a tamale vendor, scooped up two of the corn-husked meals, and retreated to a rooftop, where he chittered happily. The vendor pretended to be vexed, but was laughing at all this. Shine pitched one tamale to Childress, who discreetly hid it in his wagon. In time that heap would grow and include whatever the little monkey could lay his hands on. He was especially adept at collecting

small tools, such as knives and spoons, right before the very
eyes of the victims, who actually enjoyed the broad daylight robbery.

Shine pulled corn husks away and wolfed down the tamale, smacked his hairy dark lips, and then vanished into
a mercantile, while the Mexicans strained to see inside and
discover what act of piracy the little monkey would commit next. They were not disappointed. Shine emerged with
a remnant of blue fabric, and dropped it into the cart, while
the owner fumed and smiled, uncertain whether to laugh or
wax indignant. Childress wisely returned the merchandise.

Next, Shine plucked Childress's Panama from his head
and wandered through the crowd, holding it by its rim and
collecting reales and pesos and candy. If anyone failed to
donate, he scolded angrily, dancing from one foot to the
other, his tail lashing dangerously, until the victim surrendered. People were delighted. All of Taos was seeing not
merely a monkey, but a piratical, demanding, crafty one
as well.

When had Taos received such an entertainment? A great
sigh of appreciation went through them, children squealed,
mothers clucked and herded the children away from such a
hairy menace to good order, and meanwhile, the heap in the
red cart grew.

Shine returned, handed the Panama to Childress, whose
quick and furtive glance suggested to him that he had acquired a dollar or two of Mexican coin, a great deal, actually, coming out of an impoverished frontier town. It would
buy food.

Shine rested a while on Childress's ample shoulder, and
then plunged anew into the crowd, entertaining them as a
trapeze artist might, swinging from roof to roof, viga to viga,
while the crowd craned its necks to watch this novelty. Childress furtively counted: he now had somewhere around
three American dollars, mostly in reales and centavos. Not

enough to outfit, but it would spare him immediate embarrassments. There would not be more. Shine had pushed these people to the limits of their tolerance.

Childress enjoyed Taos, which baked in a morning sun, its people bright and happy, its views majestic, its air cool and sweet. It would soon become a part of the Republic of Texas; everything east of the Rio Grande would become a part of Texas. He might be a mercenary, but he was other things as well, and this foray had acquainted him with certain things that he would include in his reports.

In any case, he was temporarily Texan also, though he had no great loyalty to the new nation. Lamar had sent him, the eyes and ears of the strong army advancing behind him. Houston had been elected but did not recall this robust corps of Texas filibusters rolling west, all of whom bragged they could lick any ten Mexicans they encountered. Childress's price had been a thousand Republic of Texas dollars—in gold. He had brought none of that with him. He eyed the happy crowd, counting men of military age while the good burghers of Taos gawked.

But he was also looking for slaves, and found none.

All this sunny sport was interrupted by the rattle of a drum from the shadowed northeast corner of the plaza, and there Childress beheld an awful spectacle. The drummer, a soldier dressed in the blue and white of the republic, snare-drummed his way through the sunlight, calling attention to what followed, and that turned out to be poor Skye, his flesh white and naked and hairy, his arms tied behind him so he could not even supply himself the modesty of his hands. Prodding him along were two more blue-coated soldados, and finally the prefect.

A sudden hush descended, and this martial party emerged from the deep shade into bright sun. Women gasped. Who had ever seen such a thing? Most of them intuitively gathered their children and turned away, or fled into the alleys.

Some girls stared; old women in black calmly settled in to watch, licensed by age. And men drew to attention.

Now the awful parade marched slowly around the plaza. Skye's efforts to hasten his ordeal to its end were thwarted by a rope that stretched around his neck and back to one of the soldiers.

Skye knew not where to look, and stared rigidly ahead, his mortification apparent in his stiff posture. But then he saw Childress and stared, his gaze so relentless that not even a lifetime devoted to persiflage could help. Childress averted his eyes, knowing he could never meet Skye's piercing stare. Closer Skye came, the rattle of the drum shattering composure.

The Mexicans whispered: What was this? Who was this? A man from Tejas! Ah, see what happens to spies and provocateurs! A few spat. Skye passed; around the plaza he went, and passed again, and still he stared at Childress. But what did Skye know? Childress could do or say nothing. Not yet. In time, Skye's stare might be altogether different from what it was just then.

At last, after three times around the plaza, they stopped Skye and Archuleta read a proclamation: Be it known to the good citizens of Taos, that this man of Tejas, a spy and enemy of the republic, would be marched to Santa Fe to meet his fate, in the company of soldiers. Let it be a lesson to all.

An impressive display, Childress thought. He examined the equipment of the soldiers. They lacked muskets, but had broadswords and lances, and he didn't doubt they knew well how to use them. Skye had never stopped staring at Childress, and the last he saw of Skye, the naked man was still staring at him.

Childress felt momentary discomfort, but set it aside. He rarely felt any emotion and considered it a liability to his professional conduct. His storefront operation on the Arkansas gave him all the cover he would ever need.

They were hauling Skye away now; he watched sharply,

intending to find out whether Skye would be marched, bare-foot and naked, to Santa Fe, or whether they would toss him in a cart, a veritable tumbril. If they did not protect him from the sun he would surely die of burn.

He had little time. He summoned Shine, who had been bounding along beside Skye for a few moments, and the monkey landed on the seat beside him. The crowd was slowly dispersing; there would be no more shenanigans to entertain them this bright day.

"Señor," he said to an older man, "por favor, could you direct me to the residence of Padre Martinez?"

"Si, Señor Monkey Hombre, it is thus," the old man said, gesticulating. "He has a young woman who helps him keep house," he added, with a certain wryness.

The Calf had a mistress. That intelligence was not new to Childress, and no remonstrations from the bishop had compelled the priest to surrender his woman. On the con-trary, the priest openly declared that celibacy was unnatural and ought not to be required of any clergyman.

Childress found the Calle Rondo and proceeded up it, un-til he reached the place, a blank-walled adobe structure with only a door to signify a dwelling. It was not a rectory. Within, he knew, there would be a small, richly planted pa-tio with the house opening around it. The wall looked to be eight or nine feet, nothing he could look over. From his van-tage point on the street, he could see nothing of what trans-pired within.

Victoria Skye and her friend, Standing Alone, would be somewhere within, probably doing domestic chores. Padre Martinez maintained no small establishment. Childress doffed his Panama, handed it to Shine, and pointed. The monkey peered at him, uncertain of his intent, but then leaped gracefully to the parapet, and vanished. The few people on this shady lane eyed him curiously but did not question him. They had all seen him in the plaza; perhaps he would be visiting the padre.

Childress sat and sweated, the sun being high now, but all he encountered was profound silence. He feared that his monkey might have been captured, though no mortal could hold it for long by ordinary means. But at last he saw the familiar little body perched high above, still carrying the Panama. Then Shine leaped gracefully into the cart, and in one more bound, onto the seat beside Childress. Within the hat lay some round loaves, a little succor for the hard times ahead.

Victoria Skye's medicine bundle, which always hung from her neck, lay on top.

They were waiting.

28

Nothing in Skye's previous life had prepared him for the mortification of being marched naked through a public place. To strip away his clothes was to strip away his mortality, reduce him to an animal.

Some of those who first saw him turned away, and he was grateful to them. But others stared, rapt, at the sight of him, and he had no defense against it. He finally stared back, eye for eye, one by one, and many of those who watched found themselves facing an intense stare, until they too fell away, embarrassed.

But then he had come to Childress, perched on his red cart, the author of his troubles, and so he stared at Childress too, a gaze so relentless that not even that fat fraud could endure it. And so it had passed, and the harm that came to him was not to his body, but to his spirit. The guard took him back to the room from whence he had emerged, and they untied his hands. His aching arms fell to his side and he massaged them.

Larrimer was still there, compelled to translate, and Archuleta stood by, a certain amused look in his dark eyes.

"You're to put on the duds," Larrimer said.

They handed Skye some pantalones of coarse hard cloth,

and a shirt of the same material. He donned them gratefully, feeling himself a human being once again.

Archuleta murmured other things, and Larrimer translated.

"You're going to Santa Fe now for a trial. Governor Armijo will preside."

"I want my wife with me."

Larrimer consulted. "He says that's not possible."

"A man on trial is entitled to see his family."

"He says fate has decreed otherwise. Spies do not receive such blessings."

Skye started to protest his innocence, recite his intentions in coming here, but he held his peace. That litany would get him nowhere.

"Where is she now?" he asked.

This time Archuleta was more specific. "In the care of Padre Martinez," Larrimer said. "She will be employed, and her friend as well, in peaceful labor suitable for an Indian woman."

"What if she wants to go home?"

That produced a long exchange, and then Larrimer said, "She cannot, for her own good. The republic and the church must look after her body and soul, and put her to productive labor, so that she might see God."

"Slavery."

Larrimer did not translate, and Archuleta did not ask what was said. But he knew, anyway. "Slavery is forbidden in Mexico, by the republic, by the church," he said. Larrimer translated.

"Will she be in service at the padre's house?"

"No," Larrimer said at last, "she will be placed with a hacendado as soon as she shows evidence that she accepts her new life. And the same for the other woman. They will be separated, to avoid small difficulties."

"And does she have a choice?"

"No, she's in debt for her food and shelter and some clothing that was given her. So is the Cheyenne woman. He says that in Mexico these things must be paid with labor, and it is a criminal act to run from creditors. Mexican law is strict and just and virtuous, protecting all. The alcalde says that these things will all be decided for the good of the women."

"Are they going to feed me?"

Archuleta shrugged. He seemed to have understood more English than he admitted to understanding.

"How many days to Santa Fe?" Skye asked.

"Quatro, cinco," the prefect said, not waiting for translation. He turned to the three soldiers, addressed them at length, in curt tones, obviously admonishing them to be on guard with this dangerous man, and then sent them off.

They marched him south along smooth clay streets that did his feet no harm, perhaps because many hundreds of bare feet tramped them each day. Four or five days along unpaved and stony trails. Skye wondered how long his bare feet would last. Three of the soldiers were on foot, one ahead, two lancers behind. But then another, a corporal, appeared on a horse. He wore a cutlass. There would be no chance of outrunning that one. They all wore the blue and white of the republic, but not shoes or boots. These men wore sandals, as did so many in Mexico. But at least they had thick cowhide under their feet.

The countryside immediately south of Taos took his breath away. He had not expected beauty, but there it was: the dark reaches of the Sangre de Cristos to the east, the golden plain, the bright green vegetation below, the pastures of lime-colored grasses, sheep, cattle, burros.

They passed a few peasants, cheerful and sunny people who stared at him and whispered. Many carried enormous burdens on their backs. One lashed at a burro drawing a creaky carreta full of fragrant green hay.

A great adobe church loomed to the southeast, its twin towers golden in the sun, its beauty utterly amazing to Skye. This lovely building had been lovingly fashioned from the very earth by these people, and Skye found himself admiring these Mexicans for their artistry and industry.

A great peace seemed to radiate from the church, and he sensed its holiness and sacredness. Not a soul entered through its massive doors, and it seemed to slumber there in the strong light of the noonday.

The smooth path and the church lifted him for the first time, and he began to think about things: how might he free Victoria and Standing Alone? He knew where they were—for the moment. How might he escape this escort? And if he did, how might he avoid swift recapture? The odds were terrible, and even worse for finding his wife and Cheyenne friend and spiriting them all out of Mexico, barefoot.

Whatever else he needed to survive, shoes or sandals would be high on the list. He began to observe what lay alongside the trail, something, anything that might spare a barefooted man anguish. But there was only rock and cactus and sticks.

The terrain changed; the soft dusty clay of the path yielded to sharp-edged rock patched with prickly pear, and his feet knew it at once. He stubbed a toe, and limped. Then he cut a sole on a tiny shard of rock projecting upward invisibly, and left blood in his steps. His left foot hurt, and he began to limp. A soldier prodded him along with the lance, enraging him. And yet . . . he knew he had a weapon now; his own blood.

They saw the blood, spoke among themselves, and as they did he slowed. His first and sole defense was to slow to a crawl, go as little as possible. He winced as he walked; he didn't need to exaggerate the pain; feet unused to being bare are easily bruised. They prodded him again, the tip of the lance poking hard into his kidney, and he hurried for a moment, and then slowed again.

Thus by degrees he slowed them, only an hour out of Taos. The longer this walk took, the better were his chances of coming up with something, anything.

Then they prodded him again, this time angrily, and he limped forward until he stepped on a thorn, which jabbed deep into the ball of his left foot, and he bellowed. He sat down, ignoring the threats. The thorn had broken off, and was not easily removed, especially without so much as a knife.

This time the corporal shot a string of invective at him. The other two lifted him to his feet and force-marched him forward. Skye no longer had any plan at all; the pain began to rake his feet and ankles and calves, and he could scarcely imagine going through five days of this.

Two of his wounds leaked droplets of blood; no great flow of it, but enough to speckle the trail behind him. He walked as slowly and carefully as he could, ignoring the sharpness of the soldiers, who began to harry him. He had experienced much worse pain in his life, but this was repetitive, the stabs coming again and again, each step of his left foot a torment.

He sat down, and the prodding of the lances failed to budge him. They wouldn't kill him; he was certain of it. They fell into a discussion that became an argument, and though he couldn't grasp the words, he understood the gestures. The two foot soldiers wanted the corporal to dismount and put Skye on the horse, and the corporal was not about to surrender his comfortable seat and emolument.

Skye listened to the clash of wills, rubbed his sore foot, dabbed away the blood oozing from the broken thorn, and waited, all the while wondering if he could escape once he had the horse and the soldiers were on foot.

It was, in fact, a plan, but whether it was utterly foolhardy he didn't really know. What would a barefoot fugitive do with a posse of the Mexican army hot on his trail?

Then, suddenly, the argument subsided. The corporal did not dismount. One of the privates turned to Skye, talking heatedly, but Skye could grasp none of it. The man pointed at the wounded foot, unsheathed a small knife, and sent fear rocketing through Skye. But the man pantomimed what he

intended: there would be some minor surgery on the trail.
Reluctantly, Skye extended his leg, and the private placed
the foot in his lap, with surprising gentleness. He ran a hand
softly over the wounds, grinned at Skye, and held his knife
ready.

Skye clenched his teeth, waited. The soldier's deft plucking with the tip of his knife extracted the stub of the thorn,
which had run deep into Skye's sole. He held it where Skye
could see it. It looked like something off a cactus. Blood
oozed. The other private rummaged through his field kit for
a bandage, and wrapped Skye's foot tightly. He wished they
would have cleaned it first. The bandage would help, but
wouldn't last long, not in this flinty rock. They helped Skye
to his feet, a definite kindness in them, even though the corporal stared darkly at the whole process.

And so once again they began, pacing themselves to
Skye's limping. Santa Fe looked even farther away than before, but maybe there was hope in that.

29

Victoria listened carefully but could not understand a word. That didn't faze the pretty young Mexican woman though; she obviously expected Victoria to understand everything, and if she wasn't understood, then she would talk louder and faster and wag her hands and flail her arms.

Instructions, orders, explanations, sweeping gestures. All Victoria got out of it was the sense that she and Standing Alone were expected to do things. Then the sweet-voiced young woman tried talking very slowly, as if to an infant, but that did not yield understanding.

Meanings did pervade that flood of Spanish words and gestures helped. The young padre's woman was expecting help in the kitchen. Victoria and Standing Alone were supposed to toil there, peeling vegetables, cooking meat in the kettle hanging in the fireplace, shelling peas, fetching kindling, scraping pots, and in between, scrubbing clothing and hanging it to dry.

The padre had been gone all afternoon, for what reasons Victoria did not know. But that was all right: it gave her a chance to survey this place. She had swiftly learned that it was a very private and peaceful place, with a high-walled garden, and only a few small windows on the second floor.

It seemed grand; much larger and better than most of the houses of Taos. No wonder the padre wanted women to care for it.

That morning, the young woman had admitted a stiff older one dressed in black and summoned Victoria and Standing Alone. Then the dour older woman did a strange thing with a string. She took measurements; that was plain. The older woman wrapped the string around their waists, and made some marks on paper; then she did the same at the bosom and the hips, and finally she measured from the neck to the floor, and then she vanished out the barred patio door, which had a mysterious locking mechanism.

That afternoon, the stiff-backed old woman reappeared, this time with a bundle of clothing, some of it well worn and mended, some new. Now they made Victoria and Standing Alone pull off the shifts they wore and don this new clothing: drawers, a light and very full underskirt, a sort of tight blouse. The two Mexican women nodded, and with gestures told Victoria and Standing Alone to put their shifts on over all this other clothing. And so they were dressed very like the Mexican women, in layers of clothes, except that they were barefoot. The two Mexicans talked back and forth, nodding, looking pleased with what they had wrought, and then the older woman was let out into the narrow street.

As the afternoon unfolded, the Mexican woman set them to work in the kitchen, building up the fire, kneading dough, peeling carrots and potatoes, and finally slicing up pieces of beef the woman had produced from some cool place. All these went into a black cast-iron pot along with some salt. Ah! Victoria knew all of these things, and so did Standing Alone, so the work went easily. But it was irritating not to know how to talk to this woman of the padre, or learn anything. And the woman was not interested in learning Victoria's tongue, either.

But the padre's woman didn't press them hard, and there was time to explore. Victoria wandered into a large room in which the smooth walls had been coated with white, and found little niches in the walls, and carved wooden statues in each niche, each carefully and brightly painted.

"Ah! The gods of the Mexicans," she said, surveying each one. The males had black beards. One beautiful woman was larger, dressed in blue, and had a sunburst of gold behind her, and before her were two candles. She smiled into the room and blessed it with her serenity.

"The mother god of the Mexicans," Victoria said, even as she beckoned Standing Alone along. "See how they honor her. I like that one better than the one on the cross." But then she remembered the words given to her by Skye once, about this god who willingly sacrificed himself so that others might be welcomed and made whole by the Above One, and she felt a strange respect flow through her. She wished Skye could be there to explain all these mysteries.

On the wall was the hanging god, the one dying on a cross, but there were no candles before him anywhere. He was everywhere, in each room. She had seen this god before, too, and thought him very strange.

There was a table and a chair where one could make the marks on paper, and a woven basket with the money of these people lying in it. There were many coins, and some paper too, but Victoria had no idea whether this was much or little money. She had seen such things in St. Louis, but not these coins or this paper. They explored the other rooms, believing that this holy man had great wealth, and then the patio.

In the garden, she discovered Shine sitting on the high wall with the fat man's hat in hand. Shine chittered his greeting, swung down, and Victoria knew instantly what to do. When the young Mexican woman was not looking, she plucked up two little round loaves and dropped them into the hat. Then she pulled her medicine bundle from her neck and put it into the hat as a sign. Someday it would come back; she didn't doubt that. Standing Alone stared, alarmed, but Victoria laughed. In moments, the monkey was gone, two graceful bounds from a tree to the wall.

Now Childress knew where Victoria and Standing Alone were. Aiee! It was good. Skye and Childress would come. Maybe they would have rifles and food and moccasins, and maybe fleet horses and saddles and a cooking pot and flint and steel and blankets. She thought of Skye, and ached for him, and ached to know where he was. He would come for her, or she would come for him, and they would escape. But for now, she needed to plan: to know how to get food to take with them, to learn how to escape, to learn a few words of these people.

She did not see Skye or Childress during that long day, and as evening approached, the Mexican woman kept them busy in the kitchen. Then the padre, this Martinez, appeared, looked the Indian women over carefully, nodded, said things to his woman.

The women put things on a table for him, savory meat and vegetables, some hot-baked bread, which Victoria liked, and a porcelain bottle of amber liquid. She wondered what that was, sneaked a sniff and discovered a sharp tang, but she dared not drink it. Then the padre sat down alone, and poured the amber liquid from the bottle into a cup and drank.

He sighed, sipped more.

She knew what it was! Firewater! Whiskey! She could see him relax and enjoy the hour. He swept one cup and then another into him, drinking as prodigiously as he ate. She and Standing Alone peeked from the cooking room until the Mexican woman hustled them away. The holy man and the Mexican woman talked much, but Victoria couldn't grasp a word of it. She sensed the talk was about herself and Standing Alone.

The padre Martinez disappeared up a stair, and the Mexican woman watched as the dishes were cleared off. But all that interested Victoria was where that brown bottle of the firewater was going. The Mexican woman put it into a cupboard. Ah! Victoria saw the place.

At the last, the Indian women were shown to a small room where things were stored. With gestures, they were made to understand that they should sleep there. But there were no blankets, nothing but a clay floor, and it was a cold place, the chill of the evening radiating through the earthen walls. Victoria sighed; she had slept in worse places, and this one would keep the wind and rain away.

The Mexican woman padded away, and Victoria furtively watched her progress through darkened rooms and up a stairway. So she would sleep up above, like the padre. Good!

Victoria waited, but not long, and then collected the brown bottle and a cup, and made her way back to the storage place.

"See what I have," she said.

Standing Alone looked doubtful.

"Whiskey!" Victoria unstopped the bottle, poured some of the amber fluid into a cup, and tasted it.

"Aiee!" Pure fire smoked down her throat. She had never tasted anything so awful.

"Have some of this medicine," she said. "Big medicine!"

But Standing Alone shook her head, and made signs with her fingers that Victoria could barely interpret because it was so shadowed. But the Cheyenne woman was telling her that she never had tasted white men's whiskey because it destroyed her people, and she wouldn't start now.

"Take a little just to warm you. It is cold," Victoria replied.

But Standing Alone shook her head.

Victoria sighed. Ah, if only Skye were there to share this bonanza with her! She tried again, another sip of that fierce and wild amber liquid that inflamed her tongue and mauled her throat. It slid down with a heated rush, and she gasped. The Mexican firewater was ten times more violent than the American firewater.

But, ah! What a good hot pleasant feeling was building in her belly! She sipped again. And again. Finally, she fell into rhythmic sipping, letting the firewater shoot joy through her veins, and letting herself relax after a taut and terrible day. She was a prisoner, stuck inside a place from which she could not escape, but this was a solace.

"Take this," she said, thrusting the cup at Standing Alone, but the woman pushed it away.

"It is good. I am not cold now."

Victoria started laughing for no reason at all. She drank much more, for several hours, as sleep overtook her, but the good feelings gave way to dizziness and nausea, and she did not feel well at all. She tried to stand, but could not. She needed to find the place where she could relieve herself, but could not remember it.

Finally, she lay on the cold clay ground, which whirled around and around, and she could not sleep well because her head hurt and her body was rebelling against the Mexican firewater. She had consumed half of what was in the bottle.

Beside her, Standing Alone slumbered peacefully.

Aiee! She would pay for it in the morning!

30

Colonel Childress hastened back to the plaza. There was so much to do, so little time. He circled it until he discovered a tailor wedged into a southside corner, and then tugged the reins.

"Fetch," he told Shine. "I'm going inside."

The monkey plucked Childress's Panama from his master's noggin and began scouting the deserted plaza for easy marks, while Childress barged into the small, cool shop, where a horsey-faced young man, pale as a winter moon, was sewing.

"Ah, my good man," Childress began in Spanish, "I shall want you to put all that aside and perform a great service for humanity, God, and the universe. And what is your name, señor?"

"Laroccha."

"Ah, Señor Laroccha, the finest tailor, I am told, in all of Mexico, am I not correct?"

Laroccha scarcely nodded.

"I am Governor, Sir Arthur Childress, British administrator of Barbados, the Lower Antilles, British Guiana, and the Windward Islands. I was set upon by savages, as you can see, and need proper raiment at once. A black worsted suit, two white shirts, a cravat, stockings, smallclothes, and you will please direct me to a cobbler. Important! Official business. Have it all mañana."

"Mañana! But, señor! Sir Arthur!"

"Mañana!"

"I cannot do such a thing."

"Hire help. Hire every seamstress in Taos."

"But the cost!"

"Damn the cost. It's all to be charged to the government."

"The government?"

"Yes, Government House, Office of Administrator, Trinidad and Tobago. Post it the day you complete my order. I'll sign. Charge what you must! Levy extra! But set to work, man."

"But . . . I can't wait so long for payment. It will be half a year. I am a poor man."

"My friend, how well I understand all that. The queen of England will vouch for my purposes. I'm here on the most delicate of international missions, one that will benefit the Republic of Mexico, and I need a set of clothing pronto!"

"Ah . . . could you not give me a surety, say half?"

"My old friend, go to your prefect, Juan Andres Archuleta, and see about me. He will vouch for me, you can count on it."

Laroccha sighed. "I will take your measure, señor, and think upon it."

"Do that! I'm a busy man; negotiating for a large estate."

Laroccha pulled out a tape, and began measuring, mumbling to himself, penciling figures.

"Gobernador Childress, you are a hombre of heroic dimension, and you will consume a veritable shipment of fabric . . . you will forgive your poor clothier for adding something for your noble size, as well? I will require the toil of eight or ten others."

"Why, I would not want you to deprive yourself of a suitable and fitting reward, my friend."

Laroccha sighed. "Tomorrow at dusk? For the fitting?"

"Bueno, consider it an agreement," Childress said. "Be sure to check with the prefect. He will put you at ease, viejo."

Laroccha nodded tentatively.

"Now I must acquire some duds for my ladies, who were set upon by the Apaches as well. Who would you recommend?"

"Ah, Madame Vollers, wife of the late French consul, señor. Just across the plaza, and up the narrow stairs."

"Bueno. Mil gracias. You shall have your reward."

Childress hurried out into the morning sun, and cut straight across the clay to the upstairs shop of madame.

He saw Shine, hat in paw, jabbing it at people who were taking their paseo this bright new day.

"Soak 'em good," he muttered.

He hastened up the stairs, scarcely noticing the effort to hoist his bulk one story, and entered a salon with a great jangle of bells. Within were half a dozen elegant gowns, all on dressmaking dummies, all completed as far as he could see.

A birdlike woman emerged from behind a curtain, patting her graying bun of hair with feathery hands.

"Señor?" she said.

"My dear duchess," he said, "I have come to purchase two of your finest gowns, your most noble creations, for two ladies in distress, who were put upon by the Jicarillas a few days ago."

"Ah, poor dears! I trust they are brave?"

"Very brave, señora. Now I don't have their dimensions, but they are small and slender, and come up about to here." He pointed at his chin.

She smiled. "I have just the dresses," she said. "See, I have several that are ready but for the hems. Now, how shall we proceed?"

"Señora, I am Governor Sir Joshua Childress, administrator of Barbados and Bermuda and Corpus Christi, here on important diplomatic business."

"But aren't you the hombre with the red cart and monkey?"

"Why, señora, that is no ordinary monkey. It is a Frangipangi Ape, the only such creature in captivity, a rarity that your eyes will never behold again. Admire it with all your heart and soul, for you have seen one of the miracles of God."

"Well, yes . . ."

"Bill the British Government, señora. Government House, the Province of the Caribbean, Barbados."

"Ah . . ."

"And those hats! Yes, the ones with the broad brims and fruit about them, I shall require two. And slippers. Half a dozen small, medium, and large."

"But gobernador, I require cash. I will not accept any other. I am a recent widow, much abused by people of little kindness or courtesy, and therefore careful."

"But, señora, the circumstances are temporarily difficult."

She stared, stonily, and Childress knew defeat. "Very well, I shall return. What is the price of all that?"

She sighed. "For you, I will add ten percent."

"Add! You mean deduct."

"Add."

"Never mind. I shall find a seamstress with a kinder heart."

She stared. "It is an ordinary spider monkey found in Central America."

Childress retreated, and hunted down Shine, who was temporarily occupied somewhere. There was so little time.

"Shine, blast you," he bellowed.

The little monkey appeared at once, lazily swinging from roof to roof, carrying the Panama delicately, and then he dropped down to the cart. Within the Panama were several coins, some glistening gold. Two were double eagles.

"Ah! I see you have been engaged in criminal activity! I

shall have you arrested someday," he said, scooping up the coins. A swift count revealed sixty-odd Yank dollars. He handed a silver real to the monkey. "Here, buy yourself some tamales."

Shine chittered and chattered, and swung away.

Colonel Childress once again negotiated the formidable stairway, and burst in upon the frowning proprietress.

"A price! I shall pay you in advance, señora."

"In what?"

"Gold and silver."

"Ill-gotten, I imagine. I am only a poor widow, and here I am, accepting tainted money. How much have you?"

"Ah, I can't quite calculate in pesos. It appears to be sixty-three American."

"The two dresses are seventeen and eleven in Yankee dollars, and the hats three apiece, the slippers twelve, coming to forty-six in all, but I will accept sixty-three." She held out her hand.

"Señora!"

"Or I can summon the prefect."

"But, señora!"

The steely look in her eyes told him he was skunked. Dolefully he metered out the gold pieces and then the silver into her small patient hand.

"Very well," she said. "I must give half to the church for accepting your dirty money."

She plucked the dresses from dummies, folded them, added the hats and slippers, and thrust the bundle at him.

"You are a princess, a queen, and a saint," he said, backing out the door.

She stared at the coins, and as he left she was biting the gold ones.

Shine was sitting on the red cart, wiping his hairy lips.

"Well, my little pirate, you have done me a service," Childress said. "But we have more to do. This cart will never do. It is too well known."

He drove slowly through Taos, looking for a wagon-yard or livery barn, but found nothing that filled that bill. Taos was still too rude. Then, on the southeastern reaches of Taos, parked behind a sprawling house with Chinese lanterns dangling in the breezes, he beheld an ebony calash, or maybe it was a victoria. It was a thing of beauty, a don's vehicle, with facing quilted leather seats, a fold-up hood, and a raised bench for the driver. Two restless trotters flicked their tails at flies.

"Ah! Shine, we have success!"

He parked his red cart at the door of the stately adobe home, and knocked.

A young woman dressed head to heel in black opened to him.

"Are you the mistress of this establishment?" he asked.

"No, she's attending Don Amelio, señor."

"Is that his calash?"

She looked outside. "He always drives it."

"I should like to see him, if I may."

"He's indisposed, señor."

"Oh, he won't mind. I wish to offer him a favorable trade."

"But, señor, that is not possible until late in the day."

"You don't say! What is the nature of his indisposition?"

"Ah, sir, it ill behooves me to say." She smiled. "This is the residencia of the Señora Aguirre y Canales, who lost her husband to the beastly Tupamaro Indians not long ago."

"And Don Amelio?"

"He comes once a fortnight to console her, señor. She needs much consoling." She laughed merrily.

"Ah! My sweet little chickadee, I don't mean to invade paradise, but there is profit in it for you and me."

"There is? What?"

"Ah, your name is what?"

"Carmelita."

"Well, my dear, beautiful, holy, and faithful and blessed Carmelita, I am going to offer this charitable hidalgo my new red cart in exchange for his worn-out calash, and if he agrees, I will reward you handsomely. All you have to do is present the agreement to him."

"I will?"

Childress pointed. "You see that monkey? He's rare and famous. He's yours if you can keep him."

"A monkey?"

"He will help you in all your endeavors if he decides to live with you."

"I've always wanted a monkey, señor."

"Good! Now fetch me a pen and ink and two sheets of paper, so I may draw up an agreement for him to sign, and then you may present it to him for signature."

"A monkey," she said, her face ecstatic.

"Yes, and he will get a splendid red cart, and will bless me for it," Childress said. "Lead me to a writing table, se-ñorita, and I will draft the arrangement."

31

Sky limped, stumbled and fell. The trail turned precipitous as it wound through a giant defile toward the Rio Grande. It was soft clay one moment, razored rocks the next, and laden with sticks and prickly pear. His bandaged foot turned bloody, his right foot began to bleed also, leaving speckles of red in the dust behind him.

He willed himself forward, his legs punching pain at the base of each step, hot pain that shot up to his thighs, dull pain that eddied through his whole body; stinging pain as his abused naked feet hit sharp rock or debris. It was hard going, but he refused to quit. He thought of Victoria. He would keep going because of her. He thought of Standing Alone and her lost children, the reason he had ventured here. He had to keep on walking.

The soldiers, actually, were sympathetic. He had expected sadism, but found them to be gentle with him, and the more his feet were abused, the more they let him rest. He had expected the lances to prod him, but these were amiable Mexican boys, not hardened professionals, and they eyed him kindly, and perhaps condescendingly.

Any Indian could manage barefooted; most mestizos could too. But this tender-footed Anglo could not; he had lived his life inside of shoes and boots and the soles of his feet were without callus or thickness or hardening. They joked between them, and while Skye couldn't grasp the words, he knew the meaning: this tough white hombre had feet as soft as a baby's.

His struggles slowed them to a crawl, but he couldn't help it. He dreaded to put each foot down, knowing the flare of pain that would strike as his foot settled on the ground.

But they made some progress, and Skye did the best he could. He would always do his best, even if he were headed for a trial in which his fate would rest on a liar's testimony. One could live with all the courage he could muster, or not, and Skye chose to live in hope.

By late afternoon they had pierced to the shadowed bottoms of the river, and here they met small settlements, little farms, large cemeteries, and skinny cattle. And here, at last, a peon driving a creaking carreta overtook them. The vehicle was drawn by a pair of burros tugging from within a homemade rope harness, and carried within it two squealing hogs caught inside a wall of stakes rising from the cart-bed. The squeaking wheels had been fashioned from a large tree, and rimmed with iron.

The corporal halted the wizened old farmer, who was clad in rags, and addressed him harshly. The peon eyed Skye and shrugged.

The burros began nipping stray grasses and weeds as the debate ensued.

But then the old man walked around to the rear of the cart and pulled up one of the stakes imprisoning the hogs, and motioned to Skye. Within was a carpet of urine-soaked straw and pig manure, but it looked like heaven. Skye limped to the little cart, crawled through the opening, and was smacked by the sheer stink. But he settled between the snorting hogs with his back resting on the front of the cart.

"Vamos!" cried the corporal.

The privates were grinning and making jokes. Skye would have liked to know the jokes, but he could guess well enough. He stared at his bloody feet, and suddenly the pig droppings didn't seem so bad. The howling pain that had ripped breath out of his lungs settled into a dull ache, but his ears were soon battered by the squeaking of the wheels. One soldier walked at either side of the cart, while the corporal rode behind, his purpose to find anything out of order.

"Pig dung is worse than any other," Skye said to no one, since none could understand him. "This is the worst offense to my nostrils since the fo'castle where I rotted for years."

They eyed him blandly. The little old peon kept glancing at him, as if this exotic gringo would get him into terrible trouble.

The carreta creaked and groaned, the burros tugged, and the pigs pressed him restlessly, but at least he was off his bloody feet. His hunger returned and he eyed his pink and gray traveling companions, thinking of bacon and chops. The entourage proceeded peacefully until the next village, where the old peon began to argue vehemently, his gestures hot and troubled. Skye understood not a word, and yet understood everything. This had been the old man's destination. He did not wish to go further. But the soldiers were pressing him.

Muttering, he finally surrendered to the corporal, and the party creaked south again through the bottoms of the Rio Grande. Skye's porcine companions shrieked and pawed and wet the straw; they were all going to the butcher and they knew it.

By dusk of that day, Skye was as starved as he had ever been.

"Comida," he said, remembering a word.

The corporal nodded. None of these men was unkind to him; perhaps they knew he was doomed, and doomed men required the utmost courtesy.

They turned into yet another settlement, two or three adobes surrounded by crops and pastures, and the usual flower-decked cemetery because the Mexicans were so good at dying and so eager to celebrate the dead.

The corporal rode ahead to evict the tenants of one of the adobes, and soon enough a half dozen brown people, ranging from great age to infancy, hurried out of the casa with covert glances at Skye and the little swine caged behind the stakes of the carreta. Skye watched them hasten toward a neighbor's casa, laughing and chattering as if this were a normal thing. He felt embarrassed, as if he were the cause of this dislocation of a simple country family, but it was not his doing: the corporal had commandeered the farm.

They directed him inside, and he slid to the ground while the old peon held on to the hogs. He discovered a warm and bright room, with a meal of some sort boiling in a pot and some bowls upon a rude table. He sank onto a bench, aware of how much he stank, while outside the peon and soldiers were transferring the hogs into some safe place or other, and seeing to their needs.

Skye found an olla, poured some water over his soiled pantalones, and tried to wipe away the filth, to little avail. Every step was hell, but he kept at it, wanting to cleanse himself, both body and soul.

They fed him some mutton from the black iron pot, and he took a second and a third helping, feeling the ache in his belly slowly dissolve. He wondered if the soldiers would pay the family whose casa they had appropriated or if this was simply the luck of the draw in Mexico.

The old man appeared, having secured his hogs somewhere, and with him came an odor of the barnyard. He helped himself to the last of the boiled mutton as the soldiers watched. The meat rested uneasily in Skye's stomach, and he knew he was unwell.

Skye wanted to wash himself, but couldn't fashion the word, but he remembered his school Latin. "Lava," he said, experimentally.

That sufficed. The corporal nodded, led him outside

alertly, in fading light, to a battered watering trough for the animals, where Skye shed his filthy shirt, washed it, scraped offal off his stained pants, and tried to cleanse his body as well. But it was futile. His toilet done, Skye limped back inside, thoroughly chilled, to the casa lit only by the coals of the dying kitchen fire. They would all be sleeping on the clay floor.

He studied the room for anything of value: a weapon or food or clothing, but then subsided. It was bad enough that the soldiers had commandeered this family's food and shelter; he would not add to the offense by taking things not his. Oddly, he found himself wishing he could leave something for them: if he was going to die in Santa Fe, he wanted to die without debts. But there was nothing he could do: the soldiers may have been kind to a limping man, but they were no less wary of him, and alert to anything he did.

He did not sleep, but lay restlessly. The soldiers knew he could not escape, not when he could barely hobble, so they slept peacefully. The chill of the floor rose through his wet shirt, but there was no help for it. He lay taut, feeling a weariness in his body that matched the weariness of his mind. He was worn out. He had come all this way to find two abducted children, but here he was, under arrest and being taken to Santa Fe for a mock trial and probable death or certain imprisonment, his women were bound into slavery he knew not where, the man he had trusted had betrayed him, and everything had fallen apart.

He felt a turmoil in his bowels, and knew he was getting sick. He tried to ignore the torments of his body, but could not. He lay sweating and cold at the same time, feeling fever build in him and steal through his limbs. He could no longer lie quietly. Time ticked slowly, and he knew only that his body was burning, he was thirsty, his breathing was labored, and that he was gravely ill.

A convulsion twisted him, and then a rush of nausea, and he could no longer fight the violence of his belly. He crawled onto all fours, crawled away from the rest, and heaved up everything within him, a sour, vile rush of noxious vomit that swiftly stank up the dark room, and left him in tears.

He lacked the strength even to find his way to the olla and some fresh water, but fell back onto the clay, scarcely caring whether he lived or died.

And that is how he spent the night, his limbs cold, brow burning, and his spirits wavering like a guttering candle. Finally he sensed the presence of light, and opened his eyes, and stared up at solemn faces above him. There was a woman, and she was applying compresses to his forehead, and then he slid back into oblivion again.

32

Colonel Childress drafted a bill of sale in duplicate: a used calash and team for a red cart and draft horse. He waved it in the air to dry the ink.

"Now, child, I want you to take this to him. Awaken him from his slumbers, do you understand?"

"I shouldn't do that, señor."

"Why not, Carmelita?"

"He is not himself. He will peer at me with big eyes, black holes, as if all color has left them, and he will frown, groan, and fall back into his bed."

"And where is the señora? Does she sleep into the afternoons like the don?"

The girl shrugged. "Sometimes."

"My little Carmelita, chickadee, listen carefully. Tell Don Amelio that the British Viceroy of Grenadine, Grand Bahama, Great Inagua, and Rum Cay requires the calash on urgent business for Her Majesty, the queen, and in return he will receive the Order of the Garter and a handsome red cart."

"I can't remember all that, señor, and I'm afraid . . ."

"Write it down."

"I can't read, señor."

"Then remember it. Queen Victoria's viceroy. Quick now, and don't forget the pen and ink!"

She looked ready to bolt. "Remember the monkey," he said. "It's yours if you can keep it."

"Don Amelio doesn't like to be awakened after he has been smoking the pipe, señor. I might lose my position."

"It's a national crisis. I am saving Mexico from conquest."

She stared long and solemnly at him, sighed, plucked up the papers and the ink bottle and quill, and slowly headed for the stairway leading upward to—who knows what?

He hoped the señora would not appear.

It took an infernally long time, and he paced the room, oblivious of its colonial charm, the whitewashed adobe, the mission-style furniture, the bultos, and the Navajo rugs scattered about.

Then at last she slipped down the stairs, looking rumpled.

"Let me see it, child!" He snatched the papers from her.

There, in a shaky hand, was a signature, barely legible. And another, on the other sheet.

"Ah! He agrees! Take this! He gets one copy, I keep the other. Now, my child, you must tell me what happened."

She dimpled up. "He was fast asleep, señor, so I shook him gently, and he said, 'not again, witch,' and I said there is a nobleman from England who wants your calash, and he said, 'bother,' and rolled over, and I said it was a national crisis and you were the viceroy of . . . all that. And he said some cruel things to me, reached for the quill and bottle, and made the signs, señor viceroy. Do I get my monkey?"

"Of course, of course, if you can keep him."

He walked to the great front door. "Shine, fetch!"

The little beast leapt off the Clydesdale, bounded inside, evoking a squeal, and began ransacking the establishment. He fastened upon a silver salt cellar, and leaped up to a mantel to shake it.

Carmelita trailed him, twittering and laughing.

"See now, child, it is better than having a niño. Catch him if you can."

Childress hurried outside, led the Clydesdale to a nearby pen and unharnessed it, and then returned to the calash and its weary team, studying the powerful black horses and the ebony carriage with its yellow wheels. Yes, perfect. The black calfskin leather was new and soft, the shining lacquer showed no scuffs or chips, and the hood raised and folded easily.

He wondered how long the poor horses had been standing there, decided to do something about it, unhitched them, led them to a watering trough, where they sipped water furiously. When he judged that they were again in good fettle, he hooked the chains to the doubletree.

"Shine," he bellowed.

Nothing happened, and at once he was worried.

But then the hairy little rascal flew out of an open window, hung on a shutter as it swung, and landed on the ground, clutching something shiny.

But now it was confused. It eyed the ebony carriage and two sleek black trotters, hunted for the red cart, and discovered the Clydesdale unharnessed.

"Shine!" he bawled, but the monkey leaped up to the Clydesdale's broad back, patted his friend, chittered softly in the ear of the giant horse, rubbed his eyes with his free hand, combed the mane, and reluctantly swung to the ground, not happy.

The big horse nickered affectionately, and clacked its teeth.

But what did it matter? "Shine, we are the masters of our fate," Childress said. "I am Lord Childress, viceroy of the universe."

The spider monkey glared at him, and pitched the shiny object to the dirt. It was a salt cellar.

"I always have sat above the salt," Childress said, cheerfully.

He discovered Carmelita at the great door, oozing tears down honey-colored cheeks, weeping sadly. That innocent child did want a monkey and was tricked, but all that could not be avoided. He snapped the lines over the backs of the two trotters and was rewarded by a swift tug and the soft sway of the calash as it rounded the long circular drive out to the dusty road. He had things to do, and little time. Within days, his friend Skye would be drawing a black bean or a white bean.

Childress drove his fine calash back to the plaza, while his monkey sat on the seat beside him, studying his new conveyance and sucking his fingers. It knew better than to jump onto the backs of the trotters.

Slowly, the Colonel drove around the plaza looking for a cobbler. He eyed the windows, and cased the few second-floor quarters, but he could not find a maker of boots. He tried each side street, wheeling up clay alleys, stirring up the floury clay, looking for anyone who might have foot-wear. Finally he asked an old woman, and she pointed back at the plaza. He parked his calash and undertook to survey the plaza on his bare feet, but could find no bootmaker. The Mexicans mostly wore sandals or slippers that looked very similar to Indian moccasins. The few caballeros who had boots probably had them custom made in Santa Fe. Childress sighed. Very well, it would be Larrimer, then.

He entered the cool store, enjoying the redolence of leather and fabric and coffee beans.

Larrimer approached. "They let you out, Brother Childress, eh?" he said, coldly.

"Mr. Larrimer, I am in dire need of some boots, or at least shoes, and you have some ready-mades, I believe?"

"Show me some cash and I'll show you some boots."

"I haven't a cent. The Apaches made off with everything."

"Even your habit, I see. Unless you've renounced your orders and taken up with some woman." Larrimer's thick eyebrow shot upward.

"I regret announcing that I was a monk; I was desperate," Childress said.

"You might have won some sympathy by saying so. But not now, Childress. Not ever."

The Colonel knew he wasn't getting anywhere, so he tried a new tack. "Mr. Larrimer, I have a fine trading outfit on the Arkansas River, just across the international boundary. We do a business with the Utes especially. Childress and McIntyre, sir. I only regret that whatever I say will meet with skepticism because of my previous indiscretions. But it is so. And I would most eagerly give you a chit for merchandise from our stores in exchange for boots. In fact, sir, merchandise worth ten times the price of your boots."

The odd thing was that Larrimer did not laugh.

"Well? My goods are, what, a hundred miles distant? I'll add something for transportation."

"What's there?"

"Blankets, kettles, axes, hatchets, knives, saws, a few rifles, flints and steels, bed ticking, flannels, calico, salt, molasses, pure grain spirits, tobacco in plug and leaf form, vermilion, beads, awls . . ."

"I suppose you'll want some boots for Skye, too. What's his size?"

"I don't know," Childress said, marveling at the man.

"You'll want some ready-made duds for him, too, I suppose. Shoes or sandals, and some clothing. Weapons, powder, food, gear . . ."

What was this? Childress could scarcely fathom it. "I can draft an agreement, Mr. Larrimer."

"How will I know your subordinates will honor it?"

"The monkey's paw, sir. I press it into an inkpad, and press it onto the document. It's our sign and seal, the paw of Shine."

"What is the total worth of your stock?"

"Why, Sah, given that I haven't been there for some little while, I can't say. But perhaps three thousand at wholesale."

Larrimer grinned, and not kindly. "All right. You sell me your goods and the premises, and I will outfit you and Skye up to three hundred."

"But . . . but . . ." Larrimer would profit tenfold.

"I know it's there, Childress. You don't have to persuade me. Childress and McIntyre Traders. Several travelers have reported the place to me. I even know what prices you charge, how many men you have, and what tribes are camped there. I'm willing to gamble."

"Ah, would you keep my help employed?"

"Your Texas pirates? No, I'll send my own man to operate the place. He'll take inventory . . . and if there's trouble, be warned: I have my means."

"Mr. Larrimer, Sah, done!"

Larrimer grinned sardonically.

33

The padre's young woman seemed less and less friendly as the next day wore on. She raged at Victoria and Standing Alone, which only left Victoria bewildered. She couldn't understand a word. But the woman's displeasure was plain to her.

One moment the woman would be snapping; the next moment she would pantomime what she wanted: Wash those cloths and clothing in a wooden tub of water, pound and squeeze them on a ribbed board, rinse, and hang them on a line. Fetch more water.

"Agua! Agua!" the woman cried, pointing at the water.

Victoria knew that. She knew many words of this tongue even if she could not put them together.

Make the fire hot: this involved a device new to her, a lung of leather that blew air when the handles were operated. Victoria made the air come out, and the fire began to crackle. Standing Alone watched carefully. They were both studying ways to escape, ways to defend themselves.

This day the walleyed padre wandered about in his long brown robe, gazing strangely at the Indian women, his giant head lolling this way and that to see them. Maybe he could see only things that were far away, the way many old men see. His soft brown eyes studied them, the gaze poking and probing until Victoria thought she couldn't stand it. Sometimes the gaze seemed to lift her skirts, and then she looked right back at him and he looked away.

She wished he would go away, do his priestly things, but this day he hovered in the great kitchen, watching them as they scrubbed vegetables or stirred the great black pots. He had plans for them; that she knew. Maybe that was why his woman was so snappish this day. She was his woman, all right, and showing the signs of a baby, now that Victoria studied her.

Then the padre's woman took them away from the big kitchen and into the quiet bedchambers and made them broom the floors, empty pots into a smelly cistern in the garden, and shake the blankets. The padre's woman was more relaxed now that they were all away from the padre. But he hadn't left; he was there, watching.

Victoria and Standing Alone had been given no time to rest, and were fed very little at dawn, a thin oat gruel before the sun brightened the morning. They hadn't been allowed to talk, either; whenever she and Standing Alone tried to communicate in their own sign language and vocabulary, the Mexican woman started bawling at them.

Was this the future? Victoria knew that if the time came, she would fight, ferociously, no quarter, for her freedom. She would steal a knife and hide it as soon as she knew where to secret it, and one for Standing Alone, too. There were some in the kitchen; big, crude ones with dull blades, but all the better for a fight. She knew Standing Alone was thinking the same thing: sometimes they looked at a knife or a long fork and their gazes met. She knew!

A wave of contempt for the Mexican woman flooded through her: what sort of petty tyrant was this person whose strength was not her own, but the padre's? Could she not even take care of this man's dwelling place?

Victoria found reasons to head into the walled garden, always to look for the Little Person perched on the high adobe wall, but she did not see him, and her spirits sagged. For some reason, that little creature, the very one she was so darkly hostile toward at first, was her salvation. But she saw nothing, and no succor offered itself. Had that animal not taken her medicine bundle to the fat man? Didn't he know she and Standing Alone were here, behind great walls?

Then, late that afternoon, a Mexican man was admitted, and this man was dressed in a black suit coat and an open shirt, and had oily straight hair that fell away from his face. He talked with the padre for a while, and then the Indian women were summoned with a languid hand.

Victoria stared at him, wondering what this rumpled brown man would do.

The man in the suit coat addressed Victoria:

"Madam, it is I speak zoom English, and it is I am bring here to tell you zum things. For we know you habla, speak, this tongue, and do no comprende what is your mistress be saying."

Mistress? Victoria nodded, not giving the man the satisfaction of a reply in Skye's language.

"Mañana, tomorrow, a carreta, wagon, it comes and it carries you to a rancho grande, the Estancia Martinez, which is owned by the hermanos, zee brothers, of zee blessed padre Martinez. Four thousand sheep. There you will be employed for the good of your souls and bodies, and the love of Jesu Cristo."

"I think we would like to stay here in Taos."

"Stay? This place? No, no, woman, that is not possible."

"Then maybe we refuse employment, eh?"

He stared solemnly, and shook his head. "No, you cannot refuse. You go."

"Why?"

"Because zis is require."

"I am married. You must not take me from my husband. So is she."

He blinked, and shook his head. "No, not married in Me-jico. What parish? Where are zee records, zee sacrament? No, no, it is without force, like nada."

She pointed at Standing Alone. "She has a man. And children too."

"No, not in Mejico. It be no good, no good."

She pointed at the priest. "Is he married? He has a woman."

The oily-haired man glared at her.

"I heard the padre say there is no slavery in Mexico."

The man's big brown eyes blinked once, and again, as if he were careful with the words he was preparing. "Little woman, you owe much for your care. Zees things, the comida, food, the casa, the clothing on your backs, this is muy, very costly, yes, you are much in debt. So you must vork, eh? Vork!"

"So, when can we pay off our debt?"

He shook his head. "Sometime. Your vork not very valuable, si? You onnerstand, si?"

"What if we won't work?"

"Ah, pity, dolor, you taste zee whip."

"What if we go away, eh?"

He shook his head. "Do not even think of it, comprende?"

She understood and laughed at him. He seemed to puff up and withdraw into himself. Standing Alone understood little of it, and looked at her blankly.

Victoria simply laughed, the scorn in her dark features rising upward and bursting out upon the kitchen.

"Bastard," she said.

"Silencio!" bawled the padre.

She took her time. The oily man in the suit coat decided it was time to leave, and the padre showed him out. Victoria watched them at the big plank door, and she tried to understand how to work the iron mechanism that would let them out. She had seen these things before in St. Louis, but not anywhere else.

The padre's woman looked amused.

Victoria's fingers flew, and in swift gestures and their small stock of words she conveyed their fate to Standing Alone, who drew herself up proudly, unbent, unbowed, and stared at their mistress.

So she would be taken away from Skye, farther and farther, and placed into a life of grinding toil, probably worse than this light labor she had suffered this day and the day before. Tonight. Now or never. At dawn the distance between Skye and herself would stretch farther, and farther, and things would get worse, and worse . . .

Tonight.

The Mexican woman put them to work again, and set Victoria to collecting piñon wood from a large bin located at the alley wall of the patio and stacking it beside the several beehive fireplaces. She walked out there, through the serene patio with its quiet peace, past the herbs that grew in a special plot, and a lordly agave, to the place where the woodcutters stacked wood.

She plucked up a piece, and another, and then she saw the low wooden doors beyond, doors that opened on the alley, doors used by the woodcutters when they unloaded the wood from their burros and stacked the sticks within the wall for the householder. She turned and looked behind her; no, no one was watching. She stepped deep into the shadowed woodbox, and lifted a small bar. She pushed the door, and it swung a little, creaking as it did. Frightened, she peered over her shoulder, and edged the door back in place. Her heart tripped as she plucked up the sticks for the evening's dinner.

Out.

And even as she carried the load in her arms toward the kitchen, she spotted the Little Person perched quietly on the high adobe wall, watching her with bright eyes. She nodded at the fiend and continued inside, unloading her wood before the beehive fireplace.

She walked out into the garden again, and hovered around the woodbox while the little creature watched her. Then, suddenly, it vanished, and she wondered whether it understood. As soon as this household quieted, she would lead Standing Alone to this place, and they would crawl over the stacked wood, and crawl out of the walled patio.

Oh, if only the Little Person might understand. Was there anything she had failed to understand? Any message? Any sign? She saw nothing, even as she gathered a few more pieces of piñon pine for the fireplace. Anxiously, she watched the sun dive toward the horizon. Fretfully she watched the padre eat and drink and take his leisure. In agony she listened for sounds from without. Then, as dusk settled and she and Standing Alone were cleaning dishes, she beheld the Little Person named Shine on the wall again.

Her heart hammered, but there was nothing she could do, not yet, not until this house had settled, not until a great darkness could cloak them as they slipped through the house, the garden, and the woodman's gate. Sometimes she saw the monkey, sometimes she didn't. Sometimes she heard the soft clop of horses beyond the high wall, sometimes only a terrible and lonely silence. Once, a carriage wheel groaned outside the walls.

But at last the priest vanished into the darkness, and so did his woman, and Victoria and Standing Alone lay quietly in the storage alcove that had been their refuge.

Now, as the stars lit up the sky and the last blue light faded in the west, far beyond the Rio Grande, she heard the chittering of Shine up on the wall somewhere in the murky night, and she arose, and took Standing Alone with her, and crept through the garden toward the little wood gate.

34

The woodcutter's door squawked, but Victoria paid no heed. She crawled over the stacked wood, with Standing Alone right behind, and soon they found themselves standing in a dark alley with nothing but starlight to illumine the way. She peered about, seeing nothing.

"Mrs. Skye, my dear, this way."

That voice belonged to the trader, Childress, but she could see nothing.

"I shall send Shine."

Almost before the words had escaped the man, she felt the Little Person tugging on her skirt.

"Aiee!" She didn't really trust the animal.

But she let herself be led, and soon they came upon a conveyance of some sort.

"What is this damn thing?" she asked.

"It is a carriage, a calash, to be precise. Do climb in."

"Where's Skye?"

"That's a long story. First we must make haste to escape here."

She boarded the creaking carriage, barely able to see. No light shown in the streets and no moon lit the way. But she could see that it had facing seats, and that Childress was perched on a raised front seat behind some black horses, and that a sort of hood rose at the rear, making a safe black cavern there. She settled into a soft leather seat, pulled Standing Alone beside her, and instantly the faint snap of the lines over the croups of the horses started the carriage on its way.

They didn't talk and her mind teemed with a thousand questions. Where was the red cart? Where was Skye? Where did this come from? Whose was it? Where were they going? But she waited impatiently, knowing that silence was necessary just then, as the conveyance rumbled softly through the shrouded clay calles of Taos. They rolled around the west side of the plaza where a few lamps lit a few windows, and treacherous light caromed off the ebony carriage, and finally onto the camino leading south into open country.

"Ah, that's better," Childress said. "We'll go down as far as the church and wait for the moon. I'm told the road grows rough and dangerous beyond there, and we'll need the lamp of heavens to guide us."

They proceeded through a vast and cloistered darkness, and Victoria marveled that Childress would drive two horses at all upon such a night. But with each passing moment, they were rolling farther and farther from Taos, and the imprisonment there, and she felt light-headed with relief.

And worried about Skye.

She discovered the Little Person sitting beside Childress, and then felt the evil thing come sit between her and Standing Alone, as if to welcome them to this vehicle.

At last the towers of the great adobe church of San Francisco de Asis at Ranchos de Taos rose ghostly in the starlight, and Childress tugged his team to a halt.

"Now then, my dears, on the seat in front of you is a large package that contains some dresses, hats, and slippers. Ladies, please remove your present outer clothes and put these on. It's important."

"What is this?"

"You are about to be transformed. These are fine silk gowns, worn by ladies of the highest caste."

She explained this to Standing Alone, and they groped about, finding the package.

"I shall be looking straight forward, ladies, and in any case the hood behind you plunges you into perfect obscurity."

She pulled out slippery things, trying to fathom what all they were, and then began to struggle with her clothing, tugging and yanking to lift her dress over her head. But her mind was on other things. "Where's Skye, dammit?"

"On the way to Santa Fe, guarded by soldiers, to stand trial as a Texas spy. Perhaps they will execute him."

"What? How is this?"

"Madam, when we were both prisoners of the prefect, I took great pains to betray Skye, informing the Mexicans that they had nabbed a saboteur and operative of the rebel state of Texas. Of course they placed him under close guard, even as they released me to do as I choose."

"Sonofabitch!"

"Exactly. I refer to myself in just such terms, madam."

A terrible grief welled up in her. Skye in grave danger. This man the cause of it.

"Where are we going?" she asked, darkly, wrestling with clothing she didn't understand.

"Why, we're heading for Santa Fe to rescue him."

She had her dress off, and was rotating a slippery one she could not see, looking for a neckline. Standing Alone was having trouble too.

"We can't see a damned thing. What's the front of this dress?"

"Ladies, that is beyond my realm of competence."

Then Shine leaped gracefully back to them, and tugged at the fabric, and she surrendered to him. Damned Little Person was smart, but as long as he was on her side, maybe she could tolerate him. The monkey chittered and chattered, and then he held it out to her. She discovered buttons. She slid her arms under the fabric and pulled it over her head. Shine bounced and clacked his teeth and made disgusting noises.

She got her dress on and fumbled with the buttons that ran down her bosom. She had scarcely heard of buttons until she had seen them in the settlements.

"You'll find slippers in several sizes. Find some that fit, and make sure they match. I think you will be the queen of Zanzibar."

"The what of damned what?"

He laughed. "Madam, trust me. Yes, the queen of Zanzibar. You're exotic. That will do nicely. Just do this: in company, never speak to me in English. Only in Crow. And tell our friend to use only her own tongue. From now on, you are the queen of Zanzibar, and I am the Margrave Childress, royal governor of Trinidad and Tobago."

She grunted. This was all a mystery to her.

"The more exotic, the better. We will be whatever my imagination requires."

She was pawing the slippers, trying to sort them out, with little success. But off to the east, the sky over the black mountains had lightened, and soon there would be a moon. Maybe she should wait.

"What is this carriage? How did you get this?"

"By nefarious means, fraud and deceit, foul conduct, and criminal sleight of hand. Shine was my accomplice."

Big medicine. The fat man had powers she could barely grasp. She didn't know the half of what he was yammering about.

"This carriage, madam, assures our complete success. I am the queen's royal viceroy of British Guiana, and you are my ladies, and we are touring, looking for an estate."

"I thought you were the margrave, or something."

"Details, details. Trust me."

They sat quietly in the calash while the sky lightened, and

finally the white moon rimmed the skyline of distant black peaks. She stared at him, amazed. Childress wore a black suit and silk top hat, a snowy shirt and red cravat, all of it encasing his enormous bulk, and even had shiny black boots on his feet.

"Where'd you get that stuff?"

"I defrauded a tailor, my dear."

"Where did you get our stuff?"

"A seamstress defrauded me, cleaned me out of all my loot. I should say that Shine was the generous provider of the means. I did not inquire too closely where he obtained his lucre. Never look a gift horse in the mouth."

She might have laughed, had not her fear for Skye clawed so hard at her.

"What does all this stuff do for us?"

"My dear, we were vagabonds, and now we are people of great rank, and there will be much fawning and bowing and scraping wherever we go. Also, it's very important never to pay for anything. That is expected. When we're hungry, we'll demand food and that will be that. They'll bring it. Royalty never pays.

"Also, you're safe. The two Indian women indentured into perpetual servitude have vanished. Practice looking haughty."

She didn't quite fathom all this, but neither did it matter.

"Now, my ladies, if you are ready, I shall turn around and we shall have a little examination of our wardrobe. By all means, step out and straighten up."

She nudged Standing Alone, and they stepped down from the carriage. Childress stepped majestically to earth, and toured around them in the soft white light of a gibbous moon.

"Ah, yes, a little large, a little long, but we'll have your dresses hemmed in Santa Fe. Tell our Cheyenne friend she has mismatched slippers.

Standing Alone corrected her mistake.

"Yes, yes, you'll do. Queen of Zanzibar, and I'll think of something for her. Mesopotamian royalty, Pharaoh's bastard daughter. But now, the hats, don't forget the hats."

She discovered a broad-brimmed one and pulled it on, and Standing Alone imitated her.

"Yes, yes, quite excellent. Very exotic. Watershot silk dresses and hats with silk flowers on them. I think I shall call her the queen of Sheba."

"What's a queen?"

"A woman chief, or a chief's wife."

"Ah! I'm a chief!" Victoria swept around in a circle, commanding the moon and stars to obey her.

"Well, mesdames, let's go find Skye and rescue him. In that compartment under the seat is all sorts of gear, including clothing for him, sandals, a brace of revolvers, blankets, some beans and a cookpot, a few knives and other fangs, and whatever else I could commandeer from Larrimer. Step in, now."

She stepped in, amazed by the fat man.

35

S kye stared up into concerned faces. The soldiers peered down at him, but so did a slender woman who knelt beside him, studying him with tenderness.

He hurt. No part of him escaped. But his bowels especially tormented him, always on the brink of convulsion, and he was always teetering into nausea. He didn't want to be moved. He closed his eyes because it hurt to look anywhere, and the morning light tormented his brain. The woman applied another cold compress, but he was already half frozen, and he couldn't comprehend it. He tried to paw her compress away, but she held it firmly to his forehead.

The soldiers were debating; he gathered that much, and wished he could grasp their sibilant, staccato language. He knew what it was all about: to stay here and wait for him to get better, or to load him in that stinking carreta and keep on going. In the midst of all this talk, he heard the old man whose cart had been commandeered, and it was not hard to guess what he had to say about it.

"Agua," he said, and moments later, the woman pressed an earthen cup to his lips. He sipped, feeling the chill liquid slide into him, and the water convulse his stomach once again.

He had been sicker than this before, but never so nauseous, or so filthy from lying among pigs. The Mexicans continued their debate, until at last the voice of the corporal silenced them all: soon enough he would know what the soldier had decided.

The woman continued her ministrations, so Skye opened his eyes to look at her. She was young and pretty and strong.

"Gracias," he whispered. At least he knew the word for gratitude.

She nodded.

He heard the squeak of the carreta, a sound that had been the counterpoint to much of yesterday's travel, and he knew that they would be leaving soon. Sure enough, in a bit they helped him to his feet, and he stepped gingerly over the clay floor of this little jacal and out into the morning sun.

It was a fresh sweet dawn, and he would have enjoyed it but for his wasted and wounded body. Every step hurt, but he made his way to the carreta, where the proprietor of the cart, burros, and the little hogs awaited him. He crawled in, assisted by the soldiers, and discovered clean bedding there. The hogs were next; carried squealing one by one into the carreta, and then the stakes were driven into the holes in the bed, and Skye was off to the meat markets of Santa Fe once again. The dispossessed family watched cheerfully as the cart creaked and squawked its way down the clay pathway. Skye closed his eyes, determined to save his strength and ward off as much pain as he could.

The pigs jostled him, and he realized they were rooting at him with their bristly snouts, snorting softly. Maybe they considered him edible. He pushed them back, but they were curious about him, this third party en route to their executions. They seemed naked as babies.

He had never been on intimate terms with hogs before, so he watched them even as they watched him, and the carreta creaked its way south. They were all watching each other, the soldiers watching him, the weathered old peon watching his pigs, the burros, the swaying cart, and the soldiers, and the corporal riding behind them keeping an eye on them all.

They squeaked and chattered through little settlements, and on each occasion the Mexicans swarmed around the cart, examining Skye and the pigs, whispering and smiling. Skye didn't need to know the tongue to know the nature of the jokes. Swine and foreigners, they were all the same to these grinning people. They even weighed about the same, were the same color, and yielded about the same amount of meat, he supposed.

Mostly he closed his eyes because light pained his head, and he ignored this rural Mexican world, except when the pigs jostled him by rooting around in the straw, or in one case, urinating. A goodly part of the day passed, and the more he traveled on his dubious bed of straw, the more the cart hammered his aching body. His fever did not go away.

Thus the day passed well into the afternoon, and then he was aware of a commotion behind him. When he struggled to his elbows to see beyond the mounted corporal, he spotted a fancy ebony carriage pulled by two sleek black trotters. Not even the light skim of dust over this rig dulled its magnificence. A bulky man in a black suit and silk top hat drove smartly, and behind were a pair of women got up in high fashion, with wide-brimmed hats shading their Mexican faces.

He settled back into the straw. There would be more jokes at his expense, but he was too tired to cope with them, too sick to care.

There was an exchange in Spanish between the corporal and the driver of the fancy rig, and some laughter. He heard the word "Inglaterra," and the corporal said "Tejas," while gesturing toward his prisoner. Texas. England. Were they talking about him? The privates marching beside, their lances over their shoulders, were enjoying the exchange, and glancing covertly at Skye. The two hogs turned and studied this new intrusion upon their lives with alarm.

He closed his eyes and focused on gaining strength. If he was to survive, he would need to make a good case in Santa Fe, plead the truth and do it so eloquently that the cynical governor might free him. It wouldn't be easy: that miserable Childress had betrayed him so thoroughly he might not have any sort of chance.

The two-rut road wound out of a defile, passed yet another cemetery, and the country broadened into a tawny benchland above the twisting river, marked by dots of green juniper.

Here the road widened too, and the impatient driver of the black carriage eased to his right and began to pass the entourage. Skye struggled up to get a look, and discovered an apparition: driving this elegant rig was *Childress*, got up in a black suit, silk top hat, white shirt, and cravat, and sitting in the rear seat like royal princesses were his wife *Victoria* and his friend *Standing Alone*.

No! Impossible! Delusion! He fumbled into the straw, dumbfounded, and then struggled up again, disbelieving: he was sick, this was simply delusion and mirage, a trick of light. Victoria didn't look like herself; Standing Alone looked even less like herself; the fat man might have been Childress, but wasn't, and all this plainly was a cruel hoax of fate. It had to be a hoax; the women didn't so much as blink an eye, but stared blandly right through him. But yes, there was the monkey, Shine, sitting right beside Childress.

"Look at that hog going to market," Childress said in English, and a voice Skye knew well.

Skye rose and stared at him so darkly that Childress coughed, his hand politely to his lips.

"At your service, Sah. Her majesty's lord viceroy of the Lesser Antilles," he said, "and the queens of Zanzibar and Sheba, en route to the capital."

The corporal eyed him suspiciously, unable to grasp English, so Childress enlightened him in Spanish: Zanzibar, Sheba, Antilles.

"Ah!" exclaimed the corporal, impressed by these people of vast importance.

The carriage had pulled alongside now, and Skye stared at the women, his own wife in some outlandish costume that made her look like some Hottentot. She nodded slightly; an eyebrow arched.

"Sick," he said softly. He lifted his bloodstained feet.

She made no sign.

"Love you," he said desolately, something thick and painful filling his chest. Were the women prisoners of that betrayer Childress? Was the Texan relishing every moment of this encounter? Somehow, Skye thought not: this was a rescue effort. "Thank you, whatever you are doing," he muttered.

She pointed at the carriage floor with her toe, and he saw something blue-black lying there; a weapon. And wrapped parcels of provisions. How had this happened? Who had helped them? Had they really come to help him? Where did this rig and equipment come from? How was it paid for? Who was Childress now pretending to be? What would happen?

Dizzily, he sunk back to the straw.

"Which of the hogs will yield the most meat?" Childress asked. "I say, the one in the center, eh? He'll look good, hanging from a meat hook." He translated his witticism into Spanish for the entertainment of the soldiers. They laughed, but looked uneasy.

"We're going to pay a little visit to Governor Armijo," Childress said, cheerfully. To the Mexicans he said, "Santa Fe, el gobernador."

They nodded.

"You should fetch a fine price at the butcher, my good man," he said. "Good flesh, but caved in a little."

Skye felt black rage permeate him, and gathered his strength. Any more of that and he would rise, tear apart those stakes, and land on Childress before anyone could stop him. But he knew better.

Tears had gathered in Victoria's eyes, which she artfully brushed away under the deep shade of her hat.

"Tallyho, old boy," Childress said, and smacked the lines over the croups of his trotters. The black horses lurched forward, and the carriage swiftly passed the groaning carreta.

The old peon cursed softly. He didn't like rich foreigners, Skye gathered.

Santa Fe. Visiting Governor Armijo. What did that mean? He wrestled with it until he was dizzy. He wrestled with the whole idea that Childress was trying to help him, believing and disbelieving, unable to put it all together. But in the end, he thought that Childress probably was doing just that. Somehow, he had found the women and sprung them from Padre Martinez's grip, and that in itself was a feat. Where had they been hidden and how did Childress find them?

Skye lay back in the straw, his mind awhirl, barely noticing the foulness of the urine-soaked bedding. What did it all mean? He had no answers. Who was Childress? He had called himself most everything, and none of it was true. The man was an enigma; his purposes a mystery.

The swaying cart, pounding on its rough wheels, slowly lulled him into a nap, and so the day passed. By dusk, he was thirsty and still sick, but he had hope, and he knew that something was afoot.

36

The man called Childress was not a bit impressed.

Santa Fe looked to be nothing but a gaggle of one-story adobe buildings that would wash away in the first deluge. If this was a capital of a province, what did the rest of Mexico look like? He saw no brick in the streets, or good carpentry, or any sign that these people had mastered the civilized arts and crafts.

The city was perched on an arid slope and watered by a poor excuse for a creek that was largely unbridged, sawing the town in two. At least the view east and north, into the pine-covered reaches of the Sangre de Cristo Mountains, was grand.

There was scarcely a pane of glass in the city, and people employed rudely fashioned wooden shutters to keep out the cold or let in some light. The clay streets were scarcely wide enough to allow the passage of a vehicle, and his progress through the northern reaches of the little town scattered old women in black, barefoot *trabajadores,* children, and women carrying impossible loads of food or merchandise on their slim backs. Such animals of conveyance as he could see were largely burros, plus a few mules, but horses were scarce.

On the tawdry plaza, ankle-deep in dung, some Yank ox-teams stood restlessly in their yokes while the scruffy frontiersmen gawked at pretty Mexican girls and guarded their trail-worn wagons. The girls tossed them bright smiles and swaying hips and shy glances. Some of the Mexicans wore capacious straw hats against the bright glare of the day, and most wore simple sandals of leather, and not a few carried a folded *serape* over their shoulders, and so were equipped for an instant siesta, Childress supposed.

For the life of him, he could find no public building, nothing that rose above the clutter of little adobe merchant establishments. Metal was obviously scarce: the buildings had none except for the hinges on their doors, and not even all of those were iron. Where was the capitol building or palacio?

He drove his carriage round and about, exciting glances among the warm-fleshed and cheerful crowds, who studied these foreigners closely, their gazes falling upon him in his black suit and top hat, and his two dusky passengers, who managed to absorb these wonders of Mexican civilization without so much as a gesture or exclamation. They played their part well, and the effect of their haughty silence was to make them look blasé and a little bored, which was perfect.

He finally returned to the plaza, having gotten himself lost in the warren of little callejas north and east of the public square, and here he stopped next to a scraggle-toothed Yank teamster who sported a beard that reached his waist.

"Childress here, my good man. Tell me, where is the governor's residence and seat of government?"

The teamster looked amused. He jerked a dirty thumb in the direction of a low building that embraced one entire side of the plaza, a building with a shaded gallery in front of it, and loafers parked in the shade. It looked no more like a seat of government than a country church looked like St. Paul's Cathedral.

"That's the palace."

"That? That warehouse? Thank you, Sah," he said, and wheeled his calash around the plaza once again to maneuver it into a suitable place to park. There seemed to be no order at all; one put his rig wherever one could, and if that bottled traffic, so much worse for the victims.

"All right, ladies," he said, having commandeered a spot. "Step lively. Now remember, let me talk; you look royal."

"Crap," said Victoria.

He handed them down to the grimy gumbo of the plaza, and they hunted for a door to this horizontal mud palacio, and since there were several it would be a matter of luck.

They entered, found themselves within a barracks room, withdrew, and headed to the next orifice, which admitted them to an antechamber of some sort, as plain as everything else in this disturbing city. But at least an orange and green flag of the Republic of Mexico stood at an inner door, and Childress supposed that might herald something.

He tried the door, found it open, and entered upon a shadowed office, lit only by a narrow window in the thick adobe wall. He thought it might belong to a clerk, but the portly man standing within was no clerk. This one stood over six feet, had a long acquiline nose, large features, dark flesh, and straight jet hair combed back. But what astonished Childress was the man's uniform, which was sky blue with white lapels, a crimson sash, polished black boots, a sword in a gaudy scabbard, and acres of gold braid at the shoulders and sleeves of his tunic.

Childress was quite taken with him.

"Señor?" the man asked, politely.

"I am looking for el gobernador," Childress replied.

"Armijo here, come in, and how may I be of service?"

"Governor! I didn't mean to intrude."

"Think nothing of it. *Nada*. That is the way of the Republic of Mexico, which rests upon the will of the people."

Childress listened to the rhetoric, assessing this amazing apparition, and then shepherded his women in.

"Your excellency, I am Sir Arthur Childress, Her Majesty's viceroy for Madagascar and Ceylon, here on a little journey on my own account, and not the queen's."

"Ah! The English! A great nation! And what brings you to our province of Mexico?"

"Ah, Governor, first let me introduce these lovely ladies, their royal highnesses the queens of Zanzibar and Sheba, who have traveled far with me as we search for suitable investments for their endowments."

The governor bowed. The ladies nodded.

"They speak not a word of Spanish, nor do they grasp any European tongue save for a few words of English, so their purpose here is to decorate our little meeting with their dusky beauty."

"Ah!" Armijo gallantly rounded his desk, and clasped the hand of each woman, bowing gallantly to them.

"Sonofabitch," murmured Victoria Skye, which Childress thought was appropriate.

"Now, your excellency, if you could spare us a few moments, I shall describe our business here, and perhaps you can advise me as to its prospects. As part of my task of governing the protectorates, it is my duty to seek financial opportunities for the royal households, and I am here because Mexico is ripe for development. In short, excellency, we are looking to purchase a large estate, one with cheap labor at hand, for it is with such labor that large bonanzas are made."

"Plantations? Don Arturo, this is an arid climate, and not suitable for plantations."

"Ah, yes, but there are gold and silver mines and great livestock holdings, and these are of some interest to me, on behalf of these great ladies, of course."

"Ah, si, it is so. The riches of Mexico are indescribable, and there is abundant labor, and more can be gotten. But tell me, have you spoken to others about all this?"

"Indeed, Governor, we have spread the word wherever we have been, starting in Taos, the ranchos there, and we will continue southward into Chihuahua, Sinaloa, and other provinces."

"And how, Don Arturo, did you come here?"

"By steamer to New Orleans, river packet to Independence, and out the commercial trail with a caravan, past fierce Comanches and wild tribes. But we were not troubled."

"Ah! You have seen the commerce."

"We think there is great profit in it. And I have good English capital to put into it."

Armijo flashed a great smile, baring even white teeth. "Then it is up to me to persuade you to invest in Nuevo Mexico, si?"

"Well, your excellency, you can start by describing the labor situation, for there is no profit to be gotten from an estate without plenty of cheap help."

Armijo shook his head. "Oh, some merchants here profit without very little help, señor, but yes, the great estancias, or haciendas, or mines, are built upon the backs of many hombres."

"What does it cost?"

Armijo shrugged. "What is the price of food and some rags?"

"How does it work?"

"The hacendado indentures his help, and pays them in food and clothing and shelter; it is very simple."

"And they work for that, excellency?"

Armijo shrugged. "Some don't."

"And what of them?"

The governor smiled. "Ah, this is the land of opportunity, my friend. Opportunity for you, and for me. I have many resources at hand, and can find just what you are looking for. Land, labor, mines, livestock, titles to property, influence. For a small consideration to the public purse, of course."

"Ah, Governor, how secure is it? I have heard that the wild men of Texas are even now marching. I must think of the safety of our investments!"

Armijo frowned. "Any invasion will be crushed swiftly. There will only be a crowd of vultures feeding on the gibbets."

"That is good news, your excellency. The Texans are a rabble, and have no regard for human life."

"They are braggarts, too, and cannot speak without exaggerating their powers and virtues. My English friend, consider me your reliable friend and the person in office who can steer you toward a successful venture."

"Well, your excellency, yes, there is something you can do."

Armijo's eyebrow arched upward.

"Labor is the secret! I should like a list of the hacendados and mining associations that employ much labor. And these I will visit and talk to at length."

"Consider it done. Come back before the sun sets, and I shall have a list for you. Are you sure there's no more?"

"Oh, your excellency, there is always more. What does one do for entertainment in this noble capital city?"

"How about an execution?" Armijo asked. "Only an hour ago, I received word by courier that a Texas spy will be here in the morning. We handle such things with dispatch, my English friend."

"Ah, yes, keep me informed. The queens are avid for executions," Childress said. "How will it be? By shot or noose or garrote or ax?"

"We practice marksmanship," Armijo replied.

Their business done, they were ushered out of the governor's chambers, and it was then, in that plain adobe antechamber, that Standing Alone shrieked and swooned, but Childress caught her just before she fell, even as a coppery serving girl gaped.

37

Standing Alone collapsed into Childress's arms, a strange, guttural sobbing racking her. The thin serving girl stood, paralyzed, bewildered, and then began edging away.

Victoria cried out to her: "Wait!"

But the teenaged child, her gaze riveted to the woman in fancy clothes and a great hat, cried out, and then backed away.

"No!" cried Victoria.

But the girl vanished into the private rooms of the Governor's Palace.

Childress, seething with curiosity, helped the stricken woman to her feet, and signaled to Victoria, who began talking to the Cheyenne woman in the lingua franca they had worked out.

"Ask if that was her daughter!"

But Victoria had already done so. She nodded. "Yes, in all likelihood, but it happened so fast that she's not sure. The girl! Right age, right face. The strong cheekbones of her people. Little Moon is the name she was given."

"She must be sure. We need to see her. And then, if it's her daughter, we must plan. Fast!"

Standing Alone stood now, gulping air, staring at that

massive wooden door where the serving girl had disappeared. The gaunt girl was barefooted, wore only a simple shift of unbleached muslin, minimal clothing, the least possible cost for a slave.

"She must be sure. We must see that girl again. They must talk to each other! If this is her daughter, it's a stroke of luck! Maybe she knows where her brother is."

But Standing Alone was mute, staring at that forbidding wooden door with great iron straps holding it together, a door that must lead from this antechamber to the governor's private apartment in this long box of a building. Childress was tempted simply to barge in, take the women with him, and plead ignorance of local custom if they ran into trouble. Get a look at that girl one way or another. And if she was Standing Alone's daughter, begin to plan, plan, plan.

"Victoria, tell her we'll sit here in this waiting room. This is a room where people wait to see the governor. A reception room. See the benches. If this was her daughter, the girl might recover soon enough, and come peek, eh?"

Victoria nodded. She looked cross, as if Childress were intruding on some private matter, some women's prerogatives. But she led Standing Alone to the cottonwood bench, and there they sat. Childress didn't mind. His mind was teeming with ideas. He had Skye to worry about, and as yet he hadn't any notion of how he might free the man. Things were happening too fast. He had supposed he might have days, even weeks, to work out a scheme, a bribe, a trick, a political ploy, an escape. But this was Mexico, and trials and executions scarcely lasted fifteen minutes.

They sat in the anteroom, waiting. Occasionally Mexicans entered from the plaza, glanced at these exotic foreigners, vanished into one door or another. Others emerged from the governor's chambers, and left. The girl didn't return. Then, when the plaza door opened, Shine leaped in, and with a bound settled beside Childress, tugging his sleeve and reproaching him for ignoring his friend and ally. Childress rubbed the monkey's back, and the monkey chittered and delicately scratched his own belly.

The girl did not appear. Time was wasting! Childress's mind teemed with schemes, but nothing gelled. He strolled outside. His trotters were restless. They needed water and a rubdown and some good feed. But they would have to wait. He couldn't leave here. He surveyed the plaza quickly, noting its bustle, the babble of many voices from many lands, the street vendors, the carretas, burros, young women sashaying along, the dogs circling. When Skye arrived, these people would all amass right here, drawn by gossip and rumor and the thrill of death.

He returned and settled again on the bench in the anteroom. The women stared at that silent door, willing it to open, willing that child, not so much a child anymore, but a woman, to open it.

And she did, an eternity later. The door creaked. Deep in shadow stood that girl, peering at them, safe in there, ready to slam the heavy door shut in an instant.

Standing Alone had removed her hat, the broad brim of which had veiled her face during the first encounter. Now her sleek jet Cheyenne hair, parted in the center and drawn severely back, was not hidden.

They stared. Standing Alone groaned, and staggered to her feet. She said something in her own tongue, a name, Childress guessed. Little Moon. Little Moon! The girl cried out, looked about fearfully, and closed the door in the very face of her mother. But then she opened it a crack again, and Childress saw the mother reach out and touch her daughter, and her daughter touch her mother, and he heard the sound of soft keening in the gloom. Then someone came in the plaza door, and swiftly the inner one slid shut. But moments later it groaned open again, and there were furious whispers.

"Tell her we'll get Little Moon out," Childress said to

Victoria, but Skye's wife glared at him, as if he were inter-fering with something sacred. Childress sighed impatiently.

Standing Alone was crying softly, and the girl, still deep in shadows and fearful to come out of the door, stood tautly, choking back her joy and terror.

He turned to the monkey. "Go," he said. The spider mon-key sailed through the air, slipped into the darkened door, and tugged at that dim figure within, but the girl only squealed in alarm. There was a new volley of whispering between mother and daughter, and this time Standing Alone reached down to pat the monkey. So Little Moon was learn-ing about the monkey, and that was the next step: expect the *monkey*.

It seemed a long visit, growing more dangerous by the second, but then the girl begged off. Standing Alone cried out, but the girl slipped that dark door shut. Only then did Victoria help her friend back to the bench, and the monkey joined them, clucking beside them.

Slowly Standing Alone translated, with fingers and words, everything that had transpired, until Victoria got it whole.

"It's her, Little Moon. She's not sick. She wants to go. She's damn afraid. She works for the governor, makes food, cleans up, and he's got big medicine that can track her down to the sunset or the sunrise and throw her into a hole. She's plenty sick with worry."

"How's Standing Alone?"

But he didn't need to ask. She sat there, rapt, her mind a thousand years away, something so sweet and beautiful on her features that Childress marveled. For all those years she had sat at Bent's Fort waiting for news, waiting for this very moment. And now it had happened. She had *seen her daughter*, whole and unharmed.

"Tell her that we'll think of something," he said gently.

Victoria nodded.

"Did they make plans to meet again?"

Victoria shook her head.

"We know where she is. We know how to reach her. Now we've got to do some planning. Skye's coming soon. We have no time at all! I thought we'd have days to work this out."

Victoria stared at him so darkly, with so much pain in her eyes, that he was driven back by it.

"Come along outside now. It won't do to linger in here. I'm the royal viceroy. You're the queen of Zanzibar," he said.

She only stared at him. Right now she was no one but Victoria Skye and her friend was no one but Standing Alone of the Cheyenne people. Nonetheless, at his beckoning, they abandoned the Governor's Palace and stepped into the bustling plaza. No time, no time!

The horses were restless, but he chose instead to walk his women around the plaza. They needed to walk. It was as if walking was their salvation. He could not walk far, his enormous bulk paining him with every step, but this time he plunged forward, the women on each arm, Shine resting on his shoulder and drawing stares and laughter.

The plaza bustled with vendors selling dulces, tortillas filled with hot meat, and tamales, and he was reminded that he hadn't a cent. They hadn't eaten for some while. The horses needed feed and water. Yanks were haggling with Mexicans about the contents of those begrimed prairie schooners that had just come in from the States. Oxen drooped in their yokes. But no ideas came to him. Rarely had his good swift mind failed him so utterly.

They toured the plaza, and Childress settled the women in his carriage. He peered at their hungry, distraught faces, and then at Shine, who sat beside him, picking his nose.

He glanced about, fearful of discovery. "Fetch," he said to the little creature.

The monkey sprang gracefully to the clay, and then in bounds, clambered to the roofs, and dropped downward again, hidden from view. People squealed, jostled one another for a look at the little fellow, and he swung upward, the projecting vigas of the adobe buildings offering him his own walkway. Then he vanished. Childress waited patiently, trying to look as though he had no part of any of this. When the little fellow did appear, it was so suddenly that Childress startled in his seat. Shine simply bombed down from a rooftop into the carriage, one of his little hands clutching his loot, several steaming tamales wrapped in cornhusks, and carried in a sheet of coarse brown paper.

"Ah, the pirate has struck!" Childress said, his stomach growling with anticipation.

He doled out the meal, furtively watching the crowd, which had failed to notice Shine's arrival in the carriage. The monkey ate one of the tamales himself, licking his fingers and smacking his hairy lips.

And then, as swiftly, he was gone again, swinging casually along the roofs, unseen by anyone this time. Childress didn't like it. He wanted to get out of the plaza. The ebony calash and its handsomely dressed occupants were drawing too much attention in this rude frontier town. He waited itchily, irritably, and finally with anger, but the monkey did not reappear.

He turned. The women had finished eating, and were staring at him. The anguish in their faces touched him to his core.

Then Shine appeared, this time with more booty: a small burlap sack of white beans, rustled from some grocer. They would have to be cooked somewhere, but there was nourishment in them.

White beans. A plan bloomed in Childress, at last. He eyed the monkey, wondering whether there was time to train him.

38

Maybe they were expecting him. As the carreta creaked into Santa Fe, silent crowds lined the narrow streets; almost as if they knew who he was accused of being, and what his fate would be. They craned their heads as the cart and the soldiers and the old peon walked by, but they weren't examining the soldiers or the hogs or the old man; they were studying Skye, the doomed.

It was hard to focus his mind. He had been four days in the cart along with two hogs, and most of it he had been fevered. But last night, at a village north of the town, he had felt a change within himself, and within the hour his flesh was cool. That crisis had passed; he now faced another, vastly darker and more menacing than anything he had ever experienced. All because he had been falsely accused by one who called himself a friend.

He had rocked along the stony trails hour after hour, the hollow plodding of the little burros carrying him closer to his doom with every passing minute. Santa Fe was oddly silent, as if all commerce had ceased; as if even the wind had turned timid. He heard only the heavy breath of the weary burros, and the ceaseless groan of cottonwood axle against hub, as the carreta grumbled toward the Governor's Palace where matters of life or death would unfold.

The crowds thickened as he approached the plaza. Most stared silently, but then a young man spat at him as the carreta passed. And often he heard that whispered anathema, "Tejas!"

These were mild people, neither fierce nor armed. They peered at him solemnly from faces used to sunny living. The bronzed laboring men, creased by sun and chapped by wind, watched impassively, but the dons, most of them tricked out in gaudy coats and white lace and fancy boots, nodded shrewdly and whispered to those beside them.

For all Skye knew, a Texan might be as exotic as a macaw or an orangutan or a rhino to them all. A shirtless little boy picked up some dried offal and flung it, but a woman's voice halted him in his tracks. These were civil people.

Skye cringed at their gaze. Ever since he had entered this nation, he had been paraded about, subjected to stares, made to endure the most humiliating of circumstances. Were not those gazes punishment enough for any man? But there was more to come, darker, crueller, the special fate of some in this nation that celebrated death, welcomed it with flowers, let itself be riveted by it, and looked for any excuse to experience it, playing it toward a climax of terror. A gentle people with a violent lust.

The old peon, whose name Skye had never discovered, began chattering with the corporal, and Skye understood at once: the man wanted his carreta and hogs back. The corporal nodded. The peasant would receive his property in moments, as soon as this enemy of the republic had been deposited at the palacio. The pigs stirred restlessly, knowing somehow that they were as doomed as the mortal between them. They squealed and grunted, and Skye thought they were even groaning. This was the end of the road for the three penned by walls of stakes rising from the cart bed.

Then, suddenly, the entourage burst into the plaza, and the corporal steered them straight to the low building commanding one whole side. Skye saw that ebony rig there, and knew Childress and the women were present, though he did not see them. He could not imagine what they could do: even if all three were armed to the teeth, they could do nothing. If Childress intended to get Skye out of the fix he had put Skye into, Skye had not an inkling of any way to do it.

The carreta creaked to a halt and the guards formed up at either side of the cart. The corporal lifted the rear stakes and beckoned Skye to crawl out. A silent gawking crowd pressed close now, eager to see the man who was now alive and soon would be nothing but a corpse.

They escorted him into a gloomy barracks, where a dozen soldiers had collected.

One spoke some English:

"There," he said, pointing at a pail. "Clean up. Then get into this." He gestured toward a bunk where some unbleached cotton clothing lay. "The gobernador, he hate smells. He got nose bigger than you, even."

"That would be a big nose," Skye said.

These men weren't abusive, neither did they push him around. They were gentle, at least for now.

He turned his back on them, pulled off his fouled shirt and pants, and washed. He doubted that he would get rid of the pig smell for the rest of his life ... which might last one hour, maybe two.

He eyed the barracks furtively looking for miracles, loaded cannon, conspirators, rebels, hideyholes, anything. But there were no miracles in that whitewashed room. He tied the cord that held up his loose-fitting pantalones, and faced them. He felt himself tremble.

Then he waited. He sat, taut, waiting, waiting. He tried to pray, he tried to think of Victoria, of London, of blue skies. But he could think of nothing; there was only the endless waiting, and the desperate hope that he might be freed. What did they have against him?

He would make his plea, tell the exact truth, look for every chance, let nothing escape him. For he was not yet dead and as long as life pulsed in him, there was hope. But not much hope. He could scarcely fathom just how he had arrived at this place, to face this fate, when all he wanted was to free two children in bondage, and leave Mexico just as it was, a peaceful and friendly country for the most part.

The corporal nodded, and now the blue-clad soldiers formed lines to either side of him, and at a command they escorted him, boxed among them, through an interior door, into an antechamber, down a hall, and into a public room of some sort, high-ceilinged, with hand-hewn vigas supporting its roof. A crowd had collected there, and the air felt choking even though the shutters were all opened. Skye had the sense that not one more person could crowd into the chamber. They watched him silently, as the soldiers cleared a way to a dais.

On the dais there stood a tall man with hooded eyes and an air of expectancy, in a fancy blue uniform, the muted light glowing from the golden thread that decorated his epaulets and sleeves. The governor, no doubt. Armijo. The man who would turn thumbs-up . . . or thumbs-down.

The soldiers led him there, to a place before the governor, but lower, so that the governor looked downward, as if from some great height. The man smiled, nodded to a black-clad balding clerk, who rose.

The crowd hushed. At the rear stood Childress all got up in his new black suit, and Victoria, and Standing Alone. He stared at them, loathing Childress for all of this, loving his wife and their friend, seeing them for perhaps the last time, all the feeling within him caught in his throat. Victoria nodded, ever so slightly, but in the faint movement of her head lay a universe of yearning. For whatever reason, she could give him no more, and he did not question it.

The clerk addressed him: "The governor of the province of Nuevo Mexico has asked me to translate. I will truly tell you his every word, and tell him all that you say. He informs you that you are charged with spying for the army of the rebels of Texas, and that you may respond now."

Skye scarcely had time to think: all this was occurring with such breathtaking speed that he hadn't given much thought to anything.

He tried to speak, but his throat froze up; everything within him died in his mouth. He was not far from tears. Then from some far corner of his heart, he remembered a line from a psalm: "Yea though I walk through the valley of the shadow of death, I shall fear no evil; for Thou art with me . . ."

The terror lifted. He turned to the governor, who was watching him as a raptor watches a rabbit.

"I do not know why I am here," he said slowly, letting the clerk translate into sibilant Spanish. "I came here to your good nation peacefully. I am told I am a spy. I am not. I am not a Texan either. My purpose was to find two children of the Cheyenne tribe, and if possible, return them to their grieving mother. That is all . . ." He started to say he had come with his wife, but thought better of it; the statement might endanger her and Standing Alone. "I swear before God that I came here in peace; that I have no connection with the Texans, and have never been in contact with them."

He waited as the clerk droned on. The entire city, it seemed, was crammed into that tight space, and was listening closely.

"I ask you, what is your evidence? Where are your witnesses? Who accuses me? Do I have the right to confront my accuser?" He refrained from glancing at Childress with all that. "Where is a lawyer to defend me? What are the laws that I face? Can you show me any evidence? Any at all?"

He waited until that had been conveyed.

"I ask for a real trial; present your evidence; let me rebut it. Judge the case on its merit, and on its truths. I am innocent."

That was all he had to say.

They waited for more but he shook his head.

Armijo smiled and began speaking. "The gobernador, he says that the evidence is sealed and comes from a reliable informant in Taos, and without rebuttal, he finds you guilty as charged. But because there is some small chance that you are innocent, he will put the matter into the hands of God. He will count out nine black beans, and one white bean, and place them into this earthen pot. You will draw a bean. If it is white, you shall live."

That excited the crowd, which stood tautly. Skye knew how they were thinking. They were already seeing the execution, and feeling it in their bellies. They were hearing the snare drums, watching the condemned walk to the wall, listening to the padre recite a prayer, watching the jefe tie a blindfold over the eyes of the condemned, watching with morbid delight as the condemned was tied to a post before the wall, the man who was now alive, but in seconds would know nothing at all; knew the words that would come, once the soldiers lined up with their good clean rifles, and the command came . . . *fire!*

Yes, it was there in their faces, the swift intakes of air, the sweat, the eagerness, the fine, bright horror, the thrill that swirled through them all like a snake.

Slowly, the governor counted out the nine black beans and the white bean, showed them to all, and dropped them into the pot. Then he nodded.

But Skye stood still. "I will not participate in the travesty of justice. If I am to die, let the blood be on his hands, not on mine."

The clerk translated the response: "Draw a bean, or face the firing squad. If you are innocent, God will protect you."

Skye shook his head. So it had come down to that.

"If you will not, then I will," Armijo said.

Skye stared, refusing the participate in his own doom.

The crowd tensed. Armijo waited.

Then the governor reached into the pot.

39

Skye stared at Armijo's nose as the man's hand lowered into the tawny earthen pot. He could not look at the man's hand.

"Don Manuel!"

The voice was familiar. The governor paused. Childress stepped forward, pushing his way to the front of the rapt crowd. A long dialogue ensued and Skye understood none of it. But strangely, Childress kept pointing at the monkey, and Armijo kept examining the monkey, as if Fate were somehow connected with the simian.

Skye felt his knees buckle. There was only so much a man could endure.

Then, finally, the governor nodded to the black-clad clerk who had translated for Skye. The clerk gestured toward Childress. "That hombre is a high official of the government of England; I don't quite know his title. That ape of his is a prodigy. What this Englishman said is this: Your Excellency, you must not take into your hands the will of God. Only a poor dumb creature like this monkey of mine should draw the bean. He does that all the time, reaches into things and pulls them out. Let him do it, and then the will of God will truly be known. And the governor, he says, well, he doesn't like that, but maybe it is best; the blood of a man will not be upon him but upon the monkey. And so it is to be."

Skye gripped himself. He was in the hands of that miserable little spider monkey. His *life* was in the monkey's hands. Well, no; his life was already over. Nine black beans, one white. The monkey would make no difference. This was nothing but another small entertainment for the Mexicans, and they would soon be calling Shine the Death Monkey.

Skye nodded. The mode by which he was to be condemned to death, by monkey paw or human, did not matter.

And with that, the clerk stepped back and Childress led the monkey by the hand. It jumped up to the table where the clay pot rested malignantly, its earthen belly filled with death and life.

Now the silence deepened into unbearable tautness.

"Fetch," said Childress.

The monkey peered in, rattled the beans, battered the sides of the pot until it rocked on the table, thumped and hammered, a living thing as the monkey's paw pillaged its interior. And then, slowly, the monkey lifted its paw and held it open for all to see.

A white bean.

Skye stared, mesmerized. The monkey held the bean high. White, *white*, no mistake.

Armijo stared at the monkey, stared hard at Childress, stared hard at Skye, stared bleakly at the women with Childress.

Skye felt wobbly, faint, and caught himself before he fell to the floor.

"Miragro," breathed the clerk. Miracle.

The monkey chittered and grinned and licked the bean.

Governor Armijo held out a hand, and the monkey dutifully deposited the bean into the governor's hand. He inspected it, peered into the pot, squinted darkly at Childress, and finally nodded.

"Ah, señor, he says, so be it. God above has spoken. You are free."

But Armijo was still muttering.

"He says, Señor Skye, that if you are guilty, you will be found out and executed without a trial, so that no monkey can conspire against the justice of the Republic of Mexico."

Skye nodded. "Tell him justice was done. That's all I have to say."

"Ah, señor, I will say so."

The crowd didn't drift apart; on the contrary, people gathered around Skye, touching him, this man saved from death. One woman kissed the sleeve of his rough shirt, and then made the sign of the cross.

But Armijo stared, first at Skye, then at Childress, and at the monkey.

Childress pushed forward, the women trailing.

"My dear sir, let me introduce myself: Sir Arthur Childress, first baronet of Wiltshire, and an emissary of the queen. Let me congratulate you on your good fortune, Sah."

Skye was speechless. The clerk hovered closely, registering every word. It would soon be filtered into Armijo's ear in another tongue.

"I wish to introduce you to two ladies traveling with me, their highnesses the queens of Zanzibar and Sheba. I am viceroy of Ceylon and Andaman Islands, looking for investment opportunities in this magnificent land."

"The monkey saved me."

"No, my good sir, it was the will of God."

Skye supposed he should be grateful, but the bitterness at having been betrayed did not leave him so swiftly.

"I will be on my way, sir."

"I hear some England in your voice, Sah."

"London."

"I thought so! A fellow subject!"

"I am no one's subject."

Childress looked astonished.

Skye moved away, not wanting any more to do with Childress.

"Wait, Sah, how about some tea, eh?"

"Some other time." Maybe Childress thought he was acting, for the benefit of the watchful governor, but Skye had no intention of rubbing shoulders with Childress again. There would be no more deadly accusations, or rescue by means of a clever monkey.

He pushed through the gawking people and out the door. No one stayed him. He sucked air into his lungs and surveyed the deserted plaza. His knees were close to buckling. People still swirled around him, pointing, whispering, the man who had escaped death, but he ignored them.

He found Victoria staring at him, and he nodded. There were tears in her eyes. Somehow, they would need to unite, but not now; not for this crowd to witness. He saw Standing Alone there too, and there were tears in her eyes. They simply stood in the warm sun, under the free blue heavens, and stared at him, and he stared back, shaken to the core.

Childress was smart enough to stay away. Skye was ready to punch him in his fat gut.

A Mexican approached him: "Come with me, sir," he said in flawless English.

Skye did.

The thin, handsome man, with a hawk's nose and a raptor's air about him, led him into a handsome mercantile on the south side of the plaza, built entirely of wood rather than adobe, and well stocked with manufactured goods that plainly came from afar.

"Manuel Alvarez, United States consul. I am a Spaniard, actually, not a Mexican."

Skye shook the man's hand. "Mister Skye, sir. Formerly a subject of Great Britain."

"And?"

"And now a man without a country."

"You must wonder why I've asked you to come here." He

led Skye toward a large and cluttered desk in an elevated cubicle in the center of the store. "Here," he said, handing Skye a note.

It read:

Steer clear. Shine will fetch you. We are working on plans. I have asked Alvarez to help you. He has seen this.

It was unsigned.

"I don't know what it means, Mister Skye, but I will assist if I can."

"Is there anyone who needs labor?"

He surveyed Skye, who remained clad in the soldiers' castoffs. "You have no means, eh?"

"None."

"What did you do before you came here?"

"I was employed at Bent's Fort."

"Bent! He is a great friend of mine." Alvarez paused. "You are on good terms?"

"Yes, sir."

The merchant seemed to be coming to some conclusion. "I suppose you could pick out your necessaries, and I could send the bill to William. Would he honor it, and would you repay him with labor or by whatever your means?"

Skye nodded, too exhausted to talk. He was so tired from his scrape with death that he couldn't speak.

"Help yourself, Mister Skye."

"Thank you." But Skye lacked even the strength to shop, and slumped into a chair.

Alvarez took one look at him and trotted off, leaving Skye to gather his strength. When the consul did return, it was with a steaming pot of tea and a cup.

"You English need your spot of tea," he said, pouring into the cup. The smoky pungence of Oolong filled the raised office that overlooked the whole floor.

Skye sipped, and nodded to Alvarez.

"Mister Skye, if you're not occupied, perhaps you will join my wife and me for supper. We follow the custom of our old country, and eat rather late by your standards. Around nine. When the bells of La Parroquia ring at sundown, that'll be vespers, and you just show up here after that. We're upstairs."

"That's a great kindness."

"No, not really; I want to get your story. You interest me."

An hour later, wearing a blue ready-made shirt and gray twill woolen pants and some squeaking ready-made shoes that didn't fit well, Skye left the emporium.

He wandered aimlessly, still reeling, and found himself drifting along an alley.

There, before a butcher shop just off a corner of the plaza, hung the pink, fly-specked carcasses of two small hogs.

40

Jean Lafitte Childress took a swift inventory: he had nothing except time. Now that Skye was safe, matters weren't so urgent. He could go about his next steps without feeling the pressure that had harried him from Taos to Santa Fe in time to halt an execution.

The most urgent business was the trotters, which were drooping in their harness, played out by the hard trip and lack of feed. That posed a problem: that Taos seamstress and a few purchases en route to Santa Fe had cleaned him out; he didn't have a peso to pay for their care, and he knew there wouldn't be a blade of pasture grass within miles of this busy town.

He glanced at the women, who were settled back into their carriage seat awaiting his decisions. They would be all right, even though he could not put them into an inn or posada this evening. They were women of the tribes, used to hardships that would swamp white women.

"Horses next," he said to Victoria. She stared back at him so solemnly that he shrank from that gaze. Skye's ordeal had been her own, and it was not yet over for her; not until they were a thousand miles from this dangerous place.

He drove slowly through the plaza, stopping at last beside an ox-team and some Yank teamsters. The big, red-bearded oaf would do just fine, he thought.

"I say, Sah, is there a livery barn here?" he asked.

"Not as they call it," the Yank said. "But they got a yard. Just foller this creek that cuts the town, down a bit, and it's maybe a quarter mile below."

"They'll put up stock, hay, and feed?"

"They got plenty of hay, and mostly some grain too, but not oats. It's likely to be maize, or maybe barley, all depends. But it'll put some pull back into them trotters."

That was welcome news. "I, ah, haven't made my banking arrangements yet, just arrived, letter of credit to cash. Do they want something in advance?"

"Mostly, but you can allus dicker. I once traded a pound of nails for a night's feed for my whole ox-team, time I arrived late once. Nails is an item around heah, worth a plenty to people that don't have foundries."

"Just dicker, eh?"

"You got it, friend. Where you from?"

"Ah, Trinidad and the Azores."

"Reckon I don't know where that is, but I'd guess south."

"There, you know more than you think! Well, you've been a help."

The teamster waved. Childress set his weary trotters into a slow walk through town, struck the shade-dappled creek, and headed downstream until he found a large stockyard fenced with crooked cottonwood poles. A haystack rose nearby, and some rude adobe shacks lined the perimeter.

He approached the gate, and found a wiry Mexican hostler.

"You take care of these horses, hay and grain?"

The man nodded.

"How much?"

"Dos," he said. "Por dia."

"Pay you?"

"Si, Amando, that is me."

"All right, Amando, a generous feedbag for these nags, rub them down, water them, and put them on hay. There'll be a tip for you in it."

Childress helped the women down. Shine landed at his feet. The hostler drove the carriage through a chattering gate and closed it. It would be a long hike back to the plaza for a man of his girth, but he was determined to go. There was a girl to rescue, and a meal to be found, somehow. He eyed the monkey, his salvation in times when his belly rumbled and protested.

It struck him, as he stood looking at the adobes of Santa Fe just up the creek, that this was an uncommonly sweet place, nestled into the sheltering crook of the mountains. The pungent scent of piñon pine smoke filtered his way. Odd, how peaceful was this place, with its azure heavens, its pine-clad slopes, its earthen homes, its smiling warm-fleshed people. He had never been in love with any place, but suddenly this rural village smote him, and he could not say why. Only a few hours earlier he had seen this place as a miserable gaggle of mud huts.

He took in arm each of his woman friends, and strolled slowly back to the gentle village, admiring the great cotton-woods that lined the creek bank, the staircased tan adobe buildings, the velvety air, the riot of flowers here and there, where least expected, the strange light that sharply limned every building made the whole place seem almost holy, almost sacred. He wondered how such strange thoughts could stir him.

Santa Fe was an old city with old ways. They strolled up narrow streets, past languid people who were in no hurry, past a hostelry called the Exchange Hotel, and an adobe Yank store called Seligman and Clever, and when they finally reached the plaza, near dusk, they discovered that much of the town was strolling, apparently an evening diversion, many of them arm in arm, laughing, enjoying that

heady cool air and the great hush of serenity that embraced
Santa Fe.

The Governor's Palace loomed darkly, its massive doors
closed, and no light rising from any of the narrow, grilled
windows. But these public rooms were not the governor's
private apartment. They strolled by, the women on his arm,
Shine sometimes beside them, attracting much attention and
whispers, and sometimes swinging along the roofs, from
viga to viga, unseen by those below.

Somewhere, within that long low building, a Cheyenne
girl toiled and pined for another life. He scarcely knew how
to rescue her. He scarcely knew how to feed himself and
these two women he was suddenly responsible for.

Off the plaza were gambling parlors and eateries, their
windows bright with yellow lamplight. Shine didn't wait; at
the next one, a place on San Francisco Street, he dodged in,
startling people, chittering and nattering, catching bits of
food tossed at him, popping the morsels into his mouth,
licking his hairy lips, and finally absconding with some hot
buns. These he deposited at the feet of Childress, outside,
who plucked them up off the grimy clay, and handed one to
each woman. It would be the start of a meal, Shine-style,
one item at a time, rifled from a dozen sources. But they
would be fed.

The plaza darkened as the twilight faded, but the paseo
did not cease. People walked, gossiped, courted, flirted, and
maybe did a little business as they strolled the streets at sundown.

When Childress and the women next passed the shadowed Governor's Palace, everything changed. Deep in the
gloom behind a barred window, a girl cried out.

Standing Alone slipped close and whispered furiously,
even as Childress stood casually by, hoping the strollers
would not see anything amiss. They didn't. For a woman to
be talking to someone within was as ordinary as a sunset.

"How do we get her out?" he asked.

Standing Alone's powers of speech obviously weren't adequate; Victoria strained to understand. But finally, it came clear: the great wooden doors were locked with an iron key for the night. The soldiers took care of that. But one way out remained, through the barracks and into the plaza, right past the soldiers.

Childress thought swiftly: "Tell Little Moon to try it; walk out past the soldiers. Smile and walk."

Another great whispering ensued, and finally Victoria told him that the girl could not do that: the soldiers would catch her and do bad things.

Shine jumped up to the window and sat there, nattering at them all.

"Try it, take him into the barracks, let him amuse the soldiers."

The girl absorbed all that, after Victoria had conveyed it to Standing Alone. The monkey squeezed past the iron grille and jumped into the darkness within, chittering softly.

"All right! We must be quick! The barracks door is right over there," he said, pointing at a narrow orifice cut through the thick walls.

He hurried the women to where the door stood, a silent barrier between an Indian girl and her mother, and a reunion long overdue. There was a lamp lit in the barracks; light filtered under that door.

For an endless time, nothing happened. Santa Feans drifted by, though their ranks were thinning now as night enveloped the city, and they repaired to their homes for their late suppers.

The stars were popping out. The vast black bulk of the Sangre de Cristos loomed in the east, dark and mysterious. A breeze brought upon it the scent of juniper, and cooking food, and maybe even the freshness of the peaks.

He heard muffled noise within, maybe laughter, male, amused.

He eyed the women. They had heard it too. He nodded:

they would head straight across the plaza and vanish into a narrow dark alley. He didn't know what they would do if soldiers burst out, in pursuit of the little servant.

The door opened so suddenly that light seemed to explode from within. He heard laughter. Caught a glimpse of Shine, bounding out; then came the girl, stumbling, breathless, out into the dark plaza, ghostly in white. He closed the door swiftly, plunging them back into the sheltering dark.

"Ayah, ayah," cried Standing Alone, who was hugging this lost child of hers, this thin, haunted girl.

"Come," he whispered in a voice that brooked no dissent. How long would the soldiers take to decide something was amiss?

He hurried them into deepening dark. Light spilled from various windows in the plaza, but in its heart there was the sheltering gloom that fell over them now.

He heard the soft sounds of weeping, and then they were out of the plaza and into one of the little streets that would lead them downslope to the river. For the moment, they were safe.

But only for the moment.

41

As weary as he was, Skye knew where he must go and what he must do after leaving Alvarez's store. He pushed one foot ahead of the other across the plaza, and then eastward on San Francisco Street toward the twin towers of La Parroquia. He clambered up steps; the church stood on a low elevation, and then he plunged into its darkness, which foreclosed a brilliant afternoon light.

He waited just within the nave for his eyes to measure the gloom, and then headed toward the gilded altar with its glowing reredos and golden tabernacle. He chose the foremost pew, for he wanted to be as close to the Mystery as he could be, and there he sank to his knees and buried his head in his hands, and thanked his God for deliverance.

"You have spared me the eternal night. You have brought me through the trial. By what means I don't know, but it doesn't matter. I know only that I live and You spared my life. That I breathe here before You, and that I am thankful for your mercy, and for the breath that ebbs in and out of me, and for the chance to be here," he said, aloud, his voice echoing.

He tarried there in the solemn darkness, cherishing the safe silence, barely aware of the comings and goings around him, for his soul was utterly devoted to this thanksgiving.

He did not know why he lived; only that he did. He hadn't a cent, but at least he could give the thanks that rose upward through him.

He rested there in that safe pool of silence, drawing strength even as he gave thanks, and after some while he stood, bowed, and retreated through the nave, and out into the blinding sun of Santa Fe.

He was alone. His wife was somewhere nearby; the others were nearby too. But he could not contact them; they had to remain strangers. He ached to be with her, but she remained well hidden. Wherever Childress was, she would be. He could come to no conclusions about him: his rescuer, perhaps; his accuser for certain. But he was tied to him by Fate for the moment.

He trudged wearily toward the creek that bisected the town, the Rio Santa Fe, and settled himself against a cottonwood tree, wanting only to watch the clear water from the mountains shimmer by. Children gawked at him, and he smiled at a girl who was frowning. She scampered off into the safe orbit of her mother's skirts. He had no children. Victoria had never conceived. Someday, God willing, he would have his sons and daughters.

And so he rested that sunny afternoon in the dappled shade of the riverbank, alone and penniless, yet rich, for anyone who lived was by that very fact incalculably wealthy. Nothing owned by Midas could equal the breath of air in his lungs.

Something about Santa Fe reached out to him; he could not fathom just what, especially since he had come so close to doom in this very place. And yet, here he was, filled with a strange, aching delight in these warm, unhurried people, and in this pueblo that seemed so close to the sky.

Time slipped by and he never noticed. Then the bells of La Parroquia lifted him out of his reverie, and he grew aware once again that he was deep in Mexico, that the sun had fallen below the western horizon, and that he was expected for dinner at the residence of the American consul.

He stood, summoning energy. He could not remember ever having enjoyed such a pleasant sensation before; the lavender twilight, forested green slopes, golden buildings, the windows spilling lamplight, the dry, piñon-scented air, the deep peace. He stretched, and walked back to the plaza and Alvarez's store, and ascended to the second floor.

The consul was expecting him, and led him into a generous room that overlooked the plaza and was furnished with mission-style pieces and fussy bric-a-brac. Handsome oil portraits of grandees hung on the walls.

"Mister Skye, make yourself at home. May I serve you some burgundy? My esposa will be here in a moment."

Skye declined. A glass would throw him into a stupor. He wondered if he could even stay awake through the forthcoming dinner. Alvarez poured himself a generous glass of ruby wine.

The thin, hawkish consul introduced Skye to his equally thin fluttery wife, who could speak no English but welcomed the visitor with a warm smile. These people were opening their home to him. The señora vanished into the kitchen regions.

"Here's to life," the consul said, lifting his glass.

Skye nodded.

Alvarez eyed him. "I confess to some intentions," he said. "I have heard something of your story, public gossip, but I should like to hear it from you if you wish to tell it. It behooves a consul to be watchful."

Skye wondered if watchfulness was all, but he didn't mind.

"It's no secret. If you wish to know, I will tell you."

He had always been frank about his purposes, but he wondered now whether to mention Childress, and decided that for the moment, he would be cautious about that.

"I came here to look for two Indian children who were abducted from Bent's Fort four years ago by Utes, and who probably are in Mexico toiling as slaves, or indentured in some fashion. I have with me my wife, of the Crows far to the north, and the Cheyenne mother of these children, Standing Alone, who has kept a vigil all these years. At the moment, I don't know where they are. I had little enough to begin with, but we hoped we might purchase the liberty of these young people if we could find them . . . and if they live." He waited for some reaction from Alvarez, but received none. "But Jicarilla Apaches took all we possess, even our clothing. We arrived in Taos with nothing, and I soon was in trouble."

"A Texas spy, yes. They thought they had caught a dangerous man."

"I'm not a Texan. Not a Yank. There it is; there isn't much else to add."

"A strange story, a generous impulse, Señor Skye. There were more risks than you imagined."

"Still are," Skye said. He was fighting drowsiness and did not know whether he could stay awake through a meal. A brush with death had drained him.

Alvarez stared out the open windows, onto the darkened plaza. A breeze eddied piñon smoke into the room. "This nation of good people has certain arrangements that cannot stand much scrutiny, señor. The treatment of its Indians is one."

"Peonage?"

"Ah, that they defend gladly. The hacendados think it is a great kindness to the humble. The simple ones are guided; they toil, but then they are cared for until they die. But the Indians, señor, that can be another matter . . ."

"I guess every nation has its dark corners, Mr. Alvarez. Consider the Yanks and their slavery. The Texans are a slave republic."

"Mexico isn't, or so it says, but everyone knows better. And that is a warning for you. If you ask too many questions, nose about too much, you will discover enemies facing you, and they will be formidable, and if you do not flee them, you might find yourself in trouble just as grave as what you faced this day."

"Thank you for the warning."

"The Indians are used and thrown out, quite literally, in the mines. There are a few gold mines not far south of here, and there the Indians spend their lives climbing ladders made of notched logs, carrying heavy baskets of ore to bring to the arrastras, where stones grind the ore, and there the Indians waste and die for they are scarcely fed. In two, three, four years, they are gone, wolf-bait. That is the fate of so many. Terrible accidents, too. Nothing is done for their safety. The ladders fall or twist, spilling human life. A flood washes away the diggings. Dust and dirt ruins their lungs. Ah, it is a grim thing to see.

"It is worse even than the black slavery of the American South or Texas, where slaves are costly and most masters at least feed and clothe them, if only to protect their property. Señor Skye, there are many in those terrible pits who have no clothing at all, not even a cloth about their loins, and who must work in all kinds of weather, fierce heat, bitter cold, or they will not be given their gruel. There is no flesh on any of them, and within a year they are skeletal, and by the second year, they are weakened, starved, and sick, or dead."

Skye sighed. Standing Alone's boy, if that is where he ended up, would not be alive after four years.

"Ah, I have told you the worst! It is not always so bad. There is hope for you. A few captive boys are employed as herders on the great ranchos, and theirs is a better life. They eat; they are clothed and sheltered. But mostly the Indians go to the mines; the sons of peons are indentured as herders. The Indians don't seem to rebel; they work until they drop, and one hears nothing about uprisings."

Skye sighed, remembering his years of captivity, the pain, the lashes, the toil inflicted on him when he fought his masters; the small rewards that came to him for causing no trouble: an extra morsel, an occasional light task.

"But let us talk of pleasanter things," Alvarez said. "You brought your wife?"

"We were separated. I am looking for her, and our Cheyenne friend."

"In Taos?"

"I was seized in Taos and brought here by soldiers."

"Ah, she could be far away."

Skye said nothing. He hated to mislead this hospitable man.

The hostess appeared, and with a nod invited them to her table, which was sparsely set. Bowls of leek soup steamed at three places.

"The señora invites us, Mister Skye."

Alvarez led his guest to the table, settled himself, paused to say a grace in Latin, and smiled at Skye.

"Start, señor, for much more comes soon, eh?"

Skye thought he would be starved, but found himself sipping slowly, all appetite gone, wanting only the solace of sleep. His kind host understood, ate quietly, and did not press conversation upon this man who had escaped death that very day.

Skye nibbled, struggled to stay awake, and stared out the dark windows, where the breezes of Santa Fe filtered in.

And there, sitting on the sill, was the monkey, peering directly at him, waiting for recognition. Skye startled, but the monkey was already gone, swinging easily into the night.

42

There was no time for tears. Standing Alone threw a blanket around Little Moon, even as they hustled the girl away from the plaza, into the darkness of the street called San Francisco, and then the street called Galisteo, and then to the riverside street called Alameda.

There the night was so thick one could scarcely see. A little moon, only a silver sliver of itself, hung low, throwing no understanding on anything.

But at last they paused. The fat white man was puffing. Victoria of the Crows was beside them, guiding the girl. Standing Alone turned her child to her. She was a woman now, not a girl, thin, sad-eyed, but whole. The girl had scarcely spoken, but now she clutched her mother's arm.

"*Nah koa, nah koa!*" she cried. My mother, my mother.

So she remembered the tongue of the people. Standing Alone feared that she might have lost it after four winters of speaking the Spanish tongue.

"We have come," she said. "We will take you to the People. There will be great joy among us."

The girl, at last, trembled, and Standing Alone knew the tears would well up soon, but there was so much to learn.

"Are you sick, Little Moon?"

The girl sighed.

"Are you a maiden? Did you wear the rope?"

"They do not know the rope."

That was answer enough. "We will take you to the People, as one returned from the dead, and the corruption of the body will float away. The gourd singers will come and they will rattle away evil. We will purify you with sweet grass and juniper, and make the smoke flow over you, like the clean scents of the winds, and then all the People will rejoice, and bring gifts, and we will be a stronger people because you have returned, Little Moon."

The girl's great courage seemed to leak away from her.

"Quickly, where is your brother?" Standing Alone dared not name his name for fear he did not live.

"Nah nih," my brother. "I do not know. He was taken away by the men long ago."

"By the Utes?"

"No, the Utes brought us to the pueblo of the north called Taos, and then the Mexican men took us here."

"You know nothing?"

She hung her head, as if in shame for having no answer. "The last word the lost one who was my brother spoke, quickly, was that he would be taken to where the yellow metal is dug out of the breast of the world."

The mines. Victoria had told Standing Alone that the mines are bad, and now this bad news.

They hastened through the night, guided only by the burble of the Santa Fe River, the fat man leading the way, suddenly nimble on his feet. He had found a place for them to hide from the winds this night; inside the domed canvas roof of a big wagon that had rolled into town, now parked beside the yards for the horses and mules and oxen. This place he got for them by talking to one of the bearded white men who drove the oxen with whips. It would be a haven for this frightened girl, this girl of her womb, who had come back to her as from the other side, and now filled her with a joy that made her burst.

Victoria, who had excellent eyes for the darkness, led them to the place of the wagons, and soon they were sheltered within a big one. None of the bearded white men were around; they were in the earthen buildings of Santa Fe, drinking the whiskey there, and gambling away their money.

Little Moon shivered, and her fear permeated the inky place where they had found a haven. Standing Alone held the girl, her hands soothing and comforting, and felt the girl quiet in her embrace.

"Now tell me how it all happened, from the very beginning at the trading house of William Bent," Standing Alone said softly. "I will help our friends understand. We have words enough to talk a little."

"It was so long ago," Little Moon said. "These friendly old women of the Utes came to us, all smiles, and motioned to us to come with them. With signs they said they would give us gifts. Ah, gifts! We smiled back, and that was our mistake. My brother and I went to receive the gifts, walking across the grasses to the place where these Mountain People had made a camp, and as soon as we walked among their lodges, they threw blankets over us. I cried out, and so did the one who was my brother, but they wrapped us tight in blankets, and we heard the sounds of great effort: the Utes were leaving.

"And so we were taken away, the blankets over us, and I could hardly breathe, and no one cared about my tears. I was on a horse and someone was behind me. If I struggled, he beat me hard. It was a long time before I saw the sky again, and when they let us look around, I could not tell where we were, and the big fort was not in sight. And then I knew I would not see my people again, and I was a Cheyenne no more, and that I would face a new life, not a good life, very bad."

She fell silent, and Standing Alone did not urge her to talk. Little Moon was reliving so much in her mind that it was well to let her alone.

"We were watched," she said. "Always, someone was seeing to it that we could not run away. The one who was my brother tried to whisper to me, but they separated us so we could not make plans together. They gave us a little of their food, but we were not abused.

"Then, many days and nights from the white man's post, they began to slow down, and made camp, and hunted, and the band lived as if no one was pursuing them, but they were always careful. And then after maybe a moon, they started up again, and we were taken south to this land, through dry country where the water was poor, and this happened many days. I was not allowed to talk to the one who was my brother, but sometimes we waved; sometimes at night we whispered.

"We are going to the land of Mexico, he said one time. And that was so."

Standing Alone knew it had to be something like that. The Utes did that often. She listened as her daughter described the trip to Taos, the whispered bargaining with Mexicans in the night, and then the Mexicans gave the Utes four horses and blankets and axes and knives, and the powerful Ute warriors dragged the children into the light of a lamp, where they could be seen by the new owners, and then the Utes left.

"It was very dark that night; the one who was my brother was afraid of these new men who made us stand naked so they could see if we were whole. We whispered, but they told us to be quiet. Then they made him dress, and that was the last I saw of him. Just before they took him away, he said he was being taken to the place where the yellow metal is dug, and so I knew a little."

She wiped a tear from her eyes. "I have not seen my brother again."

Standing Alone translated for Victoria. The fat man, who spoke a little Cheyenne, listened intently in the dark, as the night breezes flapped the canvas of the wagon.

After Standing Alone had finished, Little Moon continued.

"I was brought here to this place, and there was much talk, and I was given to this chief of these people. He is very important, this Armijo, and he needed much help from women to keep his big house clean and his clothes washed and much food for many guests, and that is what I have done for four winters."

Her voice broke.

"What I do, it is never enough."

"Did you try to return to the People?"

"I thought much about it. But this Armijo, he has a man and woman who tell us what to do, and warn us that we will die if we do anything bad, like go away. We must be like this until we grow old, that is our fate."

"Until now."

The girl sobbed now, while Standing Alone conveyed the story to Victoria.

"We are going to find the one who was your brother, if he lives," Standing Alone said.

"You do not know . . ."

"We know it will be hard. But we have friends here, strong and wise to the ways of this country."

Little by little, Victoria conveyed the rest of the story to Childress, who sat silently in the dark. Then they talked in English, the tongue Standing Alone did not know well, and she wondered what they were saying. It was so hard, this traveling with people who did not speak the same language, and now they were in another country with still another tongue. The People possessed one tongue among so many, and that is why they were banded together, but knew so little of others.

Finally Victoria turned to her, and in their patois, she got the idea across. Childress, the fat man, was moved and grateful, and vowing to search to the ends of the earth for the missing boy. He was pleased that Little Moon was in good health, and soon would be in good spirits if that medicine was strong.

But now they needed to get her man, Skye; Childress knew how to do that. Skye would be with a merchant on the plaza if he had not found someplace else to sleep. It was time to go get him, while the darkness cloaked their movements.

And here Victoria's voice quivered, for she had not been with her man since the drawing of the beans from the jug, and there was such pain in her voice that Standing Alone grew aware that Skye had come to the edge of death, and all for her, because he and Victoria would not even be in this place if they had not agreed to help her find her children.

"Yes, go," Standing Alone said. "Bring him here, so that I can thank him and we can be together."

"I will go back to the plaza with the fat one," Victoria said. "And the Little Person, who will find my man for me."

"Ah, the Little Person! He is a great warrior."

Victoria snarled something. She never did trust that creature. "Maybe we will leave tonight. I don't know. But now I go back to the plaza," she said.

Standing Alone watched the others clamber out of the wagon and into the starlit night, and moments later their ghostly forms were gone.

She pulled Little Moon to her bosom, and held her daughter in the great sweet silence, and rejoiced.

43

The American consul Alvarez lit the way down the long stairs with a candle lantern, and bid Skye good night.

"Señor, you have no place to go," he said, questioning.

"I have never had a place to go since I was a boy," Skye replied.

Skye stepped into the dark plaza, smelled the freshets eddying down from the Sangre de Cristos, noted the deep starlit heavens, the black rooflines of buildings around the square, and waited. The little monkey had summoned him; the monkey would find him. Victoria hated that monkey, and Skye could never understand it. The monkey had constantly aided them all.

Now he heard a soft chittering. He walked blindly into the plaza, following the sound, and suddenly found the others looming out of the depths of darkness.

"Skye, dammit," Victoria cried, and she wrapped her arms about him, hugging him fiercely, and he felt her thin, bony body pressed tight against him, and her hands possessing him. He hugged her joyously, this woman who had been his friend, lover, mate all these years.

"Victoria!" he whispered.

"I think maybe I never see you again."

"I'm here."

Victoria's hands found his face, the stubble of his beard, his neck. He scraped a rough hand down her back, the embracing filling and blessing him.

"Ah, Skye," said Childress. "Come."

Skye paused, his anger welling up in him, but he contained it. The man had gotten him into mortal trouble—and then had gotten him out of it.

They led him out of the plaza. He trusted Victoria's eyes because he could see so little at night and the sliver of moon didn't help any. Santa Fe this night was as dark as anyplace he had ever been.

He felt Childress's heavy footsteps beside him.

"I will explain it all," Childress whispered. "Rejoice! We have good news."

Skye thought the man would have a lot of explaining to do to make it right.

He was being led gently downslope and south and west; that was as much as he could fathom. But eventually they struck the Rio Santa Fe, and he was oriented.

"We have recovered Standing Alone's daughter," Childress said, after they had reached the river.

Skye stopped dead. "You *what?*"

"Little Moon had been employed in the very Governor's Palace where you spent a fateful hour, working for Governor Armijo. We ran into her utterly by accident. Standing Alone started to swoon; the girl fled. But we succeeded. We have her!"

"You have her now?" It was all too much for Skye.

"We do; we executed a little maneuver this evening."

"Is she well?"

"Ah, Skye, Sah, what is slavery but the destruction of dreams and hope, eh? She was a prisoner, what they call *criados sin sueldo*, servants without hire. A convenient set of muscles to be used at labor, a mortal without the hope of a life."

Skye marveled that this self-proclaimed privateer and pirate could speak so eloquently of slavery in its various forms and subtleties. But Childress was an enigma, and there was no point in wondering about him. Nothing on earth could explain the man.

They proceeded downriver to a place where livestock were penned, and numerous wagons lurked in the slight light of a sliver of moon.

"Here, Sah, is where we are domiciled," Childress said, steering toward one big Conestoga that he somehow singled out of the gloom.

He stood outside the mammoth conveyance. "Standing Alone, we are here," he said.

The monkey bounded inside and Skye heard a rustling and voices. Victoria clambered in, and soon stepped through the puckered canvas, followed by two women.

"Hey, this here is Little Moon," Victoria said, her voice crackling.

Skye found a gaunt Cheyenne girl, fear visible in her face even in that sparse light. But her mother was talking swiftly, and soon the girl's fears subsided, and she even smiled at Skye.

He held out his hands and the girl took both of them shyly. Standing Alone clasped her hands over the girl's, capturing Skye's hands in their embrace. They were thanking him with tears and clasps and sighs.

This was a strange, sweet moment. For just this had Skye thrown aside everything else and come here. Before him was one of the missing children, a young woman now, safe and free—at least if they could smuggle her out of Mexico.

He knew that Armijo would probably put things together: Childress, pretending to be a British diplomat; a girl vanishing from his staff; and Skye, released from death by Childress's monkey. Give those odd facts to a man as alert and suspicious as Armijo, and there would soon be a platoon of soldiers tracking them all.

He held these hands a long moment, for he shared their joy, and wanted them to know it.

They repaired to the dark confines of the wagon where they would be safe from wandering gazes, and there Skye learned their story: Childress's amazing acquisition of the carriage in Taos, obtaining the dresses for the women, a suit of clothes for himself, spare goods, a little food, a few knives, even a rifle, all by mortgaging his stock of goods up on the Arkansas River. All of it the work of a self-proclaimed pirate.

Skye sighed, unbelieving. What was Childress? Trader? Texas Colonel? Filibuster? Pirate? Rescuer of Indian children, a man absorbed with slavery and justice? What sort of alchemist was he, transmuting the base metals of his character into gold?

"I accused you, Mister Skye, Sah, because one of us had to escape and deploy. It worked, eh?"

Skye felt his rage boil up, but there was little to say. The man who had put him in such jeopardy got him out, somehow. Or the damned monkey did.

"Shine palmed a white bean?" Skye asked.

"Ah, Skye, I trained him to leave the black beans alone."

"It's *Mister* Skye," he snarled. "Mister Skye and don't call me anything else."

That ended it. Skye felt his rage and terror leak away, like blood from a cut wrist.

There was too much to absorb. Skye sat quietly, leaving his fate to the rest. His weariness was telling on him again. Victoria's hands found him in the dark, each caress loving him, each touch of a finger reaching beyond his flesh and into his soul.

Finally Childress broke the quiet. "We have a good idea where the boy, Grasshopper, is, if he's alive," he said. "The last thing he said to Little Moon was that he would be taken to where gold is scratched out of the earth."

Skye sighed. Chances were, the boy would be dead, then.

But at least they had fulfilled half of their goal; they had rescued a sweet Cheyenne woman.

"I made inquiry, Skye. As a Briton looking for a good investment, I had a perfect cover. I'm now a baronet, Sir Arthur Childress. Where would a man invest in gold mining? I asked. They said no foreigner could work the gold deposits. But that didn't deter me. I said I might make a considerable payment to the governor for some land in the goldfields. Well, Mister Skye, Sah, I got the whole history."

Skye nodded. Now Childress was calling himself a baronet.

"Back twelve or fifteen years ago, Sah, a herder stumbled on some placer gold, loose gold flakes trapped in gravel, you know, not far south of here on the east slope of the Ortiz Mountains. There's plenty of it there, and it's very pure, assays at .918 pure, almost as good as it gets in nature. But there's not much water there for washing it, so mining has been slow and most of the washing's done in winter, when snow can be melted. They have chopped deep into the gravel there, and employ slaves to do it, all Indians. Much of the ore is trapped in a conglomerate that needs to be broken up.

"There were some later discoveries of vein gold farther south, but most of the work is taking place scarcely thirty miles from here. They use the most primitive methods, Sah. Wooden vessels called bateas to wash the gold. Arrastras, rude stone grinding devices powered by bullock. Slave labor hauling the sands upward in baskets, climbing ladders fifteen or eighteen feet high, nothing but notches in a log. There's a bit of a town there called Dolores, and that's where we will go."

"All right."

"But there is risk, Sah. A few years ago an American named Daley headed that way, wanting to buy in, and he was murdered. The murderers never were brought to justice and Armijo did nothing, even under the most intense pressure from the Americans in the area, including the Bents.

But what was a mere murder of a heretic Yank? So nothing happened. So the lesson was learned at the mines: outsiders are fair game. We'll need a plan, Sah. Arms, defenses, everything."

"You know how to get there?"

"Certainly. A British diplomat can find out anything."

"We go in that rig? Your black carriage?"

"It will convey us all. You shall drive; I and the three women will occupy the facing seats, and oh, what a fine sight we'll be, eh?"

"That's what worries me."

"Never fear, Skye. This little simian accomplishes wonders."

"It's *Mister*. . . ."

"Touchy, aren't you. Well, first we have a little problem to work out. I'm in hock. Have to pay the hostler here for graining and haying the nags. Haven't a cent of cash, you know. Pirates make a poor living, Skye, I assure you. It's feast or famine, but mostly famine. We're going to have to pay, or the hombre will set off alarms and we'll have a squad of dragoons riding us down."

"Daylight is our enemy, Childress."

"Can't be helped. But never underestimate my monkey."

44

Childress padded through the murk of predawn amid a hush that was not even broken by the morning song of a bird. He had Shine bounding along beside him in great frolics, plotting perfidy, and he had Skye with him as well.

"All right," Childress said. "You get out on the plaza, stay in shadow if there is any. Watch the barracks door. If any trouble starts, just drift back here and let me know, and I'll whistle Shine away from his nefarious duties."

"I don't like this," Skye said.

"Mister Skye, old friend, it's justice. We'll simply extract from the governor a small repayment for the four years of free labor he got out of that poor girl."

Skye stared. Childress knew what he was thinking.

"Sah, I know you don't approve. But we are engaged in an act of liberation, not theft. Call it restitution. He paid her nothing; now we shall extract a small price, and without his consent. Nowhere near the value of her labor, Sah, but a small recompense even so. By my reckoning we ought to extract a hundred pounds from the devil to balance things up."

Skye nodded, and reluctantly headed for the silent plaza, while Childress and his cheerful primate, who was growing agitated, circled around to the rear of the palace where there were barred windows, their shutters opened to the night breeze. The bars might foil a human but not the skinny monkey.

No one stood about. The predawn murk remained so thick on this southwest side of the mountains that Childress was all but invisible.

"Go," he said, and the monkey bounded up to the window in tumultuous leaps, peered about, and vanished within.

Childress waited nervously. Nothing stirred in the alley, but he heard the distant groan of a carreta. Some peasant on some early mission was passing by somewhere near.

Nothing changed. Childress paced. Then the monkey appeared on the sill, clutching something shiny. It leaped downward and handed Childress a silver candlestick holder.

"No, no, this will never do, you idiot. The hostler won't accept it and he'd report us. Take it back, you little bugger."

The monkey chittered and clacked his teeth. He could bite hard, and those clacking teeth were a warning that he was not to be trifled with.

"Shine, my apologies. Just try again. Something less, ah, incriminating."

The monkey bounded gracefully upward to the sill, bearing his candlestick holder, and vanished into the silent interior.

Childress thought he heard voices within, but strain as he might to hear, he couldn't be sure. He wondered how Skye was faring out on the plaza.

Then Shine materialized on the sill, clutching something dark, and jumped down to the clay. This object was mysterious, and Childress couldn't fathom what it was until the monkey handed it over. It proved to be a handsome humidor of enameled sheet metal with an elaborate design on it. Childress pulled the tight-fitting top, and discovered twenty or thirty fine cigars within, their pungence nectar to his nostrils.

"Ah! You little beggar, you've done it! Bravo, you little pirate."

The monkey bared its teeth and then sucked its thumb. Childress hastened down the alley, rounded the corner, waved at Skye, and then proceeded away from the plaza. Skye caught up with him.

"A humidor full of fine cigars," Childress said. "Now, weigh this in your scales: any Mexican male, upon given a fat black cigar, will stuff his mouth with it, light up, strut and swagger, and make a great noise so that all the world can witness his machismo. I imagine it'll pay our feed bill, and the hostler won't suppose anything's amiss, either."

"You know Mexicans better than I do," Skye said, doubt in his voice.

They were soon out of Santa Fe and back in the livestock yards, still before sunrise. They returned to the big wagon and settled in without waking anyone except Victoria, though the Conestoga creaked.

Not until the wagon yard was stirring did Childress judge the time to be ripe for the exit. He lumbered over to the ancient hostler, who was shoveling hay with a big wood-pronged fork.

"Ah, señor, I have yet to manage a financial transaction so far from England. I have pounds but I am temporarily without pesos. However, I do have means," he said in Spanish to the wary and wizened man. "Look, señor, at these fine Havanas, eh?"

Childress stuffed one into the man's rough hands. "It's yours, all yours, *un cigarro*. Sniff it, taste it, roll it under your nostrils, covet it, you lucky hombre."

"Ah! Bueno!"

"I'll give you four, cuatro, more of these fat wonders for haying and graining my trotters, eh?"

The hostler was not about to surrender. He held up ten fingers.

"*Diez!* But these are worth two pesos each!"

The man wagged ten fingers.

"Ah, very well, ten it is," Childress said.

Ten fat cigars, payment in full, and now they could leave. He doled out his pungent payment, the hostler nodded, and pointed at the harness. Childress set to work.

A while later they were all seated in the ebony calash, and Skye was driving down an obscure dirt road that would take them to the Ortiz Mountains, which formed a purple sunlit mass on the horizon. The trotters were making music with their hooves.

Childress sat facing the women, enjoying the sweet chill air of early morning and the tawny and purple vistas of this arid land. They were off on the last lap, the final mission, and with luck, they would succeed. He opened the humidor and pulled out a cigar, debated whether to offer one to Skye, decided not to, and chewed on it unlit. When they came to a place where he could employ flint and steel, he would try to fire it up. Meanwhile he waggled it with baronial vigor.

Childress was in a very fine mood.

"Give me one of those," Victoria said.

"You? But madam . . ."

She glared. He surrendered a cigar and she stuffed it into her small mouth. The sight was disconcerting, but he began to enjoy it. What better than a fat cigar for the queen of Zanzibar?

The day passed gently; the carriage making good time over a bare excuse for a road. Perhaps by mid- or late afternoon they would raise Dolores, the hamlet where they intended to sojourn. They pierced deep into arid blue mountains, passing arroyos that carried no water.

"We should make plans, I suppose," Childress said, turning to Skye.

"It's your show," Skye said.

Childress watched him, concerned. Ever since Skye's narrow escape from the firing squad, he had not seemed to be himself.

"Well, we have to find out about the mining. How the Indians are kept in line; how they're punished or enslaved. Their quarters, if they have any. Clothing. Have we spare duds? The boy will be naked or nearly so. We can't hustle him out of there naked."

"Will he know his mother?" Skye asked.

Victoria, who was listening, translated for Standing Alone.

"She says he probably would, but not in this stuff she's wearing."

"I don't want her to change, not just yet. I don't want anyone who might seem Indian looking around at Indian slaves," Childress said.

"I think we'd better wait and see," Skye said. "This is a gold mine. There probably will be guards. We don't even know whether we can buy the boy; simply pay for him and walk away without trouble. What's the price, and how do we pay?"

Skye's caution annoyed Childress. "Pah! We'll find him, just as we found Little Moon, and slide him out."

Skye said nothing and Childress took it for disapproval. Well, what did it matter?

They encountered more and more traffic, mostly people afoot, walking who knows where? But they also met with carretas, some carrying hay, others squash or produce, heading toward the mines. It would take a deal of food to keep hundreds of miners alive. Childress noted the garden patches, the adobe jacals, the herds of sheep, ribby cattle, and goats, often attended by a herding boy. But mostly this was a harsh land of barren rock, scanty grass, cactus, juniper thickets, and forbidding blue canyons that seemed to keep secrets.

The herders and peons gawked at them as they trotted by; no doubt they had never seen a rig so handsome, or men and women so fashionably dressed. The ladies looked elegant; Childress was the soul of gentility. A few of the Mexicans spotted Shine, perched beside Childress. They obviously had never seen a monkey. Shine licked his hairy lips and picked his nose, and sometimes bounced up and down on the quilted seat. That was good. Childress intended to make an impression, especially of wealth. Little could they guess, these humble, weathered, sun-stained people, that they had more wealth than everyone in that calash put together.

"Skye, we need a plan," he reiterated, annoyed at Skye's passivity.

"All I need to know is who you are and what we're doing here."

"I'm the viceroy of Borneo and Tahiti, that's who I am," Childress snapped. "And I'm here to look at obscene investments, and these are royal ladies of Timbuktu and you're my hired man." He laughed.

Skye stared at him.

They rolled into an adobe hamlet called Dolores, a scrabble of little square earthen buildings and a cantina in a gulch hugging a yellow slope. As humble as it was, it served the mines. They were in the Ortiz Mountains, and the last chapter would soon begin.

45

Skye was discovering a new way to be a prisoner. He was helpless to resist Childress's follies simply because Childress could speak fluent Spanish while Skye could barely speak a dozen words. Wherever they went Skye was utterly dependent on Childress to deal with the Mexicans. He didn't even know what Childress was saying to them.

So Skye sat in the front seat of the calash, minding the horses, wondering what Childress would say to the people there in Dolores or to the mine owners, and it was not hard to imagine a dozen ways of getting into trouble.

One American had already been murdered here for poking around too much. Gold did that. Gold aroused passions and turned men into animals. And here was Childress, fluent in their tongue, floating one preposterous story after another, poking around wealth that Mexico guarded zealously. And there was Skye and the women, inevitable victims of any blunders Childress might make.

Skye halted the coach at the mercado, which seemed to be the only store in this rude settlement.

"I'll inquire," Childress said, lowering his bulky body to earth.

"I'll go with you," Skye said sourly. Maybe someone spoke English, and if so, he wanted to know it.

"Yes, see what's in the place whilst I jabber with these people," Childress said, flapping toward the store like a penguin.

Shine landed beside his master and swiftly aroused the interest of half a dozen barefoot men, who eyed the monkey with amazement.

"Don't let that monkey steal one damned thing," Skye snapped.

"Tut, tut, Skye. You owe him your life and your liberty."

Childress plunged through a doorless doorway along with the little primate, and Skye followed. The dark interior revealed the simplest sort of store, with rough burlap sacks of beans and rice and sugar on the earthen floor, some crockery and tinware, sewing items, and little else. All lit by a late-afternoon sun.

Childress scarcely looked at the foodstuffs. He pulled one of his fat black Havanas from his breast pocket, lit it with a brand plucked from the beehive fireplace within, sucked and exhaled until the tip of the cigar glowed bright orange, and then approached a stocky woman with vast bosoms who seemed to be overseeing this rural emporium. Childress was soon talking and gesticulating and patting the stolid woman on the shoulder, while Shine cased the joint, looking for plunder.

Skye couldn't grasp a word of it. For all he knew, the Texas pirate was describing them all as buccaneers, bandits, crooks, abusers of women, escaped prisoners, heretics, murderers, and desperados. From time to time the woman glanced at Skye and at the monkey, and sometimes out the door toward the fancy carriage where the women sat expectantly.

But the Mexican woman didn't seem to grow excited. Plainly, she was giving Childress directions, pointing southward, lifting her thick arms up and down as she talked.

Childress nodded, patted her, and at the last, gave her a

fat cigar. She sniffed it, smiled, bit off the end, and stuffed
it between her stained teeth.

Skye studied her and the other Mexicans lounging about.
Plainly they were rural laborers, mestizos mostly. Nothing
about them suggesting mining, and he doubted that any
were miners. These were the weathered ones who hoed and
scraped those fields they had passed, the ones who fed the
miners if the rains came.

Childress bowed, lifted his silk top hat to the woman,
settled it again on his sweaty brow, and retreated into slant-
ing sunlight, beckoning Skye. The monkey followed, bare-
handed.

"There now, I've got what we need. There were seven
holdings originally; now it's two after some consolidating.
They employ Indian labor exclusively. She says the Indians
make good workers and don't need the whip. All we have
to do is keep on going. The first, the Blessed Saint Ignatius
of Loyola Mine, is up ahead, and employs maybe a hundred,
she thought, but counting that high taxes her mind. The
other is smaller, Santa Rosita, and she couldn't say for sure
what it employs. Ah, we'll find the bugger yet, eh?"

"Maybe. What did you tell her about us?"

"Is something wrong with you?"

"What did you tell her?"

"What does it matter? We're Finland royalty. I eat caviar. We have the queens of Van Dieman's Land and Iceland
to amuse us, and are looking for gaudy investments."

"That's trouble."

"Ah, pah! Mister Skye, you're a worrywart. Leave it to
Childress. Leave it to Shine, the phenomenal burglar."

Childress clambered into the calash, rocking it under his
vast bulk. Skye settled himself wearily in the van, and urged
the trotters forward. A thick coating of dust covered their
sleek black hair.

The canyon widened abruptly ahead, forming a plain

compassed by slopes. A dry riverbed ran beside the rutted road, and even though the summer had not progressed far, a great aridity marked the land.

A gash disturbed the rolling land just ahead, and as Skye drew close he beheld a giant pit swarming with human bodies. A single adobe shack stood on the brow of a hill. Off to one side stood some rude rectangular adobe buildings, probably quarters for the miners. A gulch had been dammed to provide some water.

But it was the pit that riveted Skye as he drove the trotters alongside the gaping hole in the earth. The solidified gravel rose in benches, which supported rude ladders of sorts, each hacked out of a single log. These were notched for the feet of those using them, but they lacked a handrail or any other means by which a person could steady himself. Yet the workers were climbing and descending these rickety devices while carrying huge baskets of ore.

"Look at those poor devils, Mister Skye," Childress said. "Swarms of them, like ants."

Skye slowed the horses. The sight horrified him. Those thin workers were bent double, no matter whether their baskets were loaded or empty. Years of brute labor and the weight of tons of ore had bowed their legs and twisted their spines, until not a one of them could stand upright.

Most were naked. A few wore loincloths of some sort. None had shoes or sandals. Nothing protected them from the harsh summer sun. They toiled ceaselessly, some at the bottom level hacking open the gravel, others loading baskets with crude wooden shovels, others parading up one ladder and another, delicately balancing the burdens while inching upward, one notch at a time until they reached the next narrow bench, and the foot of the next rickety log ladder. One misstep meant death. And there would be no pensioning of cripples. Above, somewhere out of sight, the ore was being heaped into a pile that jutted into the brassy blue sky. Skye wondered what sort of labor proceeded up there, and how the gold was extracted from this crumbling gravelly matrix.

He reined the horses to a halt, transfixed at the human anthill before him, where men threw long shadows in the low sun. These workers were small, wiry, bent, and bore terrible wounds across backs and calves and thighs. One labored with a stump of one arm. A few had tied a rag around their forehead to hold their jet hair back from their faces, but that was all the cloth Skye saw on most. He saw very little gray hair; these bent-over mortal males were young. Or were they all male? He studied them closely, his eyes uncertain. Maybe some were girls, but they all were so thin that none had breasts.

They did not notice the black carriage above, or at least pretended not to. Skye wondered where the overseers were, the ones who forced labor from this pitiful gaggle of captive mortals. He had been right; none of these had been at the mercado, and not one ever would enter those cool confines.

"The *gambucinos*," Childress said.

"Slaves."

"Theoretically not slaves. No such thing in Mexico, they insist. Indentured workers on the books."

"Can they walk away?"

Childress laughed.

Below, a thin bent man stumbled on the second notch of a tall ladder and fell back, spilling his ore. Instantly, a crowd filled the basket again. The bent man shouldered it slowly, and stepped upward on trembling legs, one notch at a time. Skye thought that man was on his last legs, and wouldn't last another week.

"Skye, get on with it. The manager's up ahead, there."

But Skye was in no hurry. He waited to see if the trembling slave would make it. He looked for water barrels to satiate the terrible thirst of these miserable slaves, and found none. He saw none of them resting or recouping. There was only the sight of shining, bent backs of coppery little men, yellow dust caking their bodies, and the big gray baskets made of reed or something similar, all of it lit by a low sun.

"Skye, blast it."

"I am looking at hell. Nothing in the Royal Navy comes close, and believe me, I'm an expert on that."

"Well, that's not important. Are we going to rescue the wretch or not?"

Skye turned to see Standing Alone, who stared unblinking at the sight below her, the lines of her face taut. Victoria was holding her arm, cursing softly. All this was obviously beyond her most terrible imaginings. Skye could scarcely turn his gaze elsewhere, knowing that this awful pit probably claimed two or three lives each day, and what lay before him was an engine of death and pain.

At last he reined the horses the last two hundred yards to the squat, sullen adobe building ahead, where a thin, hawk-faced man in a white suit awaited them, backed by two burly segundos.

46

The man in the spotless white suit a size too large surveyed the occupants in the carriage as Skye halted the sweated trotters. He did not approach the carriage, but waited, leaning into a gold-knobbed malacca.

"Ah, mi caballero," rumbled Childress, grandly, flourishing his top hat.

"Ah, the Right Honorable Lord Viceroy Sir Arthur Childress," the mine operator replied in sandpapery English. "Welcome to the mine."

"Ah, a Mexican who speaks my tongue! You have found me out with a glance. Permit me to introduce their royal highnesses the queens of Madagascar and Tierra del Fuego."

"Yes, very colorful, an entertaining idea, heathen queens skittering around rural Mexico to titillate us. I am Hector Ramon Pedro Marcus O'Grady at your service. And these gentlemen are assistant superintendents of the mine, Jesus and Pedro."

Skye thought that the assistant superintendents looked more like jailers. English! The operator spoke English and had an Irish surname. Skye supposed he ought to be glad, but already Childress was in deep trouble, and this was turning sour right from the start.

The mining man turned to him. "And you are a certain Mister Skye, the one who escaped execution by the wiles of that monkey. I was there, you know. Yes, the governor was curious whether you would all link up. It seems you have. Just what business you're about eludes us, unless it's the business of a Texas invasion after all. But I am not being hospitable. Do step down and have some tea. I saw you coming and have some Oolong steeping."

Skye's stomach churned. Had they ridden straight into a trap?

"Charmed, I'm sure, Sah," said Childress. "Ladies?" he said, holding out a hand.

"Sonofabitch," Victoria muttered, stepping down. Standing Alone followed, nervous and uncertain. Little Moon sat, frightened.

"You sit right there, young lady," Childress said. He turned to O'Grady. "We have a servant girl, Sah."

"Yes, so it seems. The governor thought she might be found with you."

Skye sighed. So even that was no secret to this well-informed man. This was more than trouble; it was menace. He set the carriage weight on the ground, hooked the lines to it, and followed the rest into the rude adobe building. It was less rude within, and divided into several small warrens. But O'Grady led them into an office that resembled a parlor, and seated them upon stuffed chairs.

He spoke swiftly to a woman servant, and smiled.

"Ah, my Yankee friends, we shall have our tea in short order."

More trouble, Skye thought.

"Sah, not one of us is a citizen of the United States. I am a peer of England."

"Galveston Bay, I hear, is only a mile from London. Did you not engage in privateering on the Thames?"

Skye squirmed. All of Childress's wild stories were coming home to roost.

"And what are you viceroy of? Zanzibar? Van Dieman's Land, Bermuda, Ceylon? Yes, and these charmers are, ah, queens of, ah . . ."

Childress laughed expansively. "You've found me out, Sah!"

Skye itched. He studied the thugs hovering about behind O'Grady, and thought he could take one, maybe both. He'd learned a few tricks in the mountains. Maybe he and the women could run for it . . . for a while. But not for long. This was looking more and more like a one-way trip in irons to the City of Mexico.

The superintendent's bright blue eyes locked upon Skye. "And you, Mister Skye, what brings the legend of the fur trade to Mexico, might I ask? You, at least, are an Englishman by birth. Have you been bought by Texas? Should you have been shot after all?"

Skye saw the question as his opportunity. "I am here on a peaceful mission, Mr. O'Grady."

"And what might that be?"

"We are looking for Cheyenne children who were abducted by Utes years ago and sold into slavery here."

"There is no slavery in Mexico, Mister Skye."

Skye didn't want to argue. Let them call it whatever they wanted, indenture, peonage. "We have reason to believe a Cheyenne boy works here. This is his mother, Standing Alone, of the Cheyenne people."

"Ah, yes, this woman is a legend. I know of her. The traders who pass Bent's Fort told us of her and her heartrending vigil. They speak of her with utmost respect."

"As long as you seem to know my purpose, and her purpose, then perhaps you'll help us."

O'Grady stared at Skye from rheumy eyes that revealed only clockwork.

Childress intervened. "Ah! Señor O'Grady, my friend Skye here is straying far from our actual purposes," Childress said. "I'm looking for mining properties, something that will make me lasciviously rich, eh? I am the fiduciary guardian of the estates of these noble ladies, eh? Gold comes to mind: lustrous, soft, pure, delicious, glittering, heavy gold, to burthen the pocket, stuff the purse, suckle the loosest dreams . . . Señor O'Grady, Sah, you might join us in a great pecuniary adventure."

"The monkey is shaking its head and tugging at the leg of your trousers."

"Ah, wretched little ape. Simian Judas, scavenger, mountebank, obscene little animal! Never trust a monkey, Sah."

Skye had enough. If they were to leave this place alive and with Little Moon and his women, there would have to be absolute truth.

"Mr. O'Grady," he snapped in a way that subdued Childress. "Have you any Cheyenne working here?"

"Cheyenne? Mister Skye, what is your interest again?"

"Charity, sir."

"Charity, is it?"

Skye was boiling. "Is that something you don't grasp?"

"You puzzle me. But no, no Cheyenne. We employ Mexican nationals. We are forbidden to employ others."

Skye stared at the man, who smiled, nodded toward the steaming teapot.

"Tarahumaras, Jicarillas, Jumanos, Suma . . ." He shrugged. "They work well and hard for a while and then grow lazy, like so many of their coppery brethren."

"Does the other mine here employ Cheyenne?"

"Ah! You are behind the time. It is closed. It exhausted itself, and this mine alone survives."

"You speak English."

"My father, sir, was from Killarney. My mother is the Doña Olivera, of Chihuahua."

"My fine friend, do you want to dicker?" Childress asked, rubbing pudgy fingers together. "What's it worth, eh? I just might plunge."

"To a foreigner, nothing. It is forbidden."

"Well, there are always ways around that. Here, have a cigar."

"Yes, I believe I shall. It's just the sort enjoyed by the governor."

O'Grady plucked the cigar out of Childress's hand, but did not light it. The cigar vanished into a drawer.

"Well, delighted we have the same tastes!" Childress boomed.

The jails of Mexico City yawned wide, always assuming they made it that far before succumbing to whatever cruelties the federal troops might dream up along the way.

O'Grady stood suddenly, his gaunt frame scarcely filling his white suit, which flowed over and around his body as he moved. "This mine barely earns a profit. By the time I acquire, feed, house, and clothe my *gambucinos*, the cost of extracting the dust from this gravel nearly equals the value of the gold. You see how it is."

"No. How is it?" Skye asked.

"Come look. But sip your tea first, and rest. You've had a long ride."

Victoria listened silently, grasping most of it. Standing Alone sat mutely.

"Tell the Cheyenne woman her son died two years ago," O'Grady said.

"What?" The bluntness startled Skye.

"He is dead. Most die soon. I have never understood it. Sickness. A weakness in savages. The will of God." O'Grady shrugged.

Skye stood abruptly. "Dead? How do you know it was her son?"

"Four years past he was brought to me by the traders of Taos. About ten years old, big enough. Armijo took the girl, the one out there. I bought the boy. He didn't last. Pity, isn't it?"

Skye nodded to Victoria, who began translating into the

argot she shared with Standing Alone. The Cheyenne woman trembled once, but she said nothing.

"Come," said O'Grady. They followed mutely out the door and down a path to a lip of a hill overlooking the mine, and just a few yards from the series of precarious ladders leading to the stockpiled ore.

"Let the Cheyenne woman see for herself who walks up those ladders," O'Grady said. "All do. They take turns, every last one."

"Why are you bothering?" Skye asked.

"So that you will see I tell you the truth. You and I talk truly, even if this Right Honorable Viceroy Sir Arthur Childress fails the test. In Mexico, honor counts. It is the honorable life and honorable death we seek."

"And what else?"

O'Grady smiled. "Eldorado."

And so they stood at the pit, lit now by a low sun, watching each bent-over, twisted Indian struggle up the ladders with his basket of gold-bearing gravel. Standing Alone stood closest, her back arched, her body pressed against a rail, her black hair fluttering in the hot breezes. As each one approached, she cried out a word. Skye didn't know the word, but surely it was Cheyenne, and surely not the dead boy's name. But none of these twisted, ruined, ribby, gaunt slaves so much as glanced her way.

Her voice shrilled into the wind like the cry of a raven, harsh, painful, sibilant, tender, and the wind only blew the word back upon her. And yet she persisted, watching wretch after wretch wrestle his basket to the pile of ore.

"Come," said O'Grady, and he led them to a different area, where squatting naked Indians, older and more adept, swirled the gravel around inside of crude wooden bowls, using tiny infusions of water to spin the gravel away from the heavier metal. A dozen of these worked ceaselessly; all were gaunt. Standing Alone held her hat to her head, and said nothing.

"Come," said O'Grady, and he escorted them, past a compound where miners lived, to a dirt-strewn field lumped with unmarked graves. One open one yawned, and as they approached a pestilence of crawling and flying things and a foul stench shot toward them, nauseating Skye. Redheaded black vultures flapped upward.

"They do not last long," O'Grady said. "A weakness of those people."

47

Somewhere in this foul field lay the bones of her son. Standing Alone was careful not to say his name, or even think it, lest she disturb his spirit. The one who was once her son had not lasted long here, in this place of pestilence and starvation. They had worked him, starved him, beat him, and he had died.

Now she knew. But somehow she had known long ago, for the medicine seers of her people had seen this in the sweetgrass smoke and had told her. But she had kept her vigil at Bent's Fort anyway, for the daughter lived and might return.

The sun's light slanted across this place, but she saw the darkness of this land, as if no sun shone here. This bone-yard held the remains of many of the Peoples, the ones who roamed this country before the white men came. She was familiar with torture, with slavery, with captivity, for her people had engaged in all of these things against enemies. But the slaves of her people, women and children taken in war, were usually treated well, soon intermarried, and became part of the band. Sometimes her people tortured enemies too. But this was different. This was endless women's work, this grubbing the soil and washing the metal from it.

But she saw no women doing it; only men, who should be hunting or warring or protecting their People instead of this shameful labor.

And this toil was destroying them, just as it had destroyed the beloved one whose name must never again pass her lips. She stared bleakly at this witch-man in white, the mine chieftain who did not know *Heammawihio,* the Wise One Above. She saw a horseman patrolling the perimeter of this place, and knew why none of these *gambucinos* ran away. She stared, and wondered if she and Skye and Victoria and the fat one called Childress and her daughter would all be put to work here too, and soon die.

Aiee, this was something to think about.

She meandered past this place of bones, toward some open-sided buildings with thatched roofs, and here she discovered a kitchen of sorts and pots of thin soup hanging on tripods over fires. Was that all those people would eat, this watery soup steaming in iron kettles? Some stocky bronzed women of the Peoples were cutting thick roots and throwing them into the pots. Where was meat, which made men strong? This was not enough in such a meal to feed an infant.

She watched, learning much of this place. She could not grasp the tongue, except a few words. She did not know any of the tongues of the coppery slaves who starved and toiled here until they died, so she could speak to no one. She wanted to ask questions.

At this kitchen place sat two boys, huddled on the earth, neither of them at manhood yet. Maybe ten or eleven winters. Newcomers. Not yet worn down. Not yet twisted. Aiee! She knew their moccasins. Yellow dyed, like most Arapaho leather. Arapaho boys. Her people knew the Arapaho well, sometimes to fight beside them against the Comanches and Kiowas. Arapahos were friends, and spoke a tongue the Cheyennes could easily learn. These boys were newcomers, brought to this place this very day by slave traders, and soon to die like the one whose name could not be uttered, who had issued from her womb.

Yellow moccasins. Arapaho boys! Sturdy, not yet ruined. Even as she studied them, an idea formed. She would snatch them from here, take them to her people and make them Cheyenne boys. The death of her son would be made right: the People would have two new boys for the one lost. Aiee! But how? She could not ask the fat one, or Mister Skye, for the want of their words. But she could talk to the Crow woman with signs and words they knew. Ah, she would do that, swiftly, for those boys might soon vanish into the pit and be lost to her forever.

They stared at her, not knowing whether she was a friend.

A fierce intention spread through her. She did not know what medicine might help her or what the augurs were. She eyed the boys again. They sat quietly, awaiting their fate, suspicious of her because she wore the clothing of white people.

But they might know the finger signs, or even some of her words. She drifted toward them, and now they studied her. They were stocky boys, still in flesh, their gazes wary. Had they been stolen by the Utes? Sold here? She made the sign for her people, the Cheyenne, and they stared at her, surprised. She saw light bloom in their eyes. She made other signs: Wait! Be ready. Friend. Run.

They stared, perturbed and silent. They were brave boys, scornful of their fate, but they had yet to lift a basket of rock, or stagger up one of those log ladders or feel the whip. How swiftly they would change under the lash of the man in white.

She did not waste more time on them. They had been informed.

The man in white was amiably escorting Skye, Victoria, and the fat one through the works, past the older ones swirling the rock in bowls, past the places were people slept. He looked like a hawk with a rabbit in its talons, enjoying the moment before he snapped his curved beak over the neck of the rabbit. Yes, that one, O'Grady, was a hunter.

What sort of man was he, who put so many men to this task? Did he care about any of them or only for the yellow metal? Did he free any? Was the only escape from this place the foul pit where sharp-toothed creatures ripped away flesh from bone? Did he have a wife and children who lived handsomely because of these men staggering up the ladders? Aiee, what a one was that man in the white suit, exuding darkness just the way this earth, here, radiated darkness and pain, so much so that it made her body ache and her own bones hurt.

She caught up with them, and motioned to Victoria, her fingers flying:

"Two Arapaho boys, friends my people. Just brought here," she said, making words the Crow woman would grasp.

Victoria glanced sharply at the boys huddled in the shade of the open-sided building.

"We must take them away," Standing Alone said.

Victoria stared at her and at the boys, understanding the urgency in Standing Alone's plans. The Crow woman would not have to be told that these would be a gift to the Cheyenne People, two boys to breed into fine warriors.

"How do that?" Victoria signaled.

In truth, Standing Alone had no idea. "Talk your man," she signaled. "He know. Don't tell fat man."

Victoria nodded and caught up with the others. The man in the white suit was pointing into the yellow pit at the swarm of men loading gravel into baskets, staggering up wobbling ladders, and pausing to catch their breath at the top.

Grief bloomed in her. Was that how her son had spent his last breaths, staggering under weight that bent him double? Was he alone, with no one to share his ordeal? Did he yearn for his people, and the tallgrass prairies, and the summer winds? Did he see the boneyards, and know he would soon be scattered across them, bits and pieces of himself whitening in the cruel sun?

Did he feel his medicine had been taken away? That he would bring no honor to the People? That he would win no girl of the People, no war honors, no admiration of the People? That he would have no reputation as a warrior? Aiee, his life was like midnight.

There was a tautness in the air. Something was going to happen and she didn't know what.

She saw Victoria whispering to Skye, and saw him listen intently. He looked strange in his humble clothes. Victoria left Skye and fell back to where Standing Alone walked.

"He says big trouble."

"I want those Arapaho boys."

"Skye says, maybe there is a way. But he don't know it. It would take money."

"I will give them to my people!"

Victoria shook her head. "Skye got taken away long ago and never saw his people again. He's not gonna help you give Arapaho boys to the Cheyenne. If he helps you, they will go home to the Arapaho."

A great rage built in her. She glared sullenly at Skye's woman, who was nothing but an Absaroka.

The wheeling vultures flapped into the field of bones again, and she knew they were feasting on the dead. She wanted to get out; if she could not take those two boys with her, then she was through with this place, and through with Mexico. Her work was done. She had her daughter.

They were gathering now around the black carriage. The man in the white suit was smiling but his eyes were cold. They were talking, but she didn't grasp any of it.

"What are they saying?" she asked Victoria by sign.

"The man Hector Ramon O'Grady is saying that it takes much labor to make gold, and he has many mouths to feed, and Indians are poor workers, and he does not get rich."

"Are we going now?"

"Soon. They are saying adios."

Standing Alone watched the hawkish man, and suddenly she knew what she must do. She raced up to him, and the words flooded out in her native tongue, Cheyenne, and she could not think of anything else.

"Take me and let those Arapaho boys go. I am strong. I am twice as strong as those boys. Take me so the boys can live. You bought them but I will do more work for you. I will carry more stone up the ladders. Take me! I am a Cheyenne and strong and I will make gold for you!"

The Mexican man O'Grady stared, and finally turned to Skye.

"You have any idea what the woman wants?"

Skye shook his head.

O'Grady turned to Victoria. "You understand her?"

"A little."

Standing Alone tried again, slow, her voice piercing, her fingers making words. "You take me. I work hard. I am better than two little boys! You trade me for them. Boys go with the carriage! I give myself to you. I do twice as much as they do!"

She stared at their faces, seeing the blankness in them. The curse of language was walling her off.

"I think she wants to trade herself for them boys you got over there," Victoria said.

The man in white studied Standing Alone. "She wants to trade herself? She's not worth two strong boys."

Standing Alone somehow understood, her small grasp of this English tongue giving her understanding.

She knelt before this man in white and clutched his leg, and wept, the hot tears rising from her eyes and flooding her face with her sorrow.

He kicked and tugged, and finally booted her free.

"Out!" he said. "Get the squaw out."

48

S kye helped the trembling Cheyenne woman into the calash, filled with pity and horror. Hector Ramon O'Grady was a swine.

"Wait," said the *mayordomo*. He stared at her, assessing her body as if she were a draft horse. "Some savage women are strong. Tell her to get out and stand."

"Leave her alone," Skye said.

But the mine superintendent held out his claw to her, and she took it and stepped down to the sun-baked clay. He walked around her, assessing, boldly examining her arms, her shoulders, her wiry legs. She stared defiantly, her gaze never leaving him.

"I'll trade her for one boy," he said. He turned to Victoria.. "Tell her."

Victoria simply lifted one finger.

Standing Alone understood, straightened herself, and held up two fingers.

O'Grady thrust up one finger. "Tell her she can choose."

He turned to one of his muscular *capataces*, addressing him in Spanish. The man trotted toward the kitchen area, where the Arapaho boys waited.

"Señores, boys that young are almost worthless to me. I offered very little. They achieve little. They won't ever work off their indenture." He shrugged sadly. "No one else wanted them. I pitied them."

"Indenture," Skye said, knowing there was such loathing in his voice that O'Grady wouldn't miss his contempt.

"Would you care to work for me, Mister Skye? Actually, I pay well for brute labor, more than it's worth to feed and house these animals. You would be useful here."

It was a smoothly phrased threat, but Skye ignored it. "I saw black slaves in Missouri, and they were decently fed and clothed," Skye said. "I'll say that much for the Americans."

"We don't have slaves here."

O'Grady's *capataz* prodded the two Arapaho boys forward. Skye was shocked. One seemed barely nine or ten; the other a little older. They still wore the yellow-dyed loincloths and moccasins of their people, but that would last only days in rough rock.

Standing Alone studied the children; they watched her solemnly, their black eyes alive with fear. She pointed at the smaller one, the moonfaced boy who was half grown and far from possessing the bone and muscle of a man.

She spoke to Victoria in that patois of theirs.

Victoria translated: "Let this one go; give the other one an easy task, and I will trade myself."

Skye hated this trafficking in human flesh. He could scarcely bear to witness this brave woman's sacrifice.

Hector O'Grady nodded. So it was done.

Standing Alone spoke volubly to the boys, wanting desperately to say something to both of them even if her tongue was not theirs; and then to Victoria.

Victoria said, "She's saying that she wants the Arapaho boy to be given to her people, learn Cheyenne ways, but if the boy don't want to stay, he gets to go back to his people."

Standing Alone nodded.

So it had come to that. Skye thought back to the time at Bent's Fort when this woman had sought his help to find and free a Cheyenne boy and a girl. Now she would take the place of one, and her life would be short and hard.

"Grandmother," said Skye, "you won't understand my English words, but let the respect in my voice touch you. You are giving your life away, not for your son but for someone very much like him, that this boy might grow strong and come into his glory. I have never known a more beautiful and sad sacrifice. May you live forever in the memory of your people, and all people. I will carry your image inside of me."

O'Grady gestured. The *capataz* started to hustle the luckless older boy away. Skye watched the boy sag and stare at the yellow clay.

Standing Alone slowly approached the calash, where Little Moon sat rigid in her seat. She reached out to her daughter, smiled, touched her child's face, wiped her jet hair away from her eyes, and whispered things not meant for other ears. Tears slid down Little Moon's amber cheeks. Standing Alone whispered furiously, conveying instructions, requests, a hundred things, no doubt including a farewell to her husband, all of which rested now in the heart of the daughter she had found and rescued.

Standing Alone looked utterly beautiful.

"Damn it all," said Victoria. "Dammit, dammit, dammit."

Standing Alone helped the Arapaho boy slide into the calash and settle beside Little Moon. Childress for once looked overwrought.

Hector Ramon O'Grady took Standing Alone by the arm. "A pleasure to show you our operation," he said to Skye.

"And a word of advice, señor. Drive straight through Santa Fe. If the governor gets wind of you, he might reclaim his property."

"His property," muttered Skye.

O'Grady smiled. "Señor, you will thank me for the advice."

Skye watched the burly *capataz* herd Standing Alone away, until they disappeared in a distant adobe shack. The world somehow seemed smaller and harsher without her in it. Standing Alone had been like a pillar reaching the heavens.

"Ah, Skye, Sah, we'd better be off," Childress said nervously.

Skye slowly lifted the carriage weight and clambered to his seat in the creaking rig. He collected the lines in his rough hands and slapped them over the croups of the trotters, and slowly the calash circled away and a few minutes later a bluff hid the mine from sight.

Even Childress looked unusually somber. A great quietness fell upon them all, as visions of Standing Alone, courageous warrior woman of her people, filtered through their minds.

They had almost reached Dolores when Childress suddenly cried out. "I say, where is Shine?"

The monkey was not with them.

"Turn around, turn around," he bawled.

Skye found a flat where he could wheel the carriage around and collect Childress's rascally simian, and they slowly wended their way back to the mine as the sun was sinking.

A few minutes later they rode once again into the mining compound, and Skye headed up the slope to the building that housed the administration.

O'Grady emerged at once and stood waiting, while his segundos filtered out.

"We're missing the monkey," Skye said.

"Yes, he's here," O'Grady said. "There's his head."

There was Shine's little head swaying on a stake off to the side, its eyes lifeless, its lips opened forever.

"We do that to all thieves," O'Grady said. "It sets an example. Every once in a while a worker takes a notion to steal some gold. This is our response."

Childress groaned. The grinning head swayed on its crimsoned gibbet.

"Feisty little fellow. Hard to catch, but we caught him red-handed. Gold ingot in his little hairy hand. Pity, Skye. Too bad it wasn't a cigar."

Skye landed on the ground.

The mayordomo stepped back. "Touch me, you'll die," he said.

"All right, I will die."

He bounded into O'Grady and slammed him hard, knocking him down. Skye hammered the mayordomo, feeling his fists mash into the man's thin frame, feeling the air whoof from the man's lungs, feeling the man's teeth loosen in his jaw, feeling the bright light of justice in every blow.

But then the *capataces* landed on him, two, three, five, snaring his thrashing arms, yanking him off the *jefe*, kicking, jabbing, gouging. They pinioned his arms and returned his punches, booted him in the privates, doubled him over until he lay on the clay, puking, coughing, and even then they kicked him hard, tormenting his ribs.

O'Grady picked himself up, breathing hard. "Mean fists, Skye. I should make you one of my *jefes*." The man wiped blood from his nostrils. He turned and spat.

Then he snapped something in Spanish, and the burly foremen threw Skye onto the calash and slapped the horses. The carriage lurched. Skye wiped blood from his lips, seized the lines, and slowed the careening calash.

Childress sat moaning, his tear-streaked face buried in his hands.

They rode down the canyon and no one followed.

He felt Victoria's gentle hands dabbing at his face from behind, cleansing him, strengthening him.

He kept the trotters to a walk, not wanting to wear them out. He needed the cloak of darkness in Santa Fe, and that meant staying on the move if the horses could endure.

They passed through Dolores again, and no one stopped

them. Below, he rested the trotters and let them graze on a patch of grass as twilight deepened.

Not a word was spoken all that while.

He studied the two Indians, the girl silent and somber and tear-streaked, the boy wide-eyed and wary. Victoria had clothed them in her love, and now they nestled into her, on either side. As always, the barriers of tongue prevented talking.

"Shine deserves the Order of the Garter," Childress said.

"I thought you were a Galveston Bay privateer."

"That, too," said Childress.

49

Skye kept the trotters to a quiet walk, conserving their strength. Childress slumped numbly, watching the hills unfold as the calash rocked northward over a rutted road. Victoria sat across from him, the young Indians on either side, each nestled into her for comfort. She was a reassuring presence to them, the one native person they had with them.

The trader quietly studied the young people. The girl, Little Moon, was composed, though he supposed her thoughts were back there at the mine with the mother she had seen for only a few hours; the blessed mother who had, after four years, come for her, found her, set her free. The most beautiful of all mothers. Little Moon now had her life before her, and would rejoin her people, marry, raise proud Cheyenne, and might well prepare all her people for the new world that was encroaching on traditional Cheyenne life.

The boy was more of an enigma. He had spoken his name this afternoon and pointed to himself, but no one could translate it. *Ouo*, he had said of himself. The meaning would have to wait. Skye would find out the name at Bent's Fort, where many knew the tongue, including Kit Carson, whose wife was Arapaho. *Ouo* was trying hard to be manly, to be

a warrior, to be an Arapaho, and often he looked sternly
about. He would become all of these now; at the mine he
would have become only weary muscle and empty dreams
and faded hopes. But sometimes *Ouo* looked ready to bury
himself in Victoria's arms. Childress wondered whether it
was all too late. The Arapaho might not yet know it, but
their life would change as settlement progressed, and maybe
they would die off, diseased and devastated.

Was it worth it? Yes, Childress thought. It had all been
worth it. Little Moon was free. *Ouo* was free. Each could
live the lives they might choose to live. And Childress had
found out what he wanted to know.

But there was one who was no longer free, and Childress
thought of her now. No doubt they had put her right to work,
and even now, in the last light, she would be carrying terrible burdens trip after trip. From this day forward, her life
would no longer be her own. And yet she had chosen it so
that the boy nodding beside Victoria in this black coach
might receive a life.

Childress studied the slumped back of Mister Skye,
knowing the man hurt from his beating at the hands of the
mine's ruffians, knowing also that without Skye's indomi-
table courage and strength, this strange rescue would not
have happened. It might yet be thwarted if the governor had
troops out looking for them.

Skye had begun this venture not for money, but to help a
suffering woman, and her suffering children. That alone set
him apart from the run of men. Childress loved the man for
his courage and his honor and his artless integrity, and loved
his wife, too, the perfect mate for a man of the mountains
who scorned the wiles of civilization.

No one had spoken a word. No one wanted to. Childress
knew that everything had changed, somehow. His work here
was over, and he must wind this business up and make his
report. His name was not really Childress; neither was it
Jean Lafitte or Sir Arthur. Neither was he an agent of the

Republic of Texas, though his crew of traders at his post on the Arkansas River believed he was.

All those things had been camouflage, just as his gaudy cart, bizarre conduct, and startling dress had been camouflage, enabling him to probe where he wanted to probe, see what he wanted to see.

The monkey had been camouflage too, and now the monkey was dead, and everything had changed. He had loved that spider monkey, and grieved its sudden cruel death as if he had lost a son or a brother. That monkey had accompanied him for years, achieving what he could not achieve, sustaining him in bad moments, as if the monkey had a human intelligence, knew what needed to be done, and achieved it without even being asked.

Ah, Shine! Childress pushed that final image out of his mind and tried to focus on the graceful juniper-blanketed slopes around him, but there was only emptiness now. None of them, not Skye, not Victoria, not the Indian youngsters, would ever know what that little rascal had meant to him.

A chapter had ended. There were things to do now, in this darker, meaner world.

Skye rested and grazed the horses at a much-used spring as the slip of moon rose, bathing this land with a ghostly glow, almost phosphorescent. The scent of piñon pine sweetened the air. Victoria let the youngsters stretch their legs. Childress lumbered to the hard earth.

"Say, Mister Skye, we should talk a little."

Skye nodded.

"What time will we make Santa Fe?" Childress asked.

"Two, three hours. It'll still be dark."

"I'll be saying good-bye to you there."

"I thought you might."

"We've done what we could. You'll be heading out the Santa Fe Trail, back to Bent's Fort. I'll be going north to my post on the Arkansas. But we've some business to transact. I'll outfit you."

"Outfit us? With what?"

"This rig. It's worth plenty. We'll go see the American consul, Alvarez, most pleasant chap."

"I already owe him."

"Trust me. There's enough in this rig to put the four of you on horses and outfit you, too."

"What about you, Mister Childress?"

"I'll go back to privateering."

Skye laughed quietly. "Whatever you are, and I haven't the faintest idea, you were never a privateer."

"Then think of me as you will."

"Who are you, then?"

"No one you've heard of."

"We're talking in circles. What are you doing here? Are you an agent provocateur of the Republic of Texas?"

"For a while. It was a useful thing to be."

Skye shook his head. "I suppose you'll tell me if you want me to know."

"I'll say only this: our meeting was most fortunate for me, and by teaming up with you, I accomplished what I set out to do."

"You mean picking up the girl and the boy?"

"That, and letting me see how it all works."

Skye waited for more, but nothing more was forthcoming, so he smiled. "I don't suppose I'll ever know, then, mate."

"You're right about me, you know. I am a Londoner."

Skye nodded. He had plainly given up, and turned to stare at the darkened slopes. "I'm in your hands, mate. You're the only one among us who speaks Spanish; you know what I don't, and you're not saying who you are. Keep us safe, put us on horse, give us a weapon or two and some food, a blanket apiece, and we'll make it."

"Consider it done, Mister Skye."

The man who called himself Childress wished he could

reveal more, but confidentiality was important, and he couldn't break the seal.

As the night-chill deepened, Skye rounded up Victoria and the two Indians. "Two or three hours to Santa Fe," he said.

They rode through a soft summer's night without incident, and at midnight Skye steered the black calash through the narrow streets of the capital city until they were again at the plaza. He halted before Alvarez's mercantile.

"Wait here," Childress said, and mounted the long stairway, one step at a time, until he reached the vestibule and knocked. It took a long while before a yawning Alvarez opened.

"Childress? At this hour? Is there something wrong?"

"A moment, Señor Alvarez. Can you spare it?"

Alvarez studied Childress sharply, and waved him in.

It took some negotiating. Alvarez agreed to supply horses, saddle, tack, blankets, food, clothing, and a rifle and powder and ball to Skye's party. He would receive two matched trotters and a calash for it, and the only calash in New Mexico.

"And what of you, Mister Childress?"

"I have business here, some things to write and then I'll see."

"Business?"

The consul was fishing. Maybe, after Skye's party got away, the man who called himself Childress would explain. But not now. There were things to do under the cloak of darkness, and Alvarez swiftly dressed, lit a lantern, headed downstairs to his shadowed store, and set to work.

He opened the front door of his store, summoned Skye, and together they hauled the outfit to the calash.

"There is a livery barn out Palace Street. I will come with you," he said to Skye.

The calash creaked through empty dark streets.

The Mexican hostler sprang to life as soon as Alvarez awakened him, and by the wavering light of an oil lamp, he caught horses and saddled them. In time all was readied for Skye and his party: the weary trotters rested in a pen, four horses stood ready, and a burro was loaded with a pack-saddle and the new outfit.

"Well, Skye, this will see you through," Childress said.

"Some privateer you are, mate."

"I'm Her Majesty's viceroy for Borneo and Tanganyika, Skye."

Skye didn't laugh. "Whoever you are, sir, you're a noble-man and a prince."

"No, Skye, I am addressing the true nobleman, the natural lord of the wilds, generous and true and honorable. And his wife, who is all of those things, herself a duchess of this great realm."

Victoria looked ready to swear, but her gaze was filled with tenderness.

"Hurry, you'll need to be well clear of Santa Fe when dawn breaks."

"Dawn has already come for these young people, Mr. Childress."

"May it come for all enslaved people, Mister Skye. Be gone before daylight!" he cried.

Skye shook hands, and the mountaineer's grip was warm and firm, and he shook hands with the consul too, and then they mounted. Childress watched Skye, Victoria, and the savage boy and the girl ride softly into the soft night, and then they vanished from his sight, and he knew he would never see them again.

50

In the Moon When the Cherries are Ripe, Skye found Black Dog's Cheyenne camped in a cottonwood bottom on Big Sandy Creek, enjoying the sweet harvest of late summer. He rode past buffalo hides staked to the earth to be fleshed, woven baskets burdened with hackberries, heaps of roots and wild onions, and racks where strips of buffalo were drying for future use as pemmican and jerky. The buffalo were thick, the berries ripe, and the People were happy.

When Skye and Victoria rode into the village along with Little Moon and Ouo, escorted by the ever-vigilant Dog Soldiers, women and children alike crowded about them, whispering furiously. Most of the men were off hunting. Little Moon cried out her greetings as she recognized childhood friends, kin, and Chief Black Dog himself, who stood waiting before his lodge as the visitors approached, lean, coppery, wearing only a plain loincloth.

Little Moon! This was news!

Even as these people welcomed the long-lost Little Moon with sharp cries, they studied the Arapaho boy, wondering about him. He came from an allied tribe, and their gazes were friendly. There were questions on their faces and Skye

hoped to answer them all, despite the ever-present barriers
of tongue.

These Cheyenne were friends of William Bent, and some
would know a little English. But many more would understand Arapaho, and between them, Ouo and Little Moon
could tell their stories. They dismounted from their weary
horses under the watchful eyes of the Dog Soldiers, no
friends of Skye or the Crow woman Victoria, but it didn't
much matter.

Black Dog made them welcome, and heard their stories,
one by one, while the Cheyennes crowded close.

Even as Little Moon was speaking, her father appeared,
and there was a long, choked moment as they stared at
each other, and his troubled gaze surveyed her strange
cloth clothing and bare feet. The father, whose name Skye
remembered as Cloud-Watcher, was a graying warrior,
flanked by younger wives, who eyed Skye and Victoria with
frank dislike. He wore a necklace of human fingers and the
ensign of the Dog Soldiers, a quilled dog rope looped over
his shoulder, the warrior society eternally hostile to all who
were not of the People.

But that changed, even as Little Moon poured forth the
story of her capture by the hated Utes, life in Santa Fe as a
drudge for the chief of chiefs, release from captivity by
Standing Alone and Skye and Victoria and a certain fat
man. She spoke of all that happened afterward, including the trip to the mountain place where yellow metal was
clawed from the earth, and the amazing, beautiful sacrifice
of Standing Alone for the liberty and life of this Arapaho
boy, Ouo, whose name Skye learned was Raven.

The villagers listened in hushed silence, and when they
learned of Standing Alone's self-chosen fate, they cried out
in anguish. For now this little bronzed boy, standing uneasily before them, was vested with great medicine and sacredness by a woman of the People who had surrendered
her freedom, indeed her life, for him.

Skye wished he could understand the tongue of these people, because some of what was unfolding eluded him. But more and more, the chief, Black Dog, eyed him and Victoria, and when at last the stories were told and retold, he motioned them to be seated in a circle, and an honored boy presented the chief with a sacred pipe of this band. Black Dog ritually pointed the pipe stem to the sky, the earth, and the four winds: "Spirit above, smoke. Earth, smoke. East, West, North, South, smoke." And they smoked quietly, each filling his lungs in turn. It was a peace offering and a bonding of them all.

Now a translator appeared, a youth who had tarried at Bent's Fort, and he explained, in halting English, that these people would rejoice for four days the return of their young woman.

"She make be purified," he said. "In a bower she be cleansed with smoke of sweetgrass, welcomed, and returned to lodge of her father. And much more happen, for the bravery and beauty of Standing Alone be honored. No greater woman ever live among our people."

"I agree, mate. She will always live on in my mind, and in Victoria's mind too."

"She make a damn good Absaroka," said Victoria, paying the ultimate homage.

"The Arapaho boy, he be gone into the lodge of his new father, Cloud-Watcher, and there he learn our ways. But in honor the wishes of Standing Alone, he be offered his liberty soon, few moons. But we hope he stay, and be a son, and replace the one who died."

Grasshopper, whose name would never again be spoken here, but who was missed and grieved by everyone in the band.

Skye dug under his buckskins and pulled out the sacred bundle that Standing Alone had given him. Slowly he lifted it over his head, and handed it to Black Dog.

He turned to the translator. "Tell the chief that I am

returning the sacred bundle of his people. I have done what I was required to do."

Black Dog took it, nodded solemnly, and pressed a hand upon Skye's shoulder.

"You carried its power; you have honored it," the chief said.

The Cheyenne people stared at the medicine bundle, which had inspired the man who wore it, and Skye sensed a gladness in them.

And so these people made Skye and Victoria welcome. They fattened Skye's rawboned horses, housed Skye and Victoria in a small medicine lodge heaped with velvet-soft robes, served them the most succulent ribs of the buffalo cow, while the Cheyenne women swiftly sewed a complete fringed and quilled doeskin dress for Victoria, and a suit of skins for Skye, dyed across the chest and back in strong red and black colors, and added exquisitely quilled moccasins for them both. Skye at once put away his cloth clothes and wore the new ones, tying back his long hair with a yellow ribbon.

On the eve of the second day, Cloud-Watcher invited Skye and Victoria to his lodge, and there at twilight, before the whole band, he adopted Skye as his son and Victoria as his daughter, clasping a hand to the shoulder of each, thus paying great honor to them both. And Little Moon proclaimed them her brother and sister. Even the shy Arapaho boy, Ouo, Raven, had a gift for them: a little medicine bundle he made for each, which he hung on a thong over Victoria's breast and the other over Skye's. The crowd admired that, and patted the boy happily.

Victoria had sighed as the boy honored her, and Skye knew how much she would have liked a son of her own, but her womb had always been empty. Now, at last, she had a son in this boy, and she smiled at him, and pressed his hands between hers, and found in him that which she had always yearned to have.

Skye noted that several of the young Cheyenne boys were paying court to Little Moon, though most stayed away. It was plain that most of the boys wanted nothing to do with her; she had in their eyes been somehow demeaned by her servitude among the Mexicans. But one youth in particular, who had a mind of his own and whose war honors included an eagle feather, was playing the flute outside her lodge, and Skye sensed that soon Cloud-Watcher would acquire a son-in-law, and Little Moon, a sweet sixteen, would begin her new life in joy, living freely within the traditions of her people.

On the fourth day Black Dog himself held a ceremonial feast, at which he made Skye and Victoria members of the tribe and of his people, with much oratory, strokes of vermilion on the cheek, and fragrant smoke of tobacco mixed with red willow bark. Victoria, of the Crows, endured this with dignity, setting aside her own passions to permit this great honor.

"Almost like Absaroka!" she exclaimed.

"For you both have brought one of ours to us, and you both helped our beloved Standing Alone to fulfil her life," intoned the youthful translator. "And so you shall always be honored among us, and wherever the People gather, your names will be spoken of with respect."

Skye thanked them simply. He was glad.

The next morning he and Victoria loaded up their burro with its pack, saddled their horses, and headed away, escorted for half a day by an honor guard of the Dog Soldiers.

But at last they rode alone, ever north, through the tall tan grasses bobbing in the breeze, toward the land of her people, the Crow.

51

Santa Fe
Province of New Mexico
Mexico

17 August 1841

Thomas Fowell Buxton, Bart.
Castle Hedingham
Essex, England

Sir Thomas:

I am pleased to report that I have concluded operations in the Republic of Texas, United States Indian Territory, and the northernmost province of Mexico, on behalf of the British and Foreign Anti-slavery Society. A detailed report will follow in a fortnight but I will write briefly at once and entrust this to merchants en route to St. Louis over the Santa Fe Trail.

Slavery in the Republic of Texas is a variant of the sort in the United States South. The black is not a citizen of the republic, has virtually no rights, and serves entirely at the whim of the master, without hope of liberty. We should call attention to this in parliament;

United States abolitionists can do little about it, operating from a foreign nation, as it were.

In the unsettled portions of United States territory, the Ute Indians, in particular, abduct children and sell them in Mexico, where there are traffickers of human flesh peddling wares to ranchers and mine owners. In this they are very like black African slavers. But the other tribes are not free from the taint of slavery, though it is milder, built around war captives, and usually results in adoption into the tribe.

A much more subtle variety of bondage finds form in Mexico, where slavery is theoretically forbidden by state and church. There are several types, ranging from the cruel and murderous servitude imposed on captive native peoples, often in the mines, to more benign versions of slavery, such as the peon system which binds the peon to his master through perpetual debt. Other forms of indenture operate in Mexico as well.

I will recount my adventures when I return to London. Suffice it to say that I employed my usual stratagems, being highly visible, even gaudy, to conceal my true purposes. I had the good fortune to obtain a commission from Texas President Lamar, which enabled me to study the new republic without hindrance, and even better fortune later on, when I encountered a famed border man looking for enslaved Indian children in Mexico. Both situations enabled me to discover everything the anti-slavery society wishes to know, while my true purposes remained undetected.

I shall drop the nom de guerre Childress, which is now worthless, and will let you know by coded letter what new one I shall next adapt to my purposes. I leave shortly for the Mexican province of California, to examine, as you wish, servitude of the local Indians at missions and ranchos, with a special emphasis on their diminishing numbers, and after that I will take ship to Australia to see about forced labor in the penal colonies, especially as it involves spouses of convicts, freed women and children, and ticket-of-leave men unable to return to England.

A full report follows. I trust the work of the society proceeds well. Garrison and others in the States are furiously arousing sentiment against the southern system, which debases masters as much as slaves, but can do nothing about Texas or Mexico. We can do much.

I will sign myself simply,

W

AUTHOR'S NOTE

This novel, like others in the series, is pure fiction, but is grounded in historical reality. The Ute Indians did abduct the children of neighboring tribes and sell them in Mexico, where the captives usually lived a short, brutal life. It is recorded that Kit Carson once took pity on a Paiute boy held captive by the Utes, and purchased his freedom for forty dollars, a large sum in those days.

William Wilberforce and others in Parliament worked diligently through the early part of the nineteenth century to eradicate slavery throughout the British Empire, as well as worldwide. His successor, Thomas Fowell Buxton, who was made a baronet in 1840, worked tirelessly to abolish slavery, and while some of his efforts came a-cropper, he exerted incalculable moral force against the institution.

Some of the characters in the story are historical. These include William Bent, Alexander Barclay, Lucas Murray, Juan Andres Archuleta, Governor Manuel Armijo, and U.S. Consul Manuel Alvarez. All of them have been depicted fictionally.

I am grateful to that formidable historian and editor, Dale L. Walker, for supplying me with ideas and material and encouragement.

Richard S. Wheeler
November 2001

The Fire Arrow

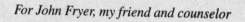
For John Fryer, my friend and counselor

1

Death rose out of the night. A rush of hooves on frosted ground. A chilling howl. Whickering horses. A faint rip, thud, gasp, and sigh. The earth trembled.

Barnaby Skye struggled awake. Violence had struck the camp. There was only the thin leather of his lodge protecting him, and that was no protection at all. Victoria gasped.

He sat up, threw the thick buffalo robe aside, jamming away the sleep. Dead ash, embers gone, only blackness inside his lodge. He peered through the smoke hole. Bright moonlit night. Stars scattering through the October skies. The Judith River country, aglow in the moon, full of buffalo, full of death.

He knew then. A raid. Blackfeet, who else? The horses already gone but now a worse evil, the enemy in the midst of the Crow hunting camp, every man for himself, death stalking the camp.

He felt about for his Hawken, didn't find it, but found his belaying pin, that weapon of choice for generations of British seamen. A polished hickory club, thick, heavy, and flared to protect the hand or stop its passage through a ship's fitting. He grasped it just in time. The flap burst open and a dark force smashed in, swinging savagely. A battle-axe slashed the lodge cover, bedded itself in the robes inches from

Skye. A knife glinted. Skye jabbed first, felt the belaying pin connect, then smashed hard just as a knife whipped by. Caught the warrior at the base of the neck. Skye jammed the stick into his face, heard teeth snap. The warrior retreated, howling, staggering out into the moonlight.

Skye sprang up, pushed outside. The last of the Blackfeet were retreating north. The moonlight caught shadowy forms retreating into the gloom. A few half-naked Crows, kin of Skye's wife, Victoria, chased on foot, carrying lances, only to fall back as arrows fell among them. One gasped and tumbled to the frosted grass.

Skye was barefoot but he scarcely noticed. He did not see a horse anywhere. His own two buffalo runners, picketed beside his lodge, had vanished. In the distance, the thrumming of two hundred hooves diminished and died. Nine lodges of Crows, and not a horse among them, unless a few escaped the herding of the Blackfeet. Crow warriors armed themselves, but it was too late.

It had happened so fast. The Blackfeet had overwhelmed or tricked or killed the night herders, the village youths not yet old enough for battle, and made off with the prized horses. But their triumph would not be complete without visiting some death or injury on the hated Crows. So they had raided the camp on Louse Creek after driving off the ponies, entering lodges, counting coup, killing if they could, making a great victory out of it. Death in the night.

The hush suddenly returned, and it was as if there had been no violence, no death, no injury. Several Crow warriors hunted for horses, trotting here and there. Women, along for the skinning and hide-scraping and preserving, peered fearfully from lodge doors. Silvery moonlight flooded the encampment, making the lodges almost as visible as in bright day. And now they wailed, for there were bodies sprawled grotesquely on the frosty hardpan.

Skye studied the murk from whence a last hurrah of arrows might come, but he saw only the silvered limbs of autumn-bare trees and brush along the creek. It had been a poor place to camp. He trotted toward a knot of people gathered around one of the fallen.

It was the boy, Knot-on-Top, and he was dead, pierced by a Blackfoot arrow. His lifeless eyes studied the moon. Hardly a dozen years had this man-child lived. Three women knelt beside him, including his mother, Wolf Dreams. She did not wail. She sat mutely, cradling her son's arm in her lap.

Grim warriors guarded the perimeter, but it was too late. Grief had come to this buffalo-hunting camp. The fletching and the dyed rings on the arrow protruding from the chest of Knot-on-Top told the story to anyone who knew of these things: Piegan. The most numerous and sometimes most pacific of the Blackfeet bands, and all the more dangerous for that.

"Aieaa," muttered Otter, the headman who had led this hunting party to this desolate end.

Skye sorrowed, and trotted toward another downed Crow, fearing the worst. He was not mistaken. Sees Dawn, the other boy guarding the herd, lay facedown, his head cleaved by a war axe, perhaps the very one that nearly chopped Skye's head in two. He would never see another dawn. He was Victoria's nephew and clan-brother. She would weep and in her own way vow death and disgrace upon whatever Blackfoot had slaughtered one of her own. Where was she? Skye didn't see her, and wondered about it.

Off in the murk, several Crow men returned leading a few horses. So some had escaped the Blackfeet net after all, slipped into brush in the night. Skye studied the small band, looking for his two dun buffalo runners and not seeing them. He owned only three horses including one for Victoria, and was poor by Crow standards, for a man's worth was measured in horses. Skye had neither the skills to capture any nor the means to buy any.

He wondered where Victoria was. She must have been

deep asleep. He would check on her. There was little he could do here in the frost, as the moon bathed the fallen. He had some small reputation among the Crows as a valued warrior and hunter, but he could not speak their tongue enough to make friends or take part in the village life. It was time to check on Victoria, whose silence worried him.

He hastened to his small lodge, a place shared only by his woman, and crawled in. Instantly he knew something was wrong. He dropped to his knees beside her, shocked by her long silences, and her brief desperate gasps for air, and the strange twist of her body, her head cocked backward, mouth open to suck life into her lungs.

Too dark! He could see nothing.

"Victoria!"

She gasped.

"Victoria! What?"

She spasmed, some sort of shudder rolling down her small, lithe body. He tugged the buffalo robe aside, and then he couldn't pull it free. The robe was pinned to her. Then he discovered the thin, cruel wand of wood rising out of the robes, the feathered end of an arrow, the same arrow that had awakened him with its soft rip through the lodge cover.

"Victoria!" The sight of her, so dim in blackness, seared him.

He needed fire!

He scrambled for wood, found some just outside the lodge door that she had gathered in the evening, grabbed some handfuls, set them upon the cold firepit in the center of the lodge, found his powder horn lying next to his Hawken, dribbled some over the kindling, hunted blindly through his possibles until he found his flint and steel, fitted the steel through his ham-thick fingers, and struck sparks savagely. The loose powder flared, blinding him.

She trembled and gasped.

One small stick caught, and then another, small blue light, and then welcome yellow. He could see. She wasn't looking at him; she stared straight up, a death rictus twisting her lips, her eyes sightless.

"Oh, no . . ."

Fire at last, tender flickering light casting its gloomy rays upon the small household of Barnaby Skye. The arrow had pierced the robe, and pierced Victoria under the robe. He could not see where and was afraid to touch her or it. She gasped again. Her lungs weren't working. Swiftly he clasped his great trembling hands over her chest, pushed air out, and let her suck air in. Something was stopping her lungs from drawing air in and out. Her face was blue. The fire wavered and started to die. He thrust more brush over the dwindling flame until it flared again.

She wasn't breathing. He squeezed her chest and she gasped. He pushed and pulled her ribs, making air move.

He needed help, but where could he turn?

He summoned words and yelled.

"Come!" he cried into the moonlight.

Someone did come, a woman whose face he couldn't see. Then he heard talk, and two women crawled into his lodge and took it all in with swift glances. He knew the women: old Makes Rain and her sister, Lifts the Doe. Makes Rain was a blessing; she was reputed to have great powers of healing. But she was also no friend of Victoria. For Makes Rain didn't believe that a woman of the Crow people should marry someone else.

She glanced sharply at Skye, and then produced a small, worn paring knife that had seen much work at this buffalo camp. Slowly she inserted the knife into the robe at the place where the arrow had punctured it, and sawed through the robe, little by little, while Victoria gasped, until at last the robe was freed and she and Lifts the Doe could peel it away from Victoria, ever so carefully.

Victoria was gasping again, and Skye slowly squeezed and released her ribs until she was breathing, if the slow suck of air into her lungs might be called breath. The Blackfeet arrow protruded from her abdomen, just under the ribs, lit by the dying flame. Blood had collected around the wide slit of a wound, staining her trade-cloth chemise. Gently, the old woman sliced away the cloth until the wound lay exposed. The arrow had pierced upward two or three inches from the abdomen, no doubt cutting into those muscles that operated her lungs. A broad steel point, probably a Hudson's Bay trade item, had buried itself in her, and there was no way to remove it without starting a rush of red, red blood.

They stared, helpless, at that fatal shaft. An inch more would have killed her but the lodge wall and robe had slowed the thrust. Victoria lay gasping, doomed unless she could breathe, and breathe soon.

2

Victoria gazed up at Skye, helpless and desolate and in pain. Skye compressed her chest again, and again she sucked air; a moment's life. But she was sinking. And he could do so little for this woman he loved so much.

Tears had gathered in her eyes; he could see the wetness in the flickering light. She was struggling for life but her lungs had quit her.

"Victoria. I must pull that arrow."

She nodded.

"More fire," he said to Makes Rain, in her own tongue. She stared, not liking the commands from a young man not of her people. But then she nodded, slipped outside, brought in wood, laid it carefully on the flames, fed it until the fire rose hot.

Skye squeezed Victoria's chest again, and again, and again, making breath with his hands. Then he withdrew his thick-bladed buffalo skinning knife and laid the blade on the flame.

Long ago, aboard the ships of the Royal Navy, he had assisted the ship's surgeon a few times. Perhaps he was chosen because he could read; most seamen couldn't. He had watched awful things, limbs sawed off, the trepanning of a skull, and the cauterization of wounds.

A red-hot knife blade was all that would stop the bleeding once he wrestled the arrow from her body. He had no curved surgical needle, no gut or string or thread to close her wound.

He waited for the knife to heat. The women stared, uncertain of his intent, waiting for death. Lifts the Doe began a low death song, certain she was witnessing the last moments of Victoria's flickering life.

The flame was slow to heat the knife, cold and smoky. Skye pumped her lungs, forcing her to suck in air, hating the pain he was causing, hating the worse pain to come, the blood, the desperation. He had only the knife. If it failed to cauterize, she would perish.

Then he took hold of the arrow.

"Victoria, this will hurt, and I can't help it."

She could not speak. She stared up at him, her desperation stamped across her features.

He tugged. The arrow didn't budge. She screamed. The women held her down. That was good. He tugged harder, twisting the arrowhead slightly, fearful of losing the point. If the shaft came free without the point, Victoria was dead.

He rocked it back and forth, trying to increase the angle each time, while she shuddered and convulsed. It did no good; the tip was buried deep in her flesh.

He wept. She convulsed now, and no grip of the women could stay her from writhing in fearsome pain.

Skye was sweating; the lodge had turned unbearably hot.

He pulled upward, fearful of losing the tip. Blood gouted from the wound. Every time he moved the shaft, blood welled up, a grim red warning of what would come.

Victoria never spoke. She didn't have air enough to speak. He remembered to compress her chest again, and felt her suck air as it expanded. She was in utter torment. He was sickened by what he was inflicting on her.

Nothing was working. Time was dwindling. He slumped over her, pressing his big stubby hands over her abdomen, quieting himself, drawing his own failing strength from some place beyond his merely mortal powers.

He lifted the arrow gently, trying to draw it out by exactly the same path it entered. It gave ground. He had not lost the arrowhead. He tried again, pulling along the trajectory of its entry as best he could tell. The arrow resisted one long dreadful moment, and then slid steadily outward. Then, at last, it came free. The tip was thick with gore. Now bright blood hemorrhaged from her, pooling outward, spreading over her abdomen, draining into the brown robes.

But she gulped for air.

He grabbed the knife, feeling the fierce heat around the bone handle. It was not cherry-hot but it would have to do. He wiped her wound free with one hand and then swiftly brought the broad tip down over the wound, or at least what he could see of it, because blood obscured it. The heated tip pressed into her flesh, spitting steam and blood and frying her skin.

She screamed, a scream so heartrending he loathed himself, yet within that scream was breath. He held the fiery tip to the puncture, feeling flesh sear under it, feeling his own sweat roll down his face. The women held her, kept her from writhing free.

He lifted the tip. The blood had stopped. The wound was a mass of bubbling, seared flesh. The cauterization had taken hold. If she didn't die from internal bleeding, and if her lungs were no longer paralyzed, she might live.

She still writhed. He put the blade back into the fire, fearful that he might need it again. But no more blood oozed from that angry patch of Victoria's side.

He fought back tears. But there was no time for tears. This camp was still in mortal peril. The Piegans might return anytime to finish what they had started.

Makes Rain stared dourly at Skye. Her face told him that this was a thing she had never seen, something sinister, something not known to the People. He didn't care. He watched Victoria's chest, watched the erratic working of her lungs, the long, alarming pauses, followed by sudden spasms of breathing. It would get better. The arrow point was gone. He picked up the bloody arrow, memorizing the thin bands of paint that circled it, the sure mark of its owner. He would remember that paint, that signature, that fletching, this very arrow. And someday when he found its owner, there would be a reckoning.

The cauterization held. Lifts the Doe was wiping away the blood. Victoria writhed, unable to cope with the pain. Gently he wiped her brow and placed his thick hand over her forehead, offering what little he had, which was only love.

The lodge was hot. But he would not step into the icy night. Not until she was quiet, not until the worst had passed, not until she could speak to him, for she had not spoken a single word from the time the arrow struck until now. He held that sinister stick in his hand, not wanting to set it aside.

He had saved her, maybe. For all these years they had walked the paths together. He was a Londoner who could never go home; she had befriended him, loved him, and also taught him to live as the Crow people lived, hunting and gathering, fending off hostile tribes but sometimes raiding other people, gathering furs and robes to trade at the posts run by white men.

He had not been a good provider. How little he knew of hunting and war when he first fled from the Royal Navy and made his way inland to this remote fastness of North America. Much of what he now knew, she had taught him. His trapping friends had taught him more about surviving in the wilds, but there was always the day of reckoning, when the pelts or hides that were the fruits of a year's hard toil were placed on a trader's counter and exchanged for a pitiful few things, powder and shot, a few knives, and trinkets for her. Trapping hadn't been much of a living.

But his free-roaming life had been immeasurably sweeter

than the one from which he fled, and each day he rejoiced in his liberty, for he was a sovereign of the wilds and she was his queen, and somehow their love, which stretched across vast barriers of understanding, had deepened and matured.

Now she hovered between life and death, her very soul afloat over her, ready to wing away into the awful void. She breathed, if raggedly. The old women sat stoically, watching Victoria wrestle with death, even as the rest of the night slipped away. Skye heard occasional voices. Several times a Crow man or woman had spoken to Makes Rain, talking so swiftly he could not catch their words. But he knew she was giving them reports on Victoria and in turn receiving word about the condition, and defenses, of the Crow hunting camp.

And so the night passed. He lay down beside her and placed a hand again on her forehead, hoping somehow to convey to her that he was watching over her and that if she had the will to live, she would live, and there would be many more sweet days and sweeter nights.

He had taken her east once, and she had seen the cities and habitats of the Americans, and that had given her understandings that eluded others of her people. She didn't like it there even though she had marveled at the wonders of the Europeans who had settled the United States. And she wasn't herself until she was back in the home country of her people, mistakenly called the Crows by English-speaking explorers and mountain men and traders.

He slipped the cooled knife back into its sheath at his belt, and sat quietly through the quickening dawn. When light poured through the smoke hole, the old women stirred, for they too had kept a vigil all through that night. Makes Rain said something softly that Skye didn't understand, but then she took one of his hands and clasped it between hers, and rubbed her cheek with it, and Skye understood.

The fire dwindled. Sun caught the lodgepoles. Outside,

the hunting party was salvaging what it could of the disaster, which wasn't very much. They would not have horses to haul away the tons of pemmican, hides, and jerky as well as the households of the Crow people.

Skye continued to sit cross-legged beside Victoria, never abandoning her. But soon after dawn, her breathing changed, grew less labored, more steady, less desperate, and he sensed she had weathered the ordeal. If somehow he could keep her quiet for a while she would heal.

But how could he do that? He and she would be alone in their lodge, on the edge of Blackfeet country, while the Crow people journeyed back to their own ground, most of them without horses. And Skye had none, not even one for a travois that might haul her away to safety. The trouble had barely begun.

3

Victoria had not spoken since the Piegan arrow had pierced her side, but some ineffable change had come with daylight, some slight progress. Skye quietly jammed his stovepipe hat on his long locks and stepped into the morning, which came late this time of year, and surveyed the camp on Louse Creek.

He counted seven horses, all that had escaped the Blackfeet herders. Nine lodges, including his own. His horses, two buffalo runners and Victoria's mare, were gone. Several young warriors stood vigil on the surrounding hilltops but this Crow camp could offer only a pathetic defense against the Blackfeet if they should return.

Skye had the only good rifle in the camp, though its headman had an old trade musket and another warrior had an ancient Northwest smoothbore. They were defenseless and the Crows knew it. Perhaps the lurking Blackfeet knew it too.

Around him, the Crows were preparing to abandon this place of bad medicine. They would walk. All seven remaining horses were being fitted with travois. These would carry the precious lodge covers, but not the poles, and what few possessions each family had brought along, including some of the abundant buffalo meat from the successful hunt.

But much would be left behind, including vast stores of fresh pemmican, some jerked meat, and scores of fleshed buffalo hides. These would be cached but no one knew whether there would be anything left when the Crows returned. Animals were skilled at breaking into caches, as were other peoples. In hours after the Crows left, this place of slaughter would be overrun by wolves that would devour gut piles, discarded bone and meat. Anything left by the wolves would be dinner for coyotes, or eagles and hawks, or a dozen other raptors and predators. All night, every night, the mournful howl of wolves had circumscribed the camp on Louse Creek.

Skye would stay. He would keep his vigil, he would sit beside the woman he loved, and if it was their fate to be overwhelmed alone, far from help, then he would die beside her. Not that he wished that result, but it was the measure of his iron-hard commitment to her. He and Victoria would walk through fortune and misfortune together.

This was a place of death. The families of the two dead youths were preparing them for their spirit journeys in deep silence. The women would wail their grief later, but now they were wrapping the poor young men, Sees Dawn and Knot-on-Top, in blankets and tying the bundles in thong. Two others were injured, sitting mutely, wrapped in bloody trade cloth, their faces maps of pain. The surviving men were lashing lodgepoles to the limbs of nearby cottonwoods, preparing a place where these young men would be given to the sun.

Grief lay heavy upon this Crow camp, but so perilous was their condition that it was boxed into the souls of the people as they struggled with death, loss, abandonment of wealth and food, hides, tallow, lodges, and horses. Bad medicine here. Something felt in their bones. The headman, Otter, lived under a cloud; he who organized this hunt had offended the powers that animated the world.

Skye said nothing. He had not fully mastered the difficult Crow tongue, though he could communicate well enough and was fluent in sign language, filling in with his hands when his tongue failed him.

He found Otter, the headman who had told them all that his medicine was good; there would be a fine hunt, much meat, many hides, from the buffalo brothers. There had been all of that and more. Otter stared dourly as Skye approached, a small curt nod acknowledging the presence of the alien Englishman in this Crow camp.

"You are leaving?" Skye asked.

Otter stared and finally nodded.

"We must stay."

"You will be alone. I cannot spare anyone to stay with you."

"I know that."

"After she dies, cache what you can. We will return for it."

"She will not die."

"I am told she will."

Skye sensed the thing that always puzzled him about the Crows, a fatalism. Once the future was mysteriously foreseen, all one could do was surrender to it.

"I will bring her when I can."

"You stopped the blood with fire, so I am told. This is a strange thing."

Skye wanted to tell this headman of ship's surgeons and what few things he had learned in the Royal Navy, but he knew that would tax his ability to convey thoughts in the Crow tongue so he let it pass. Let the Crows think he possessed medicine.

"I have seen it done," was all Skye said.

"We will leave soon. But first there is the thing that must be done," Otter said. He was alluding to the rites of passage for the dead, the surrendering of the fallen to the spirit land, the long trail to the stars. They had died in battle, bravely, with great honor, and their path would be strewn with petals.

Skye studied the anonymous ridges of the Judith country, half expecting a howling war party to crest one and
bring death to the wounded Crows. But this cloudless and
windless day was as silent as nature ever got. The Blackfeet were content with their victory, a great one. Upward of
fifty horses, many coups, and who knows what else? The
Blackfeet were a proud and dangerous people, noble in bearing, and Skye admired them. But he was a Crow by adoption and marriage and now his heart was given to these who
had taken him in and welcomed him in their lodges. The
Crow were a proud people too.

The men had finished making the palls for the dead.
These were lodgepoles tied across the limbs of the cottonwoods along Louse Creek. A silence befell the camp. There
was no medicine man among them, so Otter led the way
down to the creek, through a quick silence, as the people
collected behind him. Then, Pretty Weasel, the father of
Knot-on-Top, lifted the blanketed form of his son to the
scaffold and gently settled it there. Within the blanket was
his boy, and also his son's amulets, his medicine things, and
offerings from his kinfolk.

None of Sees Dawn's kin were present this hunting trip,
so Otter and Pretty Weasel lifted his heavy form upward
until it rested beside his friend and clan-brother Knot-on-
Top. Now the women wept while the rest stood gravely
around.

These two would be mourned in the Crow winter camp
on the Musselshell River. But now there was no time; the
buffalo hunters must walk away from the lost, whose names
would never again be spoken. Walk away, three days and
then some, walk away to their lodges and then mourn.

Hastily the small congregation loaded lodge covers onto
the travois and hoisted parfleches to their backs, and hid
what they could under a caved-in cutbank. The cache
wouldn't fool any animal, and probably not any foe either,
but there wasn't any choice.

Otter approached Skye, who watched them load, cradling his Hawken in his arms.

"If you are not back before the moon is full, we will know, and grieve," he said.

"We'll be back."

"We'll send help."

"We need horses. A travois for Many Quill Woman," he said, alluding to Victoria's Crow name.

"What are you going to do?"

"Make this camp disappear. Hang the meat as far away as I can drag it. Scatter ashes."

"And our clan-sister?"

"I will be with her night and day, and when I can move her a little, I will."

Otter nodded. Skye liked the man, who now bore a heavy burden, for nothing worse than bad medicine could life's fortunes inflict on a Crow headman.

He watched them flee, an unseemly haste in them as they staggered away, carrying too much, the horses straining under the loads of the travois. The poles bent under the overload and plowed furrows even in the thawed ground. Skye wondered how long it would be before travois poles snapped or horses broke down.

Then they disappeared over the ridge to the south and he stood alone in a ruined camp. Tonight the wolves would come.

He had heavy work ahead, but he would see to Victoria first. He studied the horizons for movement, saw only a circling of ravens, and then ducked into his small dark lodge. The fire had died and it was cold.

She lay on her back, awake, staring up at him, her body twisted slightly as if to shelter the wound in her side.

"Dammit, Skye, you hurt me," she said softly.

"I was afraid you would never speak again."

"I hurt."

"You're alive."

"Sonofabitch!" she said. She used white men's expletives promiscuously, usually to vent anger.

He settled on his knees beside her. "I had to stop the blood."

"I couldn't breathe."

He lifted the wicked arrow with its red-stained iron tip, and showed it to her.

"This far in," he said, showing how far the blood had soaked it. "We will keep this arrow."

She stared, and he saw a wetness gather at the corner of her eyes.

"Now that you saved my life, Skye, I am your slave. That is how such a debt must be paid."

"You're my slave forever," he said. "And I am yours. How many times have you saved mine?"

"I am tired," she said, closing her eyes.

4

Skye checked her wound, fearing most of all fresh bleeding. He pulled the robe back, baring her tawny flesh. It was a small wound, barely an inch across, but blistered and angry all around where the heat of his knife had scorched her. The ugly wound itself suppurated, and the flesh in all directions was red and dark. But she didn't bleed; her lifeblood was not leaking into the brown buffalo robes.

He could do no more. She lay with closed eyes enduring unimaginable pain. He slipped outside into a quiet November afternoon. There was much to do. The ribs of the abandoned lodges poked the sky, and he intended to dismantle them. His safety depended on concealment. The creek-side encampment had a haunted quality, with the cones of lodgepoles mute testimony to flight and trouble.

Louse Creek was a good place to hide because it was notched in the floor of the basin, but a bad place to be caught in an ambush for there was no way to escape the valley of death. Hide and be safe; be discovered and die. It was that simple.

Both the Blackfeet and Crows used four-pole lodge frames; that is, four poles were tied together and spread into a pyramid, and other poles laid in afterward. But there were subtle differences even in the small hunting lodges, and

Skye knew that any Blackfoot warrior would see in a glance that this was a Crow camp. Skye would remedy that swiftly by dismantling the ghost village and piling brush around his own lodge. The lodgepoles would make firewood.

There was household debris abandoned in flight, and he marveled at the number of good robes left behind, simply lying in the grass. He salvaged several and took them into his own small lodge. In all the years of living in the wilderness as a mountain man and as a squaw man, he had never slept comfortably on hard ground, especially cold ground. He thought of it as a failing. The Yank mountain men seemed to adapt to such hardship, but the hammocks on the ships of the Royal Navy were far more comfortable. Now he and Victoria would sleep on several thick warm robes and have even more to pull over them when he could not build a fire.

The Judith country was rife with buffalo this year, and other parties would be hunting here. Blackfeet most of all, but also Gros Ventres and Flatheads, perhaps Kootenai, or even Shoshones or Bannocks. This time of year the buffalo broke into smaller bands so they could forage better; in the summer they collected into giant herds. Hunters from all the tribes relished this time of year when they could surround and slaughter the smaller bands. The Crows had thought to make meat, collect hides, produce pemmican and jerky, and fill leather pouches with valuable tallow. They knew the risks of coming this far north but knew the risks were worth the reward. This time they were wrong.

Skye studied the horizons, seeing nothing. But he kept his percussion-lock Hawken close, and did not neglect his powder horn. He was a stocky man, usually clean-shaven, whose hair hung loose about his head, and whose blue eyes had a way of squinting at distant things and making out shapes and forms not visible to others.

Quickly he dismantled the ghost lodges, pulling the poles away, and then dropping and untying the four-pole pyramids that formed the core of the structures. These had been erected by Absaroka women who were very good at setting up a lodge and making it comfortable.

It took only a half hour to drop the skeletons. He dragged the scattered lodgepoles into nearby brush, hidden from casual sight. He hid debris, kicked dirt over the ash of cook-fires, buried wastes, filled two canteens with the water of Louse Creek, and saw to his meat. The Crows had abandoned two forequarters of buffalo, now hanging from a cottonwood tree, well above the reach of any animal except a bear. They were heavy, and bent the limb and threatened to break the braided elkskin ropes suspending them. He and Victoria would have ample food if these were not disturbed. But even smaller creatures, including ravens and magpies and eagles, could demolish the meat, as could a sustained chinook, or warm period. Except for some pemmican that was what would have to sustain him, for he could not risk a rifle shot.

This campsite didn't feel right. He swore a dozen eyes were studying him from the hills guarding the valley. He ached to move his own lodge deep into brush, but not yet, not until he could be sure that Victoria could be carried without breaking open that arrow wound. For the moment, he would stay where he was, keep vigil, and hope no hunting party found him during this time of healing.

His gaze lifted constantly to the ridges, knowing how many hunters were flocking through the Judith country this time of year when hides were prime and buffalo were fat. But all he saw was anonymous blue sky, an occasional crow or hawk, and all he heard was the occasional whisper of wind eddying down the shallow valley of Louse Creek, wind with snow on its breath, wind that had only recently flowed over the white-covered Moccasin Mountains as the trappers called them, or the Big Belts, or the Highwoods, not far from the great falls of the Missouri.

A flock of noisy magpies, iridescent black and white,

settled on the abandoned camp, making dinner out of scraps of meat, bits of flesh scraped from fresh hides, and a thousand bugs shaken from the fresh hides as the women worked them. One magpie stood apart on a low branch, and then flew to a perch close to Skye's lodge and sat quietly. Skye understood and rejoiced.

He slipped into his lodge and found Victoria staring at him from pain-filled eyes.

"The magpies are here, and one waits outside," he said.

She nodded, and her response disappointed him. The magpie was her spirit helper, her counselor and guardian.

"The magpies, dozens of them," he said, but she simply stared in the dusk of the lodge.

He felt a certain foreboding and placed a hand on her forehead. She was burning up. Fever, not unexpected after such a wounding.

Now the magpie outside seemed more ominous; as if this one were beginning a vigil. Skye felt a desolation crawl through him. He found a small cook pot, headed for the creek, filled it with icy water, and returned. The magpie was gone. He slipped inside, soaked an old shirt in the cold, and laid it across her forehead. She moaned, not liking the cruel chill, but he persisted. Runaway fever could kill.

Rhythmically, he soaked the rag, applied it, and soaked it again as daylight waned, early at this time of year, and settled into utter blackness. But he did not pause. She was restless, burning up, and had fallen into that profound silence once again.

"Live," he whispered.

As the northern evening fell, he thought of the lithe woman who had become his mate. How he had met her. How they had loved, in spite of all the barriers of language and culture. How she had plunged bravely into his life as a brigade leader for the American Fur Company. How he had struggled to find a home among her Crow people. How she had picked up trapper language and had become fluently profane, occasionally startling the Yanks who ventured into these wilds, the missionary, the Indian agent, the fur company owner. He smiled then. And smiled as he thought of the thousand times she had drawn him into her golden arms and held him in the sweetness of the night, or in a sunny bower on a breathtaking spring day, the two of them alone. He remembered the moments of terror and war and separation, the times white men were their enemies, the times she had cleansed and dressed his wounds, not only of the body but also of the heart, for he was a man without a country and his only home was at her hearth.

Now she was burning up. A wind rattled the lodge cover, and he felt cold tendrils pry up the leather and slide inside the black interior. He continued his vigil, applying cold compresses on her forehead one after another, hour after hour.

She muttered, and he understood. He helped her sit up, and pawed around in the darkness for the canteen, found it, opened it, and helped her drink. She drank, and again, and again, and he regretted not giving her water earlier. Then she settled back and was quiet again.

Her breathing was better but she was lost to him, deep in her own world. The stars had vanished from the smoke hole, and he wondered whether it would snow. Maybe that would be good. It would bury this desperate camp in a white blanket, and hide it from danger.

A howl lifted him to his feet. It was an eerie wail followed by short barks. A wolf was close, only yards away, summoning the pack, for the smell of meat hung in the night air here. Skye listened closely and heard an answering howl, a lonely call from some distant hill. He had heard wolves often in his long and lonely life in the wilds, but rarely so close. He settled down again beside Victoria, felt about for his belaying pin. It was a strange weapon in the wilds of North America, but a familiar one to him. A belaying pin was used to anchor ship's rigging but was a handy weapon well known to any seaman. The pin was shaped to drop partway through the fife rail on the main deck, making an anchor for the running rigging.

Now the polished pin, a relic of his days as a pressed seaman serving the king and then the young queen, Victoria, felt good in his hand.

The wolves were in camp now, just outside the thin leather walls of his lodge, talking in soft yips and growls to one another. He felt one probe the lodge, but it went away. There was meat enough for them if they dug it up: guts from buffalo, hide scrapings, offal.

"The wolves are our brothers," Victoria said suddenly.

He slipped his big stubby hand over her forehead, and found it raging hot, and felt the deepest dread he had ever known.

5

A numbing cold drifted out of the north, chilling the lodge. The small fire had long since glowed out. Victoria lay inert, and only an occasional ragged breath told Skye she lived. Once she began to shiver, and Skye tucked the robes tighter about her. But fever still gripped her body.

For a while, he heard the wolves outside, pawing up buried offal, driven by the lingering smell of meat. Sometime in the night he heard a loud thud, and another, and wondered what had caused it.

But for most of the night, time barely moved, and he fought sleep. It had been a long time since he slept, and would be a long time before he slept again. If he surrendered and stretched into that pile of warm robes, he would be dead to the world. And he could not permit that. He would watch over her, guard her, protect her with his every breath.

And so by iron will he kept himself awake, alive to the smallest change in her rhythms. She awoke once and asked for water. He held a canteen to her lips. She sipped only a little and fell back.

Dawn came late so far north. At first light he shook off his weariness, settled his black stovepipe hat on his long locks, and stepped outside into bitter air. He would soon

start a fire, warm his own numb limbs and bring his lodge
to life. He would saw frozen meat from his hanging cache,
and roast it over a small flame. A quick meal, but one full
of nourishment.

But now he consecrated himself to the day. This would
be a difficult and dangerous one. He was glad to be alive,
glad to have a home in this wild interior of North America,
glad to call the Crow people his own. But his gladness this
morning was mixed with darkness too, a loneliness that
never left him, something that would never heal because he
was the outsider. He had no country but he would make of
his life as much as he could.

He studied the murky ridges, knowing this was always
the most dangerous time, the moment when enemies struck,
when their quarry lay in their lodges at peace and unaware
of trouble. But he could see nothing. He headed for the
hanging forequarters, and found both haunches lying on the
frost-whitened ground. The wolves had gnawed hard at frozen flesh and given up; the effort wasn't worth the meal. He
lifted the end of the braided leather rope and found that it
had been gnawed in two.

The meat would have to stay on the ground. One man
could not lift a quarter of buffalo. It had taken several, and
maybe some horsepower too, to lift that meat out of harm's
way. But Skye had no horse to help him. He set down his
belaying pin and sawed at the thick haunch. It was slow going, cutting through the icy meat bit by bit, but at last he
had a small pile of it, enough to feed them both—if Victoria wanted any, which he doubted.

He built a tiny fire in the lodge, waited for it to burn bright
and bed the ground with coals, and then began to roast the
stiff and icy meat over open flame, a green willow skewer
holding it off the fire. For the first time in half a day, he felt
warm. The buffalo meat sizzled and burned, but it was soon
cooked, and its savory aroma filled the lodge.

She was watching him. She seemed the same, except a great darkness filled her face.

"Meat?" he asked.

She shook her head slowly.

"Are you feeling better?"

She stared, not replying. It was not in her to complain.

He pulled his buffalo meat away from the fire and let it cool.

"You go to the People. Leave me. It is the way of the People," she said.

She was referring to a thing the Crows and other tribes did when they were forced to: abandonment. The ill and ailing were left to die if they jeopardized the safety of the young and healthy. And now she was telling him to leave her; she would die.

He shook his head.

"Dammit, Skye, go."

He grinned at her. "It's Mister Skye, mate."

He hoped she would laugh. He had always insisted on being called Mister Skye. Here in the New World he was as good as any mister in Europe, and Mister Skye he would be. He had bloodied a few trapper noses making it stick.

But she didn't smile, and he understood that her thoughts hovered upon the end of life, and walking the spirit path.

"We will walk together," he said.

She swallowed hard. "Sonofabitch," she muttered, and closed her eyes.

He stared sadly at her. There were many things he could deal with, dangers he was ready to face if he must, but illness simply left him helpless. He could think of nothing that might heal her, not a chant or a prayer or a shout or a medicine or a magical remedy. Not an herb or a potent tea.

Then, oddly, she took the thoughts from his mind, something she often did.

"Willow bark tea," she said.

"Yes!"

He jammed his hat down and headed out, barely remembering to carry his Hawken with him, and discovered enough light to make out the trees; the majestic naked limbs of cottonwoods, irregular and rough, and the orderly, drooping limbs of creek-side willows. There were so many varieties, and he didn't know one from another, but with his skinning knife he peeled tender green bark from small branches, working savagely, as if this act alone, done swiftly, might work the miracle he ached for.

He rushed back to the lodge, built up the dying fire, splashed water into his cook pot, and while it heated he stripped the bark into small lengths until he was sure the boiling water would extract whatever powers lay within the bark. It took a long time for the water to boil, for the bark to steep, for color to appear in the water, and then for it to cool enough for her to sip.

She watched, saying nothing, and he saw the fever burning in her and thought that time was short. He finally fed her a little with his horn spoon. She swallowed, and again, and finally shook her head. It had been so little, not more than half a cup. She lay back upon her robes and closed her eyes. He could see the pain and exhaustion etching her face.

He waited awhile and then stepped out again, feeling an icy breeze threaten to topple his beaver top hat from his head. But it stayed put. All these years it had miraculously stayed put in anything short of a gale. It was time to hike to the ridge to the east and survey the countryside. This land was alive with hunters; this was the prime season for prime hides and prime meat from fall-fattened buffalo.

It was time to check the nearby world for trouble. He didn't want to think about the odds if trouble came. He wrapped a robe tight about him to ward off the icy blast, and struggled up a steep grade that ended abruptly on a plain. The empty land greeted him, its grasses brown and sere, the mountains on the horizons in all directions thick with white. A gloomy gray overcast stole the sun from the world. He let his eyes adjust, began his careful focus on distant prospects, alert to movement, but this dark October day he saw nothing but an empty world. The buffalo were elsewhere and so were the hunters. It was a blessing, but also a curse because he smelled snow in the air and knew what would be whirling out of the north soon.

There would be time enough to gather wood, bring some meat inside the lodge, and then hunker down. Wearily he retreated to the creek bottom, filled with foreboding, for his enemies were not just humans, but cold and drifts and starvation. It would be weeks before she could walk, and walking was the only way they might escape to the land of her people, far south. And if they had to toil through snow, or wade icy streams, her fragile strength would desert her.

He slid down to the bottoms, energized by fear, and hurried to the lodge. He headed for the heap of abandoned lodgepoles and began dragging them close to his own shelter, working at it until he had collected every pole in the camp. They were dry and straight and would burn well and make heat. He filled his canteens with water from Louse Creek. He heaped brush about his lodge to slow the wind. He collected more abandoned robes, which he would turn into an inner liner hanging from the lodgepoles within. He dragged the frozen forequarter to a place close to the shelter, worried about leaving it there, realized he had little choice, and then dragged the second one to the same place. The meat was close enough so he might scare off wolves.

He remembered one more thing: at the willow tree he peeled more of the soft green bark from twigs, and peeled bark from a chokecherry growing beside the creek, and bark from several other shrubs. If there was medicine to be found in this trench across the prairie, he would have it in his grasp, no matter how heavily it might snow.

He turned at last to his forlorn lodge as the brooding overcast seemed to lower itself to the very floor of the plain.

And there on a limb beside the lodge, watching him carefully, was a single magpie, her spirit animal, her own totem and fount of wisdom and hope and help.

He slipped through the door flap, settled his black top hat in its place next to the exit, and found her staring upward.

"The magpie is outside," he said.

"Tell the magpie you will bring it meat every day of the storm," she said.

He did. Outside, in the cutting wind, he addressed the bird:

"Magpie, Many Quill Woman promises meat to you each day."

The bird leaped into the sullen air and vanished.

Skye wondered, as he always did and always would, if there was anything at all to the Indian mysteries.

6

The wind ebbed, and no sound rose from the blackness outside. But then the snow came, dollar-sized flakes at first, then smaller ones, a white wall of them. Skye could see nothing when he pulled aside his door flap. If he went out, he would have to be very careful or he would lose his way and perish. He did make one last trip while he could, dragging a dozen of the abandoned lodgepoles to his very doorway. Just in case.

Victoria lay inert, in the land somewhere between the quick and the dead. The tiny flame, which he nursed carefully now, kept the cold at bay, but he would have to feed it day and night. Smoke curled lazily upward but an occasional downdraft drove it into the lodge, tickling Skye's throat and nostrils. Tricks of the air sometimes shot snow through the hole, past the wind flaps, and these showered on him, and on Victoria's robe.

With his knife he fashioned some thong by peeling it away from the edge of a robe, and then began tying robes around the perimeter of the lodge, hanging them from the lodgepoles, until he had an inner liner and the small lodge was more comfortable. The Crows often used liners in bitter weather, but this was still October, and he doubted it would grow so cold that trees would pop and crack.

That occupied him through the evening. When he noticed she was watching him, he slipped to her side, examined that cauterized wound and the angry flesh around it, found no bleeding, and felt her forehead. In the chill of the lodge it was hard to say how fevered she was.

"I brought in some bark while I could. I have choke-cherry, willow, and hackberry. I can make some tea."

She didn't respond.

"Tea, Victoria? What kind?"

He could not catch her attention.

"I'll try the willow," he muttered.

He shredded the soft inner bark of a willow and set it to steeping in hot water. Time ticked slowly. He impulsively added some hackberry bark. He would try anything, everything, carefully and in small amounts, and he would leave nothing undone that might be done.

He waited impatiently. He had never mastered the Indian way of surrendering to circumstance, and now he felt caged and restless in that small space. A gust of snow billowed down onto the robes, and slowly turned into shining droplets.

At last, the steeping herbal tea in his cook pot acquired a greenish or tan cast, and he judged that the decoction might have some value to her. But it was only a guess. He poured some into a tin cup, let it cool, and then awakened her with a gentle shake.

"I want you to drink this."

She stirred, managed to rise to her elbows, and then sat. He handed her the cup.

"Willow and hackberry," he said.

She sipped, and again, slowly, and finally drained half the contents and slipped down again.

He ached. She had no strength at all, no life force, no vitality.

But there was another tack to try, so he began some buffalo broth, steeping small pieces of the forequarter in the water until he had a thin but nourishing soup. He awakened her, lifted her head, and gradually doled the broth, sliding it into her mouth with a horn spoon. It took a long while, and his arm ached from holding her head up. Then she slid back into the stupor that enveloped her.

Maybe she would die, slide away from him despite his every effort. He thought of burning the Blackfoot arrow that might still take her life. Burn it to ash, destroy it, but something stayed him.

Time stopped. He tried to doze one-eyed, keeping up the flame while getting rest, but soon gave it up. He thought of those occasional people he met, people who had ventured into the wilderness, stuffed with romantic notions about the sweetness of the life far from civilization. In fact life in the wilds was little more than want and hardship, food uncertain, cold, heat, insects, rain, constant discomfort.

Maybe this night, when he could for a change lie on several thick robes, he might sleep a true sleep. But he would not do that, not while she was in peril.

Let them sit in their armchairs with their coal stoves snapping and cracking, a lap robe or sweater adding to their comfort, and a good two-burner oil lamp lighting the pages; let them think this life where there were no houses or stores or stoves was an easy life, full of adventure, without law. Let them think it. They all turned tail, even the Yank trappers, who stayed a few seasons if they didn't die, and headed back to the East, and the comforts of a farm.

He eyed the inert woman he loved, and knew somehow that a crisis was looming. If she saw dawn, it would be after the crisis had come and gone.

He checked the snow; it fell steadily, eight inches, ten inches on the level, and no sign of letting up. The snow was imprisoning him, and could make it impossible to move anywhere for days, maybe weeks.

Her people had a way of making time pass, of dealing with the slow dark minutes. They told stories. The Crows were great storytellers, and many of their stories were bawdy and funny. Often he had sat in a large lodge jammed with Absaroka people, and listened to them exchange stories. The old women told the best ones of all, and made everyone laugh, and soon enough a night had passed, and no one had even noticed the passage of the hours.

"I don't know how to tell stories," he said, "but I guess I will. Maybe you can hear me. Maybe I'll only be talking to myself."

She did not respond and for a moment he wondered whether she lived. But then she saw the faint lift of the robe as breath filled her lungs, and he knew she was still with him.

"I've been thinking about that magpie hanging about here," he said, "the one who's your friend and helper. I wonder where she came from and why she's here. Let's say she's here looking after you. She's the one you saw in your vision, maybe not this very bird. But a sort of idealized bird. I suppose she's up in a branch somewhere, her head tucked under a limb, the snow sliding off of her. I wonder when she was born, and when she learned she was your friend. I wonder how your people know that they can find helpers in the animal kingdom."

It wasn't much of a story. Skye was just speculating, wishing he could know more about the mysterious world known to the tribes, but not grasped by white trappers.

"I think this magpie, the one who's sitting on a twig out there in the dark, must have been told by her mama that she was to take care of you; that a certain Many Quill Woman of the Otter Clan of the Absaroka people was going to need the wisdom of the magpies, and if Many Quill Woman's plea for a spirit guide was just and good, then that little magpie out there would decide to look after you and share the magpie wisdom with you.

"And that's why she's there. She's not with her flock of

magpies, holed up somewhere out of the wind and cold. The magpies don't go south, so she has to make her living here, even on a bitter night like this one when snow covers the earth and there's little to eat and it's too cold even to find a bug or a scrap of food."

It wasn't much of a story; for the life of him, he couldn't spin a story or make a plot or put the magpie in real danger, maybe because he knew magpies did well even in brutal cold, and somehow made a living and enjoyed life and made rowdy ruckuses whenever they felt like having fun, which was often. And if they detected danger, the magpies made more noise than a steam calliope. That's one thing about a noisy flock of magpies: no creature on earth can ignore them.

"Well, this magpie should be off with her bunch, strutting and preening and looking for trouble and uproar, but she's not. She's sitting out there watching over my Victoria. Her mother taught her well, because most magpies wouldn't bother. They would be off hunting grubs or bark beetles or pestering blue jays or annoying elk. But not this magpie. That's because her mother taught her manners and duty. If she had a task, she would do it to the best of her ability. So, Victoria, this magpie out there is no ordinary bird."

He paused to slide two or three small sticks into the dwindling fire, and waited for them to catch and flare.

A puff of snow filtered down from above, and it was followed by a soft whir of wings flashing black and white in the firelight. There was the magpie, walking cockily over the buffalo robes. It headed straight toward the bits of meat Skye had cut up for broth and with a few savage jerks of its head it downed the meat.

It peered up at Skye, who sat motionless, and Skye thought he was being scolded though he couldn't quite say why. The whole episode was too startling for him to think sensibly or sort out this great oddity.

Magpie walked about the lodge, as if checking it all out. These birds had an odd, jerky walk, almost a swagger. So Skye sat very still.

Then he discovered Victoria was wide awake, not flushed or dazed but alert and aware. Magpie had waited for this moment, and hopped up on Victoria's robes, and sat quietly in the dark, its head cocked, staring at her. Then magpie lifted its wings and flapped them, as if to fan Victoria's face, and a moment later it popped up to a roost in the smoke hole, and vanished into the night.

Skye sat quietly for a while, uncertain of anything, not trusting his senses, and then he slipped over to Victoria and put his hand on her forehead.

It was cool.

7

An occasional snowflake fell through the hole and hissed on the wavering fire. Skye saw no light at all up there, and knew a heavy overcast blanked out the stars. It was dark and quiet, but something had changed.

Victoria stared at him. She had barely spoken ever since the arrow had pierced her abdomen and lodged under her lungs. She looked awful: great black circles under her eyes, her flesh saturnine and unhealthy, her jet hair matted.

He discovered the broth in the pot, heated it a while, and then crawled beside her. She struggled up upon her elbows and he spooned some into her mouth. She was swallowing better. She took the rest of it and lay back.

He rose, his limbs aching from long confinement, and pulled his blanket capote around him and plucked up his camp hatchet. He opened the lodge flap and peered into a wall of white. The snow was already high. He stepped into the night, which was not cold, and waited for his eyes to adjust. But there was nothing to see. With the flap closed behind him, he stood in pitch-dark, sensing that if he moved a few steps he would be lost. He felt the snow lick his face and slide under his collar. He probed with the toe of his moccasin for some lodgepoles and found them. He pulled one free of the snow burying it, and chopped it into three- or four-foot lengths. When he was done he could not find the lodge. Nothing revealed itself to him, not even a wall of white. He lifted the longest of the segments and slowly rotated it until it struck something soft. Then, certain he had found the lodge, he kept the pole in contact and felt his way around it until he came to the door flap.

It had been a close call. He dragged the lengths of lodgepole into the lodge. He had ten or twelve lengths and judged he had enough wood for the night.

"Dammit," said Victoria.

Skye smiled. She was going to get well.

He shed his snow-crusted capote and settled down, refreshed by the exercise. He arranged four pieces of wood so that their ends were burning, and lay back in his robes. They felt good. In all his years of life in the wilds, he had never slept in a truly comfortable bed, but this night he might.

He lay back in them, and pulled two more over him, and felt himself in a cocoon, safe enough even in this perilous place. The mystery of the magpie absorbed him. There were so many things he knew nothing of, and least of all Indian religion, if any of this could be called a religion.

He ached to know if the magpie really was Victoria's spirit counselor and protector, and whether it had powers beyond Skye's knowing. He thought back to the only religion he knew, the precepts of the Church of England that had shaped him, given him his moral and spiritual nature. Even after he was pressed into the Royal Navy, that belief was ever-present for the Sabbath was carefully observed on every ship of the fleet.

Who was God? And what was this lone magpie doing, invading the lodge of a Crow Indian woman and himself, only to fly off into a thick snowfall? He could not answer. Yet something had happened. Victoria's fever had left her. A step toward healing had occurred. She took broth, spoke a little, and lay comfortably beside him.

Was there anything in this unreconcilable with his own beliefs? He didn't know, and felt almost as powerless confronting these great issues as he had been confronting the wound that almost stole her life. He felt the comfort of a bed that gave gently under his shifting weight, the robes forming themselves to his hip and rib and shoulder, and then he fell into a deep sleep, the first since Victoria's wounding. If the lodge grew cold, he did not know it.

When he awoke a gray overcast shone through the smoke hole. He had slept sometime into the morning. He sat up abruptly, worried that he had let down his guard, that danger loomed. He hastily pulled on the fine fringed calf-high moccasins Victoria had crafted for him out of buffalo bull hide, and pushed open the flap, his gaze sharp. A foot and a half of snow, maybe more, lay on the level, and he saw nothing but aching emptiness, a white world under a gray heaven. Not a track marred the smooth surface. It did not seem like a threatening place where Blackfeet lurked, where wolves lingered. Yet it was.

"A lot of snow," he said to her.

"It will keep us safe," she replied.

"Unless it starts blowing," he said.

This could be a country of mountainous drifts, ten or twenty feet high, whipped into walls and barriers by prairie winds. There could be no passage through such a land.

The lodge was cold and clammy with their breath. Not an ember remained. He stirred the cold fire bed, and found nothing glowing, and the charred wood cold to his touch. She lay under three robes, looking no better except in her eyes, which were brighter this silent morning. He would build a fire if he could. It would not be easy.

He hunted through his possibles for his fire-making kit, and the tiny bit of bone-dry tinder he needed. He found it, and pinched some of the delicate shavings he preserved there. He dropped them into the firepit, and then carefully shaved slivers of dry wood from the lodgepoles, until he had a small nest of tinder ready. He pulled his flint and striker from his kit, and slid his hand through the bow-shaped striker. Now he was ready. He held his flint stone over the nest of tinder and scraped hard, a practiced scrape of steel over stone, sending a shower of sparks into the cold tinder. None took. He struck again and again, and then, finally, a spark caught, and another, glowing in the delicate shavings. He blew gently, watched the spark glow as air struck it. In a few moments more, he had many tiny glows worming through the tinder, and then at last one bloomed into a yellow flame. The rest caught.

Skye added thin twigs to the tiny flame until at last he had a flame he trusted to live. It brought no heat; that would come much later. For another half hour he nursed the flame until at last it was strong enough to consume the poles he pushed into the blaze. Only then did a faint heat begin to soften the harsh cold of the lodge and drive off the trapped moisture within it.

In the cities, people were using phosphorus lucifers, matches that ignited fires easily. But he could not afford them, and mostly they were not available even at the trading posts. So he lived by the means he had always used, first as a trapper and brigade leader, then as a hide hunter and occasional guide.

He cherished the warmth that gradually permeated the lodge and the robes that lay thickly about. He hurried the fire along with his breath, wanting it hot because the heavy gray smoke from cold fires was a telltale sign to enemies.

He stepped outside, knee deep in snow, and examined the smoke from his lodge. It drifted gray and heavy into the air but was almost invisible under the cast-iron sky. He studied the distant ridges, the naked limbs of trees, and every dimple in the snow, but saw nothing to alarm him.

There would be work; always work, for constant toil was the lot of anyone living far from the civilized world. He dug up poles from his stack of them and began cutting them into usable lengths, not an easy task with a hatchet. The pop and crack of his all-too-dull hatchet disturbed the deep silence, but that could not be helped. The snow itself damped sound, and in any case his refuge lay in a steep trench. In a while he had what he judged to be a day's wood, and then he cut some more while he was about it. That wondrous sleep infused him with a rare energy, and he took advantage of it to get ahead, to put in wood against a bad time, such as another storm.

He scraped the snow off the lodge, traipsed a path to a latrine area, dug his forequarter of meat out of a drift and dragged it closer, stamped down the snow in front of the lodge, and piled fuel next to the door. By the time he had finished the short November day was dying.

He found her awake.

"It is going to snow again," she said. "I feel it. Skye, go to the People while you can. Leave food and wood with me. I will make do. I have a flint and striker."

He wouldn't hear of it. "Among the British, the captain is the last man off of a sinking ship. He makes sure everyone else is safe first," he said.

"What is this thing, the captain?"

"The chief. The one who commands others."

She laughed, suddenly. "All right then, I am captain of this lodge and I'm ordering you to go."

That was why he loved her so much. He reached across and clasped her hands in his.

"We will do this together, like two chiefs of the mighty Absaroka people."

"Dammit, Skye . . ." she whispered.

"We'll wait this out. You'll be strong someday soon. If need be, I'll make a sled and pull you out."

"A sled?"

"You'll see. I will haul you out of here on a bed if that's what it takes."

He fed the flames again as the light dimmed and the fierce

November darkness settled over that small scrap of leather and wood that sheltered them.

A few flakes drifted through the vent and melted on the robes. He rose, opened the flap, and discovered a wall of white falling out of the sky, just visible in the twilight.

"See?" she said. "It's too late for you now. You're stuck with me, Skye."

"That is how I always wanted it," he said. "And it's Mister Skye."

8

The snow came down through the blackness, smothering the land. It came on the tide of deepening cold. It burdened the buffalo-hide walls of the lodge, bulging them inward. It drifted through the smoke hole, hissing on the fire, glittering white on the robes.

The fire behaved badly, wavering and smoking up the lodge, until Skye finally realized it was feeding on air from above; snow had blocked the passage of air from the base of the lodge.

He pushed aside the flap and furiously pushed the snow out into the darkness. He flailed it away from the lodge. He shook the hide until the snow skidded into heaps. After that the fire burned better, at least for a while. But he knew he must stay awake all night to keep the fire from dying.

Victoria watched helplessly, barely able to sit up long enough to take some broth. There was something eerie about this storm that fell upon them in utter silence. Skye knew that if the lodgepoles he had salvaged for firewood gave out there would be little to burn. The hunting camp had consumed every scrap of deadwood on every tree even before the Blackfoot raid.

Life was running thin, and the silent strangling whiteness was carrying death in its soft wings. He knew what he had to do: stay awake. Periodically sweep snow away from the lodge. Cut meat from the haunches and cook it. Find lodge-poles in the snow-buried stack, bring them in and break them up and feed them to the relentless fire.

And all the while he had to nurse a desperately sick woman who needed broth and warmth and shelter. He stayed awake all that night, feeling he was waging a losing war and this unending storm would engulf him. She lay quietly, awake also, caught in her private thoughts. They spoke to each other without words, and often he knew exactly what she was thinking. It was in her to be testy now; the pain at her side and deep in her abdomen was maddening. She felt helpless, even more helpless than he felt in the face of this silent suffocation falling on them.

But finally a grudging dawn came. Through the smoke hole he saw the gray of low clouds and felt their uncaring. The world had ceased to remember the man and woman in a sea of emptiness.

The lodge had a rim of snow within it. Somehow snow had collected around the periphery, blown down the smoke hole. Only in the middle, close to the feeble flame, was there no whiteness.

He drew his capote close and pushed into the white world outside. Bitter cold air stung his face and sandpapered his throat and lungs. The sky was light gray and he could see no horizons because snow and gray blended imperceptibly together. It was plenty cold for November and would get colder. He had much to do, and hoped his hands wouldn't numb entirely, or his ears freeze, before he accomplished it.

Now, with air so brutal, he needed more wood; he didn't know how long the lodgepoles would last, but not long enough. He had only a hunting-camp hatchet and no easy way to fell limbs. He struck toward the creek-side trees, wallowing every foot of the way in snow that rose to his thighs, found Louse Creek still flowing, giving off steam in the icy air, and began the hunt for deadwood. Enough deadwood to keep Victoria safe.

But every step was an ordeal. He toiled at it, chopping off limbs he wasn't sure were dead or dry. In a short time he was too numb to function, and headed back to the lodge. He would be the worst sort of fool to frostbite his feet or hands. All that effort had netted him only a few good sticks.

He slipped into the lodge, pulled his gauntlets free, and held his hands over the pitiful fire, but they didn't warm. He found some wood, built the fire up, and slowly blood returned to his hands and the stinging in them subsided.

"Cold," he said to her.

"Skye . . . if anything happens, I can't help you."

"I am being careful."

"You should have left me."

"If your magpie didn't leave you, then I won't either."

That sally quieted her.

The next time out, he found a good thick limb, dead and dry, and hacked away until he felled it. He dragged it to his lodge and worked furiously to chop it into four or five long lengths. He could do the rest inside.

He staked the meat, which rested safely under snow, so he could find it. For now, he need not worry about food, but in time scurvy would destroy them both unless he found some roots and vegetables.

Somehow his labor warmed him, and he was able to improve their lot by the time the short day turned into an icy blackness. When he stumbled in, he found her sitting up, and more. She had shifted her bed, moved herself closer to the firewood, and was tending the fire on her own.

"You shouldn't be up," he said.

"Go to hell, Skye."

"It's Mister Skye."

"Go to hell, Mister Skye."

He struggled out of his capote, pulled off his gauntlets,

thrust his numb hands into her fire, and felt prickles, and then warmth.

"Tonight you sleep. I'll keep the fire," she said. "It's no good if you're too tired to keep us going."

"But, Victoria . . ."

"English, they don't know anything."

He tumbled into his robes, thinking only to rest before he brewed her some broth or cooked a little meat, but next he knew there was light in the smoke hole and she was slumped in her bed. The fire burned steadily but the supply of wood inside the lodge was low.

He could not imagine losing so much time. Nor could he imagine sleeping so long, buried under several heavy robes. In fact, he didn't remember any robes over him when he lay down to rest a moment at the end of the day.

He got up, rested. He ventured out, and found this day cloudless and cold and the snow thick. When the wind came up, as it would on a clear day like this one, it would heap the snow into giant drifts, imprisoning them.

Even as he stood there in the early light, absorbing the white world, he felt the first stirrings of air, slicing heat out of him. In some ways this bright and glaring and windy day would be the worst of all. The firewood was almost gone, but this bitter day he would have to work through heavy snow to find some, and it would be far away.

He was rested at least, and worked north, straight into the rising wind, heading for a thicket ahead. Then he stumbled over something, and found it was a dead cottonwood, limbs shattered and scattered, but under the snow. Good. He would mine that heap of snow for all he could.

She watched him as he dragged piece after piece back to the lodge and then warmed himself. She was keeping the fire now, sparing him one worry. In deep cold it was hard to start any fire, even with dry tinder and flint and steel.

After three trips into that miserable wind, he returned to find that she had heated thick and meaty broth for him. She was well enough to stir about. He drank it gratefully and was renewed. But conditions outside were worsening by the minute. Now the wind whipped the snow into tiny bullets of ice, scouring one piece of land only to pile huge drifts elsewhere. He could no longer walk into it, and was forced to back slowly toward that dead cottonwood while the wind whipped snow like buckshot and plastered his capote with it.

When he returned it was only midmorning, but he was as worn as if he had toiled hard a whole day. He had a little wood, enough for the night, but not much more except a few lodgepoles he was holding in reserve.

She handed him tea this time, something she had decocted, he didn't know from what.

She had been sitting up most of the morning.

"Skye, if you and me get out of here, you're going to get another wife. I'm tired of doing it alone. You get two, three more wives, make me the sits-beside-him wife, so I get to boss the rest."

He stared at her, amazed.

"Dammit, Skye, you get more wives. You're doing women's work, and it ain't right. One wife gets sick, you got three more to help out."

He stared at her over his tin camp cup, feeling the steam brush his face. She was serious even if he spotted humor in those eyes that had been so dull and pain-soaked for days.

"You're all I want, Victoria," he said.

"Then you're no chief. You want to do me a favor? You want to make my life happy? You get more wives. I want some wives myself."

A sharp blast of wind shuddered the lodge, and he wondered if the wind rose so high it might tip the shelter over. There were no rocks pinning it down. This was merely to be a hunting-camp shelter, easily dismantled. There wasn't a rock in sight, and if the wind blew the lodge away, they would perish. As simple as that.

"Some wives, Skye, we could make you comfortable."

"I'll bet."

"Who ever heard of a chief having only one woman? I hold my head in shame in the village because I am the only woman of Mister Skye. It tells them you are no chief, in war or in the robes."

She laughed, wickedly. He had rarely seen her laugh like that, but it was a laugh known and practiced by the Crows, and especially old women of the People. He had heard it many times around many campfires, especially when it came time to tell stories and spin away a winter's day. Her laugh was a bawdy one, and she was thinking of what it would be like in a lodge with several comely women in residence.

Skye sat there, flustered. Where had this come from? How could she be thinking of more wives when their very lives hung in the balance?

9

Days passed, the early winter weather moderated, but the peril did not diminish. Skye scoured the valley for firewood, stamping trails that took him farther out each day. Victoria took charge of the domestic labor, keeping fires going, sawing meat from the frozen forequarters, and resting in between.

The early November sun crusted the snow so that the giant drifts no longer shifted in the wind. Some were taller than Skye. Each of them formed a wall imprisoning them, keeping them from the Crows' winter camp. Skye feared passage through a gap between the Snowy Mountains and the Belt Mountains where snow always collected and reached formidable heights, all but sealing this country into northern and southern parts all winter long. Somehow, he would have to take his fragile woman through or over that barrier. There was no good way around.

Victoria gained strength but pushed too hard to take pressure off of Skye, and then lost ground. She was right, he thought wryly: he could use a few wives, for it was the Indian women who did the hard work of sustaining life, the women who toiled from dawn to dusk.

There were other things looming on the horizon, and the worst was scurvy. How long could they subsist on meat alone, without greens or fruits? How long before they weakened, their gums bled, they lost strength and even the will to live?

One morning he remembered the cache left behind by the fleeing hunters. It was guarded by formidable drifts that stretched higher than his head but he was determined to find out what was in it and salvage anything useful. He hacked his way toward the creek, sometimes stepping into snow that engulfed him, but he finally reached the creek in the vicinity of the cutbank, and stumbled down a slope. He probed and finally located what he thought was the cache tucked under a river-washed hollow.

He chopped and hacked, using the only tools he had, a camp hatchet and a stick, and finally broke into a hollow area. A great sour odor rose out of it, and he discovered dozens of small eyes peering out at him. He had found a pack-rat city, and the insolent little creatures had made a bonanza out of the cache. He cleared away more snow and peered in. The rats had ruined the robes, eaten leather, soiled everything. There was one treasure: an axe. That simple tool would make all the difference in the world when it came to gathering and reducing firewood. He collected it gladly.

One parfleche caught his eye. It remained tightly bound, and apparently the pack rats had not burrowed into it. He dragged it out, opened it, and found it full of new pemmican. He was overjoyed. It was the great trail food of all the tribes, consisting of pounded dry meat—usually buffalo—fat, and berries. This pemmican had both chokecherry and service berries embedded in the fat and shredded meat. There could be no better food.

Joyously, he collected his axe and the heavy parfleche and wrestled them back to his lodge.

There, Victoria immediately dug into the parfleche and wolfed the pemmican, her body starved for any fruit or vegetable matter. He ate some too.

"Nothing else in the cache," he said. "The rats got it."

"Soon we will go home," she said.

He did not respond; the forbidding drifts that imprisoned them were on his mind.

"I will be ready," she said.

But he saw her weakness. She worked fitfully but always sank back into the robes and lay inert for hours. She was not ready for travel and would not be anytime soon.

He rested; fighting through crusted soggy drifts was the most exhausting labor any man could face, and he was constantly worn out, fighting for breath, needing time to recover.

Then he heard a soft clop of hooves. He couldn't believe it. Not now. He grabbed his Hawken, checked the load and the cap over the nipple, and with the rifle ready, tugged aside his door flap for a look. There, before the lodge, standing in the small area that had been trampled down, stood a gray mare and a colt. The mare had been gaunted by starvation. Her ribs showed. Her backbone formed a ridge. The flesh around her rump had wasted down to bone.

Skye thought he saw a magpie fly away, a flash of black in the glaring winter sun, but put the odd thought aside. The magpie had nothing to do with this. He peered about sharply for Blackfeet, for any living person, and saw nothing. The snowbound ridges hemming this sheltered river bottom were as bright and silent and anonymous as they had been since the storm.

A mare. And near death from starvation. Her head hung low. Brambles had lodged in her mane until it was an unkempt mess that no longer protected her long neck. Her hooves had worn down. She had an ugly roman nose and a look of sorrow in her eyes. She had once been around human beings; she was either unafraid or too starved and close to perishing to care.

"I'll be damned," muttered Victoria.

If the mare was worn, the colt was not. It was six or seven months old and still nursing, and it had robbed its mother of the last of her strength. It was truly the ugliest little beast Skye had ever seen, gray and wild, an oversized jawbone disfiguring its face. Its floppy ears sat in the wrong spot on its skull. It hung about its worn mother, butting her, dancing away.

A mare. Passage to safety for Victoria if somehow Skye could nurse the animal to usefulness, and if she wasn't a complete outlaw.

"Whoa, lady," he said, stepping toward her. He handed the Hawken to Victoria and approached gently, a tentative step at a time.

Then the miserable colt kicked. The little thing whirled, unloosed his hind feet, and caught Skye in the right thigh, rocking him back. And before Skye could recover, the colt caught him again at the groin, staggering Skye backward until he teetered into a snowbank.

Skye boiled up like a sore-toothed grizzly.

"Avast!" he bawled, determined to wrestle the offending colt right down to the ground, tie him up, and show him who was the boss. But before he even recovered his balance, the colt lowered his head, turned himself into a battering ram, and charged straight into Skye, that bonehead ramming into Skye's belly and knocking the breath clear out of him.

Skye reeled backward, gasping for air, and the colt followed his retreat, butting again and again until Skye tumbled into the snow again. Then the colt minced backward, did a little jig of victory, and stood there, watching Skye unfold himself and stand up and catch his wind.

"That's the rottenest animal I've ever seen," Skye roared. "I'll fix him."

But Victoria was laughing, and it was an unkind laugh, a cackle Skye had heard only among Crow old ladies, a cackle that said they were enjoying someone's misery. There was his wife cackling and wheezing, and there was that stupid-eyed colt with the underslung jawbone, ready to nail him again.

There was nothing to do but laugh.

Skye felt a volcano of laughter erupt from his belly; a vast earthquake of joy, which hurt his stomach where the rotten little colt had butted him. But laugh he did, laughed at the whole mad world this bright morning.

But the time came when he and Victoria were looking again at the desperate mare, her head hung low, fighting to stay alive. There was not a blade of grass to be found and the snow was too deep to paw through to feed herself.

"Have to feed her fast," he said.

"Damn lucky you got the axe," she said.

It was lucky. It was almost magical. With that axe he could offer that mare some emergency grub. Maybe the colt would nibble on it too. He circled warily around the horses and headed for the cottonwoods along the creek, where there was a stand of saplings, their bark smooth and green rather than scaled and thick and dry. The smooth bark of young cottonwoods was an emergency horse food, well known to mountain men and Indians. He struggled through deep snow, singled out a sapling, and hewed it down in swift strokes. He limbed it and dragged the green log back to the lodge, then cut a slit down the limb so he could roll the bark away.

The mare tore into it even before he had finished, her big buck teeth scraping the green bark loose and her old lips capturing every green shred. She knew instinctively that she had food before her.

Victoria stood before the lodge, a robe wrapped around her, and watched.

Skye retreated to the cottonwood stand, felled two more saplings poking from deep snow, and dragged them to the lodge. The effort exhausted him. But she was eating. She expertly worked the green bark off that thin log, turning the log somehow, chewing the pliable bark into feed.

Skye watched, gratified. This mare might be their salvation; a fair enough trade. He could feed her; she could carry

Victoria away. As for that mean colt, maybe he would shoot it. No man in his right mind wanted a colt like that, full of some insane instinct to attack everything in sight.

The colt wouldn't even let its mother eat, but butted her, poked that thick underslung jaw and snout into her bag, and robbed her of what little milk and life she had left.

Skye watched, disgusted at the little creature's greed. At the rate he was bullying his mother, she would never gain strength or put on weight or be strong enough to carry Victoria out.

He could slit its throat, or he could get the poor mare more feed. He watched dourly, and then headed into the snow once again, and spent the rest of that bright day cutting saplings, until he had managed to drag a pile of green-barked logs to her. The mare never stopped eating, stripping soft green bark off of those wands of wood, and by the end of that day he didn't know whether the tears in his eyes were from snow blindness or something else.

10

Time was running out. For days, Skye fed the old mare cottonwood bark, which he roamed wide and far to find. She prospered a little, or at least he thought she did, but it was poor food and all it did was keep her alive and allow her to make a little more milk for the ugly colt.

But with each passing day, danger increased. The mare had left a trail in the snow, and what warrior or hunter could resist the trail of a lone mare and foal? There was the prospect of another fall storm, and a hundred times each day Skye's gaze focused on the horizons, looking for an ominous bank of clouds. The forequarter of buffalo meat was dwindling; the pemmican he reserved as a travel food. He had long since consumed the available firewood. This campsite was exhausted and yet he lingered to give Victoria the best chance.

But finally he dared wait no more.

"We'll leave in the morning," he said.

"I am strong."

"We'll see when we hit the drifts. I've made a travois from the last of the lodgepoles. The mare's gentle enough; she belonged to someone once. I'll put the robes on her back, you in the travois, and I'll carry the Hawken, the tools, and the pemmican on my back."

They would abandon the lodge with its comforts. Each night they would have to stay out in the open. He would try to find cottonwood groves, so he could feed the mare more green bark. The odds were bad; he thought they had one chance in ten. Most likely they would suffer snow blindness. The whole world was still white, and only a heavy overcast could save them from ruining their eyes.

They left before dawn to gain time. The mare submitted docilely to the saddle, and then to the travois poles anchored to the stirrups. The colt butted him whenever he approached the mare, and now and then Skye roared at the miserable heavy-jawed thing that kept getting in his way. Then the colt butted him again, just to show who owned that mare.

But the colt might come in handy, especially if it would break a trail. They sadly abandoned the lodge that had kept them alive just as a faint light lined the horizon to the southeast. The snow had crusted, making walking all the more difficult as they punched through, step after step. Skye wrapped the pasterns of the mare in patches torn from old robes to keep them from being sliced to pieces.

Just as he suspected, Victoria lasted a few hundred yards walking and then settled gratefully into the travois and pulled a robe over herself. The travois was easy on the mare, mostly skidding over surface crust, but it didn't take long for the mare to weary. He let her rest. He needed her. Victoria depended on her. They had a long, long way to go.

When the sun rose his eyes watered at once. A squint didn't stop the glare, and only when he pulled the hood of his blanket capote over his face did he find any relief. The mare's eyes watered and so did the colt's. Victoria sat with her eyes closed.

At least he wasn't cold. The temperature hovered above freezing. And Skye was working too hard to get chilled. Behind them a telltale trail unfolded, hooves, moccasin prints, travois tracks. Any passing war party or loner could track them down. And yet it could not be helped. One did what one had to do, and he had to move.

They struck the Judith River, which flowed southwest, and once they reached its valley the going was easier. They were traversing game and buffalo trails, already packed. He kept a sharp eye for pony hoofprints, but saw none. The early snow was a blessing in one sense: the hunters and warriors had taken to their lodges and were probably gathered about lodge fires playing the hand games or bone games or telling stories of their people.

For a while that afternoon they traversed well-stamped ground. The mare perked up, not having drifts to fight, and the travois skidded easily over the glazed surface. The well-worn trail gave Skye the gift of extra miles, but he didn't want to exhaust the mare or Victoria, and called a halt in a fine stand of cottonwoods and willows near the fork of the Judith and Ross Creek.

There, he felled green cottonwood limbs while Victoria chopped willow saplings, wove them into a small dome, and threw spare robes over it. It was little more than a hut, but it would be far more comfortable than open ground, and a fire at its front would throw heat into it.

The ugly colt nuzzled up to his mother's bag and drained it, and then butted it for more supper, but she had given him all she had. Then it began mouthing bits of cottonwood bark, and Skye was glad to see it beginning to forage for itself. It was old enough to eat any horse feed.

"With that jaw of yours, you could eat whole trees," he said to it. For an answer, the colt whirled and kicked, barely missing Skye's shin.

"You little devil!" Skye roared.

"His name is Jawbone," Victoria said.

"That's a good name! He's all jaw! He has no brains and no back and nothing else of value. Jawbone it is, you little punk!"

They were camped in a trench cut into the plain, and Skye did not worry about a fire. They had come much closer to the Snowy Mountains and the Belts, which brooded whitely above them. In a day or two they would enter the gap between the ranges, and then there could be big trouble. But there was no sense in worrying it to death. For this night they had shelter and pemmican and plenty of green bark for the weary mare.

At dusk, which came all too early, they settled into their hut. Victoria had gathered armloads of reeds from the creek bank and these formed an insulating bed between them and the snow. But this was not the same as the lodge, and they shivered as they slipped into their doubled robes.

"I did not see the magpie," she said. "It is a bad omen."

He lay quietly, gathering what little warmth he could from within the robes. It was important to her to know that her spirit helper was beside her. In her weakened condition it could even mean life or death, despair or the will to live. And he knew he could not cheer her up with bland assurances.

"Victoria, we have given no offense to any living thing that I know of," he said. "We have given food to the magpies, fed the mare, and honored all things."

That was important: she lived in a world in which one must respect all creatures great and small.

"I am just damned tired," she said, but he knew her spirits had slipped into darkness. He rose, fed more sticks into the small fire that threw a little light and warmth into their shelter, and peered into the blackness. No stars lit the heavens, and he dreaded what might come, especially in so rude a hut as this.

He drifted into a light sleep. It was hard to sleep when you had to suck icy air, breath after breath, when your nose and cheeks ached with cold, when your feet remained blocks of ice.

A nervous shuffle outside of the hut awakened him instantly, and he felt around for the Hawken. The barrel was icy to the touch, and the stock had frost on it. He chose his belaying pin instead, and hastened out into the bitter night. Something scurried away. Intuitively he knew the visitors were wolves, and his stirring had probably scared them off. He could not see the mare or colt but knew that if they had been attacked he would have heard about it. The loss of the mare would devastate their chances of ever reaching Victoria's village. But he did not tie her up. She didn't like it, and he finally had learned just to let her be his ally and not his slave. As long as he didn't tie her, he had a partner.

By the time he shook the cobwebs from his mind the next dawn, he was surprised to see a fire burning. Victoria had lit it. She was better and more patient than he with the flint and steel, and sometimes had gotten a blaze going when he had given up and was suppressing a rage at his own ineptitude. She handed him a broth made of boiled pemmican and water, and he drank the hot greasy liquid gratefully.

He pulled on his buffalo-hide moccasins and went after the mare, wondering where she was. He was on the brink of alarm when he found her deep in brush, stripping bark off of saplings. In a place like this she could make her own living. He let her eat a while. Jawbone was butting her bag, getting his own breakfast.

Victoria had dourly dismantled the willow-branch hut and collected the heavy robes.

"Dammit, Skye, there are no magpies here."

He did not try to calm her. If there were no magpies, it could only mean trouble for Victoria. Still, he collected her cold hands in his big ones and held them. "We will do the best we can, and if we always have heart, we will go where we were meant to go."

At first light they loaded the robes onto the mare, slid the travois poles into the stirrups, and set out, following a southerly course. Skye's burdens seemed heavier this day: pemmican in a parfleche, rifle, axe, hatchet, knife, powder horn, capote, and something intangible: an added worry because Victoria was less well than the day before.

Still, they proceeded up the Ross Fork for a while before they abandoned it to head toward the visible gap between the two ranges. But now the drifts were building, and sometimes the crusts didn't hold them and they floundered waist-deep in snow. Ahead was open country, not a patch of trees, not a creek, not a sheltered hollow, not a stand of cottonwoods to feed the mare, no limbs to weave a hut, only a windy snow-covered land in which the wind had rippled the snow into ribs and ridges.

At one final patch of cottonwoods, Skye laboriously felled a few saplings, split and debarked them, feeling as worn out as the mare. He tucked the pliable green bark into the robes. It wasn't but a fraction of a meal. The mare would get no other food, maybe for days. And all that day, no magpie followed them.

11

All that bitter day they struggled south, blinded by sun-dazzle but helped by the north wind at their backs. Their course rose imperceptibly toward the gap, and the higher they climbed the heavier the snow. Sometimes Skye whacked a hole in a drift with his axe, and the rest followed single file.

The wind picked up, funneled into a ten-mile-wide flat between mountain ranges. But as long as it pushed them ever south, it was bearable. He rested the gaunt mare often, knowing that Victoria's life depended on that worn old creature. The colt seemed almost oblivious of the hardship, having milked his mother of whatever resources she still possessed.

Often the little fellow dashed ahead, as if to lead this slow procession toward a safe harbor, only to swing around and return again when no one matched his pace.

There wasn't a tree close by, though the distant mountains were black with them. Skye knew a little about this gap. It was bloody ground because it was the only passage for travelers going north or south in the whole area. That meant ambush, war, death right there, most often between Crows and Blackfeet, but other tribes had spilled blood there. It was a stark, treeless place without beauty; there was little to solace the spirit, and the spirits of the dead haunted it.

Victoria mostly traveled in the travois, enduring its lurches and bounces, but occasionally she rose and walked a little, giving the old mare some respite. No one spoke; every word was energy wasted.

They came, late in that day, to a ridge of snow as high as a house, a white wall that forbade a crossing. And yet they had to cross it, fast, before they lost the light for there was no refuge behind them. Jawbone pranced ahead, tentatively sampling the crust. And finding a crust, he began climbing that monstrous drift, ever higher. Then with a pitiful squeal the colt vanished. He had broken through the crust and was trapped in the soft snow below, thrashing about in its prison.

For a moment Skye rejoiced. Little devil! But the piteous wail of the mare filled Skye with shame and regret. He halted the procession at the foot of that drift and studied that slope. The colt was about fifty feet ahead, braying and flailing in his trap. He would soon exhaust himself, freeze, and die.

"Skye, dammit, do something," Victoria said.

"And what?" he snapped.

Skye didn't have the faintest idea what to do, so he did the first thing that came to mind. He shed his gear and prepared to go after the colt. He pulled his axe from his pack and began chopping through the crust, cutting a way to the trapped colt. It was slow, hard work, and after ten feet he was worn. He found that he had some footing well down from the crust, and if he kept knocking the crust with the back of his axe he could work along a narrow trench toward the little fellow, who was sporadically screeching his alarm, but the time between each of its struggles grew and grew.

Behind him, Victoria and the mare stood watching. Skye made slow progress and kept chopping even while his body protested, finding a slow rhythm of axe-swinging and forward movement that sustained him through another ten, then twenty, then thirty feet. But the foal was silent now, resigned to its doom the way animals are when they sense hopelessness.

Skye, too, was in a precarious place, climbing through the soft underbelly of the snow ridge until the crust came up to his chest. But at last he reached the colt, which had worked his way deeper into the snowbank.

He cleared away as much of this soft snow as he could. Jawbone could not even look back at his rescuer.

"Whoa, boy," Skye said, not knowing how on earth to free the colt.

Jawbone did not respond except to rotate his ears.

Skye tried sliding his hands around the colt, intending to lift him, drag him backward, but he couldn't get a grip, and the snow swiftly numbed his fingers.

He burrowed down and cleared soft snow from its hind feet, fearing a sharp kick, but Jawbone didn't move. Slowly he cleared the feet and lifted them, getting a good purchase on the pasterns, and tugged.

Jawbone didn't like that a bit, but it didn't matter: Skye eased him a foot out of his trap. He was so worn he could pull no more, and paused for breath. The sun was just above the southwestern horizon, and they would soon be caught in a black night with no shelter.

He took a firm grip on Jawbone's hocks and pulled steadily. The colt slid along, almost as if he were slipping out of a womb, and in a few minutes Skye, his heart hammering, had pulled the colt out of his trap, down the snow slope, to hard snowpack.

The colt righted himself, shook off the snow, overcame the indignity of it, and butted his rescuer.

"Avast!" yelled Skye, who didn't quite topple.

But the colt had already headed for his worn mother, jammed his bonehead into her bag, and was refueling.

The sun dropped behind a distant ridge.

"I think there is a crossing over there," Victoria said,

pointing to a place two hundred yards distant where some juniper seemed to grow right out of the top of the ridge. They headed that way at once, found firm footing that took them around the drift, and out upon a cold flat land.

Ahead was a dark streak, and Skye headed for it in the tumbling twilight. Soon enough he led his weary band into a sharply eroded coulee out of the wind. They could perhaps shelter under a cutbank, and there was enough juniper and other brush to sustain a fire if they could light one in the restless air.

He pushed down the dry watercourse, looking for a good place, and found one in a bend, where occasional spring floods had undercut a bank and piled up some driftwood.

"Here," he said.

They stopped. He had taken them too far this day. The old mare hung her head, her ribby sides heaving. Victoria crawled off the travois, began undoing the bundle of robes on the mare's back, and started to make a nest, gather kindling while the last light held.

The foal, wobbly from its ordeal, stood stiff-legged watching Skye unsaddle the mare and turn her free to make whatever living she could in that little ditch in the prairie. Then the little animal wobbled toward Skye and pressed his bony, misshapen head into Skye's side, and stood there, his head low and tight against Skye's hip.

"You're welcome," Skye said, and found a moment to run a numb hand under that heavy jaw, scratch it, and run his hand under the colt's ratty mane. There was something about that colt, something that set him apart.

He surveyed the cutbank. It wasn't much, but Victoria had summoned the last of her strength to spread robes, gather the heaps of dead juniper brush, and scrape a bed ground clean of stones and debris. Skye found the mare tearing savagely at bits of dried grass poking out of the snow around the juniper. He added his meager supply of green bark to her fodder.

The last glimmer of twilight faded into deep cold night by the time they had the camp readied. But they had no fire. Skye sat down and pulled his flint and steel from a small pouch he carried at his belt. Air eddying up the coulee would make a fire difficult. He settled with his back to the wind, built a little hollow out of Victoria's brush, and began driving sparks into it, with no luck. Once one caught and held, an orange glow, but a moment later it died.

He pulled the robe right over his head, making a shelter. Then he scraped steel over flint, generating a fine shower of sparks, again and again until he saw a dozen of them glowing and curling in the thumb-sized bit of shredded bark tinder he always carried. He blew softly. The little glow worms glowed the more. He blew again, and again, and then the tiniest flame embraced a straw-sized twig. He had fire if only he could keep it. Half the battle was to feed it, keep it going, helping it gain heat. A trickle of smoke stung his eyes but he did not lift the robe. Instead, he edged tiny sticks, smaller than pencils, into the guttering little flame, patiently.

It took a long time, and he coughed a lot of smoke, but at last he pulled the robe away and began feeding larger sticks into the fire, while Victoria lay on her robes, exhausted. The fire would give them hot broth made from the pemmican, a priceless bounty for numb, worn, and cold people. The cutbank at the bend of the coulee was a good place, out of the wind, blocking it from most directions. With enough robes, and enough hope, and enough courage, they would live to the morning.

He tried to heat water but it wouldn't boil. There just wasn't enough heat in that juniper debris. Still, it warmed enough so he could steep some pemmican in it, and then let Victoria drink. It would warm her. He ate his pemmican cold. Then the kindling ran out, and there would be no more light or heat that night. He listened to the night sounds, heard the mare working industriously along the coulee, wherever a sheltered corner offered some dry grass. She would do well this evening, which was not at all what he expected. The colt followed his mother, but now and then trotted through the inky black to check on Skye.

Victoria huddled in her robes. He set his beaver top hat beside him, checked his Hawken and laid it beside him, made sure his belaying pin was close at hand, and then pulled the robes up, not finding any warmth at all in them. It would be a long time, if ever, before they felt comfortable this night.

"It is bad," she said. "My helper has gone away."

"Your helper will return."

"Dammit, Skye, when we get to the village, you go to Fort Sarpy and trade these robes for a jug. I am very thirsty. Firewater! That's what's keeping me going."

"I'll get some from Chambers," said Skye. "You and I are going to celebrate."

12

They stumbled south, blown by the north wind, until at last they walked down a long draw and into the valley of the Musselshell.

Skye rejoiced. This night there would be shelter from the wind, abundant firewood, feed for the mare, and maybe even game, a welcome prospect because the pemmican was nearly gone.

The starved mare was failing again; Victoria had walked this day, but she herself was weakening. Never had a river bottom seemed so welcome to Skye. They could regroup and then head down the Musselshell. The Crow winter camp nestled another day's walk downriver, under some protective sandstone bluffs that caught the winter sun and radiated it into the village.

As the short day faded, they hurried over a snowy waste with the wind whipping them until he thought the wind would drive him mad. But when they entered the bottoms they found a great quietness there. Animal tracks laced the old and hardened snow. A lacework of bare branches stabbed the purple twilight. There were jack pines and juniper greening every hollow.

The mare paused to snatch at every dried stem and stalk that poked through the snow. Skye pitied her. She had somehow dragged that travois all those miles and all the while making milk for that boneheaded little colt who ought to be shot.

He found a fine thicket close to the narrow river, deep in a bend curtained by forest and sheltered from the cruel north wind. He unhooked the travois, unsaddled the old mare, and turned her loose. She would make her own living this night. She headed for the river, stuck her nose in the purling water, and drank. The colt followed her, poking his nose into the river and butting her bag. Skye had forgotten how dehydrated animals got in the winter and reminded himself to give Victoria plenty of broth this evening.

She was already picking up loose sticks, breaking them off of trees, for they wanted a fire at once. They hadn't been warm in days, and he was dreaming of a hot blaze that would soak heat through his buckskins. Victoria looked about ready to collapse, but sheer will kept her going. She chopped willow limbs and stripped them and soon had the framework of an emergency shelter, a small domelike affair that would support a couple of robes and give them a sanctuary.

Skye took over the firewood collecting; this grand night he would heap up a mountain of it, and they would enjoy every stick of it. There was dead stuff at every hand, and he needed only to collect it, rap the snow off of it, and drag it to the shelter.

In deep blue dusk they finished their task, scraped snow out of the bed ground, lined it with rushes from the riverbanks, and began to nurse a tiny flame that soon grew into a hot, bright, happy campfire. But no amount of heat was enough. It burned and snapped, but it did not take the cold out of his body. It scarcely even warmed his numb hands. He wished for a rocky overhang, a place that would absorb and reflect the heat through the night, but there was no rocky cliff here. The river cut through prairie and they were camping on a floodplain.

He wasn't getting warm, but at least he could heat some pemmican and make a broth. He set up his cook pot and began a meal while Victoria lay under two robes, utterly drained.

Then he noticed that the mare had stopped gnawing and was staring upriver, her ears cupped forward. He had been around the wilds long enough to respond. He found his Hawken, checked to see if there was a cap under the hammer, and slipped into shadow away from the open-sided hut and the bright fire before it. His old mountain rifle with its percussion lock had never betrayed him. It shot true and faithfully, and now he held it at the ready.

He listened closely and heard the faint clop of hooves and something else, a hiss that sounded like iron tires rolling over icy ground.

"Hello the camp," came a voice out of the darkness.

Usually a good sign. No surprises.

"Come ahead," Skye replied.

Nothing happened for some while. Victoria had slipped out of her buffalo robes, grabbed the belaying pin, and joined him in the spidery darkness of the woods.

Not one but two wagons emerged out of the blackness, following along a river road Skye hadn't discerned in the twilight.

"Thought you might be a white man. Injuns don't make big fires like that."

"Who are you?"

"Sam Fitzgerald, trading man, and my son, George."

Somehow Skye didn't like the tone of all that. He rose, rifle in hand, and walked toward the horses and wagons, which stood dimly at the edge of the orange light. Bearded men stood beside the dray horses, each carrying a shotgun.

"I'm Mister Skye."

"Saw that top hat and figured it was so," said Fitzgerald.

"Only man west of the Missouri that wears one of them things."

Skye thought it would be all right. "Fixing some broth; all we've got."

"Well, we've some meat. You have a fire. Sure is cold."

"Why are you out here with those wagons?"

"Hides. We head out to the villages and trade. Operating out of Fort Laramie. We been over to the Flatheads."

Skye nodded. This was the new thing. Traders headed out to the villages during winters, armed with goods and hoping to make a good trade for buffalo hides. It was a more aggressive and successful form of the buffalo-hide trade than waiting passively in forts for Indians to show up with a load of skins to dicker for knives, powder, baubles, and blankets.

Still, Skye was wary and intended to stay armed.

"All right; here's a fire. Warm up. We could use some meat."

"Make a camp here?"

"Maybe down a piece," Skye said. "Not much feed for horses."

"Saw that old plug. That's all you got?"

"Blackfeet," Skye said.

"Thieving bunch! We watch our topknots around them devils."

Victoria quietly emerged from the shadows.

"Ah, so you ain't alone," Fitzgerald said, surveying her too closely.

"This is my wife, Victoria. She took an arrow from the Blackfeet and is poorly. We're going to be glad to get to her village."

Victoria barely acknowledged these two, a sure sign that she didn't like their looks. She headed for the hut where she could oversee the cooking.

The traders steered their wagons ahead a bit and unhooked the dray horses. Both wagons were loaded with stiff buffalo hides, stacked like playing cards and held in place with stakes anchored to the sides.

What looked to be a deer hock hung from one, and this the son untied and brought to Victoria.

"Hey, cookum some grub, eh?"

Victoria rose and walked into the darkness.

"Feisty little squaw, ain't she?" Fitzgerald said.

Skye was having second thoughts but didn't know how to get rid of this pair. He didn't like the way the younger one was eyeing his wife. If he tried to mess with her, he'd find a lead ball passing between his eyes.

On the other hand, this pair was well armed and quick to act and dangerous. Skye settled down to a waiting game, and began sawing at the meat with his knife, gradually peeling away some steaks that could be cooked on a green stick.

"There you are," he said quietly. "Plenty of willow around; cut a stick and cook your meat."

Victoria had drifted toward the laden wagons and was floating around them, studying the contents. She was done with cooking, something he knew but the traders didn't.

"You done trading for this trip?" he asked.

"Yep, we've got over eighty prime hides, heavy devils, stacked up in them wagons. Out of trade goods, so we're heading for Sarpy to unload . . . You got something to trade?"

Skye shook his head. "Blackfeet cleaned us out. You got anything left to trade?"

"Nothing but our own kit."

"What did you start out with?"

"The usual. Knives, some trade rifles, powder and ball, blankets, trade cloth, hide scrapers, flints and steels . . ."

He left things unfinished.

"And whiskey," Skye said. "Where'd you trade?"

"West of hyar, mostly. Some Mountain Crow winter villages, some Bannocks, one Flathead bunch come over for some buffalo hunting."

Talk did not go well around that fire. The Fitzgeralds

cooked their meat until it was burnt and then let it cool, while Skye and Victoria sliced theirs into smaller pieces.

"We've got a little sipping whiskey if you can give us something for it," old man Fitzgerald said.

"No."

"Cleaned out. We was going to have us a sip and maybe trade you for a few sips."

Skye sorrowed. If there was anything that would chase away the winter chill and ache, it would be a little sipping whiskey.

"We might work a little deal, Skye," said Fitzgerald, eyeing Victoria.

"Nothing here, friend. We have nothing of value. Now make your camp, yonder, and we'll settle ours. We're pretty well worn out."

But Sam Fitzgerald ignored Skye, headed for the lead wagon, unearthed a pottery jug and a tin cup, and settled at the fire.

"Ah, man, this here's the medicine for a cold night," he said, and poured an inch and added some creek water. He sipped, gave the cup to his son who sipped, and then the bearded young man handed it to Victoria.

"Sonofabitch!" she said, and swallowed a couple of good jolts. "Ah!" She managed another jolt and handed the cup to Skye, who drained off the rest. He felt a good hot fire build in his belly. His old friends the Fitzgeralds smiled and refilled from the earthenware jug and added a splash. The cup made its rounds once again, warming up an icy night; warming up Skye's cold belly. It would be a great evening.

13

Never so cold. Skye stared into a gray dawn. He was numb. Coldness had gathered around his heart. Coldness in his belly. Limbs half frozen and not working. He didn't want to get up but lay stiff and staring at the sky through the skeleton of Victoria's domed hut.

No robes covered it. No robes covered him. No robes covered Victoria. Nothing but deep cold and gray sky. One robe under them. The other robes were gone. He struggled to awaken himself. Now it was urgent. He didn't want to get up. He rolled a little, forcing his body to move. He peered fearfully at Victoria, who lay in her buckskin dress and leggings, looking ashen, a blue pallor upon her.

Get up! He made himself sit up. They were sleeping in open woods. No flame warmed them. The fire was only ash. He did not see his Hawken. So that was it. They saw a weapon they wanted and took it. Along with everything else.

He had to move or perish. He stirred, tried to rise, fell back, and then made himself stand on aching legs. There was no heat in him. He made himself walk, one step, another, then a few. He pushed himself into a lumbering walk, faster and faster, knowing he needed to move before he could help her, if she was not beyond help. When he returned she was still inert. He rolled his half of the icy robe over her, tucked it down around her. She didn't stir. He didn't know if she was breathing. He shook her gently and was rewarded with a sigh. Alive, then. He pulled off his capote and spread that over her too. Anything to catch her in a cocoon.

The Fitzgeralds had taken what they could. Robes, axe, Hawken. But they didn't bother with his belaying pin, and he had his hatchet, which was lying beside him. They had missed it in the dark. His knife was still at his side.

Fire. Flint and steel, still in their pouch at his waist.

He stirred the ashes and found an ember buried under a heap of half-burned deadwood. One small ember. He blew softly, and it bloomed bright orange. He could not make his fingers dig out any tinder. His hands were useless. But he had breath so he blew and blew, worked his fingers, added a few dry sticks, and blew some more, because his flint and steel were worthless with hands that couldn't hold a feather. Some smoke rose but the ember didn't bloom into flame.

He found a pocket of dry leaves caught in a knothole and placed them over the ember. They smoked but didn't catch. He found some reeds and grasses but they didn't ignite. Nothing but icy ground and a tiny column of smoke.

He sat wearily, worn out by the struggle, and buried his head in his arms, hardly knowing what to do. Still, he was alive, and the living have a chance. He made his fingers work, opened and closed his hands, and found he could hold things. He fumbled his flint and steel out of their purse at his waist and began striking steadily, showering sparks upon the live coal and the bits of tinder above it. The sparks caught and glowed orange.

He blew gently, and a tiny flame rose, barely an inch high, wavering but then holding as it bit into the tinder. There was no heat in it and wouldn't be for a long time. Now he hunted for dry stuff, mostly mossy deadwood he snapped off of trees, and laid gently over the worthless little flame, careful not to demolish it. The new stuff caught. Now he had a three-inch flame that wavered wickedly with every freshet that drifted through.

"Burn!" he cried.

There was no way to speed it up. He collected a heap of deadwood and added it, but it was icy and didn't catch. What good was fire when it didn't ignite anything?

Then he remembered his powder horn, hanging from his chest all the while. He twisted off the cap and poured a few grains into his palm and tossed it. There was a satisfying flash. He did it again, and got another flash, and some deadwood caught. He did it over and over, a few grains at a time, not enough to blow the fire out, and saw his miserable little fire expand, eat wood, send up some smoke. But it didn't heat. He held his hands to it, and scarcely felt any warmth.

He turned to Victoria.

She was staring.

"Cold," she said.

Alive. He was gladdened. He stumbled to her, knelt beside her.

"Got a fire started. They stole the outfit."

It was odd how she rolled out of the robe and stood, as if her body could laugh off the iciness. She absorbed the loss: no robes except the one they slept on. Rifle gone. Parfleche with pemmican gone. Cook pot and cup gone.

"They didn't even leave the jug," she said.

"Expensive night."

"I needed that," she said. Strangely, she laughed. "That was pure spirits with a little river water. One sip kicked like a mule. Two sips, dammit, Skye, that was good stuff."

She plucked up the robe, wrapped herself in it, handed Skye's blanket capote to him, and knelt beside the cold fire. He could still feel no heat from it but she was warming her hands over the flames. He wasn't getting any benefit from the fire, so he rose, wrapped his capote about him, and walked.

The old mare was not far, greedily gnawing bark from some saplings, and the colt was butting her bag, as usual. The colt saw him and barreled straight at Skye.

"Avast!" he roared.

The colt veered away and raced off again, enjoying a fine November morning.

Skye settled beside the crackling fire, letting the heat work through his buckskins. He thought he would never be warm again, warm down inside, in his belly and chest, in his limbs, in his toes and fingers.

He had a task. Go after them. He had a belaying pin and an old mare. They had rifles, good horses and wagons, and probably some revolvers and knives too. But he would do what he had to do.

If they were heading for the Crow camp down the Musselshell, he would catch up with them. They would cough up what they stole or learn what a limey with a belaying pin could do to them.

But not now. He was with Victoria, and she was weak and his one duty was to get her to the safety of her village as fast as he could. They were still more than a day from the Crows and didn't have a thing to eat and only one robe to warm them. Vengeance would have to wait.

No food, no rifle, and that meant speed. They had a long walk to reach the Crow winter camp and he would not stop until he got there. He would somehow do it in a day and a half.

He sliced away some fringes from his buckskin shirt and tied them into a line, and made a string hackamore of it. Then he caught the mare, slipped the hackamore over her nose, and helped Victoria up. He wrapped the buffalo robe over her shoulders and she pulled it tight about her.

Skye looked longingly at the fire: it finally was throwing some heat. The Crows often transported a live coal bedded in moss and kept from the air, and used it to light the next fire. But he had no container; he would have to take his chances.

"Are you ready?" he asked her.

"We will go. I will walk when I get cold. Or the mare gets tired."

"We'll make it," he said.

She smiled. It was a beautiful smile that seemed like a blessing.

He took one last look at this bitter camp and then started resolutely eastward in the valley of the Musselshell, leading Victoria's mare while she clung to the mane.

He had starve-walked before. It required a steely will. An overcast kept him from knowing the hour. He walked slowly at first, letting the last of the spirits burn out of his body, making his cold muscles function. He set a steady pace, with the northwesterly breeze mostly behind him, his battered top hat anchored tightly in his long locks. For a while he followed the tracks of the iron-tired Fitzgerald wagons, the hoofprints fresh in the glazed snow. If he came upon the traders he would give them a fight no matter the odds. And he would have the advantage of surprise.

Maybe he and Victoria shouldn't have touched a drop of the whiskey. Maybe they would still have pemmican, robes, a rifle, and a saddle. But all the maybes in the world did him no good. He and Victoria were bone-weary. The spirits had offered a moment's refuge from cold and pain and trouble and they had imbibed the whiskey with delight. And it wasn't the spirits that had betrayed him, but the Fitzgeralds.

Just when he felt his first ebbing of energy, he redoubled his speed, leading the old mare eastward around river brush, along a natural road or animal trail on the north bank of the stream. He would not give in to tiredness. But he would rest the mare now and then, for Victoria's life still depended on that old cayuse.

The colt, Jawbone, trotted along beside, but sometimes

ran ahead or fell behind. Maybe, Skye thought, he could make something of that boneheaded beast but he doubted it.

He came to a place where the wagons turned right, crossed the stream at a gravelly ford, and headed due south for the Yellowstone country. So they weren't going to Victoria's Crow camp after all. That was smart. If they showed up with Skye's Hawken in their arm, or with that parfleche, which had classical Crow geometric designs dyed upon it, they would not have walked out of the village alive.

Skye knew what he would do: he would walk the remaining miles nonstop, through the night, until he reached safety. Only when Victoria was safe in her brother's warm lodge would he himself rest.

14

S kye walked. The mare carrying Victoria followed. He set a steady pace, letting his legs swing easily. If he was tired, what did it matter? He walked along a game trail that followed the Musselshell, thinking about nothing but making his legs work, step after step.

He stayed warm but Victoria, riding the mare, was soon chilled. Then he had to stop and let her walk and stretch, and then hand her up again. She never complained.

Skye had heard legends among the Indians of runners, of amazing young men who could run day and night for great distances carrying news. He had met some famous runners, lithe of body, able to jog along for prolonged periods. But he was not built that way. He was stocky and medium high. A man could walk if he set his mind to it; walk even when his feet began to torment him, his boots or moccasins chafed, his muscles hurt, and blood collected around his toes. Walk and not stop. Walk through twilight into night, walk through midnight and the small hours, walk into a dawn and keep on.

So Skye walked, and kept walking even when hunger gnawed at him, even when he yearned to quit. There was no shelter at the end of this day, no place to quit, no food. There was water, but no more. He cupped his hands and lifted water to his lips sparingly, knowing it was too cold to sit well in him.

The mare did not disappoint him, but settled into a rhythm that matched his own pace, neither hurried nor slow.

Whenever he tired, he rested briefly. But if he didn't walk too fast, he didn't tire fast, so he moved steadily, sticking close to the river. The wind quartered in from the left, chilling him on that side, but he ignored it. He reached some rocky bluffs and rested in their lee for a while, and then started in again. Here in the bluffs were birds, including a pair of golden eagles, making a riverside living through the winter.

He tried to think of other things, but the weariness of his thigh and calf muscles trapped his mind and focused it on his body. His hunger died away and in its place was a keen edginess, as if he were facing danger. But there was no danger in sight, only the November-quiet valley of the Musselshell with its latticework of tree branches and a gloomy sky.

At twilight he rested in an undercut cliff, not a bad place to camp if he needed to. He lifted Victoria off the old mare and set the horses to scrounging in the brush. Jawbone was learning to get his own feed, and he gnawed beside his mother, finding sustenance in twigs.

"Are you cold?" he asked Victoria.

"Keep going, Skye."

That was answer enough.

He collected the old mare and hoisted Victoria aboard once again, and then set off into the deepening shadows as the November night fell. The next lap was going to be hardest of all. There was going to be no moon for the first half of the night, and when it did rise, it would be nothing more than a fat sliver. This night he would stumble through utter dark and hope he didn't meet disaster, such as falling into the river, which would probably kill him.

He chose open country this time, north of the dense river-

bed brush and trees, believing he could make his way better back from the tangle of foliage. And that proved to be
true. Nights with open heavens are not black, and the dome
of heaven sheds its own faint light, so he walked on, the
mare somehow keeping pace. He was never sure about Jawbone, but the little fellow managed to keep track and checked
in now and then.

Night travel was not new to Skye but he had rarely traveled in this sort of cold, nor had he ever attempted to cover
so much ground. The wind picked up now and then, filtering through his blanket capote. But he kept on. Step by step,
through the night. Then the moon rose and he had a little
more light and could see the dark wall of timber guarding
the river.

He lost track of time. He could walk or he could try to
hole up. The buffalo bull-hide moccasins Victoria had
crafted for him were slowly opening along their inner seam
and he wondered whether to stop for repairs. Some thong
cut from the remaining robe might lace up the growing
gaps. His feet ached but he would continue. Something in
the rhythm of walking kept him going, even if every step
shot pain through each foot.

For brief periods Victoria dismounted and walked with
him, but she had no strength for it and retreated to the back
of the mare. He sensed the mare was slowing now, and he
let it happen and slowed his own pace to hers. The goal was
not speed but to keep on going.

The landscape was changing and the river was running
in a narrower valley flanked by high sandstone bluffs. That
was a good sign. But he questioned whether he could go
much farther; his body was finally rebelling. He sensed he
might be within five miles of Victoria's village, maybe less.
He had no way of knowing.

He heard the distant howl of wolves high up on the ridges
to the north but heard no answering howl, and then heard

only the silence of deep night. He thought it might not be long to dawn, but he saw no streak of light on the southeastern horizon, only the slow-ticking darkness.

The hunger pangs were returning now, not sharp as before, but cold and sullen. His body was telling him it needed nourishment or it would quit on him.

He ignored the trouble; there wasn't a thing he could do about his hunger except push it aside, pretend that his body wasn't howling at him. He was arguing with his body now, trying to impose his will upon it, as if it somehow would heed his wishes. But his steps were shorter and slower, and he knew he was reaching the end. They would have to quit. For a day and much of a night he had walked.

The mare snorted. Then whickered softly.

Skye stopped cold. That was horse talk. He had heard it a thousand times. The mare snorted again, a soft low rumble down in her throat.

Victoria came awake, slid off the mare, and took the lead line, holding the horse in place. Jawbone stood, questioning his mother. Skye edged forward, seeing little, unsure of what he was looking for. Jawbone danced along beside him, sometimes sniffing the night air, smelling something that Skye didn't smell.

Then the colt cut to the right, down a grade, and squealed. Skye hated to be given away by that miserable renegade but padded softly down the slope toward the river, which ran through grassy bottoms. Then he saw the shifting shapes of horses, lots of horses, some of them edging close to him. The colt stopped and snorted.

Now there was a great stirring of the herd. Skye thought he might be in real danger. In a moment he was surrounded by horses, which stared alertly at him, ready to break away, stampede. But they didn't.

Maybe Crow horses. He tried a few words of the tongue they might know: hello, friend, four-foots, and finally Absaroka, the name Victoria's people gave to themselves.

She came up beside him. "We have come," she said.

"How do you know?"

"I know."

These pronouncements had always mystified him. The Indians knew things in ways he could never grasp.

"We're likely to get shot."

"I will walk among them. They know me."

"How can they possibly know you?"

"We are sisters and brothers."

She handed the mare's lead line to Skye, and wandered slowly into the mass of animals, talking softly to them. They did not bolt but soon collected around her. He heard one tiny squeal, and that proved to be from Jawbone, who was being examined by the boss mares of this herd.

He tried desperately to see whether there were herders on this wintry night and worried that they would shoot first and ask questions later. But he saw no mounted form rise out of the dark.

"Come," Victoria said, a sudden lilt in her voice, the song in it celebrating her safe return to her people. She walked ahead, this time with Jawbone cutting through the animals like a ship's prow, and on across a broad but protected grassland bordering the river.

The pale slice of moon caught the quiet cones ahead, which were arranged in a great arc under the shelter of sandstone cliffs. Skye followed; this was now out of his hands. The herd mysteriously stopped, as if some invisible fence lay between the village and the pasture, though no fence did. And then they were clear of the village herd.

Before them stood the stately Crow lodges. Smoke eddied from a few, caught by the pale moon, but most stood silent and dark, the thin walls of buffalo hide protecting these people from all the evils of the night.

She knew exactly where to go, her step lithe and purposeful, and he followed slowly, aware that the mare's clopping behind him must sound like an invading army to these

sleeping people. But no one exploded out of a door flap. And
then she stopped before a certain lodge. He could not tell
one from another, yet he knew this would be her brother's
lodge. She scratched softly on the door and waited, while a
small cloud slid over the moon and took away the light.

15

A gain, according to the polite Crow custom, Victoria scratched softly on the lodge door flap of her brother Two Dogs and waited. Victoria's other kin were with the Kicked-in-the-Bellies band on the Big Horn this season. To Skye, feeling his own weariness soak him, the wait seemed interminable. But at last the flap parted slightly, and Skye recognized Night Stalker, one of Two Dogs' wives. She stared, absorbing the pitiful sight, and muttered something. The flap closed. Skye heard stirrings and the flap parted once again.

Two Dogs had awakened and was tossing dry grass onto the coals of the fire. It smoked and then broke into a small flame, immediately lighting the lodge. The other wife, Parts Her Hair, was hastily pulling a robe over her hips. Two Dogs had chosen her for his mating this night.

Two Dogs summoned his sister and Skye with a wave of the hand, and Skye crawled into the warm and fragrant lodge, which also contained this family's three children ranging from infant to teen.

"Ah! Many Quill Woman! We may say your name at last!" said Two Dogs, a greeting that acknowledged that this family thought she had died.

Victoria sank into the robes, and Skye settled down beside her.

Then Jawbone poked his head and neck through the door.

"Aaee!" said Parts Her Hair, scrambling up, mostly naked, to chase the animal out.

Two Dogs stayed her with a barked word.

"Who is this?" he asked Skye.

"It is Jawbone, the foal of a mare that brought us here. He is a horse with medicine. His mother came to us, brought by the magpies, and saved my wife. She has great spirit."

"So he is. Welcome him," Two Dogs said to his wives.

They pulled the flap open and the colt stepped in.

"He is not a handsome horse but he is a horse that is destined to serve you well. Now, Mister Skye, tell us your news while my women heat some buffalo stew."

Skye did not mention his hunger or that neither he nor Victoria had eaten in two days. Their plight was obvious to this family. The children lay wide-eyed in their robes now, studying the visitors.

"My blessings upon this lodge of Two Dogs," Skye said.

It was this ritual that smoothed over the life of the Crows, and Skye remembered it now.

"And the blessings of Two Dogs goes out to his sister and her man."

This called for tobacco, so Two Dogs motioned to Night Stalker for his beaded pouch. She handed it to him, careful not to touch the pipe within, and he tamped tobacco into the pipe, with its bowl of red pipestone, and then lit it with a coal. He puffed and handed it to Skye, who puffed, though he hardly had energy for it. He wanted only to collapse into a warm robe in this safe place.

But there were rituals to perform, and only if they were performed could the peace and safety of the lodge be kept. And so they kept the ritual. It was also a way of preparing the lodge for the story that would follow. These kin and all of Chief Robber's village knew of the disaster up in the Judith basin, but none of them knew Skye and Victoria's story and believed they had perished.

Skye felt the tobacco quiet him, and struggled to stay awake while Two Dogs studied him calmly. At last Skye was able to narrate the story of their struggle against the north wind that had brought down an early winter upon them. How close Victoria was to death. How slowly Victoria's wound healed. How weak she remained. His Crow was rudimentary, but they sat patiently as he struggled for words. His tale of hardship, of wolves, of cold and heavy snow, of hunting for firewood, and of the miraculous appearance of the bony mare and her ugly colt, all caught their fancy, and they listened soberly. Skye told of being robbed by the traders named Fitzgerald and did not neglect to tell how ardent spirits had been employed to rob them.

Victoria, he saw, was falling asleep. No one awakened her.

When the stew was steaming, Parts Her Hair, who didn't bother with her fallen-down robe, ladled it with a horn spoon into two bowls. She shook Victoria gently and when Victoria emerged from her stupor, handed one bowl to her and the other to Skye. He ate gratefully, relishing the hot meat broth. He spooned it into him, admiring Parts Her Hair, whose honeyed flesh glowed in the firelight.

The Crows never bothered with decorum, and Skye had been a long while getting used to it. Unlike other tribes, the Crows mated anywhere and everywhere, in public or in private. Skye's whole instinct had been to back away, turn his head, retreat, but that had only won hoots from Victoria, who thought Skye was being prissy. She often teased him about it, and Skye didn't mind the teasing because it always led to good times.

Two Dogs spoke to his older son, and the youth, clad in leggins and breechcloth, rose out of his robes, steered Jawbone out the lodge door, and pulled the robe from the mare.

"He will take your horses out to the herd, and we will

see that they are watched over," Two Dogs said. "When sun
returns to light my way, I will go out to the herd with you,
and you will show me this medicine mare and this colt you
call Jawbone. For mark my words. There has come into my
lodge this night an animal unlike any I have ever seen. We
Absaroka know more about horses than any other people.
We have more and better horses. They live in the mountains
south of the Yellowstone River. We have beautiful horses,
sleek and fast. But this ugly one . . . it is upon me to tell you
that I felt the presence of a power I have not before experienced."

Skye nodded. In truth, he could no longer keep his eyes
open. Food, warmth, safety, comfort, all conspired against
wakefulness. Two Dogs watched him sharply. "We welcome
our friend and kin Mister Skye, and honor the Great Walk,
for it will always be known to us as the Great Walk," Victoria's brother said, and Skye's last recollection was someone
drawing a robe over him on the right side of the lodge, the
place of honor, and then he was lost to the night and to the
great village of Chief Robber.

When he woke the next day he was confused, hardly able
to sort out the scents and sights around him. Clearly it was
midday, not morning. He did not see Victoria. He was uncertain about the young Absarokas who studied him solemnly.

Two Dogs' lodge. Safety. Warmth.

He sat up, rattled, ashamed of oversleeping and impeding
the daily life of these people. He wrapped a robe around
him and poked his head out of the door, surprised to find
the sun behind him. This east-facing lodge had seen the sun
rise and begin to set as he slept.

Outside, sitting on a reed backrest, was Two Dogs,
wrapped in a red Hudson's Bay trade blanket and enjoying
a mild November day.

"Ah, Mister Skye! You have returned from your long
trip," he said. "Come enjoy the afternoon. Your story has

won the hearts of the People and they wish to see you. All day they have walked by here, looking for a word with you, a chance to see the Walker."

Parts Her Hair, now dressed primly in buckskins, smiled sweetly and began warming some ribs of buffalo for Skye.

"Where is Many Quill Woman?" Skye asked.

"She has gone to the sweat lodge to purify herself. She has some sweetgrass to put on the fire, and its scented smoke will drive the sickness out of her."

Skye settled down beside his host. He discovered both the mare and Jawbone tethered to the lodge and eating some dry grass that had been harvested for them.

"That colt, Mister Skye. I see wings in the sky above it. I see lances and battle-axes. It is a warhorse. It is the greatest of warhorses."

"Your vision is larger than mine," Skye said. "I see an ugly little gray thing with a jaw that is too large for its head, and a madness in its eyes."

Two Dogs laughed. "We shall see," he said.

"I am indebted to you," Skye said.

"There is no debt among kin. You were dead and now are alive. The women are sewing skins and before the sun sets they will have a new lodge for you. My sons are gathering our horses and you will take your pick. You will need four or five. We are rich in horses and you are not. Chief Robber's wives have brought you two robes, and his sons have brought you a forequarter of buffalo cow, killed only two days ago. There will be other gifts in your lodge, including a hackamore and other horse tack, and parfleches filled with pemmican, and a spare dress and leggins for your woman."

"I have no way to repay you."

"You already have. Your Hawken barked many times, felling buffalo for this village, protecting it from the thieving Blackfeet. Someday, we hope, you will have enough robes to trade for another rifle. I hear tell of a new Buffalo gun called a Sharps, but it is only a whisper. No one has ever seen one."

"Never heard of it," Skye said.

Even as he sat, blotting up the mild sun, a band of ponies wended its way through the village, driven by half a dozen Crow boys. Skye knew they would stop before him, and he would be given his choice.

Two Dogs rose and waited, and then nodded to Skye when the herd reached this warm place in the sun, milling and churning, restless at being in the middle of Chief Robber's village. Skye's brother-in-law nodded. Skye stood slowly, doffed his top hat, and studied the horses. He was a seaman, a mountain man, not half the expert with these animals as his hosts, who knew everything there was to know about horseflesh.

Jawbone trotted into the herd, began butting animals, and in a minute had isolated four quivering ponies, a mare and three stallions, two of them yearlings, one older. They were fine animals.

Skye marveled. Two Dogs laughed softly.

"He is telling you," Two Dogs said.

Skye nodded, and watched that colt butt the older horses until they were out of the herd. Jawbone was no horse; he was something Skye couldn't explain, something that had no words to express it.

16

W alks to the Top was in no hurry to receive his visitor so Skye waited in the winter cold. The old man held the office of Tobacco Planter, and thus was deeply esteemed among the Absaroka. He was also a seer, a visionary. Skye had little to give this eminent man but had brought him an armload of firewood for a gift. It wasn't much of a gift from a male, because the gathering of firewood was woman's work. But he had nothing else to give, being a pauper. A gift of tobacco would have served better. A haunch of buffalo still better for the old man was totally dependent on the village to keep him alive and warm and well.

Jawbone didn't like the cold wait, and butted Skye.

"Avast!" Skye bellowed.

Jawbone only laid back his ears and lowered that thick skull and pushed at Skye's midriff. The little colt didn't want this interview.

At last the arrogant old man deigned to open his flap, eye his visitor and the colt, stare at the modest heap of small sticks, and nod. It was not an invitation to enter.

Skye summoned up his rudimentary Crow tongue. "I have come to seek your wisdom, Grandfather."

"I have no wisdom for you."

"It is about this colt."

"That is the worst excuse for an animal I have seen."

"A magpie, the spirit guide of my wife, brought this colt and his mother to us at a time of great need. The mare saved the life of my wife."

The Tobacco Planter stared, and then Skye saw mockery in the man's face. He didn't believe a word of Skye's story.

Jawbone detached himself from Skye and pushed toward the old man until he stood inches away, his muzzle almost in Walks to the Top's face.

"He has something else. Something rare. A will, a force."

"Cut its throat."

"I am seeking your counsel about him. I have given him a name. He is Jawbone. What will he be? A buffalo runner? A warhorse? A hunting horse?"

"No good will come of him. This I see. This animal should be driven from the village. Give him to the Piegans so they may suffer this colt's evil."

Jawbone lowered his head softly and pressed it into the old man's chest, pushing him back toward the lodge door.

"Jawbone!" Skye yelled, and grabbed the colt by the mane and pulled him back. But the insult had been done. The wizened old man, prominent and powerful among the People, had been offended by a colt.

The old Tobacco Planter straightened himself and drew a blue and black trade blanket about him, eyeing the colt, and Skye, with an obsidian gaze that raked them both. He wore the insignia of his rank, including a bear-claw necklace, a powerful reminder that he was not to be trifled with.

"Tell this to The Robber; tell it to the headmen, for I have said it. This village will know no peace, no comfort, no food, no heat, no buffalo, no safety, no new children, no honor until this monstrous creature is removed and the village is cleansed with sweats and prayers."

Skye stood frozen. It would be up to him to report, faithfully, the exact words of the old Tobacco Planter to the headmen.

"I do not want your wood," the old man said. "Bring something that does you honor. Not this." He pushed his moccasin into the piled wood and scattered it.

"Suppose I don't bring this colt into the village but keep him and his mother in the herd . . . I am indebted to the mother. She carried Many Quill Woman all the way here, though the old mare was perishing from the want of feed, and because she was nursing this colt."

"I have spoken," Walks to the Top said, cutting off all further discussion. The old man's eyes betrayed something that Skye had not fathomed before: a contempt for strangers in the midst of this Absaroka village. For a pauper.

He leisurely turned, showing his blanketed back to Skye for too long, and then slipped into his cold lodge. Skye stood there, ripped asunder. Behind him stood the village, nestled under the snowcapped sandstone cliff lining the north bank. Here in a peaceful bottomland the Musselshell River meandered through lush grasses and cottonwood and willow groves. A low autumnal sun heated the sandstone cliff each day, and far into each night the cliff radiated its stored warmth upon these fortunate and comfortable people.

It was Victoria's home, or at least her brother's home. Her own Kicked-in-the-Bellies band was down on the Big Horn River. He wondered whether she would agree with the old Tobacco Planter that the colt must be destroyed or exiled. That its presence would invite disaster upon her People. That he must do as the old man directed or be driven out of this place.

He was a pauper now. The Hawken rifle that had won meat for the whole village had been stolen and he had no weapon save for a knife and his ancient belaying pin. Those were good enough for close-quarters war, but of little value here in this vast plain. He had no grasp of archery and could not hunt with bow and arrow, the way any Crow boy could. Bows and arrows were not weapons known to a British seaman. Just now he was dependent on these people for everything. For every scrap of food. For the lodge the village women were sewing together for him and Victoria. For clothing, moccasins, safety. He had gone from being an asset to a serious liability, someone who needed to be cared for. His rifle had meant meat and hides and a trump against the more numerous Blackfeet and Sioux. Without it, and without skill with a bow and arrow, he was . . . nothing.

He stood in the warm sunlight, absorbing his new status of beggar. The colt edged in and rubbed against him. Well, he would destroy the colt. Slit its throat. Worthless ugly thing. Kill the mare too, because the old creature would be frantic about the colt. Mercy killing. She was starved anyway and her teeth were no good. She couldn't gain weight even if he fed her buckets of oats. He would collect his courage, his ability to do hard things, and do them. They were just strays who happened upon his desperate little camp up in the Judith country. So do what must be done.

But first there were obligations. He walked slowly toward the great lodge of the chief, The Robber, a famed and revered leader of the Absarokas. The Robber and his wives had already given him four lodge skins, and these were even then being sewn into the new lodge that the village would give him and Victoria.

Skye found the fat graying chief warming in the sun before his lodge, enjoying an idle afternoon along with three headmen, every one of them a noted warrior. He paused, waiting for the invitation that would permit him to approach. It came at once, for Skye was still a respected man among them.

He approached, and found the chief and headmen waiting. They had been playing a stick game to while away the sunlight hours. In the evenings they often told stories. The headmen glanced at Skye, but their attention was focused on the audacious colt, which dogged every step and presented himself to the chiefs just as Skye was presenting himself.

Skye studied them, aware that his broken Absaroka tongue was not adequate to the task. But he knew the sign-talk, and decided to employ it.

"I have visited the Tobacco Planter," he began. "The elder has pronounced what he believes. It is this: he says that this colt beside me is a curse upon the people and must be destroyed. He will bring evil upon the village. He will unloose trouble."

"And?" asked The Robber.

"And so I am first to tell you every word of what Walks to the Top has said."

"And?"

"Then I must decide what to do."

"Is there any decision to be made?"

"Yes, sir, there is."

"And what might that be, Mister Skye?"

"To spare the lives of this colt and its mother, who brought Many Quill Woman to safety."

That met with dead silence. It would be an act of defiance. It would signal trouble and sorrow.

"We each must follow our own path, and we each must bear the consequences," said The Robber. It was not unkindly said.

But Otter, the headman, had other ideas. "If that is what the elder believes, then the colt must die."

"Or leave, or be given to other people," Skye said.

"I personally will destroy the colt for the sake of the People," Otter said.

"It is . . ." Skye caught himself. He was going to tell Otter that it was not his to destroy. It was something Skye alone had to do.

Skye glimpsed the black and white flash of a magpie, and remembered suddenly that it was Victoria's spirit helper, the magpie, who had somehow driven and pecked the mare and the ugly colt to Skye's lodge on Louse Creek, clearly a gift of Victoria's helper.

"The horses were the gift of magpie," he said. Every headman knew whose spirit helper the magpie was.

The colt stood quietly and then walked boldly to the headmen and studied them. Skye had never seen such a fearless colt.

Otter didn't like it and growled at the colt. Jawbone didn't budge, and slowly lowered his head and pushed straight at the headman, who was surprised and then enraged. Otter lashed wildly at the colt, who danced away unharmed and bleated cheerfully.

Chief Robber raised a weathered hand. "It is so," he said. "The elder has shown it. Take him from the People. I do not wish to see this colt again, and if I see it, I will have it killed at once."

17

S kye walked away from The Robber's commodious lodge with the strange colt prancing beside him, butting him, and otherwise making a nuisance of itself. Behind him, the chief and village headmen stared, and their gazes were not friendly. Something sour had happened, and Skye couldn't fathom it.

One moment Skye was a hero, renamed The Walker for delivering Many Quill Woman to safety even though she was weak and had been at death's door. Now the village glowered at him and his colt, the foal of the very mare that had borne his wife all that distance.

Was it the colt? The elder had condemned it out of hand, employing his authority as a shaman, to sentence Jawbone to death. And for what? Because Jawbone was unlike other colts? Because Jawbone was fearless? Fear is what governs horses. They sense danger and they run, for their safety lies in escape. But this little fellow marched right into Two Dogs' lodge, butted people, pushed the shaman backward, and didn't behave like a horse. Was that it?

Skye knew it wasn't. An obnoxious horse might be welcomed in a village, but there was something more, something having to do with medicine powers known only to the grandfathers, that had set this village on edge. Jawbone was a dark force, a looming danger, and The Robber had condemned the colt to die, for not even a chief would overrule the verdict of a Tobacco Planter and elder such as Walks to the Top.

Skye didn't know what to do. He could slice that colt's throat, but he knew he wouldn't. He knew somehow that Jawbone was a magical colt who would bring great good fortune to him. The ugly little thing was a gift to a pauper, and it had come to him in a moment of crisis. He would not kill it, nor would he kill the old mare that had rescued them.

Magpies burst away from him, and he thought to tell Victoria who lay abed in the lodge, weakened by the long and desperate trip from the buffalo hunt. But as he walked through the village he felt the hard stares; men who yesterday had honored him and hunted with him and welcomed him now stood silently, their gaze on him and on the condemned colt.

It was a rare and warm late autumn day, with the village nestled comfortably under the yellow rimrock, soaking up the low sun. It was a good day to be alive. Most of the men were out hunting. The disaster up in the Judith country had depleted the supply of meat and hides and robes, as well as horses. The buffalo were nowhere near here, but deer were abundant, and there were elk too. The women were gathering firewood in the thick woods along the river or tending to their cook fires or lacing new moccasins together, or collecting in knots to dress skins and scrape hides and enjoy the mild air. Some of them were out in the woods, cutting willow saplings that could be employed as lodgepoles. Old men and old women, dark and wrinkled, wrapped themselves in grimy blankets and watched the world go by. Blue smoke drifted up from the lodges, which were blackened on top around the smoke holes.

But it was no idyll for Skye, for people paused and stared at him, the executioner's glare in their faces. And some turned their backs, not on Skye but on the condemned animal, who it was believed carried a bad spirit that menaced the village.

Not far from Two Dogs' lodge a dozen women were lacing hides together, making a lodge for Skye and Victoria. It was a tedious process but with so many hands patiently lacing one hide to another the work was progressing rapidly. By nightfall he and Victoria would have a home of their own.

If he slit Jawbone's throat.

He paused at the lodge door, scratched, for he was a guest, and received a word from within. He entered. Jawbone followed.

"Get him out!" said Victoria, who was sitting up in a reed backrest.

Skye grabbed Jawbone by the mane and evicted him. Jawbone contented himself by poking his head inside and observing. Skye thought it was funny but kept silent.

"I have heard it," she said. "You will do it?"

"No. This is my own spirit horse. I won't do it."

Victoria stared, bleakly registering that. It meant trouble, or worse, it meant Skye might be banished from this place.

"I am going away for a while," he said.

"You will not return."

He saw a sorrow in her face and knew what she was thinking. So many women of the People had married a white man only to have that man abandon them and their children and go back to the place where white men lived. She had seen the East; she knew its comforts.

"I will be back, Victoria. I'm going to the American Fur post on the Yellowstone and see about a job. I've traded pelts for years and I think I can get a wage there."

"You will buy a rifle," she said.

"Yes. I'm not much good without it. Without my rifle I am nothing here. I can't make meat. I can't feed us. I can't get hides and trade them for a rifle and powder and ball. I can't help your people in war."

She nodded sadly. "Dammit, Skye, take me with you!"

"I will come for you."

He saw tears collecting in her obsidian eyes, and reached across to her, slipping her cold hand into his big rough ones.

"Every hour that we are parted, I will be thinking of you and dreaming of the time I will send for you. It will be a while. I must earn enough to buy a new rifle and all the rest. But someday I will have what is needed."

"And you will take the mare and the colt?"

"Yes. We are all exiled."

"Exile, what does that mean?"

"Banished. We must leave."

"I am glad. Magpie brought them to us."

"Today, a magpie was flying and flitting around the colt and me."

She nodded. "But you cannot bring them back to this village."

"First I'll get some work if I can at the trading post on the Yellowstone. Fort Sarpy, out on the plains. Get a rifle and an outfit. Then we'll go to Long Hair's village on the Big Horn River, the Kicked-in-the-Bellies, and we will be with your kin. Then I will come for you. We'll end up with your people."

She sighed. "It is so far away."

"It will take one or two moons for you to gain your strength. It will take me that long to buy a rifle."

"Dammit, Skye, you think I am an old woman?"

He laughed, his big voice booming in that small, enclosed cone of leather.

She grinned. "Maybe I will show up at the trading post. Maybe I will surprise you. Maybe I will catch you between the robes with some girl. Maybe I will crawl between the blankets with you. Then you'll see I am well and strong."

He touched her face with his thick fingers, gently rubbing the tears away.

"Will I ever see you again? I am feeling so bad."

"I will be coming for you soon. I must have a rifle. Tell Two Dogs I will come for my ponies some other time. And thank him for caring for them."

It was a painful moment. He kissed her. She smiled at him. He stood, gazed down at her lithe but gaunt beauty, and knew he would never leave her.

He collected his few things: a robe, hatchet, blanket capote, saddle, halters, belaying pin, and some pemmican, enough to keep him going for two days. There were two dangers: cold and Blackfeet, and he would not be well armed against either.

He shooed the colt away from the door flap and crawled into the beautiful afternoon. People had halted their labors and were staring at him. He nodded curtly, not explaining himself though the things he carried told the tale. The colt trotted along beside him, inseparable, and drew cold glances. He continued beyond the village, walking through open bottomland, past young herders riding slowly around the horse herd. The colt squealed and barreled straight toward his mother, who turned her head and watched. She remained gaunt, but somehow looked better.

Skye saddled her, not to ride her but to carry his few possessions, and when he was ready, he walked her to the river, looking for a ford. When he found it he mounted her and she carried him across a flat gravelly shallows. Then he dismounted; from now on, he would walk.

He didn't know this country well, but knew there was a low divide between this river and the Yellowstone, and once he had topped it he could follow any watercourse south and he would end up at that majestic river, one of his most cherished streams and one where he had spent his happiest times.

In all his years with Victoria he had scarcely been apart from her, and only for brief periods. But now he would be gone awhile. He made his lonely way south, a solitary man, half trapper, half native, wearing buckskins, moccasins, capote, but also wearing his battered beaver top hat.

He hoped to earn his way back. He needed a whole outfit, but especially a rifle. With that, he could be a valued guest among the Crows. Without it . . . he was a parasite. He didn't know whether the fur post, Fort Sarpy, would hire him; and if he could not find employment there, he would head for another, either Fort Union at the confluence of the Yellowstone and Missouri, or Fort Laramie, far south. And every step would carry him farther away from his woman.

18

He raised Fort Sarpy just before dusk, when the cold was setting in along with a knife-edged wind. The fur-trading post stood on the north bank of the Yellowstone, below Rosebud Creek, like a grim and solitary prison. It was nothing but four picketed walls of wood, and its bleakness matched the surrounding country.

Skye led his mare and colt along the brushy river bottom, alert for trouble. The Blackfeet had made winter sport of killing any man who dealt with the Crows, and there were often two or three Blackfeet lurking around Sarpy, looking for a chance to bury an axe in the skull of a trader. The little graveyard behind the post had seven mounds of clay in it.

Skye knew that a belaying pin was no match for one of these assassins so he trod gingerly, keeping out of sight in brush, avoiding open trails as much as he could. The forbidding fort rose starkly ahead, on a hill above the floodplain. There was abundant forest in the bottoms to feed its fireplaces and stoves, and river transportation to Fort Union, down a way, where robes and hides could be shipped to the States. It was the most solitary and desolate post in the Northwest.

He saw no Absaroka lodges at the post, but the old, glazed snow was dimpled with hoofprints and other signs of life and passage. The purple twilight settled gently over this land of long rises, tinting the gray smoke rising from the post's chimneys. He walked in utter silence, the sort of quietness imposed by late November on an empty land, hearing not even a crunch of snow under his moccasins.

He had been here several times, usually in fall or summer, when Crow lodges filled the whole plain below the post, like a fleet at full sail. But now he saw not even a raven perched in a branch. He knew the post's bearded and long-haired factor, John Chambers, who scorned and ridiculed the Crow people but was perfectly at ease driving hard bargains with them, a few pennies worth of trade goods for a good robe or hide.

No one greeted him as he walked across the flat in a lavender dusk.

"Hello the post," he bawled.

He saw no one manning the walls.

"Hello the post!" he yelled.

"Someone is talking a strange tongue. We haven't heard it in a long time," a voice returned. "Would you be talking some fool language called English?"

"I am Mister Skye."

"Oh! The damned limey! Living in sin with a Crow slut."

Skye kept the peace. He had heard it all before. It was a way of testing and provoking him. When he was younger, an insult like that always got a fight from him, and he usually gave more than he received. His broken and pulpy nose was mute testimony to his brawling. But now he lifted his old top hat from his head, let them stare through the deepening murk.

"Guess it's himself, all right."

"It's Mister Skye, you bloody damned yellow-bellied Yank."

He heard only a maniacal laughter, but moments later one of the ten-foot-high double doors creaked open and a pair of traders motioned him in.

"We don't let Brits in here," one said. "Now if you were a good honest upright Crow chief with a dozen daughters, we'd let you in."

The other laughed.

The post was typical, with an open yard surrounded by lean-to sheds around the walls.

"Welcome, Skye. I suppose ye want us to put you up."

"You can feed me, water and hay my horses, and give me some floor to sleep on. I want to talk to Chambers."

"That's me, Skye."

"So it is. The darkness fooled me. It's Mister Skye, mate."

"Lord Admiral Skye if you insist."

Chambers opened the gate, let Skye through, then slammed it shut and dropped the bar to keep the redskins out.

"I keep forgetting, you put on them English airs," he said. "We're a little shorthanded here. Lost two men a few days ago. Pesky Blackfeet. You'll have to put up your beasts yourself. The stew pot's full of meat. Good to see you."

That sounded good to Skye, who had subsisted on pemmican for two days.

"I'll be with you directly," Skye said. The horse pen was on the west side. Any animal left outside the walls would vanish and never be seen again. He put the mare and Jawbone in, watched them stir up the half a dozen other horses, and watched Jawbone horn in on some prairie hay that was lying in a manger. Skye found some more hay and fed the mare, hoping she would get it before the others crowded her out.

He watched them a moment, satisfied that his animals had food and drink, and then hiked across the yard to the one lit room, the light radiating from windows plugged with leather hides scraped so thin they were translucent. They were a thousand miles from glass at this lonely place.

He hoisted his few belongings and headed for the common room, a kitchen and dining and social place, the only one in the post. He walked into a wall of warmth. They weren't lacking wood, anyway, and the brightly burning fire in the hearth was throwing heat into every corner.

He set down his robe and saddle and small travel bag and belaying pin and top hat.

Chambers watched him intently. "That's all you've got? No rifle?"

"Two traders named Fitzgerald stole it. And everything else. And I want to talk about that. You got any outfits out in the villages?"

Chambers squinted at him, spat some tobacco, and shook his head. "That'd be the Opposition. Probably the two working for Carson and McCullough. They're hitting the winter villages."

"Father and son?"

Chambers nodded.

"Well, if I find 'em I intend to get my piece back, one way or another. And maybe bang a few skulls."

Chambers looked impatient. "It ain't us and don't you blame us, limey."

"You got any rifles to trade? Real rifles, not muskets?"

"You got any hides or cash?"

Skye laughed. That was a thing about him: anger washed away as fast as it rose.

He discovered four others, mostly so young they looked fresh out from the States. One scarcely could raise a beard, by the looks of the boy.

"I'm Barnaby Skye," he said. "Call me Mister."

They didn't introduce themselves but he would put names to faces soon enough. The stew pot was hanging on an iron hook over the hearth fire. He hunted for a ladle and a bowl, finally washed out some dirty crockery and spooned the broth into it, savoring the smell.

A much-hacked haunch of buffalo hung from a beam. Meals around Sarpy were plainly self-accomplished. He lifted the bowl, sipped from it, and finally ate with his fingers for the want of a spoon. But it tasted just fine, good meat and salt and some sort of root vegetable tossed in. The rest watched glumly and he wondered just what had gone wrong with this meeting.

Skye finished a hearty meal and took a second bowl for good measure. He hadn't eaten like that for a long time. He wiped his face and turned to his hosts.

"Blackfeet trouble?"

"Never stops. Those two hunters vanished a week ago. We don't know whether they're alive or dead."

"Two of your engaged men?"

"Yost and Parsons. They went out to make meat and never came back. Now we're down to what you see here. No way I can defend this place anymore."

"Crows been around?"

"All the time, but that doesn't mean there ain't times like this when this post's naked."

"You want another man?"

"You?"

"I'm wanting to work to pay for a new outfit. Rifle above all else. But also powder, ball, and all the rest. I don't have a shilling to my name. I've done a lot of trading and trapping for American Fur, the Upper Missouri outfit. You'll get an experienced man."

Chambers eyed him. "I was thinking of quitting here. Just four men and me against the whole redskin world."

"Nothing I can't do."

"Skye, that's fine, but you'd never save up enough for a rifle and a kit. Not with them horses you'll have to board with me."

"If I cut enough cottonwood bark every day to keep my horses without using your hay, then what do I make a month?"

"Thirty dollars and board."

"And what does a new rifle cost?"

"More'n you'll ever earn here."

Skye laughed. "Then I'll buy a used one. I'll just have to make myself profitable. By the time I was a brigade leader during the beaver days, I was earning a thousand a year. Put me on, Chambers."

"It's Mister Chambers, Skye."

They laughed uproariously, as if that were the funniest thing all fall.

"Now, Skye, I have a question for you. That's the sorriest mare and colt I ever did see. Mare might make a pack animal, but that colt; there's no help for an ugly little cuss like that. What you should do with them is slit their throats and turn 'em into jerky."

Skye stopped his merriment cold. "Anyone who harms those animals will be dealt with in kind."

"That's mighty peculiar, Skye."

"You heard me," Skye said. "In kind. A life for a life, a wound for a wound."

"Mind telling me why?"

"They came to me out of heaven," Skye said.

The factor and his four men stared at the newcomer, hardly knowing what to make of such a man.

19

S kye woke up that mid-November day to find himself an employed man. The American Fur Company owned him now. He had risen high in the ranks of that company, becoming a brigade leader back in the beaver trapping days.

Now the beaver days were gone. The beaver had been trapped out, but fashion had changed also, and the beaver felt top hat had given way to silk. The company had drifted into the buffalo robe trade and continued to dominate the unsettled American West.

Skye felt at home. He knew his value: he could speak Crow, was married into the tribe, and was a veteran of the fur trade, knowing the whole business. He didn't doubt that he could be of service, especially when the rest of this crew seemed to be green youths fresh out of the border towns of Missouri.

Chambers probably thought more of Skye than he thought of Chambers. Through those November days Skye listened to the factor's unending litany of contempt for the Absaroka people. Thieving rascals he called them; immoral, gross, childish. He had a way of condemning everyone and everything about the people who traded at Fort Sarpy. Skye simply shut up and did his work and waited until he could trade his labor for the new outfit he needed.

The morning after Skye arrived, Chambers took him into the trading room to familiarize Skye with the stock. There were the usual striped trade blankets, kettles, awls, knives, arrow points, powder, pre-cast bullets, lead and bullet molds, calico, flannel, beads, thread, needles, flints and steels, and rifles. It was those rifles that absorbed Skye. His old Hawken was gone, though he intended to get it back if he ever saw it again. He knew that rifle better than he knew his own face. But here was a battered Hawken and assorted muskets and Indian trade rifles perched on a rack.

One new rifle caught his eye instantly: it had an octagon barrel and was made of blued steel, and was unfamiliar.

"A Model 1852 Sharps," Chambers said. "Fifty-two caliber. Anything hit with a ball that size stays down." He lifted the rifle off its rack and handed it to Skye. Everything was unfamiliar. It had a sliding breech action and used linen or paper cartridges. When the breech closed it tore the paper, exposing the powder to the cap. But even the caps were different; they came ten to a small rotating disk.

"A man can fire this rifle ten shots to a minute," Chambers said.

"Ten shots? One minute?" Skye had never heard of such a thing.

"The capper rotates. You slide in a cartridge, close the breech, aim and fire."

"A shot every six seconds? That's faster than an Indian can nock an arrow and shoot it."

Chambers nodded. "Evens the odds, don't it?"

It certainly did. Skye thought through the long roll call of dead trappers he had known, men who died because it took so long to pour powder down a muzzle-loader, jam the patch and ball home, pour powder in the pan or slip a cap over the nipple, aim and fire.

Skye hefted the rifle, felt the sliding breech snap shut,

dry-fired, and suddenly wanted it worse than he had ever wanted anything in a trader's store. "How much?"

Chambers laughed. "More'n you'll ever earn, Skye. Over a hundred dollars for the bare rifle, and the rest, the caps and cartridges, cost a pretty penny."

"We'll see about that. Now, Mr. Chambers, what's a carbine like this doing here? Not an Indian on the plains can afford it."

"Wrong, Skye. The fur company knows better. Some chief walks in here, finds a rifle he can shoot like that, every six seconds, and he wants it so bad he'll bring in a thousand dollars of hides and pelts, kill half a buffalo herd, and throw in all his wives in the bargain. Company figures one of these will fetch a thousand percent profit."

Skye didn't like that. Chambers probably wouldn't sell him the rifle even if Skye came up with the cash.

"If I bring in enough hides, you'd sell it to me?"

Chambers just laughed. "Skye, those shelves need cleaning. Pesky thieves made off with half our sugar and coffee last time."

"I'll hunt, Chambers. You need a hunter?"

"They'd kill you too."

"Not if I use the Sharps."

"I'm not letting the Sharps out of here unless it's paid up. A Sharps in the hands of some Piegan or Blood could just about knock the props from under the fur company. Bad times, Skye. No one's making much."

"I've heard that before," Skye said.

Skye found himself doing whatever needed doing. There were hides to be graded and protected with bug powder. Firewood to be felled and chopped and hauled. Stores to be inventoried. And once in a while a Crow party showed up, wanting sugar or coffee or candy or firewater. The spirits were illegal, but Chambers no doubt had a private supply hidden somewhere. Skye guessed it was kept in a cellar under the factor's own room. Skye wished he could trade a few hides for some of that stuff himself. But he knew if he just waited around that post, there would be a fandango sooner or later. Meanwhile, he went dry.

Chambers soon gave Skye the tasks that required some experience. Skye sometimes did the trading, but Chambers didn't like it: Skye always gave an honest weight of gunpowder or coffee or sugar, and failed to stick his thumb into the measuring cup.

"Skye, you'll never earn anyone a profit," Chambers said.

"It's Mister Skye, mate."

So Chambers pulled Skye from the trading counter and sent him out to make meat while the greenhorns around the post did the menial work such as loading in the firewood and bug-powdering the hides in the storeroom and feeding the horses.

Skye borrowed one of the Leman muskets to hunt with; it was made for the Indian trade, and shot true enough. There weren't any buffalo close to the post this winter, but he found plenty of elk and a herd of antelope.

Whenever he headed out, he took the mare and Jawbone with him. They always enjoyed themselves, nipping at dry grass and twigs, enjoying the liberty of the open country. Skye kept a sharp eye for trouble but the November days paraded peaceably by, absorbing him in the routine of the trading post. It took an awful long time and a lot of labor to fetch thirty dollars.

The darkest days of the year arrived, and Skye heard nothing of Victoria. Was she healed? Did that wound and scrape with death change her? Did she still hurt? There were some wounds that never ceased to torment. A deep December cold settled over the north country, temperatures far below zero on Fahrenheit's scale, and Skye hoped she was warm in her brother's lodge, or her people were caring for her in her own lodge. This winter the Blackfeet were especially aggressive, and reports filtered in from all over, Piegans, Bloods, killing a Crow here and there, stealing horses, causing trouble.

Evenings, Skye listened quietly in the small kitchen room but said little. Chambers mostly railed against the Crows. For most of a week he complained about Crow mating habits, calling the whole tribe debauched, corrupt, scandalous. Skye listened irritably. The man was applying his white man's morals to a people who lived and believed other things. The Crows were a bawdy tribe, and none more so than the old grandmothers, who could tell yarns that made him blush. But Skye had rarely seen the sort of open and public mating Chambers claimed was commonplace.

"Them Crows, they got nothing else to do all winter, so that's why they get a mess of babies along about October, November, December," Chambers said.

Skye kept his silence. It wasn't so different among European people. The greenhorns, Rufus and Jasper and Billy and Ezekiel, mostly listened and blotted up the lore of the fur trade. They were all good enough youngsters. But they had little commerce with a squaw-man, and Skye let it stay that way.

Each day, Skye headed into the trading room, hefted the blue-steel Sharps, slid a cartridge into the chamber and slid it out again, lined up the sights, learned how the rotary capper worked, and ached to own the rifle that would make him king of his world once again.

"Forget it, Skye," Chambers said, just as Skye dry-fired at a raven outside.

"I will own this rifle," Skye replied.

Jawbone began filling out as he headed into his yearling stage. The colt put on weight and began to bully the other horses in the pen, especially his mother, who wouldn't take it and nipped Jawbone hard. Also, he began to grow in his adult hair, and began to show the color of a blue roan. If anything, he turned even more ugly. That underslung jaw projected outward from his muzzle. His narrow-set eyes seemed to bore into the surrounding world and intimidate it. He learned to bare his teeth and squeal, and that was all it took to stir up the post's horses.

"Skye, if that colt causes me any trouble, or I end up with injured stock, I'm holding you responsible," Chambers said one day as they watched Jawbone herd the rest of the animals round and round the small corral.

"That's fine. He's my responsibility," Skye replied.

"I should charge you for feed."

"Every day I bring more cottonwood bark into this pen than both of my horses eat. Look at your stock. They're fat, and it's the leanest time of year for horses."

Chambers wasn't done with ragging Skye. "I'll tell you, Skye. That colt is nothing but trouble. You'll wish you took my advice and knocked its head in. The first time you climb onto that outlaw, that's gonna be the last day of your life."

"Good," said Skye. "Then no one else will ride him. And call me Mister or I'll quit."

Chambers backed off. Skye was obviously his most valuable and experienced man. But Skye had his fill of Fort Sarpy and Chambers, and thought maybe it was time to move on, rifle or not.

20

Skye preferred to hunt alone. It had fallen to him to keep Fort Sarpy in meat, especially on days when no Indians drifted to the trading window. Chambers saw the value of it. More often than not the former mountain man returned with a deer or an antelope, and sometimes even an elk. The others were mostly hooligans recruited from the waterfront dives of St. Louis, and likely to scare game off.

But there was one of those young ones who wanted to hunt, and resented it when Chambers sent Skye out. His name, Skye gathered, was Rufus. He particularly didn't want Rufus along. The young man had killer eyes. Dead eyes. What was there about some males that gave them that look? Skye couldn't imagine. He only knew that some men liked to kill, and he usually could see it in their faces, in their cold dead gaze, in their view of animals, and sometimes in their view of people as well. He did not want this dead-eyed Rufus with him or around his mare or Jawbone.

He did not want Rufus killing more meat than he and Skye could haul back to the post. He did not want Rufus orphaning a fawn. He did not want Rufus standing around and gazing at the birds while Skye butchered and loaded meat.

When it came to killing animals, Skye preferred to be alone. Long ago, he had adopted the Indian ritual of asking forgiveness of the creature whose life he was about to take. He wasn't sentimental; a quick death from a bullet was easier than the torment of wolves. But Skye had come so close to perishing so many times that he respected the living, and honored the living, and took no comfort in destroying any creature's life.

He set out most days with the mare and Jawbone, often under low gray December skies, and usually headed downstream into country less traveled by the Crows or others. It was always a relief to escape Fort Sarpy and the endless scornful comments about Victoria's people. Skye endured it, kept his mouth shut, and saw his back-wage build. He was getting close now, close to abandoning this melancholy place, this lonely life, and rejoining Victoria.

From time to time he did receive word of her. The Absaroka bands did not neglect each other during the long winters. She was well. She was even more crabby than usual. She was living with her older brother and making her sisters-in-law unhappy. Those snippets of news heartened him. He had come to the realization he was more at home with his wife's people than he was with these white men, no matter that they spoke his tongue. His beliefs had changed and he would never be wholly a European again.

On this overcast morning just ahead of the New Year he set off once again. Chambers usually required him to stay close at hand when there was trading to be done. But on this morning what little snow remained on the flat was glazed, dimpled, and devoid of life.

He set out with Jawbone, who carried an empty packsaddle, and the bony old mare, who dragged an empty travois. By these means he brought meat home and sometimes that saved him a return trip.

"I'm tired of antelope, Skye," Rufus said just before Skye let himself out of the gates.

Skye lifted his top hat and settled it. "It's Mister Skye, mate."

"Putting on airs, that's what."

"No, it's my way of saying I'm worth something in this world. In the Royal Navy no man was mister except an officer."

"So you deserted, and now you can call yourself whatever you want, and bring us rabbits for dinner. If you was a Yank, we'd be eating buffler hump every night."

Skye smiled and refrained from a retort. If Rufus was the post's hunter, they would be boiling bones for some thin soup most nights.

Rufus laughed nastily, no doubt feeling he had put the Brit in his place, and slammed shut the massive gate behind Skye.

Skye headed east again into a desolate emptiness. The river bottoms bristled with a latticework of naked branches. Animal trails laced the rotting snow. He studied them, wanting to know what sort of creatures had threaded through.

The lonely white ridges that guarded the broad valley blended into a gray sky. He saw no movement this morning, not even a raven or the flash of a magpie, both of them wintering birds. No wind plucked at him, and he knew he would be warm this time. Some hunting trips had left him so numbed he thought no fire on earth could restore his heat.

His horses followed dutifully behind. He didn't need to lead them. Jawbone had accepted his packsaddle easily and seemed proud to carry meat. Sometimes Skye would hang two quarters of a deer from the pack frame. The little fellow was filling out. He was still fearless, facing danger by plowing toward it rather than fleeing, the way any ordinary horse would. That worried Skye. But something mysterious still clung to Jawbone, as if there was a Destiny about him beyond Skye's fathoming.

He checked his borrowed Leman rifle now and then, making sure a cap was seated and no snow or mud plugged the muzzle. It was a good enough weapon and he could afford to buy it now, after almost six weeks of service. But he wanted that Sharps and the cartridges and caps that it required.

He walked quietly, his gaze alert for the flash or color of game. In their winter pelts, animals blended into the black and white world they inhabited. Hunting always made him lonesome. He enjoyed being out on a good day, matching his wits against a wily deer or a distant herd of antelope. And yet there was a sadness weighing it not because the animals anticipated death, but because he did. Animals lived in the moment. It was he who foresaw the yearling without the mother, the calf without the parent, the pregnant mother carrying a creature that would be born only two or three months into the future.

He topped a rise and was startled to discover a dozen buffalo a thousand yards away pawing through crusted snow and snatching at prairie grasses. They were black dots in a white hollow. It had been weeks since he had seen a bison, and now he had a chance to kill two or three and bring in meat for two weeks. He would carry what he could and send an *engage* back for the rest. They were all facing away from him, save one. He saw no calves. This probably was a bachelor band, yearlings or two-year-olds, driven off by the old bulls, awaiting their turn to lord over a harem. Good tender hump meat tonight! Buffalo steaks for days to come!

He felt no breeze, and wished he might because he didn't know what direction the air was eddying. The animals were not on the alert, and were placidly pawing and eating, black behemoths under a leaden sky. He could not get close from this point of view, but to the left an intervening slope would give him cover. He backed off until he reached a coulee with brush in it, and tied his horses there, out of sight.

Then he slipped leftward and worked around the slope until he found a small dip where he might approach without being seen. He wanted three or four good shots and he would have them. He stayed low, out of sight, knowing that buffalo had weak eyes and an excellent nose. As far as he could determine the air was lifeless. No breeze would carry ahead of him.

When at last he spotted them again, two or three hundred yards away, they had stopped grazing and were all staring southward. He feared it was too late. He readied his Leman, choosing a big male on the far side of the herd, when on some sort of signal they all snorted and ran, scattering east and northeast. And moments later half a dozen Indians pursued on horseback, each after one or another of the buffalo. He could not make out who they were; only that he was in some company he may not wish to entertain. Men clad in buckskin; men with black hair, some braided, some loose, some pinned in place with red headbands. Men on good ponies.

The ponies were slower than the buffalo, which were now running swiftly and oddly silently. Skye had always associated the sound of a buffalo running with thunder, but not this time. They were phantoms, easily racing away, with the Indian hunters not far behind. He could see several rifles and one or two bows among them.

There went the buffalo steaks. He would have relished dropping a haunch of buffalo in Rufus's lap this evening.

He backed off and circled around the slope. He might yet bag a deer if he was lucky. He rounded the bend that led down to the coulee and froze. Two of the Indians had found the mare and Jawbone, grabbed the leads, and were hastening over the top of a grade and out of sight.

Skye started to yell, and curbed the impulse.

Not the mare, not Jawbone.

He ran, his body thumping through brush and up the far hillside, his heart banging, his lungs pumping. He would stop them. He would catch up. He would shoot those thieves off their ponies. He topped the grade and saw them again, maybe a half a mile distant, mounted now, dragging their prizes behind them, looking backward to see if they were followed.

Skye raised the Leman, sighted on the more distant of the pair, and lowered it. He didn't know how many more were nearby, friend or foe. He hadn't the faintest idea who they were.

An anger welled through him. He was a walker. He would walk. There would be a trail. He would follow. He knew Jawbone's hoofprint. There was a little snow to reveal it. He would walk until he dropped. But he would get his medicine horses back. He peered about carefully, looking for trouble, saw none, and began a slow, steady, methodical pace that would mount into miles and leagues. So far, at least, the thieves were sticking to the valley of the Yellowstone, and heading toward the fort. That was a bit of luck even if he was out of luck.

21

kye stopped dead. He had neglected a cardinal rule.
Now he studied every ridge and valley looking for the
rest of them. He didn't know whether he was among
friends such as the Crows, or foes. The hunting party could
have been Sioux, Blackfoot, or Assiniboine, and not a bit
friendly.

So he stood quietly and took the measure of the land and
all upon it, noted places he might find cover, places that
might conceal danger. But he saw no more movement this
overcast day when the snowy ridges evanesced into dreary
cloud. The rest had been chasing buffalo and were probably far away. Far enough so that he heard no shots, no rumble
of hooves.

He checked his Leman rifle. A cap rested over the nipple. He studied the route taken by the thieves, one that took
them through river brush, concealed them from view, and
afforded them endless opportunity to ambush pursuers. He
would need to be doubly careful because he would not be
trailing through open country with good views, but through
the dangerous woods of the river bottom.

Satisfied, he began the long walk. The prints were easy
to follow, fresh in patchy snow. He walked into the river
flats, wary of every thicket, every chokecherry or willow

copse, every fallen cottonwood. But then he realized he would do better on the bluffs where he could see the whole country again, so he abandoned the trail, headed away from the great river until the land rose and the forests gave way to grassy slopes. He saw no evidence of the thieves and knew they were well ahead now, mounted and making good time.

But he walked. He liked it better there just above the bottoms, the formations distinct, his gaze able to measure what came ahead. Now and then he could see the river, a great gray slab of water hemmed by timber. What he did not see was his horses or the thieves. But he did not give up hope. A man who had been left with nothing as often as Skye had realized that luck turns, a determined man rebuilds. Even so, this loss was acute. His medicine horse, his mare, his future . . .

Then he did see them a mile or more ahead, fording the river, distant dots so small he had to focus hard, strain to make out what he was seeing, for the tiny figures working across that wide flowage could have been anything, elk, buffalo, even mustangs. But it was the thieves, both mounted, both leading Skye's horses. That deepened his melancholia. Unless the ford was shallow, and there were few of those on the mighty Yellowstone, he could not wade across. It was one thing to cross a river in winter on a horse that never got belly-deep in water. Another thing to wade across naked, carrying one's rifle and clothing high above one's head, hoping to build a fire and dry out on the other side before freezing to death.

He continued along the bluffs until he came to the place where the thieves had forded, and there he cautiously descended into the thick cottonwood forest, and made his shadowed way to the riverbank. It didn't take long to find the place. Prints in rotting snow told him what he needed to know. The Yellowstone was wide and ran fast there, rippled by a few rocks that broke the surface. But on the far side was a deep channel carrying gray water topped with foam. Death to a man on foot.

The thieves had escaped.

He stood at water's edge, aching to cross, watching the turbid water roll by, and then slowly backed away. This was not done. Somehow, some way, he would find Jawbone and the mare and he would care for them the rest of their days. Somewhere someone would know, would show Skye the way.

He took off his top hat, wiped his battered hand through his mop of hair, and stared across the barrier. He was familiar with water. For years, water was what imprisoned him. He could always jump off the ships that carried him; it was the water that robbed him of life and liberty and hope. Now he was thwarted by water again.

He studied the distant ridges, and then began the slow, steady pacing that would take him back to the fort in perhaps three hours. He didn't walk easily, the way some Yank frontiersmen walked, with a swinging gait and a way of galloping over the surface of the earth. But he walked, stocky, solid of limb, determined as a bull moose, and gradually he covered the miles that had separated him from Fort Sarpy. This night he would bring no meat. A pity, too, because he had buffalo in the sights of his rifle. Rufus would scorn him. Lost his horses! Returned empty-handed!

But Skye knew something about young men like Rufus. They didn't last in the wilds. They were killed as the result of their own recklessness, or driven out of stockades and posts by others, or they wandered back East to brag about their times out beyond the borders.

He reached Fort Sarpy an hour before dusk. The gates were still open. There was a scatter of Absarokas outside along with horses and travois. Skye looked sharply among these but did not see his mare or Jawbone. He hailed a warrior he knew, one of Long Hair's band, an Absaroka version of Beau Brummell who was parading his new red and black blanket before his woman.

"It is a good day when I see you, Little Horse."

"Ah! It is the man named after the heavens above."

"Have you word of Many Quill Woman?"

"I hear nothing, man named after the heavens."

"Or her family? Are they here?"

"No, they are in winter camp. We came to trade."

"Did some of your party hunt this day?"

"No, Sky Man. We came to trade. Why do you ask?"

"I saw some hunters and they had found a few buffalo."

"The shaggy ones? Are they near?"

Skye pointed downriver. "Half a day," he said. "Are there any other of the People nearby this day?"

Little Horse pondered it and finally shrugged. "It has not come to my ears," he said. Skye thought his response was oddly secretive. But he knew he was in no mood to judge others fairly.

"We are preparing for a great feast," Little Horse said. "Our son is coming into his manhood. Even now, he is doing the manly things the elders and Tobacco Planters have given to him to do, and when he is called he will go upon a vision quest, and if his pleas are heard, he will receive his protector and learn of his medicine. And then we will hear what name he has taken."

"Congratulations," Skye said. "Is he with you?"

"No, he is preparing his way."

Skye nodded, bid the Absaroka good day, and headed into the post, where the high stockade was throwing cold blue shadow across the court.

"Make meat?" Chambers asked.

"Lost my chance at some buffalo."

"That's not good, Skye. I've been feeding these big-bellies whatever chops we had lying around, so's to get more trade. You know how they are. Give 'em a rib and they'll eat a haunch. If I don't watch 'em, they make off with half my stock. Bunch of thieving redskins."

Skye had heard all this before and turned away. Chambers wanted to gouge some headman a thousand percent profit for the Sharps, but complained when an Indian lifted an awl.

"Where's your plugs?" Chambers asked.

"Stolen."

"Stolen? You let 'em get away with it?"

Rufus, at the hide press in the court, stopped his labor and stared.

"If that's how you want to put it, yes."

"Well, as long as you're not doing anything, go cut some cottonwood bark for the rest of the nags. That's a good little way to keep some meat on 'em in the winter."

Skye nodded. He returned the Leman rifle to the trading room, and dropped his powder horn and other personal gear in his bunk, which was fashioned from some buffalo hide strung between two poles. The employees shared a common, ill-heated lean-to room against the rear stockade. Only Chambers had quarters of his own. Skye was weary after the long hike back to the post.

Skye found an axe among the post's tools and headed out the gates, his destination a thick grove of cottonwoods near the banks of the Yellowstone. Cutting bark for horse feed was hard work. He didn't shy from it. But Chambers's command was spiteful and had little to do with the welfare of the post. The Absarokas had pulled out, and the river valley was a solitary place now, in the lavender shadows. He found some suitable saplings, smooth green bark all the way, and slowly hacked them down and limbed them. Then he dragged the three poles back to the gates, carefully slitted the bark, and then peeled it off in large chunks. By the time he had finished and fed the fodder to the post's horses, it was dark.

"I want some more bark, Skye," Chambers said.

"In the morning?"

"Now. There's a moon coming up."

There was a post rule against needless night activity when Blackfeet and others were waiting their chance. Chambers was deliberately flouting his own orders and ragging him.

Skye lifted his top hat and settled it again.

"I guess I'll be drawing my pay. There's over six weeks of wage owing," he said.

"Draw your pay? You quitting me?"

Skye nodded.

"Your pay comes outa St. Louis. You walk out, you walk out with nothing. I always knew you couldn't be trusted, Skye."

"Forty-five dollars," Skye said. "And it's Mister Skye."

Chambers laughed and walked away.

22

Forty-five dollars would buy him an outfit even if it wouldn't buy him the Sharps he coveted. For starters there was the battered Hawken on the gun rack, not in the excellent condition of the one stolen from him, but a Hawken even so, rock solid with the thirty-four-inch barrel, low sights, and a fifty-three caliber bore. Seventeen dollars. The back wages would buy him that, a one-pound can of Dupont, a pound of precast balls, a box of caps, and some patches. And a pair of five-point blankets thrown in. He knew the prices; he worked most days in the trading room. He would take his wage in goods.

He collected his capote, belaying pin, and buffalo robe, the meager possessions he could call his own, and headed for the trading room. There he lit an oil lamp with a lucifer and began laying out what he would take. He hefted the old Hawken. He had looked at it a dozen times before. Its stock was battered and the basket protecting the nipple was damaged. No matter. He set it on the counter along with the rest and began scratching a receipt. Let no man accuse him of theft.

At that moment Chambers roared in, saw what was in progress, and yelled at him to stop right where he was.

"This comes to thirty-nine dollars and forty cents worth of trade goods, and I am taking my pay this way," Skye said.

"You are not. You walk out of here and you get none of it."

Skye thrust the receipt at Chambers, who backed away from the counter and reached for a huge dragoon pistol he kept under it for emergencies.

Skye's belaying pin pushed the factor backward so swiftly and steadily that Chambers found himself staring helplessly at the pin as if it were a snake, lashing slowly back and forth.

"Sign here," Skye said.

Chambers twisted free, bolted from the dimly lit room, and Skye heard shouting. The factor was marshaling his troops, who were in the common room starting in on an evening's meal.

It would be no easy task to get out of Fort Sarpy along with his new outfit. He would have to take what he could on his back. There would be no second trip to pick up anything left behind. He slid into his capote, rolled the blankets into his robe for a bedroll, and hung it around his neck. He stuffed the powder and ball and caps inside his buckskin tunic and didn't forget the unsigned receipt. Then he plucked up the Hawken and the belaying pin, one in each hand, and emerged into the court just as the engaged men burst out of the common room. Skye backed steadily toward the gates. Unbarring them would be a problem. He needed an extra pair of hands. But he would deal with that when the moment came. First, he would show them what a limey seaman with a belaying pin could do in close quarters. This was familiar ground to him, up close, his wooden club against sharp-edged steel.

He dropped his gear before the gates and watched them boil across the court, the dim light from the hearth of the kitchen turning them into bobbing light and shadow. He didn't wait; he pushed into them, bulldog strong, jabbing and whacking, spinning to crack one over the head. Chambers stood aside, watching, a coward. These were young-sters mostly, tough as warts on a toad, but they had never brawled on the bobbing decks of a man-o'-war. It was Rufus who worried him. Rufus didn't plunge in but circled be-hind. Skye caught the glint of steel. Dead-eyed Rufus, the killer.

Skye danced away from the rest, took a hit on his right shoulder, and almost dropped the hickory stick. Then he cut it upward into Rufus's groin just as the lout jabbed with the cutter. The knife ripped leather in his sleeve. Skye jammed the belaying pin into the man's crotch and watched him fold up. Rufus tumbled to the icy ground and howled, the big knife lying ten feet away. Skye took a whack along the head from one of the others, lifted his belaying pin into the man's jaw, and heard the crack of teeth and bone. Then suddenly they quit.

And Skye found himself staring into the bore of Cham-bers's hogleg pistol.

"Very good, Skye. You've disabled more of my men. Now walk out and leave the goods."

Skye laughed suddenly, relaxed his stance, and reached into his pocket. "Sign the receipt," he said. "Trade goods for labor."

"You step back now, step toward that gate, lift that bar, or you're dead."

Skye started to obey, took one step back, and then dodged to one side and plowed into the factor, knocking him over. The piece exploded with a flash. Skye felt the burn of gun-powder sear his face, but Chambers was disarmed and sit-ting on the cold and filthy ground.

Skye's top hat lay on the clay, a perforation through its crown.

Skye pulled out his paper and a stubby pencil. "Sign here, Chambers," he said.

Chambers glowered. "I will hunt you down. The com-pany will hunt you down."

"For what? Taking my wages in goods after you stole my labor? Let me tell you something, Chambers. I was pressed into the Royal Navy, and for seven years the Admiralty stole my labor. I'm a little tired of people stealing my labor. I'm so tired of it that I'm ready to knock your head in. So sign."

Behind him, one man was sobbing. Two stood apart, not wanting to try Skye again. Rufus clutched his groin and groaned softly. Chambers still exuded contempt, but now it was leavened by a little respect.

He turned the paper so it caught the light from the kitchen hearth. "All right," he said. He scribbled a signature. Skye took the foolscap and studied it. He had seen plenty of Chambers's signatures. There was nothing tricky about this one. Now he had a bill of sale, one expressly saying his wage was paid in goods. The paper vanished into a pocket within his tunic.

He tucked it into the quilled buckskin tunic that Victoria had lovingly fashioned for him. He felt alone here, alone among these English-speaking white men.

He turned to them. "Remember the Golden Rule," he said. "Treat others as you want to be treated."

They stared.

He tested his limbs. Except for a hurt shoulder and a nasty welt on his head, he was whole. He deliberately turned his back to them, a sign of his triumph over them, and unbarred the massive gate. Then he collected his gear, the old Hawken, the bedroll, the rest, and stepped into the cold March night.

A deep chill had settled over the flat. There was little light. Behind him he heard the gates creaking shut and the heavy bar fall, locking him out. He didn't mind. He had a kit, the result of toil and insult. He was alone now, but he had been alone ever since he had been snatched off the streets of London's East End by a press gang. He knew where he would go, straight upriver to the Big Horn, and then start looking for the Kicked-in-the-Bellies band, Victoria's people. Her younger brother, Arrow Giver, was there, and her younger sisters, Makes-the-Lodge and Quill-Dye-Woman were there also, married to warriors he knew. But they were a long way away.

He carried a heavy burden. The bedroll on his shoulder consisted of two new blankets and a robe; the belaying pin hung on a leather thong from his waist. His capote kept him warm. The Hawken felt good in his hands. He had his knife, hatchet, flint and steel, powder and ball, as well as the powder horn that hung on his chest.

He hadn't a lick of food but he wasn't worried. The river bottoms would provide. He knew of an excellent emergency food sometimes used by the Indians. Cattail roots were thick, starchy, and filled the belly. They were awful, redolent of the swamp, but they would serve. Ideally they needed to be mashed and boiled into a white paste that was edible with the fingers, and served to stay starvation and weakness. But for the moment he needed nothing, and was anxious to put miles between himself and the rotten traders at Fort Sarpy.

He did not mind the wintry night in a land without shelter. He had begun his career in the mountains thinking of wilderness as a hostile and alien place, as most white men did. Now, many years later, he viewed the wilderness as his natural home, friendly, embracing, filled with resources. He had begun not only to live in the manner of the Absarokas, but to think in their fashion too. The Crows treasured this very country as the very best place on earth, neither too hot nor too cold, with abundant game, mountain vistas, rolling prairies, and endless comforts.

He was weary. All day he had hunted, lost his horses, walked back only to find the factor resentful because he had not made meat that day, gotten into a brawl, and now was walking west through the thick darkness with only an occasional howl or the bark of a coyote to tell him that others, too, were out upon the night.

He felt the belaying pin thump against his leg. The Yanks

thought it was merely a stick. It was a long shaft of polished hickory, slippery and hard to grab. Any good British seaman knew how to use it with great effect. And fists were no match for it, which is how he settled the question of whether he would leave Fort Sarpy with his wages.

When dawn broke he had made another eight or ten miles upriver. He located a cattail swamp and soon was pulling the sere brown cattails out of the half-frozen muck, collecting a heap of their thick roots. He built a small fire, nursing a spark in the bosom of the dry inner bark fibers of a dead cottonwood until it flared into flame. Then he patiently cleaned and mashed the roots with the back of his hatchet, and roasted them on rocks set close to his cheery fire.

His cheer departed when he tried to eat the stuff, but it would do, and keep him alive another day, another week, another month until he could find the treasured old mare and Jawbone. In a day or two a new year would begin, and he would make it his own best year.

23

Skye worked west along the great river, at one point circling widely around an ice floe dam that had backed water across the entire valley. The weather held. But he had seen no game and subsisted himself on roots. He was so sick of roots that he yearned for meat, any meat.

His wish was granted, or so he thought. Ahead, motionless, white on white, sat a snowshoe hare, almost invisible on a snow patch. Dinner. He lowered his plains Hawken, lined up the low sights until the hare was directly in line, and squeezed. The Hawken bucked. The hare raced away. Skye peered about sharply, looking for observers, but saw only a crow or two riding an air ladder. Missed. He had not test-fired the weapon but knew he needed to, at once, to find out what was wrong. Carefully, he ran a patch through the rifle to clean it and then measured powder and poured it down the barrel. Then he jammed home a patched ball and slipped a cap over the nipple, making sure the nipple was not fouled. He gouged a cross in a cottonwood tree and paced a hundred yards, found a log for a bench rest, settled onto the hard frozen earth, and aimed. He took his time, resting the heavy barrel on the log, until he was satisfied that his sights were squarely aligned with the mark on the tree. He squeezed. The Hawken bucked. He carefully reloaded and then walked to the tree. The ball had struck three inches low and to the right. He felt betrayed. Hawkens shouldn't do that. His own had shot true. Still, it was valuable knowledge and he was glad he had taken the time.

The next hare might not be so lucky.

He soon found himself in deep woods across from the confluence of the Big Horn and the Yellowstone. He continued upstream along the much diminished Yellowstone, looking for a ford, usually a wide place, often braided, with rills showing, and water only a few inches deep this time of year. But he had no such luck. A man with a horse could have crossed at a dozen places; a man on foot would have to face the worst ordeal that winter travel could offer.

He studied the river, selected a spot that was shallow except for the far side, where a channel of clear green water ran swiftly. He could not fathom how deep. One misstep would send him into a hole, up over his head, drenching everything he would carry, including his blankets. That would probably prove to be fatal, though some of the hardiest of trappers had survived similar drenchings.

He studied the far bank, wanting plenty of firewood, and saw an abundance of ancient cottonwoods. He hated what he had to do, but did it. Crossing would require two trips. He stripped, rolling his clothing and capote into the bedroll. He felt the icy air upon his flesh. He left his moccasins and hardware on the riverbank. Then he waded out, feeling the numbing water pour over his feet and ankles, wobbling as he walked over slippery rock, step by step. The water did not come to his knees but even so his lower legs were afire with cold. He reached the channel. It looked mean and swift. He tentatively stepped out, holding the roll high above his head. He felt the bottom descend swiftly and ice water boiled over his thighs, making his heart race. His whole instinct was to retreat, but he felt his way along, dreading a hole. The water slid up his torso, maddening him with its cruel cold. He almost slipped as the swift current tugged him, but then he stepped to higher ground, rough gravel that hurt his feet. He took three bold steps and a lunge and clambered up the south bank. The blankets and clothing were dry.

He was tempted to wrap himself in his robe for a while, but resisted the seduction. Instead, he steeled himself, stuck his numb limbs back into that brutal current, and made his way to the north shore. By then he was so numb his muscles weren't working, but he had no choice. Every stitch of clothing and warmth lay on the south side. With a thong he draped his moccasins around his neck, then his belaying pin and hatchet, flint and steel, and knife and powder horn. He picked up the Hawken last, checked its load, and started for the brutal river. He had never known such dread of cold. He stood on the bank in browned grass, unable to make himself step into that current; not even the shallows that would take him three-quarters across. But he knew he was not far from the sort of cold that kills, and if he delayed he would never see another sunrise. He was quaking now, unable to stop the shudders that were unbalancing him.

There was only will, the steely determination to carry through that is our last resort. He stepped again into the river, forcefully strode through the shallows, stumbled once and again, righted himself, and came at last to the grim channel. He did not stop, for stopping would have paralyzed him. He felt the bottom decline away from him, stepped fiercely forward as ice water rose to loins and belly, and then at the middle, he did step into a hole, felt himself submerge, ice water over his chest and neck. He thrashed, plunged his Hawken into water, and made himself continue. The shore was only yards away. He stumbled up and out, shaking so hard he could not control the spasms.

There was no time. With water rivering off of him, he reached his bedroll, yanked it open, dumped his burdens, pulled the buffalo robe fur-inside around him, and shook violently, feeling no heat at all from it.

He thought he was a dead man. He felt ice clutch his heart. He clung to the robe, but it did little for him. He found his moccasins, which were largely dry, and somehow tugged them over his feet, and swiftly knew that was the right thing to do. It was as if his feet governed the rest of him; warm them a little and the rest would follow. But he could not stop his violent shaking. He rose, kept the robe wrapped tightly around him, and walked, kept on walking, made his body work. Some while later the quaking diminished to tremors. But he was still so cold he knew he would not live long without fire.

There was plenty of deadwood everywhere, but whether he could make something of it was the question. Much was half wet or icebound. He found a knothole in a willow trunk, and gingerly reached in, finding soft dry debris. This he tenderly placed under a heap of thin sticks. He found his powder horn and poured a bit of powder into the tinder. He could not control his shaking hands and arms, and feared he had poured too much, so much it would blow the tinder apart.

He found his flint and steel in their wet pouch, and now began the hard part. He could not make his hand strike the steel against flint in the practiced way, but he had to. There was, again, only will, the fierce determination to make his muscles obey him. Three strikes failed even to yield a spark from the wet flint. But then the fourth strike shot sparks into the tinder, into the powder. It hissed, flared, flashed, but did not blow the tinder apart, and suddenly he had a tiny, tentative blaze.

"Burn!" he cried hoarsely, for there was nothing he could do but wait and see. His hands trembled too violently to be adding twigs. He wrapped his robe tight again, protected the tiny fire from the breeze with his bulk, and waited an eternity, shaking badly, growing more and more weary. Would his body fail him even as the cold little fire burned?

He watched smoke curl upward. A twig flared and another. A tiny piece of deadwood caught. Then the flame seemed to retreat, and he feared it would die. He made himself rise up, dig for more tinder from any likely spot, the fiber under dead bark mostly, and fed it into the struggling little flame. It caught at once, and he knew he had won. The fire flared orange and another half a dozen deadwood sticks caught. He could live now on hope. It would be half an hour before he had heat, but he had hope and hope preserved life.

There was no warmth. He shook inside his robe. For the first time he surveyed his situation. His goods were safe; his rifle wet and probably useless. He had two blankets he didn't touch because he didn't want his wet body to dampen them. He saw no one. It was not yet afternoon. A weak sun, obscured by a veil of cloud, cast cold shadows.

He fed his flame more sticks. He rose, still trembling, and gathered a pile more. He would burn this whole cottonwood grove if that would warm him. He would build a bonfire ten feet around and ten feet high if that would warm him.

He jammed his beaver hat onto his head again, over wet hair. Maybe that would warm him. It did warm him; he felt it almost instantly.

He fed the fire, returned to its side, opened his robe to its radiation, and let the snapping little flame ply his damp icy flesh with the first friendly warmth it had felt. He opened his robe and spread his arms, making bat wings out of his robe, collecting every scrap of warmth coming his way. His flesh dried. He bathed in the heat, heaped more deadwood into the fire, breathed the foul cottonwood smoke, the bitterest of all wood smokes but didn't mind. Smoke was fire, fire was life.

He brought his clothing to the fire and let it warm. He brought his Hawken close, and let it dry, making sure the octagonal barrel was pointing safely away.

He felt prickles in his flesh, but his inner torso remained numb. He needed hot liquid and had no way of heating any. He needed food, something to heat his body from within. He had seen Crows heat water within some curving green bark placed close to flame, and knew he would try it when he was able to make his arms and hands cut a piece of green bark. But for now he had nothing.

He found more firewood and added it. The fire leaped high now, sending telltale smoke high, but he didn't much care. It was fire or death.

For an hour he sat absorbing heat, gaining ground, staving off a weariness that made him ache to lie down and tumble into oblivion. But finally, he dressed in his warmed and smoky buckskins, swiftly feeling warmer for it. Then he wrapped himself in the two new blankets as well as the robe. He had crossed the river. He was alive.

A while later he lifted the warmed Hawken, sighted on a distant tree, and squeezed. The cap popped. A faint smoke leaked from the nipple. The ball remained in the chamber, and behind it a mass of soaked powder. He had no extractor, a corkscrew-shaped device one could use to pull a ball. His Hawken was useless.

24

The trick was to heat the barrel without scorching the half stock or stock. It needed doing at once. A working piece was more important than his own comfort. He found some flat sandstone that might shield the half stock from the glowing embers, and devised a way to heat the Hawken and draw off the water in the powder. He hated doing it. This was no way to treat the finest rifle ever made. He was so weary that the slightest effort drained him of what little reserve he had, but bit by bit he gathered some sandstone, fed the fire, and finally laid the barrel over hot coals while the flat stone protected the rest of the weapon.

He sat and watched. He knew he should try to make a cup from green bark and heat some water and warm his innards. Instead, he slipped into his capote, rolled up his bedroll, and sat and waited, so devoid of energy that he could do no more. From time to time he fed small sticks to the flames near the barrel. Nothing happened. He hoped for a small, satisfying snap, a puff of smoke belching from the muzzle, a sign that the piece had discharged. But even after what might have been a half hour of careful roasting, nothing happened. Wearily, he found a small copper cap, slid it over the nipple, burning his fingers, and then hunted for his gauntlets. He could not handle that hot steel with bare hands.

At last he was ready. He pulled the hammer back to cock, held the weapon, and pulled the trigger. It cracked. He felt the soft recoil. He set it aside, even as the barrel heat threatened to burn through his gloves. He would soon arm it and have a weapon again.

That heartened him. He found his hatchet, headed for a grove of young trees, found an elbow in a limb, and began slicing the bark from it. The task exhausted him but in time he had a hollow green-bark vessel. He dipped it into the icy river and then settled it on some of the burning-hot rock, just apart from the flame. A while later he clumsily drank warm water. After a second try, in which he heated the water longer, he downed a gill or two of good hot water, and rejoiced. He felt that heat work through his middle. He started another gill of water heating on the hot rocks, and carefully reloaded his Hawken after swabbing it. He was armed.

Three more times he heated water and downed it, and felt his strength tentatively return to him. But the river crossing had exhausted him and he could not travel until tomorrow. He judged that he was one full day's walk from the Absaroka village. He hoped so, anyway. He found cattails in a backwater, roasted as many of the knobby roots as he could manage to push down his unwilling throat, and called himself fed, though it wasn't much of a meal.

He knew he shouldn't stay there in plain sight beside the river. Blackfeet prowled. He studied the country. Heavily forested bottoms, steep lightly forested bluffs, maybe some good cover from predators and weather.

He trudged slowly into the bare-limbed forest and then found himself walking onto a lush meadow. A log structure loomed ahead. It was roofless but had a sandstone hearth at one end and thick cottonwood walls. Some history came to him. This confluence with the Big Horn was where several trading posts had risen and fallen, including the earliest of all. Soon after the Lewis and Clark Expedition Manuel Lisa of St. Louis had come upriver to this point, and did a lively trade.

Skye entered, found the enclosure empty except for a scatter of animal offal. Others had long since burned the fallen roof in the hearth. He examined the hearth and chimney, well aware that such a structure could hold fire and throw heat at him all night. He decided to stay. It took his remaining strength to drag deadwood and driftwood to the hearth, build up a fire there, carry his few possessions, cut some boughs for a bed, and start more hot water heating, for he was still bone cold. But at last, as the afternoon light waned, he was settled there, out of the wind, the entire heat of the fire thrown his way by the hearth.

He was grateful and felt a kinship with those who long ago had felled these logs, raised these walls, built a mud-mortar and sandstone hearth, and did a business here. He realized he did not feel alone at all, though he was a solitary man in an empty place. He felt a kinship with so many people. He remembered his parents and his sister in London. His testy father who was always lecturing him. His ironic mother, love and mock in her face as she dished the porridge. How could memories so simple give him so much delight? Who was alive and who had died he did not know and might never know. But he remembered their hopes for him, their patience with his youthful foolishness, their belief that in him something of themselves would be passed along to the future. And he remembered their furrowed brows and sly humor. They were present here. They were beside him when he crossed the river, as was his beloved Victoria.

He felt his own goodwill being returned to him. Those men at Fort Sarpy, Chambers and the rest, they were the true loners, for they had nothing to share with others and were divided between themselves and apart from all the world by their own sourness. They might have a wage and live in a safe place, but he would not trade his life for theirs. For he had friends. For he loved. And they could not. And finally, as he sat there absorbing warmth in the twilight, he felt that he had never been alone, that some great Being was his friend and companion, beside him even in his most harrowing moments.

"Thank you," he whispered. It was a prayer.

Night settled, the stars emerged, and the sandstone hearth threw heat his way. He liked it there. A good buffalo hump steak might have helped, but he was alive. He had Victoria. He had an outfit. He could make his way, care for her now with that old Hawken lying beside him.

He picked up the weapon, rubbed the soot off the barrel, sighted down it. If he could find a file among the Kicked-in-the-Bellies, he would file down the bead and alter the notch a bit, and then it would shoot true.

He was rich. What more did a man need than friends, a good rifle, two blankets, a robe, and a hearth with a good fire throwing joy at him?

He slept well and undisturbed, though once when he replenished the fire he saw a pair of eyes glowing in the dark, outside of the open door. A wolf maybe; coyotes were too shy, and no deer or antelope or buffalo or elk would come close. By the time the slow dawn of a winter's day quickened the world, he was rested and his worn body had recovered from the crossing. With luck, he might reach the camp up the Big Horn River and find succor among Victoria's kin.

He was ravenous, but thought to make time during the short cruel winter's day rather than wait upon his belly. He loaded the heavy burdens over his shoulders: bedroll, belaying pin, powder horn, and hung other things from his waist, including his fire-making pouch, hatchet, and Green River knife. He felt like a beast of burden.

He thought of Jawbone and the mare, and knew his life was not complete. Somewhere not far away were his medicine horse and the mare, and he sensed they were eager to return to him if only they could. He did not know why he needed them so much. Horses were horses. And yet, something that reached into his very heart told him he must find the pair, that he and they were destined to face the world together, that Jawbone was more than a horse; he was, in the terminology of his wife's people who had condemned him, a medicine animal.

He hiked slowly south along the Big Horn River, itself a formidable stream oxbowing northward toward its marriage with the Yellowstone. There were easy trails to follow, showing signs of passage by horse and man and wild game. He had to rest every little while. A man who had come so close to perishing the day before was a man whose heart and limbs and lungs had not yet restored themselves. But he soldiered on, resting at midday beside a giant slab of sandstone that had caught the sun's heat and was warm to the touch.

Later that afternoon he began to find signs of traffic, and walked warily, his old Hawken at the ready. Then he passed some women who were gathering firewood in the cottonwood timber. They stared. He raised his hand, palm forward, the Friend sign. Soon some boys swarmed up to him, several armed with bows and arrows that were not toys.

"I greet you," he said in Crow.

They swarmed beside him, sometimes tugging on his bedroll, mocking him with drawn bows. It was not comfortable nor was it intended to be. But then he rounded a river bend and beheld the village, spread comfortably against deep woods and under protecting northern and western slopes. The blackened peaks of the lodges leaked gray smoke. But around the bright tawny bottoms of the lodges life teemed. Women scraped hides or sewed with their awls. Oldsters wrapped in blankets or robes sat idly, taking the sun and smoking. An arrow maker patiently anchored metal points to the shafts with slippery wet sinew.

Young men greeted him. He was known at once, and the

youthful warriors greeted Many Quill Woman's man with delight. Ahead, a town crier, already informed, proclaimed the visitor. People swarmed about him now, delighted at this novelty, a white man and friend who had come to the Kicked-in-the-Bellies. One of their own.

Their gaze noted that he carried his burdens, that his step was unsure, and that fatigue lined his face and furrowed the brow under that famed black top hat. They waited silently, for he first must seek Long Hair's permission to stay among them. He saw his brother-in-law Arrow Giver, and then spotted one of Victoria's sisters, Makes-the-Lodge, and they greeted him with a slight nod. Soon he found himself before the great lodge of Chief Long Hair, whose locks had never been cut, so it was said, and extended many feet when unbound.

The chief was waiting; he, too, had been apprised by the crier, and now greeted Skye, observed Skye's desperation, and invited his guest to have a smoke, which was a way of preparing to receive Skye's news. Skye lowered his heavy burdens, nodded, and followed Long Hair into the great lodge. There would be much to talk about.

25

Chief Long Hair was obviously a vain man. He bestowed glimpses of his legendary hair, folded into hanks and tucked into a quilled pouch he carried around with him, all the while grilling Skye. His vanity extended not only to his odd affectation, but to knowing more than anyone else in the band knew, so that he might be the fount of all knowledge.

Thus did he detain Skye through the rest of the afternoon, oblivious of Skye's hunger and weariness. Nor did it matter to Long Hair that Skye might want to see his in-laws and discover if they had news of Victoria.

"It is said, pale man among us, that you worked for the traders at Fort Sarpy. Tell me what you think of them. Are they just and good, and do they treat us well?"

Skye, whose stomach churned just from the scent of boiling meat wafting through the village, thought over a judicious reply. He had been thinking up judicious replies for what seemed like hours, but wasn't that long a time. The ritual smoke, the slow deliberation of Indian social commerce, seemed lengthy to any white man.

Skye decided on candor and summoned up his limited Crow words, which he supplemented occasionally with fingertalk. "I left them after a fight. It was about my failure to bring back meat. But it was about much more."

"Ah, a fight! And you won this fight?"

"No one ever wins a fight for little is settled by one. But yes, it was necessary for me to tame them in order to receive what was owed me and leave. That very day I lost my horses, a mare and yearling colt. So I walked away."

"And how many of them were there?"

"Some fought. Some didn't. I fought two or three."

"And then you walked for days. And how did you ford the river?"

"I almost didn't."

"It has been said in this village that your mare and colt rescued you and your wife, Many Quill Woman."

"They appeared in our camp when I needed a horse to carry my wife. A Blackfoot arrow almost killed her."

"So it is said."

The conversation droned on. The chief never let Skye go. The chief's appetite for news exceeded even his appetite for food, wives, honor, and notoriety.

By the time evening settled in, the chief had acquired an exact knowledge of the Blackfoot raid, Victoria's wound, surviving alone through the blizzard, the miraculous appearance of two nondescript horses somehow steered there by her spirit helper the Magpie, the trip south, and the encounter with white traders who stole Skye's outfit. There, at least, Skye learned something.

"They passed here, heading for Fort Laramie," Long Hair said. "We did not encourage them to stay. They tried to trade the rifle for robes, but it was recognized as yours."

"I am not finished with them," Skye said wearily.

The chief questioned him about the horses, their color and looks, and turned oddly silent. Then he elicited from Skye the whole story of his hunt for buffalo, the discovery of other hunters, and the theft of his horses, taken by two Indians who crossed the river at a place where Skye could not follow. And then the chief kept returning to the fight, the unhappiness at the post, and what might have caused it.

Some intuition told Skye not to tell Chief Long Hair about Chambers's contempt for the very people he traded with, but the chief relentlessly ferreted it out, mostly by saying it himself.

"This headman Chambers has the bad eye for us," he said. "This man tries to steal robes and pelts from us by cheating on weights. His thumb is always on the balance. My people trade for one cup of sugar and get less. One cup of the bean that makes us crazy, you call coffee, and get less. He is a thief."

Skye couldn't agree more.

This consumed yet another strand of time, while the evening deepened. Skye had received not a drink of water, not a dish of stew, not a slice of meat. Long Hair's wives sat patiently, eyeing their guest with blank faces.

Skye decided it was time to escape, knowing he might well insult the chief. But he could no longer endure the grilling, or sit still, and he was dizzy with hunger and need.

"It is time to see my kinfolk," he said.

The chief stared sharply. "Is the company of Long Hair not enough?"

Skye was afraid of just such a response, and met it head-on. "It is always enough. But I wish to see my kin."

Long Hair nodded curtly, a dismissal that boded ill for Skye in the future. Skye had arrived with no gift for the chief and that didn't help either.

Gratefully, Skye nodded, retreated through the lodge door and into the night. Arrow Giver beckoned. Skye followed, and his brother-in-law steered him into a commodious lodge where two wives and a younger woman and two small boys crowded around the fire. He barked some commands and the younger of the wives ladled some steaming venison stew into a wooden bowl and handed it to Skye. He lifted it, sipped, felt hot nectar slide down his throat, and rejoiced. It didn't take long for him to demolish what lay in that bowl.

He would have liked a few more bowls but no more was offered.

"Long Hair talks," Arrow Giver said. It was a way of saying more than the words implied.

Skye smiled.

"Now you will have to talk all over again," he added.

"Have you word of Many Quill Woman?" Skye asked, relying more on his sign-talk than on his limited Crow tongue.

"She lives alone in the new lodge and puzzles the people," Arrow Giver said.

"Is she well?"

"It is said her mind is changed. The wounding and the visitor from the other side changed it."

"How changed?"

"She is very cross, and uses trapper words, bad words, upon all the people there."

Skye started to laugh and then contained himself. "That is a sign she is getting her strength back."

Arrow Giver tamped tobacco from a pouch into a long-stemmed pipe and lit it with a coal he plucked from the fire, and then handed it to Skye, who drew the tobacco into his lungs and felt its calming.

Once again Skye told his stories, while Arrow Giver listened. When it came to the story of the mare and the colt, Victoria's brother had Skye repeat it again, though Skye was so weary he thought he would tumble to the robe he was sitting on and fall instantly asleep.

"This colt, is it the very colt that the Tobacco Planter, Walks to the Top, said would bring great trouble to the Otter Clan people?"

"It is."

"And this is the very colt he said must be killed for the sake of the People?"

"It is. But I would not permit that. I left instead. It is my medicine colt. He is unlike any other horse. Other horses run from trouble. This horse heads right into it. I knew at once that this horse was destined for me. If a white man can also have medicine, then this horse is my medicine, for it will bless me all of its days."

Arrow Giver stared sharply at Skye. "But now the horse is stolen?"

"I will find that colt and that mare. The mare brought my wife to safety, dragging her by travois and carrying her. It was our salvation. My wife had no strength. The Blackfeet had taken the horses. We were alone and surviving on our last meat and wood during a blizzard. But then just when she was well enough to be carried, and the weather warmed enough so it was possible, there came the mare, and the colt I have called Jawbone in honor of his great jaw, which protrudes from his head and makes him look misshapen. I would not let our medicine horses perish. So there was no choice. I left the Otter Clan people, and brought my horses this way, intending to come here. But my rifle and most everything else was stolen by white traders. I headed for Fort Sarpy, where I hoped to earn enough as a trader to outfit myself again."

He wasn't sure whether his words and signs were fully understood. How could he explain about Jawbone, a horse unlike any other, a horse that was meant for him, and only him.

Arrow Giver stared into the dying flames. The night had thickened. Some of his wives and children and nephews had slipped into their robes.

"The mare and the colt are here, in the herd," he said at last.

"Here?" Skye's spirit soared.

"Here. But it is not possible that the horses will ever be returned to you."

Skye stared, unhappily, wondering what was happening here.

"It was taken from you by the son of Little Horse, Badger Tail, and his friend Wolf, son of The Hawk Watcher. They are both boys entering manhood. They have gone to the hills to seek their spirit guardian, which is also part of becoming an Absaroka man. They will cry for a vision high in the high place that is known only to the People. They have done all else to enter into manhood and into the warrior society. Taking horses from others was the act of war and bravery both needed to enter manhood. It is the most important thing they have ever done, and celebrated by all the People."

"But I am one of your people by marriage. And adoption."

Arrow Giver ignored that. "What is done is done and cannot be changed. If they took your horses, those horses are theirs. There is nothing you can do. The young men will be honored. If you shame them upon their passage to manhood, the People would not forget. You will have bitter enemies. Do not shame them. Let the horses go. They no longer belong to you. If the issue is pressed, Mister Skye, there would be no welcome here or in any Absaroka village for you . . . or for my sister."

26

Soft light in the smoke hole awakened Skye. He had slept badly in spite of his exhaustion. A lodge filled with people always left him restless. There were usually noises in the night he could only guess at, people moving, slipping in and out.

Now they all lay motionless, the fire down to a few coals, a dawn coldness heavy upon the air. He threw back his robe and blanket, slid on his moccasins and tied them, found his capote and threw it over his shoulders, and slipped into the gray morning light. Smoke lay heavy over the village, drifting lazily from dozens of lodges. He saw no one about, but there were always a few, the warrior clan acting as village police and guardians, watchful even in the dead of winter.

A deep peace reigned here. He stretched and headed south along the purling river, seeking the horse herd. The Crows were rich in horses, which is one reason other tribes were constantly raiding them. He realized he was not alone. An old woman bathed at the river. Several young men stared. He found the herd grazing semitimbered meadows half a mile south, dining on leaves and bark as well as grass and sedges along the river. There were all sorts, lineback duns and grays, paints and spotted horses, a few blacks and some chestnuts. They weren't pretty horses, and yet they seemed vital and capable. Some had potbellies or oversized heads or broom tails. They served their purpose, which was not only to provide war and hunting mounts to the men, but travois and pack transportation to the whole village.

He walked quietly among them, and they didn't stir; it was as if they knew him, though most didn't. Then he spotted Jawbone and his mother just as they spotted him. The yearling raced to him, squealed, lowered his big ungainly head, and pushed it hard into Skye's midriff, forcing Skye back.

"Ho, there, you bloody devil," he muttered, overjoyed at the sight of the medicine colt Skye ached to call his own. He knew he must be patient, cautious, and terribly circumspect if ever he would get his horses back. Anger filled him. These were his own horses! He pushed back a fierce notion to take them and get out. The Crows would catch him in no time. This needed diplomacy, something he hated.

Jawbone kept butting Skye and expressing his joy with odd little bleats until the mare whirled, planted both rear hooves into Jawbone's butt, and drove the little rascal away. Then she bared her teeth at him just to show him who was still boss.

Skye laughed, albeit sadly. There was now an aching void between these horses and him, a gulf he had no way of bridging.

He knew he was being observed. Warriors, herd watchers, studied him. This was no secret. Everyone knew whose horses they had been, who took them, and what Walks to the Top had said about the colt in that faraway village on the Musselshell. So, if anything, young Crow males watched and waited, and Skye felt himself being weighed. He ran his hand under the mane of the colt, and then turned to leave. The colt followed.

"Avast!" he growled.

The colt, looking wounded, stared. Skye walked away and downriver, feeling miserable. The only good thing was that he had seen his horses and they were healthy. Maybe he should just try to forget, abandon them. But he knew he could not. They were his. There was some strange destiny about them, something larger than the reality of the day or the hour could voice.

He performed some simple ablutions at the river's edge and walked back into the village. It still barely stirred. Especially in winter, people slept late, except for the ever-busy lesser wives, who were constantly burdened with dreary tasks, such as gathering loads of firewood and hauling it on their backs.

He would talk to Long Hair. That would be the first step, but he had no illusions about any of it. It would be late morning before he would be admitted to the chief's presence. The legendary chief followed a well-known ritual. He slept late while his several wives did the drudge work. When he arose, his first business was to primp. His wives unfolded his hair and spread it on the ground, and sometimes measured it to see if it had grown longer. Usually this was done out of doors unless the weather was bad. After the hair was stretched, the wives curried it with a porcupine-quill brush until every strand was unknotted. Woe to the young wife who pulled a strand out of Long Hair's head.

Then the wives folded his hair into hanks and returned it to his carrying case, which he kept at his side, or on occasion slung over his back. After the wives had attended him his next ritual business was gossip. It wasn't called that, but that's what it was. News givers brought him every detail of life in the village, every scrap of information. This morning they would tell him all about Skye's trip to the herd, and how the medicine colt butted him and was disciplined by the mare. This morning Chief Long Hair would learn who visited whose lodge in the night, what the medicine seers had said, who was out of meat, whose wives were quarreling, what children were teasing whom, and on and on. By late morning the chief would know everything worth knowing, and everything not worth knowing, and he would use his vast knowledge, brought to him by a whole network of talkers, to lord over his people in ways that seemed miraculous to them.

So Skye waited. Back in Arrow Giver's lodge he noted that Victoria's younger brother was paying close attention to his youngest woman, with smiles and merry little jokes, and Skye surmised who was his host's favorite at that moment. But if anything was true of the Crows it was their fickleness. Tomorrow that wife, Sow Black Bear, might be flirting with someone else, and Arrow Giver would probably be favoring two or three others.

Meanwhile, he had a rifle to look at. The Hawken didn't shoot true. He pulled the charge and studied it. The rifle had been abused by someone, and its bead, the little ridge of metal at the muzzle used for aiming, had a left tilt to it. The rifle had been used to pry something and the bead had been damaged. Actually, Skye's heart lifted. If he could find a file he would reshape that bead. It took some while to convey to Arrow Giver what he wanted, but in time Victoria's brother produced a rough wood file. It would have to do. Skye found some sunlight and patiently scraped away the cant in the bead, and hoped he could center on his target. Then he scraped at the top of the bead to lower it, hoping that would raise his aim slightly. It was good steel and his work went slowly, and the sun climbed and arced around the southern sky.

Something changed in camp: it was, in fact, the time when Chief Long Hair would hear petitions or counsel of whatever a Crow wanted to say to the headman. But this time there was more: the whole of the Kicked-in-the-Bellies were waiting for Skye to make his petition. This moccasin telegraphing was a thing Skye hardly understood. How could everyone know his business?

He finished his work on the rifle and thought to aim and shoot it later, but now he had a case to make. He wondered how to make it. He set the rifle aside and started toward the chief's oversized lodge. There he discovered the village elders gathered outside in the bright winter sun, and all of them in ceremonial dress. This was no ordinary occasion.

Skye stood and waited for the summons, which came at once.

He knew there would a great deal of talk. They would seek to hear his case, there would be a lengthy debate, and then a verdict. He would need to summon all his Crow words and add some sign language too.

He decided on a simple approach: the young men took his horses, the horses of a friend and adopted son of the Crows. He wanted them back. He would honor their bravery, but he wanted his horses back.

Thus he approached the chief, who sat in a reed backrest, with several robes scattered about him. His hair pouch rested in his lap.

"You who married one of my people, approach," he said. "I have heard your story and will decide now."

"But I haven't told it . . ." Skye suddenly realized he would not be allowed to tell it. This was not a matter for debate nor did he have standing. This was going to be something directed at him, and he would have only the choice of heeding it or leaving the village.

Skye stood awkwardly and removed his hat. He was the center of attention. Headmen at the innermost circle, then warriors, and then women and children, as was the custom in Crow life.

Long Hair was plainly enjoying the moment.

"Our fine young men, Badger Tail and Wolf, have acquired a mare and a colt. This mare and colt were taken in an act of war, and now belong to these young men, who are entering into the manhood of the Crow people. These horses are said to be medicine horses by the visitor among us." He did not refer to Skye by name, which was a bad sign. "But we know that the Tobacco Planter, Walks to the Top, has

said this colt is a bad omen and will bring evil to the Otter
Clan people who are wintering on the Musselshell. He required of you that you destroy the colt so to spare the people
his evil. You brought the colt and its mare here, intending to
escape that verdict.

"Some of my headmen think it should be heeded. The
colt should die. Others say that Walks to the Top was speaking only about the fortune of his village, not ours. And so
we are divided. Some say when Badger Tail and Wolf return from their crying for a vision, they should heed what
was said by the Tobacco Planter. Others say that the young
men won war honors, and the horses are the sign of it, and
it would dishonor their victory and dishonor us if we require
them to destroy their prize.

"I have decided. Let my word be heard. The horse colt
will belong to Badger Tail, the mare will belong to Wolf. I
will wait and see whether the presence of this pair of horses
harms my people. You visited the horses this morning. You
will not visit them again. They must be left to the young
men. If you visit the horses you will not be welcome here.
I trust you have listened."

Skye nodded. "I have listened," he said, "but I wish to
talk about those horses. They were the gift of Magpie to
Many Quill Woman and me."

"Enough," said the chief.

The horses would live for the moment but only until the
next trouble. Skye turned slowly and walked away. He had
not been allowed a word of explanation, not a word about
how Victoria's life had been saved. Not a word. It was most
unusual and bespoke some strange chill, or fear, or dread,
soaking through these people. How could a feisty little colt
like Jawbone evoke all that? Skye didn't know, but he knew
he must not say a word, not a whisper, to anyone.

27

So the day had begun badly but it was to grow worse. Later that morning the young men who had been on their vision quest returned a day early. They should have stayed four days, fasting and praying to the Above Ones and the spirits in all the directions of the winds for their vision.

It was unusual for them to seek their vision in winter, unusual to go together though nothing forbade it. They had been boyhood friends and were warrior-brothers now, bonded by vows to defend each other. So they had headed up to the sacred bluff in the Pryor Mountains, through which the Big Horn River passed in a deep canyon, there to fast and thirst and beseech their helpers until they should receive that which came out of the mists.

And now Badger Tail and Wolf limped into the village, each carrying the heavy robe that was their sole comfort in the mountains. And even as they entered, a wail rose, for the youths were injured. Both had been bitten around the face, and Badger Tail on his calf and forearm as well.

Skye followed the crowd as it collected around the young men, back early from the sacred mission.

They looked frightened and desolate. Already the women had surmised what had happened, and began a quiet moaning.

The men stood silently, absorbing the tooth marks and blood that covered those youths.

Little Horse, powerful and sinewy, approached his son.

"The time of pleading has not passed," he said.

"Father, a wolf came. We thought he was our spirit helper."

"A wolf came so close?"

"He came right up to me and was not afraid. I saw madness in him, but then it was too late. He was not a spirit helper, but a wolf with the madness. Foam and spittle dribbled from his jaws. And then he shook his head back and forth and pounced, biting my cheeks, my jaw, my nose, and for a moment I did nothing for fear of angering him, for this might be a dream and I was waiting for the vision."

Skye listened sadly. Hydrophobia. Rabies. A rabid wolf had bitten the boys, and he was staring at two doomed youths, barely reaching their manhood.

The women keened. Badger Tail's mother rushed to him with a sopping deerskin rag and washed her son's blood away. The tooth marks, especially those of the fangs, remained clear upon his gray flesh.

Wolf, the other boy, seemed less bitten, but bore the marks of his fate as well. Both youths stood there, knowing their fate, frightened and yet brave, their gazes almost defiant. What terrible thoughts were running through their minds now? They had sought manhood and a name and protector, and found only doom.

Skye puzzled over it. Hydrophobic animals usually showed up in the summer, not winter. But no matter. If these lads had been bitten by a rabid wolf, they would perish in the midst of excruciating pain and thirst. It would take the disease only a short while, a few days, because of the head wounds. If they had been bitten on a limb or foot, they might survive as long as two months. Soon they would face fevers and convulsions and pain in the throat and esophagus that would make them unable to swallow, and no matter how much they craved water, they could not stand to drink it. It was an awful way to die and there was no cure.

Some of the trappers believed in a madstone, a porous stone that was to suck the lethal poisons from the body. Others believed in bloodletting. Cut open each puncture, where the infected tooth had pierced, and let the blood carry away the sickness. But Skye had never heard of a success. Everyone who had been bitten by a rabid animal, wolf or skunk usually, perished.

And here were two boys, the very boys being celebrated by the entire Crow nation, stepping from boyhood into the adult world where they would help the People and keep them safe.

This great and saddened crowd had at last attracted the attention of Long Hair, who made his stately way, his wife carrying the hair chest behind him.

"What is this? What do I hear? Tell me," he said to the young men after inspecting them.

They slowly described the bites of the rabid wolf, which they had thought was only a dream, a vision, the strange initiation of their spirit protector who was testing them.

Now a great circle of villagers surrounded the youths. Chief Long Hair walked slowly around them, two wives dutifully carrying his sacred hair, until at last he stood before the young men.

"This has never happened. Not in all the winters of our lives. Not in all the stories handed down by the grandfathers. No young man seeking a vision has ever been hurt by anything. Some came back defeated; no vision came to them. Others came back weakened by fasting, but they soon recovered. But this is different. The Other Ones must be displeased with us. Those who inhabit the west winds and the south winds and the other winds have found fault with us. We harbor evil in our midst, and must purify ourselves. The whole People must purify themselves and drive out evil."

Skye suddenly intuited where this was going though Chief Long Hair had not yet gotten down to specifics.

The youths stood somberly, in need of rest and attention but unable to move until they received permission. The chief scarcely noticed their distress or the pallor in their faces.

Long Hair repeated himself several more times, as if he wanted his message ground deep into the heart of every listener, while the poor youths endured in the chill air.

Then suddenly Long Hair paused and faced Skye and pointed.

"He brought evil here. The very horses condemned by the Tobacco Planter, Walks to the Top."

Skye felt the gazes of scores of his friends, his adopted nation, his wife's family and kin, and the somber suspicious study of impressionable children, and all their gazes hammering him like sledgehammer blows.

At that moment the old seer, Red Turkey Wattle, most revered of all the Absaroka medicine men, raised his old hand, palm forward, and such was his authority that even the chief fell silent.

"Our friend Mister Skye, husband of Many Quill Woman, did not bring the horses here. The horses, sacred to him, were taken from him and brought here. I have burned sweetgrass and heard the whispers. The colt, named Jawbone, will live to be a great ally of the People. In the troubles that come, he and his owner, Mister Skye, will be like a hundred warriors fighting for us. The mare has already spared one of us, carrying Many Quill Woman to safety. Do them no harm. That is what I have seen, and what I say."

Contradiction. Skye found himself witnessing a struggle of a sort he had never seen among the Absaroka. There was the word of the elder, Walks to the Top, a Tobacco Planter, considered wise and all-knowing by the People but not necessarily one who communes with the Other World. And there was Red Turkey Wattle, a true medicine man, venerated for his insights, one who did receive gifts from the

Other Ones. And now the chief, once a war leader, powerful, whose word was law, following yet another course. And
it was the chief's own words that Red Turkey Wattle had
challenged. Jawbone and the mare had not been brought into
the village by Skye but by the youths who stood miserably
at the center of all this. Skye waited uneasily, knowing that
whatever happened, his own fate lay in the balance.

The chief took offense, glared at the seer, but did not dare
challenge the old man. Instead he whispered to his wives,
who withdrew the long hair from its casement and slowly
spread it until it trailed behind the chief, an amazing hank
that ran perhaps fifteen feet. This was his medicine, and
now he was displaying it. He walked slowly, letting that cas-
cade of hair pull along behind him for all to see. He circled
the young men once again, so all might see his hair, and
then paused before Skye.

"The People will suffer for as long as you and the cursed
horses remain among us. Go," he said.

Skye stood there a moment. "It will be as you wish," he
said. "I will make it my first business to track down the rabid wolf, and if I find him, I will kill him. The wolf will be
glad of it. And the People will be released from danger." He
paused, gazing at his many friends, hunting companions,
kinfolk by marriage, and others who had shared village life
with him. "You are my only nation, and I remain your
friend."

He was alone again. Ever since he had been ripped out
of London, he had been alone. He walked through the
crowd, which parted, and headed for Arrow Giver's lodge,
where he gathered his few belongings. He headed for Little
Horse's lodge to collect what the boys had taken and found
his packsaddle and tack awaiting him outside the lodge
door.

These things he lugged out of the village and into the
sheltered bottoms of the Big Horn, until at last he reached
the sunlit herd. He spotted Jawbone and the mare and

headed their way. Jawbone squealed and raced up to him, butting him and making himself obnoxious.

"Avast!" Skye bellowed. But in truth, he was grateful the little fellow was alive and returned to him, even at the terrible price of his exile from the Crow nation.

Skye settled the packsaddle on the mare, tightening the cinch and tying it. Then he anchored his bedroll on it, along with the few things he still possessed, preferring to carry his Hawken in hand. He had his colt and his mare. He had, in a distant village, his wife, and she had a new lodge, and there were four ponies there awaiting him, the gift of her elder brother. All that was wealth. And he had a Hawken, shot and powder, to make meat and collect hides and protect himself. He was whole again, but once again he was a man without a country: not an Englishman, not a Yank, not a Crow, not a fur company employee, not any damned thing at all.

28

H e followed the trail into the Pryor Mountains the youths had taken. He didn't know where it would lead. The Crow people didn't say much about the place where their young men pleaded for a vision.

Occasionally he saw the fresh imprint of a moccasin in soft earth or mud. Through the afternoon he ascended into an upland desert and sensed that these mountains were in the rain shadow of the Rockies to the west. Juniper flanked these slopes, but little pine, and some brush in the watercourses. This country was arid, but fine horse pasture and it offered the Crows an almost endless pool of ponies.

Jawbone trailed behind, delighted to be alive and snorting with joy at everything that should have alarmed him, while his patient mother brought up the rear. Skye was looking for the hydrophobic wolf, as he promised he would do. The offer had not been accepted. Long Hair had a different agenda. But Skye felt obliged to find the wolf and kill it before more tragedy struck.

It was a strange story, these youths thinking the wolf came to them in a vision and the biting of their faces and legs was part of a wolf-dream, an ordeal that would lead to the fulfillment of their quest. Not only did they have no weapon to fight it or drive it off, but they were disposed by their innermost belief to welcome the rabid animal. They must have cried out with joy at the sight of it.

In some ways, the Crows puzzled him. Why did they interpret these things as omens, the wrath of spirits, things amiss in the harmony of their lives, rather than simply what this was, a rabid wolf on the loose who happened on two unarmed, vulnerable youths? He had no answers. These were another people with a different way of seeing the world.

Had that wolf wandered into a rendezvous, the trappers would have taken after it, would have hunted it down because it imperiled all of them. Maybe the Crows would too, but he doubted it. Their world was wrapped in mystery and fear of powers that rose like whirlwinds out of the little-known. He sighed. It wasn't only a matter of reality on the one hand and superstition on the other. There were times he thought the tribal seers had something just right, some gift of discernment that seemed to probe the very soul of other life, something that Europeans did not have. But that was balanced by the sort of thing he saw today, the chief acting on a set of invented or imagined beliefs.

Skye knew he'd never understand it so there was little point in wrestling with it. He and Victoria's people lived in different worlds. He hiked up the trail into the Pryors, hardly knowing where to look for the rabid wolf, and growing ever more aware that he hadn't a scrap of food. He was far from the plains and river bottoms where he might find some emergency roots.

He rounded a bend and saw the wolf. It stood directly in the trail and did not run. It sat on its haunches, unafraid, usually a sign of hydrophobia. It was in terrible shape and looked more dead than alive. It did not slobber but he had seen rabid animals who had not a speck of saliva on their jaws. He would shoot this one, and brought his Hawken up.

Then Jawbone squealed and bolted straight at the wolf.

"No!" Skye roared.

It did no good. The colt raced forward. The wolf stood and snarled, its great murderous jaws snapping. Jawbone whirled, presenting his rump to the wolf, and kicked. The hooves caught the wolf amidships, even as the wolf clawed and snarled and snapped. The kick tossed the wolf into the air, and then it fell in a heap and shuddered. It did not attempt to get up, except for some weak pawing of air.

"No, no, no!" Skye bellowed, and Jawbone pranced aside, for once heeding a command.

Skye saw that the wolf was all but dead and had been even before Jawbone planted two hooves in its side. Skye lifted the heavy Hawken, aimed, and shot. The ball hit the wolf in the chest. It convulsed once and went limp.

Shaking, Skye reloaded at once and turned to Jawbone.

He caught the colt and led him to a rotting snowbank where he scooped up snow and ran it over the colt's forelegs and pasterns and then the rear legs and pasterns, looking for blood. If the snow reddened, Jawbone might well be doomed. The colt stood still, submitting to all this as if it were the most natural thing in the world, though Skye had never before handled his feet and legs.

There was no blood, not a trace of pink or red in the snow. Maybe it would live. Maybe Jawbone was destined by some sort of fate Skye couldn't imagine to survive all manner of troubles. He eyed the strange colt, wondering what fate had given to him.

Skye was done here and it was time to head north. He had killed the wolf, as he said he would try to do. The Crows would read the evidence soon enough. He stared at Jawbone, wondering what sort of horse would run straight at a wolf and not flee it.

Skye took stock. He was high in the Pryor Mountains, which were arid and grassy, almost devoid of forest. To the north lay the Yellowstone and far away, Victoria with her people on the Musselshell. He decided to descend a long coulee, perhaps fifteen miles in length, that would take him to the Yellowstone or one of its tributaries.

It was a good choice. The descent was easy. He was soon out of the snow and into dried-up grassland. An hour later he spotted half a dozen antelope herded up in a swale, enjoying some good grasses. They spotted him, broke for cover, and he swung up his Hawken, gave the rear antelope a good lead, aimed a little high, and squeezed. The recoil slammed his shoulder. All the antelope continued to run, but then the rear one staggered, tumbled, and sprawled on the grass, thrashing. It was trying to get up and run again. He would have to put it out of its misery, and fast.

He hurried to the animal, a young buck that was breathing heavily, and cut its throat with his Green River knife. His shot had pierced the buck's belly, missing the heart-lung area by several inches. It had been a lucky shot at well over two hundred yards.

Jawbone approached the dead antelope and sniffed, and Skye let him. He wanted the little horse to get used to the smell and sight of blood.

Skye was ravenous but there wasn't a stick of wood anywhere near. He would have to wait.

He wrestled the buck antelope around, found it was all he could do to handle it, but forced himself to lift it to Jawbone's packsaddle. He thought the colt would go crazy, as most horses do at the scent of blood, but Jawbone accepted the burden. After balancing it as best he could, Skye anchored the carcass on the packsaddle and he continued his long downhill journey through a waning day and twilight. It would have been convenient to find firewood before nightfall, but there was nothing but grassy slope and some occasional low chokecherry brush in watercourses.

Darkness fell, and now Skye saw Orion in the southwestern sky, a winter visitor who vanished in the warmer seasons. The horses trailed along through the darkness. It was so black that Skye feared he would tumble into a trench or hollow, so he slowed down. Nothing but faint starlight showed him the path.

He began to feel faint, and knew he must do the thing he had seen his trapper friends do time and again, though it repelled him. He halted, slit open the belly of the antelope, tore its guts out, and then probed the bloody interior until he found the liver, resting high under the rib cage. He pulled and cut it free, not even sure in that deep darkness he had what he wanted. His hands were sticky with gore but he ate the raw liver, bit by bit, finding it shockingly tasty.

He sat in the cold grass, feeling icy air eddy down the coulee, and rested awhile. He wiped his sticky hands on dried grasses, with little effect. He had rarely felt so befouled, and yet he had been nourished. His horses nibbled grass nearby. He still had a long way to go to find shelter and some firewood. The raw liver worked its peace upon him, and he ached to curl up right there within his robe and blankets, and sleep. But he didn't like this naked place and somehow didn't trust it either.

He found Jawbone, led the colt to where the antelope lay, and hoisted the carcass to the colt's back. It was noticeably lighter this time, disemboweled. He floundered about but finally caught the mare, and set off down that long dry coulee once again. It was not late, maybe nine in the evening. He was thirsty now, but there was no water anywhere, and no snow here. That, too, would have to wait.

The stars vanished behind a cloud bank and it became much too dark to travel, so Skye stumbled along until he found a level place, pulled the antelope and then his bedroll off of Jawbone's packsaddle, fumbled the packsaddle free and lifted it from the little fellow's back, released the mare, and made a cold bed in utter darkness.

He pulled the blanket and robe over him, grateful for the small nest against a wintry night. Beside him was his loaded Hawken. The nearby carcass might attract coyotes or wolves. But he would deal with that, just as he had dealt

with trouble for as long as he could remember. The odd
thing was, life was good in spite of every trouble that had
befallen him. Soon he would be reunited with Victoria, and
she would be strong and well.

29

Skye awakened to a winter fog that obscured the whole world in a veil of white. Dew covered the top of his robe as well as the brown grasses nearby.

He sat up, feeling weary after a fitful night. He could not see the horses and knew he might have trouble finding them. There were beads of moisture on the barrel and stock of his rifle. It plainly was above freezing but not by much.

He didn't know where he was, except in the most general way: on the north flanks of the Pryor Mountains. Somewhere above there was blue sky. These winter fogs hung low upon the land. They often didn't burn off until afternoon. He would make his way downhill, that being the sole compass available to him this day.

He would have liked some fire to drive the aches out of him. He would like some water. He noted the beads of moisture covering the stiff carcass of the antelope. He ought to cut it up, carry what he could, rather than try to load that ungainly weight on Jawbone's back. Always assuming he could find the colt.

He had the odd sensation of being the last living person on earth. He had never quite gotten used to being so small a speck of life in this aching wilderness.

There he was, utterly alone, without direction. Surely that

was how his life was playing out. Everything he had done had been simply a struggle to survive. He rose, stared at the walls of white that sealed him in this lonely place, and saw his life in it.

In short, his whole life was as fogbound as he was this day, and he ached for some goal, some purpose, some understanding of what he should do with his life. Where was he? He didn't even know that. He felt like roaring so he roared. He howled at the fog, he howled at the white sky. Then he laughed just because he felt like it.

"You bloody horses, fetch your blooming asses here," he yelled into the whiteness.

He scarcely dared move. It would require only a few yards to separate him from his bedroll, his rifle, and the antelope.

He saw and heard nothing.

He walked a small circle, hoping to drive the chill and stiffness from his body, and then he set to work on the antelope, slowly sawing it open, peeling back hide, and severing slabs of meat from bone. It was slow, dirty, mean work.

He sensed the slightest shadow, looked up, and discovered Jawbone studying him and the mare quietly overseeing her wayward son.

That heartened him. He rose, let Jawbone smell his bloodied hands, and then gently stroked the rambunctious fellow.

Soon he had some meat wrapped in green hide. He loaded his few possessions onto Jawbone's packsaddle and started downhill, scarcely knowing what he would run into a hundred feet away. It wasn't particularly cold, but there was something about fog that chilled him and made him crazy. Still, there was nothing he could do. He had discovered long ago that surviving in wilderness required a sense of one's own helplessness. And now he was as helpless as he ever got.

He hiked through what might have been morning, and

walked down the coulee through what might have been afternoon, and then discerned naked cottonwoods looming out of the mist. Wood. Maybe if he was lucky he'd find some dry wood somewhere, and have himself a fire and some antelope meat. The land leveled and the woods thickened and he sensed he had reached bottoms, maybe even the Yellowstone River's bottoms. But he still could not see ahead and nothing offered any clues. He found a rotted snowbank under some trees and swallowed some snow, alleviating his terrible thirst.

Now that he was on a flat he had no sense of direction; he could as easily be going in circles as heading north toward the river, which is where he wanted to go. Give him a riverbank and he could follow it somewhere. But the fog swallowed up his immediate past. He could not even tell where he had been two or three minutes earlier. And as he maneuvered around fallen logs, deadwood, and brushy thickets, he knew the chances were that he wasn't traveling in a line at all. He was meandering.

Maybe that was a good description of his life, he thought. It was an odd thing: the fog had started him thinking about who he was, where he was going, whether he was going anywhere at all. And the best he could manage was that he had been going around in circles for years.

Then, to his astonishment, he hit the Yellowstone River. He almost stumbled into it. He could not see to the north bank. He was somewhere upstream from the Big Horn River and north of the Pryor Mountains, but that wasn't helpful knowledge. He cupped his hands in the icy water, lifted water to his parched lips, and drank. And again and again.

Still, though he didn't know where he was, he was gladdened. He turned west and kept the riverbank in sight, working through mist, looking now for a place where he might harvest some firewood, anything that hadn't been soaked by cold droplets all over it. His hunger fevered him now. He needed food. He would eat most of the meat he had carved out of the antelope haunch. Meat! The sizzle of it caught his imagination.

But whenever he stopped to hunt for firewood he found only cold, wet deadwood, soaked and soaked again. He would go on as long as he could, and then try to masticate raw meat if he must, a sliver at a time. He couldn't endure much more.

A mirage ahead stopped him cold. Wavering in the fog was the yellow light of a large fire. He must be demented. Not here. But he continued. Jawbone whickered softly. The mare pushed forward too. Yes, a fire, but he needed to be careful. Not every fire offered friendship and safety. Now he discerned figures, blurs wandering about. He worried that his moisture-soaked Hawken might be useless. He paused. It was time to take careful stock here. He might still escape if this was big trouble. He stood stock-still and squinted into the fog, trying to make sense of the blurs ahead. He held Jawbone back and the mare stopped on her own.

They were talking now and then but he could not make out the tongue. He would have to take his chances. He edged closer. The fire cast eerie orange light, though it was still daytime.

Then: "Hey, Mister Skittles, the horses are staring that way."

"Must be something out there. Better go look, Mister Grosvenor."

Skye yelled. "Hello the camp."

The shadowy figures paused. "Who is it?"

"Mister Skye's my name. I'm alone with a couple of horses."

"Come in, then."

He pushed ahead, almost tripped over a slippery dead-wood log, and continued onto a treeless flat beside the river. Now he saw white men, maybe a dozen, waiting for him. Some had weapons in hand. They were taking no chances.

"Gents?" he said. "I'm glad to find some company."

They looked him over, examined his colt and the weary line-backed mare, and at last studied that battered top hat. He saw them relax. One, with a neatly trimmed red beard, hiked over to Skye. "Joshua Skittles here. These are my colleagues. We're pelt and hide dealers. And you?"

"Well, mate, I'm a loner traveling through. Trapper, hunter, fur business trader. All that."

"You Canadian?"

"What you hear, mate, is some London in my voice. I was born there. No, if anything, I'm a man without a country."

"Not a Yank?"

"No, not a Yank. I've a little antelope steak I'd be pleased to roast on that fire if you'd allow me. I'm more than a little past a meal. And there'll be some for you if you want it."

"Help yourself, Skye. We've eaten."

"I prefer Mister Skye, mate. And you're Mister Skittles?"

"Good! I always use the polite form with my men. It's Mister Skye, then."

Skye was amazed. The place seemed safe enough. The men emerging from the fog were outdoor types but with a difference. These men seemed well groomed, in clean clothing, with trimmed beards and hair, and green flannel shirts that showed signs of having been dipped in a river now and then. He studied them all, not recognizing a face. They were young, except for Joshua Skittles. He met a few. Mister Oliver, Mister Parsons, Mister Richter, Mister Balsamwood, Mister Mendelhoff. There were others out there.

Some had heavy dragoon revolvers hanging from their waists, others the new Colt Navy, a sidearm Skye had barely seen.

"Where's a good place to put the horses?" Skye asked.

"Wherever you want, Mister Skye. We've got draft horses here. We're pulling some wagons. Only a couple of saddlers in this outfit."

Skye wandered toward the wagons, curious about them.

One was filled with flattened buffalo hides and robes and other peltries. One stood empty and another apparently carried gear, such as tents, mess equipment, and food. One carried little more than medium-sized casks, maybe fifteen or twenty gallons each, carefully packed in rows and wedged tight.

Traders indeed, Skye thought. There would not be a license from the Indian Bureau in this lot. He knew what was in those casks. Pure grain spirits, two hundred proof. Mixed with river water, molasses for taste, a little pepper or paprika for seasoning, and maybe a pinch of strychnine to make the tribesmen crazy, this was the most brutal of all ways to extract pelts and robes from Indians at almost no cost. Get 'em drunk for two bits, walk away with a hundred dollars of robes.

Skye unpacked and picketed his mare and Jawbone, and returned to the campfire to fry some meat.

There would be some interesting talk soon.

30

Skye cooked his antelope steaks at the welcoming fire, aware that these men were watching him, and maybe more: they seemed to be assessing him as well. While he ate, slicing thin bits of meat and masticating them, he observed them as well.

He had never seen such a well-groomed, well-mannered bunch in the American wilderness, and it intrigued him. A few even shaved daily, no small feat in a place like this. Now, in the deepening twilight, they were busily policing the camp, gathering firewood, or attending to their personal toilet. Some washed their green flannel shirts in the river and set them to drying on limbs close to fires, while others aired bedrolls. One man attended to the tin messware, polishing it with river sand, rinsing and stacking it in the Studebaker supply wagon.

As soon as Skye had finished, Skittles approached him.

"You're welcome to stay the night, Mister Skye," he said.

The offer surprised Skye. He thought he was already welcome.

"I'll take you up on it, Mister Skittles."

The boss pulled out a pipe, loaded it, lit it with a lucifer, and settled beside Skye at the fire. He did not offer tobacco to Skye.

"I'm curious about what you do, Mister Skye."

"Well, I'm curious about you, sir. I've been a trapper, a brigade leader, an employee of several fur companies, and I've lived with the Indians."

"That commends you, Mister Skye. We're in the fur business ourselves, as you no doubt noticed when you passed our wagons."

"I did notice."

"We collect hides and furs in the Indian villages, turn them over to the trading posts for delivery in St. Louis, and collect our pay at the end of each season, back in Missouri."

"You turn them over to the posts?"

"American Fur Company, yes. They give us receipts for each hide and pelt, and these are as good as money in St. Louis. We work for a gentleman who prefers to remain anonymous, but who has generously financed our winter expeditions. The men know him only as Mister Quiet, an invented name, of course, but as good as gold."

"And why did he invent it, sir?"

"It is simply his choice."

His choice to ship spirits out, dodge the licensing, and turn over the pelts to licensed fur companies to bring downriver. Skye thought it was clever enough. Ever since the opening of the Oregon and Santa Fe Trails, the Yank government had lost its control of spirits destined for the Indian trade. And here was a simple but effective scheme to circumvent the government.

"We're paid in gold. There's an incentive on each pelt. These incentives are shared equally by my men here back in St. Louis. They contract for one winter season, coming out here in October and returning in June. We have written agreements, detailing exactly what rights and duties each participant must perform."

"That seems to include grooming, Mister Skittles."

"Indeed it does, sir. We're professionals, and I insist on appropriate dress and conduct and idealism on all occasions. Our goal, sir, is to make money, and lots of it, but there's more: our goal is to liberate the tribes from their ancient bondage upon hunting and gathering, and steer them toward a free and better life, with more personal choices and chances of fulfillment. Let them look at us. They see clean, proud, groomed, disciplined men. In short, sir, we are apostles of liberty and democracy."

"And how's this accomplished?"

"Trading, sir. Our goal is to show them that they can have a more abundant life by becoming animal husbandmen and farmers. We trade sharply, for as many pelts as we can get in exchange for goods they wish to have in exchange, and at the same time, we present ourselves in our dress and demeanor as representatives of a higher nature and calling."

Skye listened, amazed. If his eyes were to be believed, these were cutthroats who despoiled every Indian village they visited, made off with every robe and pelt in the village after soaking the whole village in spirits.

Skittles sucked his meerschaum and surveyed Skye. "I see skepticism written all over you, Mister Skye. Let me say, simply, we are doing the tribes a favor. Only when they see the futility of resisting the modern world will they come to the cast of mind that is open to new things including the blessings of our world. That requires that they know they face a superior race of people, and that their old tribal superstitions will only fail them as time goes by."

Skye laughed softly. He'd heard enough.

"Ah, Mister Skye, think it over. As it happens, I'm shorthanded. Every time I send some wagonloads of pelts to a post, I'm shorthanded. I have two wagons out now, carrying pelts to Fort Sarpy, and that occupies four men. I'm a victim of my success. The more pelts I get, the more men I need. I'm prepared to offer you a secure and lucrative position with us for the duration of the season, June thirtieth.

Less than six months. That wouldn't be long. You would receive two-thirds of one share in the proceeds because you started late. But it happens that I could use more men, and with your experience you would be most valuable to us. Sometimes new men don't grasp the opportunities and perils of life here. A veteran of the mountains, why, sir, you'd be worth twice a share, and if you prove out, I'll be sure you get a bonus."

"And what are the terms?"

"Why, you can read them anytime. I have several blank contracts which only need to have the blanks filled in. You'll get a copy, of course."

"And my duties?"

"Why, obey my direction always. Assist in the trading. We especially need a man who speaks the court language, or can employ the hand-talk. That's why I'm interested in employing you."

"And obligations?"

"To keep yourself immaculately attired and groomed always. It is a professional statement we make to the tribes. You may shave every other day, or keep a closely trimmed beard. We have a small cache of spare clothing, and will sell you enough to suffice, and you can abandon the buckskins."

"And you mentioned privileges?"

"Of course, of course, Mister Skye. We're not martinets here. We're quite able to enjoy ourselves and I encourage my men to make the best of each trip west. Each man gets a gill of spirits each evening as his due. And Kentucky whiskey, too, not spirits used for the robe trade."

A gill was two good drinks, not bad at all, Skye thought.

"As soon as the men finish their duties, we'll all have a gill, save for our sentries, and that's a task that rotates night by night, Mister Skye."

"And what happens when you approach a village, Mister Skittles?"

"Well, for professional reasons we forgo our evening libations, Mister Skye. Our task then is to encourage trade, inviting men and women of all descriptions to join us for some pleasant conversation. They bring us robes, and we trade for those, and supply them with just enough spirits to make a cold night pleasant."

Skye had seen this sort of thing, but never so veneered over with high talk of liberty and democracy and being a part of modern times. And what he had seen, from rougher and harsher traders, had sickened him. He had seen villagers shivering in their worn blankets or devoid of any cover, children desperate for food and warmth, sickened men and women, their bodies ruined by the debauch, despoiled girls hanging their heads. Some usually died, frozen or choking in their vomit, or ruined in spirit. And in the aftermath of these drunken orgies, the villages remained demoralized. Headmen's warnings went unheeded. No one hunted and so they starved. Skye didn't know why Indians were susceptible to spirits, but he knew the results.

He faced Skittles. "No, Mister Skittles, I'll decline. I am headed toward my family, and the life I know."

Skittles seemed unfazed by that. "Why, that's fine, Mister Skye. I thought I'd inquire. You'd be a valuable asset to me. But in our world, liberty and contract are paramount, and it always takes two or more to make a contract."

Skye nodded. He wasn't sure he should stay the night among these well-dressed, well-disciplined ravishers of a whole way of life. He thought of Victoria and her people, wandering freely over the open prairies, troubled by many things, but always sovereign, always free.

"Well, Mister Skye, the hour's at hand for our gill of spirits. Would you care to join us? The gill's on me this time."

Skye thought of the aches of his body, and his long starvation, and the pleasure of letting some spirits steal into his belly and bring him peace.

"I'll accept with pleasure, Mister Skittles."

A master of revels, of some sort, handed each man a tin

cup and filled it exactly half full, working around the circle with a one-gallon cask in hand. Some men sipped their ration neat, but most added some cold river water, and settled around one of the three mess fires for a social hour.

Skye sipped, relaxed, and enjoyed himself while Mister Skittles played the affable host. And when Skye had drained his gill, Skittles added a bit more with a gracious laugh.

"Tis a rare night in the wilds of the Northwest when a man can have a drink or two," Skittles said.

Skye found his cup refilled again, and again let the spirits flow through his veins, until at last he had reached oblivion. Lots of talk, lots of amusements. Those Yanks were a peculiar bunch, all right, with an opinion about everything, especially what they knew least about. He would undo his bedroll and plunge into a most pleasant sleep among all these good blokes.

And that was all he remembered.

The next dawn he awakened with a dull ache in his head, and a sense that something about him had changed. Yes, indeed, it had changed. His beard had vanished. He slapped his bare face. His hair, usually shoulder length, had been carefully shorn. His neck was naked. He wore a green flannel shirt he had never before seen. His old Hawken still rested beside him.

"Ready for work, Mister Skye?" asked Mr. Skittles.

31

Skye bolted to his feet. Skittles was standing there, an amiable smile on his chiseled face, while around the camp, the men were packing up.

"No," Skye said. "I'm not. I'm not working for you."

"Oh, but you are, Mister Skye. You signed the contract last night. Your copy is tucked into your shirt."

"You don't get yourself a man that way, Mister Skittles."

"Oh, now, Mister Skye, that's really not a wise choice. According to the contract, which was carefully explained to you, if you leave—and you are perfectly free to do so— you forfeit all your possessions."

"What contract?" Skye dug around in the flannel shirt, found a folded sheet of foolscap, and opened it. The printed form was actually quite long. There was something at its bottom that might or might not have been his signature. "Sorry, Mister Skittles," he said, and tore it in two.

"Not a good idea, Mister Skye. By your own free will you chose to join us, and you're now committed to service until the thirtieth day of June. Over five months. Two-thirds of a share, which is generous, considering you're working less than two-thirds of a full term of service, as defined in the agreement. Now, I'd suggest that you pack your bedroll and eat the porridge at the mess fire, and then set about learning our ways. You can begin by harnessing the draft horses."

"No. I'll be on my way. I committed myself to nothing."

"Ah, Mister Skye, I'm afraid that would be difficult. There's a dozen men in the company, and they'll hold you to the forfeit. I should tell you, sir, that the language is precise. It says all your possessions. And that is perfectly clear. All is all. Your horses and tack, weapons, bedroll, tools, and of course your clothing, including those excellent moccasins. You may walk away wearing nothing at all, because your possessions are forfeit."

He eyed the rest, knew their attention was on him, knew that a dozen men could swiftly overwhelm him, knew that Skittles meant it: he could walk away stark naked. In the winter. He knew the old trappers' lore. How John Colter ran naked from the Blackfeet and survived. How Hugh Glass crawled and hobbled hundreds of miles to safety. But not in winter. Not in January.

He eyed his Hawken. He could grab it, stuff the muzzle at Skittles, hold him hostage until the rest put his outfit together, and then walk out. But he knew better. Under that hammer, the cap would be off the nipple, and they were all waiting for him to do just that, and then give him a little lesson.

Talk, then. Talk until he took the measure of all this.

Skittles watched him intently. "Not a good idea, was it, Mister Skye?"

"A contract isn't a contract when one of the parties is impaired," he said. "You know that."

"Oh, yes, impaired by nature. A contract involving a madman would be a scandal. Contracts must be forged between competent adult people, wouldn't you say? That's the whole future, Mister Skye, and the bedrock of the American Republic. A society forged on contracts between equals, enforced by courts. We've no court here, of course, but a clear contract can be interpreted by our little community here. What a pity your copy lies on the ground. Perhaps you should collect the pieces and read it."

"I was impaired. Unaware of what you were fobbing off on me."

Skittles smiled. "Impaired is a good word. Drunk, you mean. No, Skye, your argument doesn't hold. You are not impaired by nature. In fact, you're the most competent man in the party, which is why I agreed to hire you. My signature's on there too, you know. By your own free choice you chose to have a drink. By your free choice you chose to have another. No one forced you. You were perfectly free to refuse my hospitality and walk away from here this morning. You are a competent man, Mister Skye, and if you chose to sign the contract, it was as a competent and equal man. That's ordinary logic."

"Skittles, a man who doesn't know what he's signing or doesn't remember it is not a man bound by anything."

"It's Mister Skittles, Mister Skye. We are all gentlemen here. This is a company of American gentlemen and capitalists."

"Slavery," said Skye. "You are coercing labor from me against my will."

"That's a quaint interpretation of entering into an agreement, Mister Skye."

"You support black slavery back in the States?"

"Good heavens no, Mister Skye. I'm an abolitionist. I believe in freely negotiated labor, not servitude. No man here believes in servitude, and that includes serfdom or any other form of bondage or semislavery, including debt-slavery. That's what the Republic's all about. What separates us from the rest of the world. Each person is his own master."

"Except when he works for a master who won't release him."

Skittles laughed gently. "You'll find, Mister Skye, that there are other clauses that now bind you. One deals with insubordination. At my discretion it can be punished by flogging. The other deals with laziness, for which there are several remedies, such as being denied meals. But the main one is simply that one's share of the proceeds is forfeit. No work, no reward. Perfectly sensible."

"And of course you make these decisions."

"Who else? A contract is an agreement between a master and employee. If the labor is performed to my satisfaction, you receive your reward. That, Mister Skye, is the law of God. St. Paul said, in essence, let him who doesn't work, not eat." He paused. "Well, sir, enough of this. We must be on our way. Are you going to forfeit your worldly goods or join the company?"

"Why the pretense, Mister Skittles? You knew perfectly well I don't want to work for you and would leave if I were not being coerced. So why do you pretend I'm not being coerced? You're coercing me with my life. You call it forfeit of my possessions, but what you mean is that if I leave I die of exposure. Why not call it what it is? You want me to be a bondsman, a slave."

"You're a card, Mister Skye. All Brits are cards. Here in the States, each man shapes his own destiny, out of his own free will. It is my will to shape your destiny, as long as you don't care to shape your own. It's the fittest who survive and prosper. The dregs are fated to work for masters. Eat the porridge if you want, or don't eat it. And then harness one of the teams. We're leaving."

Skittles smiled cheerfully and walked away. Skye watched him. The man certainly commanded the company. A word from him sent men into feverish preparations. This was a clear, cold winter day and would be a good one for travel.

A slave once again. When he was a boy a press gang had yanked him off the streets of London, and he was a slave in the Royal Navy. They didn't call it slavery, of course. The crown opposed slavery. They paid him a pittance and called it a wage and took it from him for any infraction, and wouldn't release him. He had been a boneheaded youth then, and fought it every way he could, fought it until they all but threw him overboard. Then he came to his senses and began to make himself a reliable seaman, valuable to them, and was watched less and less as he proved himself an able man.

Now, after four decades of hard living, he had absorbed a lesson or two. He wouldn't fight; not yet. He would make himself an able man and trusted man in this company, and as soon as he had his chance, he would be on his way. This was a big land and there would be plenty of chances.

He spooned gruel into a tin mess plate and ate it. It tasted like paste, but it would serve to fuel him. No sooner did he finish than one of the men, Mister someone, snatched his plate, washed it, and stowed it away. Mister this, mister that. Mister master, who pretended this was a company of equals in voluntary alliance with one another.

He rolled up his bedroll, stowed it in the supply wagon, checked his Hawken—which indeed had no cap on its nipple but was otherwise loaded—and slid it into the wagon as well. For the time being, until he was trusted, they would keep weapons from him.

The draft horses were picketed on good grass. He looked for the mare and Jawbone, and found that they had already been tied behind a wagon and loaded with goods not his own. For a moment his temper flared. Skittles had no scruples about commandeering labor as well as property. Skye's horses were simply something to exploit, and what did it matter that Skittles didn't own them? Skye choked back his rage and collected two draft horses, big black geldings, and began harnessing them, remembering from times past how it was done. He dropped the collar over their necks, strapped the surcingle in place, and slowly readied each of the docile, well-groomed, and muscled horses. This outfit used tugs, and each wagon was teamstered by a man walking beside the paired draft horses.

They were all furtively observing him.

"Mister Skye, we require that the horses be brushed before they're harnessed," Skittles said. "It saves us sores and cankers and trouble."

Skye nodded, unharnessed them, found a currycomb in the supply wagon, and carefully groomed the big, friendly horses, who obviously enjoyed the attention.

This was a disciplined outfit, and it left nothing to expediency. He hated to be among a bunch of easterners, no matter how disciplined, when his own weapon lay useless until they gave him his ball and powder and caps.

Around ten in the morning Skittles pointed, and the wagons rolled along the Yellowstone.

"We'll cross when we find a good ford, Mister Skye," Skittles said. "There's some Crows up on the Musselshell we plan to trade with."

32

Skye studied his captors. It paid to know who he was dealing with. This outfit was proceeding with military discipline. Each man knew his tasks and did them. The young men functioned as a unit. They knew how to live out of doors. That was it! These were Yank soldiers, either in civilian duds or else recently discharged. He studied their faces, seeing men in their twenties and thirties.

They didn't carry rifles but there were several in the supply wagon, and these were the new Sharps, the very model Skye had coveted. So they could deal with large threats.

These men had teamster skills too. The harnesses were mended. Axles were greased. Draft horses were carefully brushed and doctored and shod.

He studied the wagon carrying the twenty-gallon casks, no doubt of pure grain spirits. Pure alcohol is flammable, and the walls of this wagon box were thick plank able to stop a ball or an arrow. A wooden box at the rear of the wagon probably contained trading trinkets. That wagon was heavier than the others and was in the hands of a veteran teamster, whose task was to preserve the strength of the heavy draft horses dragging the payload.

Ahead, one of the men rode a saddle horse, picking out

a trail along the riverbank. He was also obviously looking for a ford, and occasionally wandering out into the river, over rocky shallows, and probing channels with a long pole. He rejected several fords until he found one where the channel itself was spread wide over a gravelly flat. At no point did the water reach the horse's hocks.

Even so, the rider poked and probed with his pole, looking for holes or surprises, and then shouted back to Skittles. They would cross here. There would be a steep rise on the far side, but otherwise a good crossing.

Skittles approached Skye. "Well, how are you faring, Mister Skye?" The question was merely a courtesy. Skittles had come to give instruction. "You'll ride in the supply wagon," he said.

"That brings up a point, Mister Skittles. I would have ridden my mare across, but she seems to be laden with your company's goods. Now where in the contract does it provide that your company can use my stock?"

Skittles's response surprised Skye. "Why, you have a point, sir. There is nothing in the contract that permits it. Mister Grosvenor and Mister Parsons were remiss, commandeering your horses. We'll pay you a small stipend for their use. I'll write it up as an amendment to your agreement with us."

"I'd rather carry my own outfit on my own horses, Mister Skittles."

"As you wish, sir. At the crossing here I'll have your mounts unloaded, and you can put your own goods on them, and we'll proceed without a stock contract."

Skye pondered that. What sort of world did this man Skittles live in, where he was ruthless about commandeering Skye's labor and expertise, but meticulous about the details involving property? What sort of men were these, who would illegally pour whiskey into vulnerable Indians and walk out with every robe and hide in the village? It was almost beyond fathoming.

When they reached Otter's camp on the Musselshell, he would need to signal Victoria. He needed to work up a plan. He had to let her know he was captive, had to let her know what these trim-bearded and well-groomed traders were going to do. His only advantage was that Skittles had no idea Skye had connections there. He thought uneasily of the medicine horse, Jawbone, and the mare, suddenly appearing in the very village where Walks to the Top had told the people these horses would bring evil upon them.

The crossing was done in masterful fashion. Skittles sent two horsemen ahead to look for surprises. Then the teamsters drove the wagons across, never wetting a foot. Skittles brought up the rear, making sure everything was in good order.

On the north bank, Skittles talked briefly to Grosvenor, and then approached Skye.

"Mister Grosvenor will unload your horses, sir, and you may put your outfit on them if you wish."

Skye did so, taking a moment to let Jawbone butt him. The colt had a way of lowering his big ugly head and gently pushing Skye backward. A bad habit, thought Skye, in any colt but this one. He laughed. Skittles watched dourly but said nothing about it. Skye tied the lead lines to the back of the supply wagon rather than letting his horses run free.

"You'll be my relief man, Mister Skye. You'll relieve each of my teamsters in turn, so they can take a break on one of the wagons."

Skye nodded.

They set off to the north, toward what appeared to be a gradual incline out of the Yellowstone Valley, and soon were in jack pine country. The boss man seemed to know where he was going. This route to Victoria's village was as good as any.

He felt melancholic, being a part of a trading outfit that intended to debauch Victoria's people. And yet, maybe he ended up in this place for a purpose. He eyed the wagon carrying the grain spirits, wondering how to set it afire, how to destroy these traders' entire stock of goods. They'd kill him quick if they had any idea what thoughts were teeming in his head: finding some way to spring a leak in a keg. Some way to ignite that pure alcohol. Some way, without being seen.

When it came his turn to relieve the teamster who was guiding the whiskey wagon, Skye began to study how that wagon was put together. This one had steel axles and wheel hubs, well greased. The barrels were wedged in and could not roll around. And around the casks was a wall of wood that would turn a ball or arrow.

"You're admiring my wagon," said Skittles.

"It's stronger than the others," Skye said.

"It has to be. The value of the goods in there can be multiplied between one and two hundred times if we succeed. The wagon is heavy, but armors the goods against disaster."

"Am I hearing right? A hundred dollars of whiskey can be turned into ten to twenty thousand?"

"Minus expenses, Mister Skye. Your pay, your share, the cost of doing business."

"I'm in for five months. What are your plans, sir?"

"To make us all rich, Mister Skye. It takes only half a cask of grain alcohol, properly diluted, to clean out most any village. Ahead is a fortune! Crows! Piegans! Bloods! Kainah! Flatheads! Kootenai! Assiniboine! Gros Ventres! Not to mention Bannocks and Shoshones and assorted mountain tribes."

"What's the procedure, mate?"

"You certainly sound like a man from the sea, Mister Skye. And I prefer to be addressed as Mister."

"Probably Captain unless I miss my bet."

"You missed your bet, Mister Skye."

Skye thought the boss wasn't going to say more, but instead he began instructing Skye. "We stay well outside of the villages, in a spot where we are in absolute control. Then we invite the chiefs in for some gifts. I have a stock of those. Then we open the trading window. One robe, one drink. After we soften them up, two robes for one drink, then three robes for a watered-down drink. Sometimes some politics are involved. An old man starts railing against us, or the young bucks get into a brawl. Shamans complain. Chiefs give orders. That requires some skills I don't have. That's where you'll come in handy. You can talk; you can wiggle your fingers. You can give some outraged old man or woman a good hunting knife to quiet things down. That's why I hired you, Mister Skye. But sooner or later, we clean 'em out and head for the next village. I cut a wagon loose and send it to a trader, Fort Union, Fort Sarpy, Fort Laramie, Fort Benton, whatever. And we take nothing but a receipt. So many hides, pelts, robes accepted. We head back to St. Louis with empty wagons and not a shilling on our persons. And then, after the reckoning, sir . . ." He smiled broadly.

They toiled up a vague trail toward higher ground. Skye could see that Skittles had outriders keeping an eye on the surrounding country.

"I see you observing how we do things, sir. You've been with us a day or so. Tell me, do you see any vulnerability? Things I should do?"

"I'll know better after you make camp tonight, Mister Skittles."

"A good answer, Mister Skye. You are thinking about the horses. Whether we make an adequate defense. How we protect them. Loss of these horses would be a disaster for us, wouldn't it?"

Skye smiled and kept silent.

"This is the season for horse thievery, isn't it, Mister Skye? A mild winter, that's when all the braves are out, seeing what they can harvest. But I doubt that they'd much care for our big draft horses. Slow beasts."

Skittles seemed to be testing him, and he rose to the challenge. "No, sir, they'd prize the big horses above all else.

The horses are most valuable to them for hauling. Long ago they carried everything on their backs or the backs of dogs. Horses changed that. Big horses . . . maybe you'll see how hard they'll try for some big horses."

Skittles smiled. "Capital, Mister Skye."

He walked away, and Skye sensed he had passed some major testing. Skittles was no greenhorn and was familiar with the tribes and their special way of making war. Who was he? Who was this Mister Quiet, as he was called, who employed this man and this crew of ex-soldiers? And why were these men so rapacious, planning to ruin one village after another, and despoil one people after another, and yet so obsessed with rules?

Skye planned to find out. The trail had a way of opening men up, forming friendships, and revealing secrets. He needed to know fast. Two days ahead was an unsuspecting Crow village, and there was the woman he loved.

33

The closer Skittles's trading outfit came to the Crow village on the Musselshell, the more it was observed. Skye noted distant warriors quietly watching from ridges. These were hunters or men from the village policing society, and it was their task to protect the village from surprises.

Later, as they descended a long, gradual prairie slope into the Musselshell River bottoms, several warriors he knew well approached the wagons and waited. They recognized Skye and were soon wreathed in smiles. Skye waved. That was all it took. They broke toward the camp, bearers of news.

Soon The Robber's winter camp would know that traders were coming and Skye, husband of Many Quill Woman, was with them. Skye wondered how they would feel about all that in two or three days, after an orgy had shamed and impoverished the whole village.

He was in a spot so painful to him that he could barely imagine how to deal with it. And he had little choice, at least for the moment.

"They seem to know you, Mister Skye," said Skittles, who had approached the wagon that Skye was teamstering.

"They do," Skye said.

"All to the good. We'll make camp and then go visit them."

Skittles certainly knew the ritual. There would first be a parley with the chiefs and headmen, some gifts, maybe a smoke, and eventually the trading windows would open. The Robber would certainly want to know who had come and how Skye fit in.

Skittles took them across the shallow Musselshell, so dry this time of year that men and horses could cross without getting soaked, and then headed east, along the riverbank, where a thin blue haze just above the horizon suggested the smoke of a large village.

By now, Skye thought, Victoria would know of his presence. He wondered whether the advance guard of village police had spotted Jawbone and the mare, the very horses condemned by Walks to the Top as bad medicine.

Skittles halted his wagons at a good place perhaps a mile from the village, a meadow near firewood, close to the river, and sheltered from wind and weather. The low sun was heating the sandstone bluffs nearby and at night that pleasant heat would radiate back upon the camp.

Almost without direction, his men formed a camp, unharnessed the wagons, picketed the big draft horses and saddle horses, collected wood, and quietly unloaded a single cask of pure grain spirits, along with the paraphernalia to turn that into Indian whiskey.

People collected now. Warriors first, watching benignly, some younger women, children, a couple of headmen Skye knew. They said nothing, smiled, and Skye waved to acknowledge their presence.

"Well, Mister Skye, we appear to be ready for action. Come with me to translate. And ride your mare."

"That's not a good idea, sir. My horses are considered bad medicine in this village."

"Bad medicine? How so?"

"A certain seer proclaimed that their presence was a bad

omen and that I must either leave with them or the horses must be killed."

"A marvelous superstition, Skye! All the more reason for you to ride the mare. We'll show them we're not bound by such nonsense."

"Sir, it will affect your trading. And it would endanger my horses."

"You will ride the mare, Mister Skye."

"Sir, my mare and colt are my own property, and not leased or sold to the company, and not available to you without my consent. No contract exists concerning them. So I must decline."

Skittles smiled quirkily at Skye, eyed the mare and Jawbone, and came to a conclusion. "It doesn't matter, Mister Skye. You will ride the mare. And bring the colt. It is exactly the display of powers belonging only to white men that I wish to convey to them."

"Sorry, Mister Skittles. They aren't your property."

Skittles smiled, and Skye saw a flash of menace in his eyes. Skye had him. The man who was so punctilious about contracts had no right to those animals. Skye was not going to risk the lives of his medicine horses.

Skittles didn't waste a moment. "Mister Skye," he said softly, "according to your employment contract, you can be flogged for insubordination."

There it was.

"Thanks, mate, that answers a lot of questions. Now I know where I stand."

"It's Mister, sir, not mate."

"Sorry, mate, you don't deserve the courtesy."

Skittles's temper leaked from him.

Skye waited quietly. He was in for it. But with half the village watching, whatever happened here would send a message swiftly to The Robber. He glanced quickly through the gathering Crow people, looking for Victoria, and didn't see her.

"Go ahead, mate," he said.

There were a dozen of these men, mostly ex-soldiers if Skye had it right, and they would overwhelm him and it would hurt. But he wasn't without a few resources. Two steps away, on his mare's pack, was his belaying pin. Probably not a one of these Yanks knew what it was. But he thought he'd just show them what a limey tar could do with a piece of polished hickory.

Skittles eyed them, and him, and backed down. "Later, Skye," he said. "I have a long memory and not an ounce of forgiveness."

"Thanks for letting me know."

Skittles collected a small sack filled with gifts, and started toward the village, hiking through rich pasture along the riverbank. Smiling children paraded beside them. Boys staged mock ambushes. The village policing society formed a rank, escorting Skye and Skittles along the river meadows. Skye knew most of them. They walked buoyantly, fulfilling their office of protectors and peacekeepers. Girls smiled and whispered.

The Crow village lay just around a bend. Its tawny buffalo-hide lodges bled smoke from blackened tops. Here were old people, wrinkled and bronzed, warming in the midday sun. A dozen women scraped fresh buffalo hides, while others were tanning and working two other hides. Smoke permeated the air, along with the scent of stews and other less pleasant odors.

Chief Robber's lodge stood at the center of the arc, somewhat larger and more formidable than the others. It was decorated with brown stick figures, each symbolizing an event in the chief's life. He was waiting there, his hair in glossy braids, his expression benign.

Skye searched anxiously for Victoria, and spotted her. She came running, her eyes bright, her cheeks swabbed with vermilion in celebration of his arrival.

"Skye!" she cried, working through the gathering crowd. "Skye!"

She burst through the police guard, threw herself into Skye's arms, and he hugged her mightily, dancing over the ground with her, knocking his top hat to earth. She was laughing.

"God damn," she said.

"A squaw man, Mister Skye," Skittles said. "I should have known. Man like you wanders around out here with a squaw in every village."

Skye drew himself up swiftly. He would not let that pass.

"This is my wife, Victoria, or Many Quill Woman of the Crows," he said. "Victoria, this is a trader, Skittles by name."

She caught whatever was in his voice and stared at Skittles, suddenly reserved.

Skittles laughed. "Then I've brought you your husband," he responded. "All the better."

"Skittles here is a trader, Victoria. He will trade spirits for robes."

"Aiee! We'll have a good time tonight!"

Skittles watched her, amused, perhaps contemptuous. He urged the party forward. Victoria squeezed Skye's hand and then retreated. There would be time for a reunion later— maybe. Skye had a bad feeling eating at him, and didn't like any of this.

When they reached The Robber's great lodge, the blanket-wrapped headmen had gathered, and were cheerfully awaiting their guest.

"All right, Skittles, I'll translate. They don't know much English."

Skittles nodded.

"Chief Robber, I am honored to be among you, and pleased to tell you we will be trading for robes and hides and pelts and all manner of furs," he said. "My name is Mister

Skittles, and my company of traders has settled a little way up the river. Tell them that."

Skye did, translating into Crow as best he could.

"We will be trading many things and offering good prices," Skittles said. "We are pleased to be in this camp of the mighty Absarokas."

Skye translated. The Robber asked him a question.

"The chief asks whether you brought gifts for him," Skye said.

"I have gifts! A mighty knife for the chief! Green River knives for these gentlemen!"

The Robber nodded. "Ask the trader if he will trade with our enemies next."

"The chief wants to know whether you'll be trading with the Crows' enemies next."

"Tell him we only trade with our friends the Crows," Skittles said.

Skye paused. It was always a temptation to add or subtract or comment on what had been said. But a translator has a sacred duty to be exact. Mendacious translators cause more grief than the harshest truth. Skye knew he must honor what was said. In any case, there were some in the village who knew English.

"The trader says he only trades with his friends, the Absaroka," he said.

The Robber nodded, pleased with this pledge.

34

Chief Robber was a discerning man. He was given to the Indian way of weighing words carefully, often with a silence that white men found disconcerting. He stood there in quiet contemplation, aging but with unlined features, as keen a man as Skye had ever known.

The villagers waited quietly. The Robber gazed at Skye, who stood two or three paces from Skittles, rigid and stern.

"It is said among us that you have in your wagons the spirits that make men mad. Is it so?"

"Oh, yes, Chief," Skittles replied. Skye translated.

"I do not think these things are good for the young men. It makes them bad," The Robber said.

Skittles listened to Skye, and nodded.

"I think these traders are welcome if they agree not to trade the spirits that make men mad for robes. Tell the trader this. Ask him if he agrees."

"Chief Robber says you are welcome to trade if you agree not to trade for spirits. He wants your agreement."

"Why, tell the esteemed chief that we will trade only for those things his people wish to have."

Skye translated and The Robber was not satisfied. "Tell the trader he must agree to serve no spirits. That is my word."

Skittles bowed slightly, smiled, and nodded. "No spirits," he said. "But I can't always control my young men."

Chief Robber's eyes turned merry. "Tell him I can't control my young men either. That is why there will be no spirits."

Skittles smiled easily, enjoying the joke. "Tell the chief we will be ready to trade as soon as I return to the wagons."

"We will see," said The Robber, a sudden smile on his face. Skye sensed the agreement would not be taken seriously by either party.

He followed Skittles back to the wagon. Victoria rushed up to him, alarm in her eyes, but a gesture from Skye quieted her. She sensed trouble.

Skittles's men had set up shop. There was a paltry array of small steel items: awls, knives, fire steels, and arrow points. In addition there was sugar and coffee, hard candy, some one-pound casks of powder, small pigs of lead, caps, vermillion, beads, needles and thread. That was it. But nearby was a great black kettle brimming with firewater, hastily manufactured while Skittles was parleying with the chief. A dozen tin cups and a stack of hollowed gourds were at the ready.

Skittles looked over the array, nodded, and gave his men a thumbs-up.

"Mister Skye, you'll translate. The price list's on that tailgate. One good robe for a drink. If it's mangy or worn, half a drink. No exceptions. The rest, awls, knives, and all that, it's there. Tell 'em, and don't back off."

"No," said Skye.

"What do you mean, no?"

"Didn't you just make a contract with Chief Robber?"

Skittles smiled, dangerously. "No, a little palaver isn't a contract. Now, if you want to stay out of trouble, do as I say."

"No," said Skye.

A flame leaped up in Skittles's eyes. "No? No? You're saying no?" Then he saw the villagers drifting close. Everything was set. "You'll learn the hard way," he said. "If I deal with you now it'd disrupt my business."

"Do that."

Skye had the measure of the man now. For Skittles, a contract was a means to take advantage of others. It wasn't an agreement for mutual gain. If a contract was inconvenient, as far as Skittles believed, it didn't exist. In Skittles's new world, powerful combines would force the weak or the wounded into contracts and use contracts, enforced by courts, to bleed the world's laboring classes white. It all came clear to Skye. He saw enough of that in England. He was seeing even more of it in the Yank republic. A contract was nothing but a serfdom agreement when it was negotiated between a humble man and a rich combination. Slavery, papered over by the notion that both parties going into a contract were on equal footing.

But there was not time to ponder that now.

"What, what?" cried Victoria.

He saw her reaching for him, mystified by all this. He caught her hand and held it. "No time. It's a long story. There's something you must do. These are bad men. I'm their prisoner. I'll explain that later. Tell every woman in the village to hide robes. Take them out of the lodges. Hide them away from the men. Hide them!"

"But, Skye . . ."

"Do it!"

"Who would listen?"

"Try!"

Something steeled within her. "I will."

"Good! Then help me escape. I'll tell you later."

"Escape, Skye?"

He saw wild fear in her now. It matched his own fear. "Save your people from death and grief," he said.

She glanced bleakly, then walked away, her pace urgent.

Behind Skye, the trading had started. Young men were the first. They heaped luxurious buffalo robes, thick with curly hair, onto the back of a wagon, where one of Skittles's smooth-shaven men lifted it, examined it, and then gave the young man a chit. Already there were twenty splendid robes laid flat in the bed of the wagon, and more pouring in.

Skye glanced at the rest. A few of the women were trading pelts for sugar and beads and needles and thread. An old man, wrapped in a blanket, was trading an otter skin for a knife and ten arrow points.

Skittles smiled blandly, glanced maliciously at Skye, and urged people to step right up. The firewater flowed. Tin cups, handed down to grinning youths. One sipped, coughed, whooped, spit, and downed the entire cupful with a gasp. That had cost him a good buffalo robe.

"Oheeee!" he howled.

A toothless old granny dropped a worn and hairless robe on the wagon gate, and waited patiently. "Half a cup, grandma," said Mister Balsamwood, who appeared to be doing most of the evaluating. She nodded. He gave her a chit. She traded it for a tin cup and sipped, sputtered, and then smiled. She sat down and sipped slowly, nodding and smiling at the passing parade.

There went her winter night's warmth, Skye thought.

He saw a headman he admired, Talking Drum, glaring thunderously at all this.

"I wish to talk to you," Skye said.

"My ears are stopped. I will not listen."

"I tried to prevent this."

"You lied to us."

"I translated truly."

"You will never be welcome again among The Robber's people."

"I was brought here as a prisoner."

Talking Drum's scorn laced his face. Then he smiled cruelly, the sort of smile that mocks and destroys. "I will tell The Robber. The Robber will be entertained," he said.

The powerful headman abandoned Skye, walked slowly and massively through the throng, eliciting swift sharp glances. He headed toward a young warrior, Eagle's Claw, and slapped the spirits from the youth's hand.

The boy's temper rose until he saw the massive headman looming over him, ready to deliver ten times more than he got. The youth slipped away.

Talking Drum cut a swath through the crowd, slowing things down, until Skittles approached, with a smile and a gift.

"Here's to the chieftain," he said, handing the headman a good hatchet.

Talking Drum took it, threw it into the soft earth, where its blade sank up to the hilt. In an instant, half a dozen of Skittles's smooth-shaven men surrounded the headman, and handed him a cup of spirits.

Talking Drum poured them into the ground and walked away.

Skye took his chance during the confrontation and hastened out of the trading camp, trotting toward The Robber's village, eliciting stares as he passed scores of people lugging heavy robes and lush fox and weasel and mink and wolf furs, or elk hides, or deerskins.

They greeted him cheerfully. He hurried into the circle of lodges, found it half deserted, headed straight toward the small lodge of the Tobacco Planter, Walks to the Top, collected his breath, and scratched.

No one responded.

He scratched the lodge door again.

"I see no token of your esteem," the old man said.

Skye had nothing. Then he thought of his green flannel shirt, and swiftly stripped it off and laid it before the door. The winter air chilled him at once. After a long wait, the door parted, the seer beckoned him in, and took the shirt.

"Your vision came true," Skye said, preempting the talk

and cutting straight to the heart of things. "You said that if the mare and my medicine colt remained here, disaster would strike The Robber's village. That is happening."

The old man stared, swift and sharp and also startled.

"I was brought here as a prisoner by bad men who plan to take away every robe and pelt in the village, and debauch the young men. Now I am trying to prevent it."

"A prisoner, Mister Skye?"

"They gave me the option of leaving them one bitter cold day. Naked."

"What are they doing?"

"They do not have a license, a permission, from the Fathers, and they are ruthless. There will be much weeping."

"What do you want of me?"

"The headmen think I'm one of the traders. They are deaf to me. I cannot tell them of the trouble, or what has happened to me, or what will fall upon this village. You can. You are an elder. Chief Robber and the headmen can stop this."

Walks to the Top stared into the ashes of his fire, and then into the warm winter day.

"That which I saw in the sweetgrass smoke and the clouds will come to pass," he said. "I will do nothing. Who can resist an ill wind?"

35

He felt the cold air on his back. He needed a shirt. It was a bright winter's day. If Skittles's men hadn't made off with his buckskin shirt, it would be among his things. But first, find Victoria. She needed to know the whole story.

He hunted through the village. A few women were indeed carrying the heavy robes away. Somehow Victoria had talked them into it. He found her collecting robes in her brother's lodge.

"Oh, Skye!" she cried, and flew to him. They hugged with all the pent-up love that months of separation had built in them.

"Oh, Skye," she cried, touching his face, running her hand through his shorn hair. "What? What?"

He pulled her down to the robes and sat beside her. "Too long to tell now. No time. I'm a captive, or they think I am. These traders are evil. They are not offering a little whiskey and a lot of other goods. They mean to make The Robber's whole village crazy and walk off with every robe and pelt here. The Fathers in Washington don't know about them. The traders think they own me. They said they'd keep my possessions, Jawbone and the mare, even my clothing, if I didn't obey. I'll need your help. My rifle and gear and the horses need to be taken away and hidden. The Hawken's one I got at a trading post.

"We need to let Chief Robber know. And the headmen. Maybe they can stop this. Let them know that evil is here among them. And beware. These men are armed and capable of anything."

"Skye, what first?"

"Talk, Victoria. Tell them. Tell everyone. Warn them away. Hide robes. Stop the young men from drinking the spirits."

"How did you lose your green shirt?"

"Gift to Walks to the Top."

"Did he believe you?"

"Yes, but he says it will all happen just as he dreamed it."

"Sonofabitch!"

Skye laughed suddenly. Victoria was an army.

"Come," she said.

He followed her to their own lodge, which he had never seen. Its new hides shone golden in the bright light, and smoke had not yet blackened the top of the cone. There were half a dozen robes within, but little else. All this had been a gift of her brother and his wives.

She plucked up a buckskin shirt.

"Try this."

"Victoria—"

"I was making it for my brother. Maybe it fits."

The shirt had been sewn of the softest doeskin he had ever felt in his fingers, fringed and partly quilled. There was a red geometric design over the heart.

He slid it on, feeling its soft silkiness cover him against the winter air.

"Damn! I make good shirts!"

This one had an irregular hem that followed the contour of the hide, dipping low on the left side. It had long sleeves, fringed all the way to draw off water.

"I feel like a chief," he said.

"You're my chief. Ho ho, Skye, let's get those bastards. Now you got medicine. This here shirt, it's big medicine."

He didn't need an invitation. He stepped into the light somehow transformed. Now he was a man of the mountains again, not some interloper in a green shirt, like all the others over there in their green flannels.

"I go talk. Then we see what we can do," she said.

He watched her race toward a knot of angry headmen, who plainly didn't like what was being purveyed over at the trading camp.

He had his own business to attend, and headed along the riverbank to the trading camp. He had to acknowledge there were a lot of happy people on the trail and around the camp. He had never seen so many smiles in a village. Young men swaggered expansively, parading themselves before the maidens. But so were cheerful wives and sisters, old warriors, and scores of older wives, who had bargained for sugar and needles and thread and awls, but also tried a cup of the brew.

In a glance Skye saw that one wagon was nearly filled with robes, carefully laid flat. And that Skittles's men were busy brewing another batch of firewater, this one no doubt thinner and meaner than the first. Less of the spirits but more of the cayenne pepper and maybe now a pinch of the bug powder used by fur outfits to control insect damage to hides and furs.

The camp was perfectly orderly. Young men stood around in circles, sipping out of gourd cups, horn spoons, and sometimes a tin cup. They were at ease, laughing, enjoying the crisp bright afternoon. In small knots old men wrapped blankets tight, folded their arms, and glowered at those who were abandoning the traditional Crow ways.

Skye's plan was simple. Spirit his horses out of there, along with everything in his packs, especially his rifle. Victoria would hide them. Then he was free. Nothing Skittles might throw at him would compel him to stay. After that, somehow, wreck the trade as much as possible, get these people back to their lodges.

And after that . . . he eyed the well-guarded wagon with the casks in it, knowing he would have his hands full. But if he could destroy that pure grain alcohol, trading would come to an abrupt halt.

He headed into the traders' camp only to run into Skittles.

"Where've you been?"

"In the village."

"Why aren't you in your green shirt?"

"I gave it to a powerful man."

"Gave company property away, did you? That's going to cost you. You're out of uniform. That's going to cost you. All my men wear green shirts. That's so the redskins know we're a company. Now what'm I going to do with you?" He eyed the beautifully made shirt. "Put that in the wagon, Skye. You just traded it for the green shirt."

Skye started to walk away, but heard the snick of a revolver being cocked.

"No you don't, Skye. I'm not done with you."

Skye doubted the man would shoot. It would start a riot. But there was no telling about Skittles. He stood quietly, not liking that black bore pointed at his midsection.

"You don't seem to understand, Mister Skye. You're my employee."

"Slave."

"Go to that wagon and start spreading those robes flat. I want every robe just as flat as it gets. We can put a lot more robes into a wagon if they're loaded right."

"Slave," Skye said.

Skittles laughed. "I can read your mind, Mister Skye. You're wondering where your nags are, and your outfit and your rifle. I don't know what you see in that ugly colt and spavined mare, but they make handy hostages, don't they? They're well guarded, Mister Skye, along with your other truck. If you even approach the pen we've put them in, the first bullet goes into them, not you."

"Thank you for warning me, mate."

"And don't suppose you can send your little trollop after them. The guards are well aware of the slut."

"Victoria is my wife."

"Ah! Wife! A squaw in every camp. A sailor has a whore in every port!"

"Wife," said Skye.

He smiled brightly, walked toward the wagon where two other Misters were spreading robes, tossing a little bug powder on them, and coughing. In the other wagon a few uncured hides were being laid flat.

Skye stepped up to the wagon bed and began the labor. Skittles watched, and then slid his dragoon revolver into its nest at his waist.

The trading was going smoothly. An endless stream of Crows, most of them lugging valuable buffalo robes, or elk hides, or wolf or mink or ermine furs, wound toward the trading area. The Crows were colorfully dressed, as if this were a festival occasion, many in deerskins decorated with bright ribbons. The older ones were wrapped in blankets, and Skye was glad. They, at least, would sleep warm this night.

To the casual observer, it looked more like an idyllic rural fair, with laughing Indians telling their usual bawdy jokes, and orderly lines of people waiting their turn to bargain a robe or a pelt for a cup of brew.

But this was only prelude. He eyed the sun, slowly sinking now, and knew that when dark fell, so would all civility, and before the sun rose again, the ground would be soaked with blood and the wealth of a village would be lost.

He furtively studied the whole scene, looking for ways to do what must be done, and found none. Skittles and his ex-army bunch would not be taken by surprise.

He spotted Victoria wandering in, her eyes bright, her

greetings to all around her cheerful. But what set him to worrying was not her presence, but what she carried in her arms. She had a prime robe with her and it would buy her a cup of that brew, and he knew he had to stop her.

He jumped down from the wagon, raced to her.

"No, Victoria!"

"Skye, dammit, I will have a drink."

He clasped his hands about her shoulders. "If ever I need you, I need you now."

She smiled gently and worked free.

"Ah, the little Missus," said Skittles. "Welcome, welcome. I see you've brought us a good robe."

"Her name, to you, is Many Quill Woman, Skittles."

"Why, Many Quill Woman, we have a treat just for you. A little drink back here, with your mate. A little jug just for the two of you."

Skye knew suddenly how Victoria was gaining access to the traders' camp.

36

Skittles led them behind the wagons to a quiet spot near the traders' campground. Skye didn't like it. The mob around the trading wagon was safety of a sort, but here, fifty yards away, whatever happened would not be noted. There was plenty of daylight now, but in a couple of hours whatever happened here would be cloaked in night.

"Now, little lady, you just settle yourself and have a drink. If you're Mister Skye's friend, you get all the spirits you want for that robe. We treat our friends just right."

"Hot damn!" she said. "Wooee!"

"Victoria, we'll go back to the lodge now," Skye said.

"Dammit, Skye."

He tried to lift her up, walk away with her, but she fought him off.

"Maybe you'd care to join her, Mister Skye?"

"No thanks, mate."

"I've just decided you'll join her. This is quite perfect. If you were elsewhere, I'd have to keep track of you. An unhappy employee can cause problems. So, have a drink on the house."

Skye grinned and refused to sit down. He was as vulnerable as Victoria. They both could wrap themselves around a jug and enjoy the whole shot. Many a rendezvous, back in the trapping days, they had whooped their way into oblivion. But not now. Not when everything was at stake.

He heard shouts. The party was becoming a little frolicsome around the trading wagon. Someone had brought drums, and now the throbbing beat was hammering the village. One young man in a red blanket was parading himself back and forth before some bright-eyed girls.

"Skittles, I quit."

"I thought you might, Mister Skye. A pity. According to the contract, you surrender your worldly goods to us. The ugly horses you put so much stock in, your outfit, your rifle . . . and the little Missus here. We'll enjoy her."

Skye swung, caught Skittles off guard, knocked him to the turf, but Skittles was an army man and up like a cat, his revolver blooming in his hand.

Skye didn't much care. He swung again. The revolver barked. Skye felt the ball part his hair. He jammed in, wrenched Skittles's arm just as the next shot sailed by. Then half a dozen green shirts landed on him, yanked him back, threw him to the earth, and twisted his arm until he thought it'd break. These were skilled brawlers.

Victoria howled, and dashed her jug over one of them. Then they caught her and pinned her down near Skye.

Skittles rose, dusted himself, smiled blandly. "Why, Mister Skye, you've mussed up my attire," he said. "We don't want to give the redskins the wrong impression."

Skye felt a half a dozen hands and arms pinning him to the cold meadow. Victoria was caught in the same vise. Some Crows stared. Mostly they kept on sipping, peddling furs at the wagon, and courting each other.

Skittles gazed blandly about until he was satisfied that the uproar behind the wagons had scarcely been noted by the Crows.

"It seems we have the upper hand, Mister Skye. We always do. But you're a little slow to learn."

Skye stared up at him.

"Let him get up," Skittles said.

Skye was lifted to his feet. Arms continued to immobilize him.

"As it happens, I need you, Mister Skye. The traders have trouble with the Crow tongue. You'll come and translate."

Skye started to object but Skittles cut him off.

"Don't say no. Don't ever say no to me, Mister Skye. The only words I plan to hear are, 'Yes, Mister Skittles.' That's what you'll be saying from now on."

"Let her up and let her go," Skye said.

Skittles smiled broadly, revealing those perfect teeth. "She has a new name, Mister Skye. The name is not Victoria, and not Many Quill Woman. The name is Hostage. We now hold everything you care about hostage. Your ugly colt is a hostage and so is the mare. Your, ah, wife is our hostage. Your miserable possessions, a battered Hawken, a bedroll, a few tools, those are all hostage too. You must be in your forties. That's not much for a lifetime, is it?

"It's all hostage now, Mister Skye, and you will say 'Yes, Mister Skittles' whenever I ask you to do something. If you say 'Yes, Mister Skittles,' maybe your squaw won't get hurt. Maybe you might even get your horses back. And your rifle. Maybe. Only maybe. It will all depend. You are going to be a slave, Mister Skye. You are going to say yessir, yessir, and you are going to smile, and you are going to invite your old friends from this village to the trading wagon, and smile at them. And if you don't, Mister Skye, the things that will happen tonight, once the orgy starts, oh, yes, there's usually an orgy and a few redskins dead by dawn—the things that will happen to your squaw, and your animals, won't even be noticed."

Skye nodded.

They stepped back. He stood free. He could run. He could howl. He could maybe even walk away.

Skittles smiled again. The man worked at smiling, had a smile for every occasion, a bright smile, a condescending smile, a triumphant smile. He flipped open his revolver and ejected the two spent shells and reloaded from a handful that fit into loops on his belt.

"Time's a wasting, Mister Skye." He pointed toward the trading wagon.

Skye watched them steer Victoria toward the traders' camp, and then she disappeared inside a tent. He watched the flap close. She was in there with a couple of green shirts.

He clenched and unclenched his hands.

"Mister Skye?" Skittles asked. He pointed gently toward the trading wagon where two or three green shirts were still raking in pelts and robes and pouring out watered-down spirits. It was not yet evening, but soon would be.

He saw no quick or easy way out. But he would await his chances and break when he could.

"Why, it's Mister Skye, going to help us out," said one of the green shirts, Mister Oliver.

A familiar old woman was approaching. He knew her; he was acquainted with most of the people in Otter's band. This plump old lady was Little Red Fox, a graying widow who made and decorated cradleboards and gave them to young mothers. Her bead and quill designs were famous for warding off dark spirits and bringing luck to the infants in the cradleboards, and she was revered for the goodness she brought to the newborn.

"So it is you, Mister Skye," she said in her own tongue. "I heard it was you. You're a trader now?"

"What's she saying, Skye?"

"She's asking after me."

"I am not a trader, mother. But I will translate."

"That is good, Mister Skye. I brought this good robe, which has served me well for many winters. I want to trade it for some needles and thread, a new awl, a new knife, and many bright beads."

"What's she say, Skye?"

"She wants to trade her robe for needles, thread, beads, an awl, and a knife."

"Tell her to take the robe over there to have it looked at. We're not trading for the hardware now, Skye. We'll trade her for a cup of lightning."

Skye didn't like what he was being forced to do. "Mother, they say to take the robe over there, where the men in green shirts will look at it and offer a price for it. Then they say they'll give you some of the water that makes people crazy. They say they won't trade for the things you want now."

She sighed. "Are they out of these things?"

"She wants to know whether you're out of the things she wants."

A green shirt grinned. "Just tell her we want her robe and we'll give her a treat."

"They want your robe and they'll give you some of the water that makes you crazy."

"I think not, Mister Skye." She smiled and walked away.

"What'd she say? You let her go!"

"She said no."

"You let her go!"

"She makes beautiful cradleboards and decorates them and is famous in the village for the things she makes with her hands. It is very good luck to get one of her cradleboards."

"Go tell her we want that robe."

Skye shrugged, and hastened after her. "They said to tell you they want the robe."

She paused. "I wish you and Many Quill Woman would make a child. I would make the most beautiful cradleboard I have ever made. I would weave powerful signs into it."

"I'll tell them."

He returned. "She said she wishes my wife and I would have a child so she could make a cradleboard for us, and for our baby. She said it would be the most beautiful one she has ever made."

"Damn you, Mister Skye, take this hooch to her and snatch that robe."

Skye stood paralyzed. He thought of Victoria, in that tent. He thought of his medicine colt, and the mare. He thought of Victoria at the utter mercy of those green shirts. He thought of the colt and mare lying dead, their throats slit.

"No," he said. "She doesn't want your spirits. She wants what she wants. And we don't steal robes."

The green shirts laughed but let it go. Skye had won a tiny victory but he was losing the war.

37

Chief Robber himself showed up with three of his youngest wives beside him. He paused, rocked on his heels, studied the bacchanal, looped his way around the trading wagons, and then discovered Skye.

"Ah, it is you, Mister Skye," he said. "Are you working for the traders?"

"I am their captive."

"What's the chief want?" asked a green shirt.

"He's inquiring about my employment."

"Tell him, he's got robes to trade, we'll give him some good brew. Nothing but the best for old Robber."

"The traders wish to trade robes, and will give you the best of their water that makes men crazy."

"Why are you their captive?"

"They have taken Many Quill Woman and my horses and my rifle from me."

"That is a good joke."

"What's he say, Skye?"

"He asked me about my employment, and I told him."

The Robber smiled. "It is a good evening," he said. "The young men drum and dance. The girls flirt. Friends sit around the big fires and laugh. It is a good time. I was wrong about spirits."

"Translate," yelled a green shirt.

"He says it's a good evening, and he was wrong about spirits."

The chief studied the cheerful crowd. "I like this. I see no harm in it. I will trade. I want a big jug of crazy-water. Here are my three youngest and prettiest wives. They will make the traders happy. Say this."

The ladies smiled seductively. Skye noticed they were all gotten up in their best, with vermillion on their cheeks, and wearing their finest quilled dresses. Their eyes shone.

Skye didn't want to translate. He coughed and hemmed and settled his top hat on his locks.

"Come on, Skye."

"Chief Robber wishes to trade for a large jug of your best stuff. His payment is to lend you his three youngest and prettiest wives."

That caught their attention. The green shirts suddenly quit grading and loading robes, and rushed to the women, who were delighted with the attention. To be lent out by their husband the chief was a delicious honor.

"No," said Skittles.

The boss appeared out of nowhere and grasped the transaction instantly.

"Mister Balsamwood, go back to work," he said. "Mister Skye, tell Chief Robber we'll be delighted to give him our very best spirits, one cup for one prime robe."

"But, sir," said Grosvenor, "that's a dandy offer."

"Business before pleasure, Mister Grosvenor. After we clean out all the robes, then I'll consider it."

"Yes, sir."

Skittles turned to Skye. "The squaw's enjoying a drink or two. Behave yourself, Mister Skye."

"Same to you, sir."

Skittles clouded briefly, smiled, and wandered off.

Night was falling. The incessant drumming was affecting Skye's heart, making it beat to the rhythm of the drums.

Some of the Crows were chanting, their hard voices violating the twilight peace. A few young women crowded about the trading wagon, where they were disposing of ermine and mink pelts, each for a half cup of the hooch, poured into the gourd bowls they brought along.

Green shirts tucked the mink and ermine hides into the corners that no buffalo robes filled. The wagon with cured furs and pelts was full; the other wagon, with raw buffalo hides, was not. The green shirts were making a haul. And this was but one village. The outfit planned to visit several more. It was working north toward Blackfeet, Gros Ventres, and Assiniboine villages. It struck him that the owners and their employees would split upward of twenty thousand dollars from a winter's work.

One by one, the young men slipped away, dug up another robe somewhere, and returned. Now it bought them watered-down spirits, and with a pinch of bug powder to make them crazy. Skye didn't need to translate. They dropped a robe before the traders, who examined it by lamplight, and the warrior walked away with another cup of the rotgut steadily being stirred up by a couple of expert green shirts.

It seemed an idyll. A mild winter's night. Some good drumming. Stars popping out. A few warming fires. Some flirting, some giggles, some couples meandering away from the light and into their own world. The spirits were dissolving restraints. Men laughed. The girls turned seductive. Even the chief was joining the revels.

Skye thought of Victoria. Was she guarded? Was she bound or constrained? How could he free her? How could he free the mare and Jawbone, corralled in a makeshift pen? How could he get to her? He didn't even know which of the traders' tents she was in. But nighttime was a good cloak.

Chief Robber's women showed up, each bearing two robes, which was all most women could carry. These were prime robes, luxuriant and thick.

One came to Skye. "Jug. He wants a jug."

"The chief wants a jug," he told Mister Oliver.

Skittles materialized out of the dark. He had been prowling, ever alert, ever aware of everything in the camp.

"Six prime robes, Mister Skittles," said Oliver.

"All right, six cups."

"Of this?"

"What else?"

He motioned toward the kettle of watered-down muddy-water stuff, spirits and pepper and whatever else the traders felt like tossing in.

It was Skittles's deliberate act of disrespect for the chief.

Skye watched the green shirts prepare a jug and hand it to one of the wives. She beamed and hurried away with the two other women, and were soon lost in darkness.

He felt bad. Everything about this was bad, and he included his own yearning to settle in a corner with some of that rotgut somewhere and pour it down his gullet.

In an hour or two the sober green shirts would be absolute masters of this Crow camp. Many of the younger Crows were plainly drunk. But they seemed cheerful enough, and Skye thought maybe the night would pass without tragedy.

But then in a flash of flame everything changed. One young man wrapped a blanket around a young woman, an old courtship ritual, and a rival howled, drew a knife, slashed, and all Skye saw was blood gouting into the old blanket. The girl screamed. She raced into darkness, spilling her blood and covered with her swain's. A young man fell, rolled across cold ground, and lay in a widening black pool. Other young men howled. Firelight glinted off of naked knives.

He didn't know their names. He only knew that brothers and friends were fighting brothers and friends, old men were wrestling with young ones. The beat of the drums stopped cold, but now there were howls and shrieks terrible to hear.

Skye raced into the melee.

"Avast!" he roared, the roar erupting from his belly.

He threw men apart. But drunken warriors howled at him and slashed the air with cold steel.

"Let them brawl, Mister Skye. It's all part of their nature."

Skye turned on Skittles, only to see the man smiling, the revolver casually in hand.

"There now, Mister Skye, you step back and let them destroy themselves. It is destined, you know. The inferior races will fade away. The superior races will triumph and possess the land and its wealth. That's historical reality. There's nothing we can do to change it."

Some few youngsters were still brawling, but now village headmen were pulling people away, clustering around the fallen, stanching blood. And the wailing had begun.

Skye smelled death in the air. Along with vomit, fear, and maybe something like hysteria. He itched to land on Skittles and thrash him into the cold ground, but he knew better. It was a good thing he himself had not been drinking. He would be among the dead.

In time, the Absaroka people, those who could still function, came for the sick and the dead and hauled them away. Chief Robber was not among them. One or two headmen, including his testy old friend Otter, had restored order. Now there was a lonely gulf between the village and the traders' camp, a no-man's-land where no one dared venture. An aching silence.

Death and grief had come. Skye didn't know who had perished. What boys lay wounded. What girls wept into their cold beds, for there were only a few blankets to warm these people this winter's night. They would lie on cold ground where robes had once protected them from the earth. They would shiver, not only from cold, but from the evil unloosed in their camp. They would remember the prediction of Walks to the Top, that Skye's medicine horse Jawbone would bring down the wrath of the spirits upon them.

He thought that in the morning they might come to kill

his horses, or even kill him, for had he not assisted in the trading?

And even if he might escape with Victoria and his animals, would he ever be welcome in a Crow village again?

But there was not time to ponder that. The traders were working by the flickering light of two fires as they closed up shop. They had filled one wagon; the other was nearly full. There were no doubt few buffalo robes left in The Robber's village.

"Time to be moving, gentlemen," Skittles said. "We've done all the good we can."

38

By the light of the bonfires, green shirts dismantled the trading camp. Two canvas tents had already vanished into the bowels of the supply wagon. All that was left was blood and vomit on the grass.

Skittles obviously planned to make time this night, putting distance between his outfit and the Crow village they had debauched.

"Mister Skye, you'll harness the teams," he said easily.

He had an air of total triumph about him. The outfit had raked in a small fortune, almost without cost.

Skye nodded. If he was going to make a break, it had to be now. But where was Victoria? The tents were packed and the wagons were loaded almost to the bows and canvas tops.

One green shirt stood at guard before the wagons, his rifle at the ready. The rest were packing up. Some lifted the empty booze kettle and stowed it. Others collected tin cups, gourd cups, wooden cups that littered that bloody ground, and piled them into a burlap sack. Others raised the tailgates of the wagons carrying the ill-gotten robes and hides, and levered them tight.

Skye started toward the rope corral that contained the draft horses and the saddlers, as well as his captive colt and mare. The harness would probably be lying there, ready to drop over the big draft animals. He would have trouble in the dark.

His mind seethed. Another guard stood at the horse pen, rifle at the ready, no doubt to prevent theft of the stock. Skittles was not one to let anyone or anything slip through his hands.

Two green shirts were already harnessing. Putting eight draft horses into harness and hooking them to wagons was a tough task, especially at night. Add to that the loading of the packhorses, and you had a half hour of hard labor by several men.

Skye looked toward the dipper, trying to tell the time as it rotated around the north star. The night had turned wintry and dead quiet. He was grateful that no wind stirred, so that his hands wouldn't go numb as he dropped collars over those thick necks and tightened bands under their great hairy bellies.

It was perhaps midnight. An eerie silence lowered over them all, all the louder for the drumming that had shattered the peace only an hour or so earlier. Now not even the wail of the mothers of the bloodied boys caught the tendrils of winter air.

He clambered under the rope fence and found a heap of harness awaiting him.

"Good evening, Mister Skye," said one of the green shirts. "You can start on that big black over there."

Skye thought it was Oliver, or maybe Parsons. Men who were groomed alike were hard to pick out. Jawbone discovered him, trotted up, squealed, and butted him.

"That miserable thing should have its throat cut," said another of the green shirts. "Makes trouble."

Skye nodded. He found the mare now, faint firelight reflecting off her side. She whickered softly and drew close. But there was little Skye could do for the moment. The firelight revealed too much. He needed darkness, real darkness, a cloak of darkness, the kind of night where a man can't see ten feet.

Where was Victoria? How could he make a move without knowing? Had they knocked her in the head and left her in the woods?

And where was his kit? His bedroll, his rifle, his pack-saddles, his gear? He hadn't the faintest idea. He found a collar, which felt icy in his hand, and found a halter. These teamsters rarely used bridles with these superb animals. They walked beside their teams, lead rope in hand. The big draft horse stood quietly, letting itself be haltered. Then Skye dropped the collar over its thick neck, and led it to the heap of harness. A belly band would be next.

It was then that he heard the harsh whistle of a magpie. It was a thing unknown in the night, but apparently not a thing that troubled the green shirts anyway.

He felt a surge of joy. She was there.

He finished with the big black's breeching and led it to one of the pelt wagons, backed it into place, and buckled the traces. Skittles was watching him. Skye walked slowly into the darkness again, entered the rope corral, and found another big draft horse. The two green shirts from the rope corral were each leading a harnessed draft horse toward the wagons.

No one was watching him. It was the moment Skye needed.

He collected another halter and belly band and headed for the next draft horse, only to bump into a small person in the moon-shadow side of the horse.

"Dammit, Skye, don't step on my toe," she said.

Skye's heart raced.

"Come."

She led him to the rear of the corral, closest to the naked cottonwoods that lay fifty yards away, and they simply walked through the darkness. Somehow she had discerned that the fire-blinded night guard could not see them. Skye followed silently, his heart banging, not knowing what to think but filled with joy.

They raced into the naked trees, the distant firelight eerie on the web of limbs. And then they reached the sandstone cliffs, and she headed through brush toward the village, well screened from the river.

She paused at a niche in the stone and pulled him down beside her.

"I hide here," she said. "See, a cave. I got that jug. They gave me a jug of the good stuff. They put me in the supply wagon, guard in front so I couldn't get out. But they don't know Absaroka. I got my knife from my moccasin and cut through the canvas at the other end and walk out as soon as it got dark. They never knew. Dammit, Skye, I got a whole jug here, big enough for us to have a good time. But not now."

"You rescued me."

"Hell, yes. Maybe I'm good for something, eh?"

"Can we get my gear? Rifle, bedroll, packsaddles? Do you know where they are?"

She didn't respond. She didn't know. One of the wagons.

"We need to get the mare and the colt."

She pressed a hand over his. "Let them go, Skye. We can't go back. They're hunting for you now."

Without a rifle once again. Without means to make meat. Without weapons. Without horses. All that time at Fort Sarpy lost. But he had escaped.

"We'll head for the village," he said.

"The hell we will, Skye. They're looking for you there. Why do they want you, eh? You never told me."

"At first I thought it was because they wanted my labor. They're shorthanded and don't have a good translator. Now I think it's because I'm a witness. What they're doing is against the laws of the Fathers. Any white man who doesn't go along, he's dead." He turned to her. "Maybe you saved my life."

"Witness?"

"Someone who would talk in St. Louis. Someone who would tell the Indian agency about them. Name some names."

"You people crazy."

"I'm not a Yank, Victoria."

"You want a sip?"

"Yes, soon as it's safe."

"Who died, Skye? I heard the wailing."

"I don't know. One of the young men drumming."

"Sonofabitch," she said.

"Let's work back and see," she said.

He nodded. They left the sheltering sandstone and worked back at the base of the bluff until they were opposite the traders' camp, and then slipped like wraiths through the naked forest until they could peer out onto the meadow.

Nothing. Gone. All the wagons, all the livestock. But for the trampled brown grass that whispered of large events, it was as if the traders had never been there.

"Don't go out there," he whispered. "It would be just like Skittles to leave a man behind, his horse hidden, waiting for us. They know I'll come looking for my kit."

"I won't."

They waited an eternity, it seemed. A cloud canceled the moonlight. The meadow of sorrows lay in deep darkness. A deep predawn cold settled over the meadow, frosting the broken grasses. And still they waited.

Then, soft as the flapping of an owl through night air, the clop of horse hooves. The horse moved upriver, away from the village. Probably the direction the traders went.

He didn't know where they would go next. Skittles would have to send his two loaded wagons to a fur post. But he was expecting two wagons back, and there must have been some agreement about where. If he sent the two full wagons out, that reduced his company by four men.

Skye sighed. His Hawken, powder horn, caps, lead and

patches, and all the rest were moving away from him in the cold night. He and Victoria slid onto the meadow, searched it closely. Searched with dread for the bodies of his colt and mare, their throats slit. But they found nothing at all in that sad flat beside the river.

They walked toward the village, knowing it was forlorn and defenseless, that its men slept with vomit on their shirts, that they would wake up sick and listless, that many a lodge was shivering this night, that in some lodges bloodied young men were lying in the vise of death. The village was naked to its enemies. A raiding party could sweep through it. The entire pony herd, pride of the Crow nation, could be swept away.

The Robber's village was a desolate place. Something foul hung in the air. Little smoke ebbed from the blackened cones of the lodges. One drunken man sprawled on the ground. Skye wished he had a blanket or a robe to cover the wretch.

Victoria steered him toward her own small lodge, but when they entered they found nothing at all. No robes, no blanket, no parfleche with her things in it. Nothing but frozen earth.

Victoria scratched on the door of Two Dogs' lodge. No one answered. She tried again. The smell of vomit eddied from the door.

Skye knew what he had to do. He was going to follow that trading outfit, he was going to do it, and he would do it even if he didn't possess a weapon to his name.

39

Something frightful had passed through The Robber's village. Skye and Victoria crawled out of their small lodge in the gray light of a winter's dawn and saw a deadness everywhere. No smoke was eddying from the lodges. A desolation hung over what had been, only hours before, a vibrant and happy place.

Skye and Victoria had survived the cold by building a lodge fire and feeding it all night. She had gone to the sand-stone bluffs to recover a robe she had hidden there but it was gone, and so were all the other robes the village women had hidden there. Each had been pawned for a drink of the rotgut. So Skye had dug into his fire pouch at his waist, struck steel to flint, and eventually they had a hot fire in their naked home.

Now he braved the cold, wandering through the forlorn village, wondering who lived and who didn't. Victoria muttered softly, wandering from lodge to lodge, looking for life. They rounded a lodge and saw a girl. Victoria knew her. She lay across the frozen ground, her skirts hiked high, her face staring at the dawn.

Victoria plunged to her knees and shook the girl.

"Get up! Get up!" she cried. "Broken Wing, wake up!"

Victoria shook hard, but the girl did not move.

Victoria and Skye lifted the girl, but the girl did not sit. She was stiff, frozen solid, and life had fled her. A rime of vomit clung to the girl's lips.

"Aiee! Broken Wing!" Victoria cried.

Victoria pressed her hands upon the dead woman, and sobbed softly.

When at last she had wept away her grief, she looked up at Skye, and at the other person who now stood over her. It was the old Tobacco Planter, Walks to the Top, wrapped in a bright thick Hudson's Bay blanket.

"I saw this in the smoke of the sweetgrass," he said. "I warned the people. Now it has been as I saw it."

Skye nodded. Would the old man blame all this on the medicine horse?

"The traders are gone. They left in the night. They have almost every robe and hide that was the wealth of this village," he said.

"This I saw in the smoke."

"And it's not over. There are the sick, the dead, and the ones who fought each other with knives. And the girls who were violated. And the old men sleeping half frozen in their cold lodges."

"I went before The Robber and I told him. Do not let business be done with the traders. This I saw."

"Here is The Robber's oldest daughter," Victoria said. "The one he loved most."

The Robber's lodge rose nearby, as cold and quiet as the rest in the village. Someone would have to tell him that his daughter had perished of spirits and cold.

Tenderly, Skye lifted the frozen girl. She seemed so heavy, but probably didn't weigh a hundred pounds. Then he lowered the girl to the trampled earth before the chief's lodge, and Victoria straightened the girl's soiled skirts. Walks to the Top, wrapped tightly in his red blanket, his face dark with pain and anger, came along.

Skye scratched at the door, but this evoked no response.

Victoria slapped the doorskin hard, repeatedly. They heard a stirring, and finally the chief's old sits-beside-him wife, Stirs the Water, poked her head out.

"Mother, we have bad news," Victoria said.

The woman squinted, caught sight of her daughter's frozen body before the lodge, muttered a cry, and then retreated inside. The lodge's door flap slapped shut.

The village was stirring at last. Skye stood unhappily at The Robber's lodge, noting that old people were heading for the bushes, women were building lodge fires, a few shivering children were solemnly wandering about, some of them in tears.

Some wore spare clothing. A few had blankets. One wore a blanket capote. A few did have some worn or torn buffalo robes, somehow salvaged from the devastation that had whirled through this village.

The Robber poked his head through the door, studied the frozen body of his daughter, and groaned.

"She was over there when we found her," Victoria said, pointing.

The chief nodded and dismissed them with a wave.

He looked ill. Skye thought the chief was barely functioning. Whatever it was, headache, nausea, the aftereffects of indulgence, he wasn't ready to cope with this.

Now a crowd gathered, and Victoria told of finding the chief's daughter frozen to death.

Walks to the Top whirled away, exuding anger and sorrow. Skye followed. There was nothing more he could do for The Robber and his family.

"This is the beginning of the end of my people," the Tobacco Planter said. "I have seen it."

"I'm going to try to stop it."

"How will you stop it?"

"I'm going to go after them."

"More traders will come with this poison water. Nothing in the stories of the People prepare us for this. It is a new evil that white men bring. Look at them! They are dazed. They are sick. They hurt. They lost their manhood. A man is a man when he commands himself. But they swallow this poison and they no longer command themselves. They fight like rutting elk. They stab each other, brothers fight, friends fight. And now the mothers and widows cry. Our chief himself drank the poison, and he is helpless now. They will wait for the next traders to give them more, and they will kill buffalo and tan robes so they can trade them for more and more and more!"

The Tobacco Planter saw the thing Skye dreaded.

"Look at them!" Walks to the Top shouted. "We are naked before our enemies. They still stagger. They cannot put one foot in front of the other. Who cooks the morning meals? Who cares for the horses? Who polices our village?"

The elder stopped suddenly. "What are you going to do?"

"Follow them, stalk them, find some way to destroy their spirits. It's pure grain alcohol. It burns."

"You will take a war party?"

"Many Quill Woman and I will go alone. It is better that way."

"With what?"

"That is a good question."

"We will see," the venerable man said, and walked away as suddenly as he had approached Skye.

The village was stirring now, sullen, hungry, cold, and ashamed. Skye spotted Otter, the headman who had suffered ambush at the hands of the Blackfeet.

"It is true, then. You are the cause of this," Otter said. "That's what is whispered."

"Otter, I was a prisoner. My wife was held hostage, along with all my things. My horses were held hostage. I did not sell any of the spirits. I only translated."

Otter eyed him malevolently "We will see," he said. "I took none of the spirits. I alone am fit and able this morning. I have chosen my way."

"Then you must put this village together, Otter. Put guards out. Start the village police. Watch over the horses. See about firewood. Start hunters. The village needs a thousand robes and hides."

Otter stood, his arms crossed before him, looking truculent. "It is said you should leave here. You were with them. You are a white man. You brought this upon us."

One could not argue with something like that. Skye knew it, knew he would be wasting his breath. This would soon snowball into an exile.

"I have some business to attend, and then I'll leave the village," he replied. "And if I return, I will have good news for you."

Otter simply glared. A storm was gathering over Skye.

He trotted to his lodge and found Victoria there.

"I'm being blamed. We need to leave. The ponies that Two Dogs gave me; are they still in the herd? Do you know them? Can we borrow a few things?"

"I know them, Skye. I don't want to leave my people. I don't want you to be disgraced."

"We have nothing. Food, robes, weapons. Whatever you can scrounge from your brother . . ."

She nodded.

They didn't even have saddles. He could ride bareback, but only for a while, and when his back split in two he had to dismount. They could get hackamores easily enough, and with luck, a packsaddle. But they would be leaving The Robber's camp with barely enough to survive on in wintertime. And Skye had a mission in mind, no matter that he even lacked a rifle.

Victoria begged all that morning, and somehow put together a small outfit. She and Skye caught the horses in the village herd. They were good sound animals, and that was a start. And on a venerable pack frame they loaded their few things: some parfleches of jerky and pemmican, a worn blanket apiece, a hatchet and spare knife, Victoria's bow and quiver filled with arrows, and the small jug of spirits that Victoria had not sucked dry while she was imprisoned by the green shirts.

They rode out amid dour stares, silent curses, grim glances, and deep silence. For most of the village he had called his home, and the people he had called his own, somehow connected him with the darkness that had fallen over The Robber's band.

Victoria sat bareback, her skirts hiked, tears forming in her eyes. These people were her own, but wherever her man went, so would she.

Skye rode straight upriver from the stricken village, reached the somber meadow where the traders had milked the people of all they had, and then picked up the trail of the wagons, fresh still in the frosted ground. He didn't know how he was going to do it, but he intended to put Skittles out of business.

40

Skye felt like singing, so he sang.

As I was a-walkin' down Paradise Street,
To me way! Hey! Blow the man down!
A pretty young damsel I chanced for to meet,
Give me some time to blow the man down.

Oh, blow the man down, bullies, blow the man down,
To me way! Hey! Blow the man down,
Oh, blow the man down, bullies, blow him away,
Give me some time to blow the man down . . .

Victoria was cross. "Why are you singing?" she asked.

"What else is there to do?"

"You should be watching for the wagons."

Indeed, the furrows of the wagons ran straight ahead, cutting deeper and deeper in the thawing mud. Skittles might end up mired if this winter day warmed much more. That would suit Skye fine.

"What is that song about?" she asked.

"It's a sea chanty. Paradise Street is in Liverpool."

"Where's that?"

"In the country where I was born."

"We should be crying instead. People dead. My family, everyone, sick."

He lifted his battered top hat and settled it again. There were times so dark that all he could think of was singing, as if melody might kill a little hurt in him. Sometimes it did.

He sang because everything had gone bad and he was worse off than he'd ever been. A man likes to make some progress, but here he was, almost as poor as the moment he jumped ship at Fort Vancouver with little more than the clothing on his back to sustain him.

He thought over the past months: a devastating Blackfoot raid that almost killed Victoria. His good old Hawken stolen. Everything else stolen. His horses stolen. A new colt and mare with strange powers. Distrust in her village and exile. Work for a rotten fur company post to get himself a new outfit, and that got him fired for being fair to the Indians. Then some time spent in the Kicked-in-the-Bellies band of Crows, only to get himself kicked out because of a rabid wolf. Then Skittles's imprisonment of him, loss of his kit again including the replacement rifle, loss of his medicine horses, and distrust once again in The Robber's village. All his fault. It was time to sing!

She hailed me with her flipper, I took her in tow,
To me way! Hey! Blow the man down!
Yardarm to yardarm away we did go
Give me some time to blow the man down.

"What does that mean?" she asked.

"It means the singer's about to be shanghaied."

She sniffed. "Talk about something I know about, dammit."

"Did you bring that jug?"

"Yes."

"We'll drink our dinner tonight."

She grinned.

He got tired of riding bareback. After a couple of hours the spine of the horse sawed his crotch in two. So he stopped, slid down, grabbed the line, and walked. She thought that was a good idea and joined him. They were trailing four horses, all good ponies.

They approached a grassy rise dotted with jack pine, and he handed her the lines and told her to wait. He hiked to the ridge and peered over, studying the country ahead. The prairie was surrendering to rougher country with sandstone outcrops and piney ridges. The ruts of the wagons continued straight, generally northerly. But the warming ground was starting to claw at those iron tires, and Skittles's traders were no doubt slowed, and their big horses would be wearied. It was time to be careful.

Skittles was probably too contemptuous of the Crows he left behind to post a rear guard, but he also was an army man and one could be sure of nothing. So Skye settled into the dry grass, studied the country ahead for a while, spotted nothing but cloud shadows cutting across the aching open country, and finally decided it was safe to proceed.

He didn't know what he would do when he found the traders. He lacked so much as an old rifle. They were well armed with short and long guns, some of them the new fast-loading Sharps. And Skye knew they could use them all to good effect. If he had any success, it would be entirely by stealth.

He thought he heard a distant crack of a rifle, but the wind was tricky, and he heard nothing more. His imagination, then. He studied the empty land one last time, then slid down the rise and joined Victoria.

"Looks all right. They're struggling with mud now. Frost's out of the ground. Maybe they'll hole up before dark to let their plugs rest."

"What the hell is a plug?"

"Horse."

"You white men have ten names for everything. I gotta learn the whole damn business over again."

All that afternoon they pursued Skittles's wagons. Skye was sure from the freshness of the ruts that they were gaining ground, and now he paused at every hill for a long look. But Skittles was driving hard.

They came to a low pass of sorts, with a saddle to the northeast. That's where the ruts parted. Skye studied the place. Two wagons were cutting northeast for the Missouri River. The rest continued northward and would hit the big river somewhere west of the badlands, maybe Fort Benton. The great river wound through impassable canyons for a couple hundred miles. There probably would be a flatboat waiting on the river somewhere to carry those hides and robes to Fort Union.

Skittles was down to two wagons and eight men. But he had two empties and four other men coming his way, and they would rendezvous somewhere and then hit another Indian village. It could be Blackfoot, Gros Ventre, or Assiniboine, but who could say?

Victoria studied the diverging ruts.

"There go the robes," she said. "There go everything they could take from my people. Are you going to follow the robes?"

"No, I'm going to follow the booze."

"Goddamn, Mister Skye, are you sure?"

Skye knew she was seeing those robes and hides as a Crow woman would; hundreds or thousands of hours of patient scraping, softening, tanning, the brutal work of generations of women. He wondered how many hours of miserable bent-over labor was expended for each cup of rotgut hooch the Absaroka people got in return.

It was something he didn't want to think about. There was another reason to go after the kegs. He wanted his outfit back. His rifle, his horses, his packsaddle, his bedroll, his powder and shot. They had it all.

And they had all the odds on their side too. But they could get too cocky in a hurry.

He wondered how Skittles felt right then. The man had made a killing. Did he consider what he had done to the Crow village? That the youths especially might acquire a taste for that booze? That he left the village naked and demoralized? Was he so oblivious to the needs of native people that he didn't know or care? Or was he just another avaricious Yank, making a buck and the hell with scruples?

Skye thought the man did have scruples of a sort, which he heeded when it was convenient to do so. That was the odd thing about Skittles. He was full of ethics.

They followed the wagon ruts into a broad valley hemmed on the north and west by a sandstone ridge. Skittles's bunch were pressing straight down the valley toward what Skye believed were the Snowy Mountains, blue, white-crowned, and distant.

Skye called it quits well before dusk. He didn't want to walk into an ambush. He wanted plenty of light around him for now. A need for the dark would come later, when it would shroud him, cloak them both, conceal their design.

He found a side canyon in the yellow sandstone and went up it, being careful to keep his horses on hard ground. He didn't want hoofprints to tell tales. There were scores of shallow wind-carved caves in the whole region, many of them dandy shelters. He picked one deep in the side gulch, far below the rimrock capping the bluffs. There he could build a good fire that would not be seen, and its heat would radiate off the cave walls, warming them all night.

There would be plenty of grass for the ponies too. He and Victoria picketed them on buffalo grass and gathered wood for the camp. He found plenty of fallen deadwood and built a fire. He had no weapons at all and intended to whittle a belaying pin from a dead limb.

They settled down to a miserable meal of pemmican, but even so, the fat and ground meat and berries in it filled his belly.

"You have that jug?" he asked.

She laughed. This was the jug Skittles's green shirts had handed to her to keep her quiet while she was a hostage. Now she dug it out of the gear on the pack frame.

"Sonofabitch!" she said, pulled off the cork, and sucked.

She gasped, wheezed, howled, growled, and handed the jug to Skye.

He let that awful, treacherous, vicious stuff slide down his gullet. He whooped, groaned, sucked again, and sighed.

But then she plucked up the ceramic jug and hurled it into the darkness. It shattered.

"The whole damn world is broken," she said, and began to weep.

41

Her tears fell into the hollow of his shoulder. Skye pulled her tight with his big hands until she was wrapped into his side. He could not comfort her. She wept softly, sometimes muttering in her Absaroka tongue, her English abandoned now.

But he could follow her every thought. It wasn't just that her world had shattered when the green-shirt traders had debauched her village; it was much more. Her life had changed with the wound in her side. It had shattered when he had left her to put a new outfit together. In all that time they had struggled on alone and apart.

"You have not touched me," she said. "You don't want me."

How could he tell her he had feared to touch her? That the terrible wound in her side might yet torment her? That he had been waiting, almost forever, for some hint that she wanted him? Some little flash of light in her eyes?

"I am ugly now," she said.

He slid his hand to the place where he had pressed a red-hot knife into her almost fatal wound to cauterize it, a place of corduroyed and corded scar tissue under her ribs.

"You are beautiful," he said. "This wound is where life

is, not death. Without this wound you wouldn't be here in my arms."

"Oh, Skye."

She wept, her hot tears soaking through his buckskin shirt. She was weeping not only for her village, which she saw in its shame and ruin, but also for herself. She had suffered a loneliness just as terrible as his own.

"I love you more than ever, Victoria." It seemed a lame thing to say to her.

"But you haven't had me."

It had been a long time. Some eternity ago, when she was slowly mending, he had left her in her brother's care, headed out to get a new rifle and outfit, and now, months later, he was with her and still had not touched her and it was tearing her to pieces.

He caressed her softly, and felt her torn spirit quiet within her. He had not let her know how he ached for her. He had been away too long. He kissed her. Her hands found his well-shaved cheek and jaw, and he felt the joy in them as she caressed him.

She nestled herself into him, and he held her until the fire dimmed and the cold began to creep into this perfect hideaway, wind-hollowed and peaceful. Then, softly, he rose, built up the flame so the warmth would again echo off the sandstone, and returned to the old robe and blanket they shared. Now his hand found her and slid over her and possessed her, and her arms found him, and her lips and her heart too.

They made love softly, awakening ancient memories. He kissed the scar on her torso. It was his way of saying something to her, that he loved her whole, all of her, and she was as beautiful to him as ever.

Her hands found his back and drew him tight and Skye and Victoria renewed the bond that had brought them together long ago. And so they passed the night. From time to time he rose, built up the fire, and then they came together again, scarcely noticing when the flames played out and only embers lit their night.

At last he pulled the old blanket over them, but they didn't sleep. She wept again, her tears watering his bare shoulder. He knew she was thinking of other things now. Something had happened to her people. The proud Crows, able to hold their own against the more numerous and more dangerous Sioux and Blackfeet, had been ruined by a poison brought by the white men. And now she wept.

She had long experience of it. At the trappers' rendezvous she and Skye had bought the spirits and sucked their jug dry. But after those rendezvous everything returned to the way it was and the party was over. It was a weakness in both of them. He knew how hard it was for him to resist a good howl with a bottle, and sometimes that's what he wanted more than anything else.

But she was right. This thing done by Skittles was different. The booze was meaner and was used systematically to ruin her people. There was nothing in their entire history to help them deal with this; it was a new menace for which they had no defense, not even a legend, a story with a moral to it. In the world of white men there were hundreds of mocking stories about drunks, a thousand jokes, a folk wisdom about spirits, and these were an inheritance he had that she didn't. None of her people had heard stories or jokes like that, or listened to the wisdom of their parents or their priests. The Crows were naked before this new thing, but so were all the Indians. Would Blackfeet or Sioux fare any better?

They kept to themselves and hugged through the chill, but then she rose until she was sitting, looked at him in the ember light, and said, "Thank you."

Oddly, he knew what she was thanking him for. It wasn't the union they had shared. So close had they been for so long that he fathomed her thoughts, even as she fathomed his. Her thanks were not for the love they had renewed that soft night, but for his resolve. He would destroy the destroyers of her people. Somehow, powerless as he was without a weapon, he would stop these traders in their tracks.

"There will be a way," he said.

And that was all they had to lift them; a sense that there would be a way. They fell asleep at last in the small hours, when the chill descended on them, and their thin old robes were not enough to keep the cold at bay. But the warmth of their bodies was enough, and so the night passed into faint dawn, and the embers had died away with the dimming of the stars.

They dressed quietly, aware that their lives had changed; that they were mates, that they had a great task before them, one that might kill them both. In a way, they grew aware of the danger they faced and resolved to face it.

There was nothing but more pemmican, cold and cruel on the tongue, and they gnawed at the fatty stuff, knowing it sufficed to sustain life.

The ponies had passed the night grazing. Skye collected them and eased the packsaddle over one. They would need watering soon. Then he lifted Victoria onto one of the ponies and he pulled himself over the other. Riding bareback was never easy. Getting aboard a horse without a saddle was hard and he had never mastered it. But soon they descended the side canyon and picked up the clear trail of Skittles's outfit. The ground stayed frozen and Skittles would be making fine time this morning, but the ground would soften that afternoon and then things would be different. The trail had turned mostly west across rolling land, south of the Snowy Mountains.

So Skittles was heading for the Judith country, the very area where Blackfeet had made off with Crow horses and wounded Victoria. Skye eyed his wife, who was riding with steely determination. She was well aware that they were retracing the route from the buffalo hunting camp to her village many months earlier.

There was no sign of the traders but that didn't mean much. They were ahead. What worried Skye was that they had at least one brass spyglass in the outfit, and an ex-army outfit like that would be using it, studying the country from every rise. The chances were that Skittles already knew someone was following him. That would make it tougher, and also raise the prospect of an ambush. There was little Skye could do about it.

Still, stalking an armed body required more than a tracker's skill. Skye wanted to know where Skittles was going. Once he knew that, he could quit following and circle around. Skittles was heading for a village of the Piegans or Gros Ventres, and probably would take those robes and pelts to Fort Benton, the American Fur post on the Missouri.

But all that was guesswork.

They rode across a vast land, with the noble Snowy Mountains, white-topped, guarding the north. Then, late that day, Victoria pointed.

Skye did not see what she was pointing at, but it was something far west.

"Flash of light," she said.

Light? Sun off brass? "Where?" he asked.

She pointed, but he saw nothing. A chance flash had caught her eye. But it was enough to make Skye wary.

"They're heading for the Piegans," he said.

"Maybe we should let them."

Let this southernmost nation of the Blackfeet suffer the fate her Crow band had suffered. Let them drink themselves into a frenzy, kill one another, disgorge all their robes and pelts for another round of spirits, and end up sick, ashamed, broken, and impoverished.

There was something flinty in her face.

"Each time Skittles succeeds, he'll gain strength. He'll come back time after time and destroy your people."

She nodded.

They would continue, demolish Skittles's wagonload of

spirits if they could. Only then would the northern tribes, all of them, be safe from him.

But he was certain Skittles knew someone was behind him. Several times more that day they saw, or at least thought they saw, observers on ridges or peaks. One thing for sure, Skittles was not far ahead. Three, four, five miles. As the day warmed, so had the soil softened, and his big draft horses would have a tough time dragging wagons through the mire.

It would pay to be very careful. In fact, Skye thought he would wait for dark and then work north a few miles, and find shelter in one of the giant coulees issuing from the Snowy Mountains. There would be no safety now; no night of bliss, like the last one.

42

Victoria was yelling at him, but the wind whipped her words away. He slowed the pony, and she caught up with him.

"Stop," she said.

He did. The packhorse behind him bumped into the rear of his pony.

She pointed at a distant ridge to the west. He saw nothing.

"Riders," she said.

He still saw nothing, but employed his old way of scanning one sector of the horizon at a time, piece by piece, until he might see what she saw. Her eyes were often better than his.

Then, he made out two moving dots, slightly blurred. He watched them closely.

"Coming our way?" he asked her.

"Damn right."

"Two. Probably sent by Skittles to see what's on his back trail."

They waited quietly until they could get a clearer picture, and then a trick of light showed the distant riders clearly. Green shirts. Rifles.

Skye examined the nearby terrain. They had been crossing giant coulees and ridges that stretched like claws from the Snowy Mountains. But the country was naked. It was a bad place to be caught unarmed and defenseless by armed riders.

This was a day of sunlight and shadow, of fast-moving clouds driven by high winds, whose dark shadows plowed coldly across the endless open land. It was a day full of tricks of sunlight that made things appear to be moving, when only shadow and wind were galloping along the earth.

They were atop a ridge. Skye retreated from the riders, and descended a shallow grade into a broad, grass-bottomed coulee that had its origins many miles away, and would carry water in the spring. He turned north, sticking just a little off the bottoms even though the going was slower. The passage of four horses through the dried grasses of the bottoms would give them away.

He desperately needed some little side gulch or a gentle turn in the coulee to hide himself, Victoria, and the ponies. To preserve their lives, he thought. He kicked the pony into a slow trot, the fastest he could travel over a rough and eroded slope. At least they were below the ridge, and maybe had not been seen. That was optimistic, given the spyglasses that outfit owned.

For a time he found no place to hide, but then the coulee's west wall retreated slightly, and he found himself riding around a slight bend, and in a moment he and Victoria were riding into a small, shallow side gulch, not much deeper than a mounted rider. He slid off his mount, and she did too. They pulled the horses farther up, past chokecherry brush that would help hide them, and into a shallow hollow that ran only six or eight feet below the surrounding rolling prairie.

Victoria held two horses, ready to slap her hand over their nostrils if they were about to whicker. Horses, famously gregarious, loved to greet other horses. Skye handed her hackamore loops of the two other ponies, removed his plug hat, and edged upward until he could see.

At first he saw nothing, but then he found them, not half a mile off, drifting up the coulee.

"We may have to run," he told her.

It was an impossible situation. They without a firearm, the riders with rifles. Victoria had her bow and quiver but that would offer no help at all, not here.

More cloud shadows rolled across that vast country. One could watch them come and watch them slide by, mile after mile. The riders were identifiably green shirts and in no hurry. But they were out in the middle of the coulee, not on its western edge, and missing the plain trail. They approached another quarter of a mile, quit, and rode south. Skye watched them shrink back to black dots and then vanish.

It had been close.

He turned and found her just behind him, an arrow nocked in her bow.

"They quit," he said. "But there may be more. Skittles knows someone's behind him."

He retreated into the gulch. A pony yawned, baring yellowed teeth. A heavy cloud rolled over, spitting pea snow from its belly, and then it passed. Skye found himself taut and sweaty, even in that chill.

He was a damn fool, going after Skittles this way. He knew it. What did he think he'd accomplish except to get himself and Victoria shot in some lonely gulch and left for the ravens.

"Don't cuss yourself," she said, reading him.

"I've been stupid."

"What is stupid? I don't know this word."

"Dumb. Crazy."

She walked up to him, touched his cheek, running her fingers gently along his jaw, and said nothing.

He didn't want to move, not yet. Not with two snipers drifting nearby. It was cold in that little gulch. He turned his back to the blustering wind.

"Sometimes we are given to do things," she said. "We must do them. We must try to do them even if the end is bad. Sometimes it leads to bad things. Sometimes we are given to do something and we die. Or fail. I think this is given to you to do. If it is given to you, then we will do it."

He clamped his hat down when a gust threatened to whip it away. The wind was rising, and he sensed warmth in it, warmth that would slow down Skittles's wagons when the frost went out and the iron tires of his wagons cut deep furrows.

"We'll get in front of them," he said. "We'll find a place to camp and wait for the warmth to mire them."

"It is coming," she said. "It's in the air."

Skittles would be slowed, and Skye would get around to the front where maybe with some stealth he could slip into the camp and do what needed doing.

They worked patiently up the coulee to the timber and snow, and then cut along the foothills of the mountains until twilight veiled them and they could carve a camp out of a rocky grotto after brushing the snow away.

About midnight the warm winds eddied in, woke them both, and Skye didn't hesitate. By the light of a tiny fire they collected their gear, loaded the packsaddle, clambered aboard their ponies, and set off across tumbled country, with nothing to guide them except the looming presence of high country on their right.

The temperature shot upward so fast that suddenly the air was delicious, the breezes almost tropical. Within the passage of an hour Skye felt his pony pulling mud with every step. The ponies labored but kept on. He heard dripping water. He listened to the thud of snow sliding off of pines just above.

"Sonofabitch! It's getting hotter than you in the robes, Skye," she said.

He laughed.

If Skittles had any sense, he wouldn't travel much during the coming day. And if the thaw lasted, Skittles might be rooted to the spot for many days.

Dawn caught them several miles west and in rough country, but now it was their turn to study the surrounding land. The first sunlight poking out of the southeast, horizontal orange light, caught something at once: a column of gray smoke a mile or so away and down the long swales to country where wagons could move.

Skye exulted. He knew where they were. For a while, anyway, they could ride in sun-shadow, invisible to anyone down there. As they came abreast of the camp, he could see but two wagons, and a few men. One wagon held the spirits; the other held the gear. He itched to ride down, throw a lit torch into that wagon full of casks, catch them shaving and squatting and rolling up their bedrolls, and howl his way out.

"I just thought of a good way to kill myself," Skye said.

She smiled.

He took some more long looks, and hurried by, wanting to get ahead before that horizontal light caught them and turned them into bull's-eyes. They were protected by a long ridge clawing the prairies to the south, but even as they worked west, the rising sun narrowed the shadow they were racing through, and in minutes they would be exposed to its bright and deadly glare.

"We've got to drop," he said.

She nodded.

He turned the pony downslope, ever closer to Skittles's camp, down into timber that was even more dangerous than open country because he could not see ahead. But at least they were still shrouded by dawn shade.

They burst out of timber not half a mile from Skittles's camp and could see it and its men clearly. But Skye and Victoria hurried west, racing past the camp, hoping his ponies wouldn't betray him, and hoping that their big, stolid draft animals wouldn't stir.

He could see the horses in a rope pen.

Jawbone squealed. Skye knew that sound as well as he knew his own voice. They hurried west, needing the safety of the next woods or ridge or whatever might shield them from those prying spyglasses.

Jawbone whirled around and around in the rope enclosure, and then bolted straight through the rope. The old mare, suddenly as wild as the colt, bolted with her colt. They raced straight toward Skye and Victoria, who froze in the deep shadow.

Skye heard a shot and another, and then the faint sound of laughter and annoyance. Jawbone and the blessed old mare kept going, and no one was coming after them.

43

J awbone kicked up his heels, bounced and leaped, and danced his way up the long grade, and then quit the sun and plunged into deep shade, the very shade that hid Skye and Victoria and their ponies.

Skye dreaded what would come next. Jawbone and the resolute old mare were racing full tilt toward them and would give them away. He was in more than enough peril from the rising sun, which in minutes would bathe the slope he stood on, leaving him exposed to every eye below.

And now this boneheaded colt was frisking and kicking and squealing his way up the long grade while men watched.

But a sharp command below set the green shirts to work. They had draft horses and their own saddlers to round up. For a moment Skye stood, paralyzed, and then began looking for cover. There wasn't much, copses of naked-limbed trees, a few swales. He would edge toward those.

Jawbone danced and pranced his way uphill, ever higher, ever closer, until he was only a few yards away, squealing his greetings.

"Avast!" Skye bellowed.

The colt bucked, kicked, whirled, and plunged right past them, with the laboring old mare behind. Right past Skye, right past Victoria, right past the ponies, and bucked and kicked his way upslope until suddenly he was caught in the morning's glare again, a bronzed horse bounding along a ridge.

Then the colt headed straight for the pine forest above, and plunged into it, bucking through the heavy snow at its base, while the razor-backed old mare followed. The sun caught them pushing into the forested flank of the mountain, and then they vanished.

It was beyond explaining. Skye stood, shaking, aware that if that colt had paused, had rushed up to Skye and butted him, started his ponies milling, it would all be over. Down below men were collecting the straying stock, but also glancing up the long grade straight at Skye and Victoria, who could not remain hidden in shade for long as the sun began its swift ascent.

Skye collected his animals and walked along the path he had chosen, desperate to find cover. But far above a strange squeal echoed down the mountain, and Skye found himself staring at the tiny figure of the colt, bathed in bright sun, on a small promontory overlooking the vast country below.

Down in Skittles's camp men paused, pointed upward, and then resumed their business. They had stock to harness.

Skye shivered. What possessed that colt? What strange medicine, or luck, sent the little fellow straight up the mountain, far from Skye and Victoria? Were they free and saying good-bye?

They hurried to a place where a slope hid them in trees and soon they were out of sight of the camp. But not safe. They were leaving a plain trail that anyone, even a Yank soldier, could follow. Skye hurried westward, for distance was the sole protection he had.

Victoria followed, her gaze slipping upward, searching the empty mountain above, even as the shadows dropped lower and lower and eventually vanished. They were walking in full daylight now, the dawn was a thing of the past.

Victoria paused at a ridge and studied their back trail, but no one followed. Skittles had probably abandoned the ugly colt and scrawny mare. Good riddance.

That suited Skye just fine. Good riddance indeed. Even if he never saw that colt again, his spirits lifted at the thought that the mustangs had found their liberty. Let that feisty creature and that faithful mare escape snares the rest of their days. They had blessed Skye, saved Victoria from death, and deserved whatever goodness nature had in store.

He began at last to relax. He was where he wanted to be, ahead of the Skittles party, riding the flank of the Snowy Mountains. Ahead was the gap, the broad flat between two ranges that permitted travelers to move north or south through country where the mountains ranged east and west Skittles would enter that gap sometime soon, depending on whether the ground would stay firm under the iron tires of his wagons.

Skye reached a ridge where he could see the gap, which spread below him, naked rolling prairie between the ranges. This was bloody ground. Here, Blackfeet pounced on unsuspecting Absarokas heading north, or Crows ambushed Blackfeet pushing south. Nature had conspired to funnel all manner of life through this hole in the wall of mountains, and war parties took advantage of it.

Victoria squinted at the place.

"Bastards," she said.

Skye grinned.

They descended to prairie country along the flank of the Snowies, and turned north. Skye was looking for the right place to pounce on Skittles, but right places were in short supply. He didn't know where Skittles would go. For that matter, Skye didn't know just how he was going to jump Skittles's company. But it would have to be in the dead of a moonless or cloudy night, when a man could hardly see ten feet. He was going to have to slip through Skittles's defenses and torch that whiskey wagon. And collect his kit if he could. And do it without so much as a revolver to help him. And get Victoria, himself, and his horses away to safety.

He had one advantage. He had been here many times over his long life as a trapper and denizen of the wilds. He doubted that Skittles knew the country.

The more Skye thought about it, the worse his prospects looked to him. The best he could do would be to shadow the trading outfit and wait. Somewhere along the way there would be a chink in Skittles's armor, and it would be up to Skye to find it and exploit it.

No wonder Skittles had recruited former soldiers. Somehow these traders understood that they might need to be a small army. Might have trouble with boozy Indians. Might have trouble with tribal leaders. Might have trouble with rival companies, of which there were several roaming the Northwest hunting for robes.

Skye wondered how he could shadow an outfit like that, especially with his pemmican running low, two more horses than he should have, and a lot of open prairie ahead where a man could see everything for miles, and a man with a spyglass could keep track of movement everywhere the lens could reach.

Nighttime, then.

He paused at an overlook and waited for her.

"I want to catch them here. Once they get through the gap, they could head any direction."

"This is a bad place."

"It will be for them."

"We need a camping place on the flank of the mountain," he added.

She nodded. They moved slowly upslope, studying the land, and finally selected a rocky ledge a couple hundred feet above the valley floor. It would do nicely, and was watered by a runnel from above. They picketed the horses on good grass nearby, made camp, and settled down for a wait. It had turned warm, and Skye didn't doubt that the wagons would roll slowly, if at all this day with the mud so thick.

He settled back to wait, letting the intense sun warm him. He had never seen such a clear day. The air was so transparent it drew everything close. The Belt Mountains, on the other side of the gap, seemed so near he could touch them, though they were six or seven miles distant.

Victoria joined him, sitting cross-legged with her skirts hiked, as she often did. He was glad she was there. The horses grazed contentedly on the slope behind them. The air was warm, and he felt good.

He remembered how, only a few weeks earlier, he had wandered through a winter's fog, not knowing where he was going, and thought that was how his life was playing out. But the important thing was that he kept on going through the fog, through the air filled with ice crystals.

She touched his arm and pointed. Across the southern heaven were sun dogs, bright miniature suns at the exact altitude of the real one, shimmering and sometimes shifting color, a phenomenon he had never before seen.

"It is a sign," she said.

"I know where I am going now," he said.

"I wondered if you ever would."

"When I lived for myself I walked through fog. When I give myself away, I can see to the farthest horizon."

"Damn, you better tell me that in my tongue," she said.

"Your people are my home," he said.

His response was enough for her. She caught his big hand and held it.

They waited through the warm, bright day, but Skittles and his wagons never came.

44

Skye and Victoria sat on their cliffside rock and watched and waited until the sun plunged toward the western rim of the world. Skittles's party should have rounded the flank of the mountains and headed through the gap. Skye didn't know what to make of it.

"We go look," Victoria said.

"Leave the horses," Skye said.

Stiffly, they began back-trailing along the rough foothills, pausing at every promontory or spot that afforded a view. Then she pointed at a distant collection of moving dots. They hiked another half mile eastward until they could get a better look from a ridgetop.

Disaster had struck Skittles's party. They had started their wagons across a shallow coulee, little knowing that the earth beneath its grassy surface was water-charged gumbo the consistency of jelly. The whiskey wagon had gone first and was mired up to its bed, its wheels mostly lost to view. Worse, the noble draft horses hauling that heavy load had mired, fought their fate, and now were bloodstained bodies lying in the muck. They had obviously been shot when it became plain to the green shirts that those big, gentle, hard-working beasts were doomed.

The supply wagon, behind it, was mired too, and its giant draft horses also lay dead. No legs were visible from any horse. They had sunk to their bellies, struggled against their fate, and were put out of their misery.

Skye thought that he had heard no shots, but that was not surprising, given the brisk wind and the distances.

"Dammit," Victoria said. "If we were down there we would have been caught too."

Skye nodded.

Off as far as his eye could see even on that bright day, he could make out the green shirts salvaging what they could. They had pulled the walls off the supply wagon, along with its tailgate, and made a sort of ramp back to safe land on the east side of the grass-topped river of mud. They had salvaged the whiskey barrels, which stood like stumps on safe ground. They had rescued a pile of gear, perhaps including Skye's rifle and his bedroll and packsaddle.

The outfit's saddle horses were safe, picketed on the east side. Skittles would probably build packsaddles and load as much whiskey as he could, leaving his men to carry their own kits. But there weren't enough saddle horses for all that whiskey. He would have to cache most of it.

Unless Skye could destroy it.

"Sonsofbitches got what was coming," she said.

"They're not licked yet. They'll clean the mud out of their revolvers this night. Tomorrow they hunt for more horses. Skittles will send men to look for Jawbone and the mare."

They needed to know what Skittles would do. They sat quietly, watching the rescue efforts. In time, a horseman started off, heading southeast.

"Skittles has two parties out somewhere. One's delivering the robes he got from your village, and the other party's returning empty or maybe with some supplies from a trading post. That means he still has four wagons and four teams. He just has to wait."

As if to confirm Skye's judgment, the green shirts threw packsaddles over the remaining two saddle horses and began shuttling the whiskey kegs toward a copse of cottonwood trees perhaps a quarter of a mile from the disastrous crossing. There would be firewood and shelter there. The men would tote their gear to the cottonwood grove and move the whiskey and wait for help to arrive.

"See that horseman? Skittles is sending for help. He's got wagons coming and going. Looks like that rider is headed for Fort Sarpy."

"He's headed for hell, that's where," she muttered.

"Well, they're stuck in that grove. They might be there for weeks," he said. "They can't do much until they get some wagons and teams."

"And every day they stay in that place, they get stronger," she said. "They wash away the mud, clean their guns, start hunting for meat, and maybe get that whiskey hidden somewhere."

The men were frantically dragging everything to the cottonwood grove. They were obviously tired, yet seemed impelled by something menacing. In the grove, two tents rose. Skye could not fathom what was happening; it was all too far away, but the distant green shirts were obviously in a hurry.

A darkness was descending too early. Skye whirled, discovered behind him a massive gray overcast rolling out of the northwest from behind the Snowy Mountains, galloping across the heavens.

"Trouble," he said. "I should have read the sun dogs. They were telling me something but I wasn't listening."

Victoria's single glance took in the weather. They needed to get their horses and find shelter, and there wasn't much of that. Swiftly overtaking this country was a massive spring storm, the type that could dump feet of snow on the high plains. They abandoned the overlook and hurried back to the rocky ledge to the west, found their horses nervously tugging on their pickets, released them, and headed downhill. They needed to get to woods and find shelter from the wind. They needed firewood and a place to keep a fire going. But there was nothing, only the anonymous rolling foothills on the south flank of the Snowies.

No wonder the green shirts were throwing up tents and heading for the cottonwoods. A cold wind plucked the warmth out of the air, and eddied through the slopes and hollows, brooming away a day's work by the sun. Not bitter yet; that would come later, maybe after snow.

The land descended for miles and Skye had only to find a coulee and it would eventually deposit him in the valley of the Musselshell River where there would be shelter. But that was a ten-mile hike through the night.

They simply could find no place to go to ground.

The massive dark reef of cloud was wiping away light, turning a lively day into an iron-gray twilight. When dark finally fell, it would be pitch-dark, not even starlight, and they would be stumbling through inky night.

They had reached the gumbo-bottomed coulee but on the opposite side from the traders.

He surprised himself: "Let's get into that camp when this storm hits and burn the booze."

She stopped suddenly, laughed, and the gusts whipped her laughter away.

They turned into the wind, into the iron twilight, until they had gained ground and reached the foothills. Then they turned east, cut past the head of that evil coulee, and started their descent on the same side as Skittles's men.

Skye began laughing. They were in peril from a cruel storm, but laughter bloomed through him and she joined him. They laughed as the wind at their backs bullied them south toward the traders' camp. They laughed when the wind plucked Skye's old top hat and sent it sailing. He roared, recovered it, and anchored it to the pack frame perched on one of their ponies.

"Maybe we can save out a jug, Mister Skye?"

"Maybe we can!"

Behind them rose a great commotion. Skye turned to find two equine specters galloping down on them.

"Ah! You've found us at last!" he bellowed.

Jawbone jammed to a halt, butted Skye in the belly, disturbed the ponies, and began pushing Skye backward, while the mare stopped just short of Victoria and bobbed her head up and down in wild greeting.

"Oh, ho! You've come to join the fiesta!" Skye said.

The first blast of icy pellets smacked into them. Not snow, just slivers of frozen moisture that stung their faces. Skye ached for his capote, but the green shirts had it. Maybe he could get it back. Maybe he could get his bedroll, his rifle, his kit, his packsaddle back. Maybe he could grab something for back wages. Maybe he could find a shelter-half or some canvas to crawl under until this storm blew past.

But maybe that was all wishful thinking. The only reality was the blackening heaven, the sting of ice in the air, a wind that probed through his shirt and numbed him, and a skiff of snow on the ground that could swiftly heap up into impassible drifts.

They almost ran into the traders' camp. Off ahead they caught a glimpse of things that didn't fit in nature. They halted. Jawbone had the good sense not to squeal. Skye strained to see, and finally made out a mesh of black limbs. They were on the west edge of those trees. Nearby were heaps on the ground. Off somewhere just beyond the wall of night were the two tents.

Mister Skittles, Mister Grosvenor, and the other misters were huddled within. There would be no fire on a night like this unless they had found some protected hollow out of the claws of snowy air. But there was no sign of light. The gents were rolled up in their bedrolls, safe under canvas, and glad to be halfway warm.

Skye began howling. Victoria joined him. They laughed and the wind whipped their every sound away. He lumbered from one heap to another. The whiskey casks were collected in one place. The company's supplies were stored under a canvas tarpaulin. Somewhere in the woods were the company's saddle horses. And the seven remaining men were locked into their tents.

Snow was beginning to build around every barrier, along the sides of the tents, around the casks, around the supplies anchored under the tarpaulin.

It was time to get to work.

45

Nature helps and nature hinders. Anyone living in the wilds knows that. Skye worked frantically to strap his own packsaddle on his pony before the light failed entirely, while Victoria probed under the tarpaulin to see what was there. By the time he finished buckling the packsaddle, he could no longer see anything. He worried about losing Victoria.

The wind helped. It rattled the cottonwood branches, whispered and yowled across the earth, and flapped the canvas of the traders' tents. There was no silence to expose Skye's activities.

"I found the rifle," she said. "Lotsa stuff."

"You'll have to load in the dark."

"I can do it. I got a bedroll too, maybe yours."

"Good. It has my powder horn and a hatchet in it."

She began loading now, working in full blackness because all light had fled the world. Snow stung Skye's face.

Skye tried to remember where the casks stood. He hardly dared venture that way. He could move twenty feet from Victoria and lose her entirely.

The barrels were a few yards out from the supplies, about where they had been rescued from the gumbo.

"Talk quietly, Victoria. Just talk," he said.

She took him up on it, cussing steadily, trapper cussing, the oaths rolling out of her like a waterfall. He laughed softly.

He stumbled and fell upon the casks, felt them with his big hands, brushed snow away, and tried lifting one. Oaken staves, iron hoops. It was all he could manage, maybe seventy or eighty pounds. He lifted all he could find, hoping to find a light one. After lifting five, he did lift a light one and he rejoiced. Now he began probing and patting it, and found a bung faucet in it. More good luck.

Victoria was cheerfully cussing away, the oaths peppering the air. He carried the light cask over to her.

"This one's been opened. We'll use it to burn the rest. Unless you can find an axe."

"Dammit, Skye, how am I supposed to find anything?"

"Is there an old blanket I can soak?"

"How am I supposed to know, eh?"

They were fighting nature now. He hardly knew what to do. He didn't even know whether he could start a fire in all this wet wind. He wanted an axe. Maybe a swift blow to each cask would open it. He thought that maybe he could start a fire if he could strike some sparks into a rag soaked with pure spirits. But a fire would bring them all boiling out of their tents, and they would shoot at anything that moved.

This was proving harder than he had wanted. And now he was getting numb. His hands would quit him pretty soon.

He felt his way to the packhorses and found that Victoria had anchored his Hawken on one. He could tell it by its feel. He found his bedroll, opened it, and pulled out his powder horn. He found his capote in his saddle kit, and gratefully put it on, feeling its welcome warmth at once. He had everything: his rifle, his kit, his horses.

There was only one task left, but it was the reason he came, the reason he was here on a black night in a storm. The only thing was, he didn't know how to destroy those casks.

A light bloomed behind him. He whirled, and found

vague yellow light emanating from one of the tents while shadows bobbed on its canvas walls. Someone in there had lit a lamp. He saw Victoria, who was holding the reins of two horses, whirl them around so their eyes would not pick up lamplight. And just in time too. A figure parted canvas and emerged into the night, bearing the lantern in one hand and a revolver in the other. Skye was sure he and Victoria had made too much noise, or disturbed the rhythms of nature too much. A veil of snow, blowing horizontally, obscured the man. Skye knew that the trader was seeing little but the white wall of snow. The man stood before the tent, uncertainly, and then jammed the revolver into its holster and relieved himself.

Skye took the opportunity to orient himself in the lamplight. The casks stood in a cluster, mostly snow-covered now. The supplies remained under the tarp, which was a salvaged wagon sheet. Skye wanted that tarp; it would give them shelter. It wasn't particularly cold, but it would be plenty cold when this storm blew over. A wagon sheet was twice the canvas he wanted, and three times heavier than he wanted. Maybe he could slice it in two.

The trader finished. From the dark tent, two others emerged and relieved themselves. They were talking but Skye could not make out any of it. Then they retreated to their respective tents, and Skye had one last chance to study the layout before they blew out the lantern. He and Victoria were plunged into utter darkness once again.

"You there?" he asked softly.

"Damn right."

"I don't know how to burn this booze."

"I don't either. It's snowing too hard."

"I don't think I can bust these barrels with a hatchet."

"Shoot them, Skye?"

"In the dark?"

"One, maybe?"

"Shoot one and hope it leaks enough spirits to burn the rest?"

"We ain't gonna hang around and let them shoot us, are we?"

"They won't see; they'll be blinded."

He found Victoria holding the ponies. Somewhere out in the dark Jawbone and the old mare were standing.

"The only thing I can think of is to start a fire beside a barrel, get away, and then shoot one barrel and hope for the best."

"So what's gonna happen."

"They'll see fire, come busting out of their tents, maybe shoot into the dark, try to put out the fire. I shoot a barrel. More spirits out, more fire."

"Damned waste of good booze, Skye."

He could feel the snow caking on his capote. It would be caking his horses, caking Victoria's robe. It was a wet warm snow, plastering whatever it touched, including those barrels. That was good, white on white.

He fumbled his way to the casks, began lifting and rocking them to find the light one, and located it. He lifted it easily and was immediately worried. Was there anything in it? He found the brass bung faucet, turned the cock, held his hand under the spout, and felt nothing. Empty.

There went his only plan. Worse, he had been counting on some firelight for a getaway. He knew he was next to a cottonwood grove, and next to a coulee that could mire him. He needed light enough to get away, get out of rifle range, escape those deadly Sharps.

"Nothing in here," he said.

"Sonofabitch!"

"We're in trouble."

He felt her draw close, something intuitive because he could see nothing. They could not even see the white canvas tents a short distance from them.

"We got to wait for the first light and hope we can escape," she said.

He felt the warmth of the horses she was leading, or was it their moist breath? Who could know?

"We got that wagon canvas to keep us warm," she said.

That was a good idea. He didn't know where the heap of supplies was, but she seemed to, and eventually she stumbled, cussed softly, and drew him toward her. They clambered under the canvas. She held the lines of their horses and hoped the others would linger close. In truth, he had no idea what direction he was facing. He couldn't remember a night so black, or being so lost.

The wagon sheet served well to shield them from the pelting snow, though he insisted on keeping his head in the open, relying on the hood of his capote for warmth. If the traders lit a lamp again, he wanted to know it.

It would be a long, long wait. It wasn't far past dusk. And first light wouldn't come until six-thirty or seven. And then they'd run the risk of being seen, and they would leave a plain trail in the snow. Well, that was war, won or lost by weather, or an unshod hoof, or bad luck.

"Victoria . . ." he started to say, but couldn't continue. He just wanted to tell her it had been a good life and she had made it so.

She found his hand and squeezed it.

The minutes dragged. An hour passed by his reckoning, but maybe it was only five minutes. The snow diminished. He couldn't see it but he felt it. The men in the tents had buried themselves in their blankets and Skye heard no talk from that quarter, nor did he see any lamplight.

He was growing stiff, but at least under that sheet he was dry and not cold.

"Sonofabitch, look," she said.

She turned his face with her hand. There was a slit in the sky. Off to the north eerie moonlight shone on the white peaks of the Snowy Mountains.

46

Everything changed. That crack in the sky across the north was his compass, his lantern, his escape. He knew where he was. He could see his way out. The snow glowed eerily.

Such was fate, where the fortunes of war hung on chance.

"Get the horses together. I'll cut my way through a barrel with my knife."

"Wait," she said, touching his arm.

She crawled out of their canvas shelter, hastened to one of the packhorses that stood dimly visible as a silhouette, and returned with something. She stooped, flexed something, and he realized she had gotten her bow and quiver.

Maybe it would work. Her reflex bow, made of yew wood wrapped in sinew, was as strong as she could draw. Her arrows, with iron points, were carefully crafted by Crow artisans and had grooves in the shafts to draw away the blood of animals she pierced, thus killing them faster.

He followed her to the stockpile of whiskey, praying that they would not be silhouetted by that crack of ghostly light to the north.

She cut around to the side, making sure no arrow, if it careened off a barrel, would pierce the tents. The moonlight from the distant mountains quickened just enough so they could see the barrels, snow-clad on their tops, dark bulks gathered together.

She nocked an arrow, drew and aimed easily, and loosed it into a cask. It hit with a thump, and Skye turned sharply to see whether it had stirred anything in the tents.

She slipped close to the barrel to see the effect. There wasn't enough light to know, but when she slid her hand around the arrow she raised her arm high, to touch sky.

She beckoned, and drew his hand to the arrow, which projected from the cask. Wetness. The grooves were drawing the spirits out.

She danced a little jig in the snow. Then he beckoned her close, so he could whisper.

"We'll get the horses ready first. At the edge of the woods. They'll come out shooting."

She nodded.

They led their horses around the cottonwood grove, just out of sight of the tents. Jawbone and the mare followed. The colt butted Skye, who butted back.

The crack of moonlight to the north widened. The snow-clad peaks of the Snowy Mountains shot white light under the massive storm cloud. Light glistened off the thin snow covering the land.

"How we gonna light it?" she asked.

"Flaming arrow?"

"I can do it."

They hastened back to the casks. Victoria nocked arrows, sped them into the oaken staves. They checked each one, running their hands around the buried shaft, finding wetness as the spirits slowly drained to the snowy earth.

The moonlight brightened. Skye kept a sharp eye on those tents. Snow was now the enemy, bouncing pale light everywhere, wiping away the cloak of blackness. It was only a matter of time, maybe only minutes or seconds, before one of Skittles's men crawled out of a tent.

Still, their luck held. There were seven casks, and Victoria punctured each one. These were slow leaks, and not much of the grain spirits was puddling on the ground, and that worried him. He tried pulling an arrow, but its iron head locked it in. He would just have to trust.

Skye cut a strip of wool from the bottom of his blanket capote, and cut some fringes from his buckskin shirt, and Victoria wrapped the wool around an arrow and tied it tight with the fringe leather. Then they prepared a second arrow, and soaked both in the spirits.

Victoria slid her bow over her shoulder, lifted her hands to the black sky, and supplicated the Other Ones, singing softly. It was a pleading, a soft song of empowerment. Jawbone arrived, sniffed the barrels, and tried to butt her.

Skye grabbed his mane and yanked him away.

They retreated twenty yards in the direction of their horses. Once that flame bloomed, they would be easy targets. It was a risk they had to take.

Skye checked one last time to see whether the barrels were still leaking spirits. They were. Their staves were wet. But he could find no pooling on the soft ground.

No matter. It was now or never.

He retreated to where Victoria stood, her bow ready.

She held the fire arrow.

He slid the curved steel into his hand, and held the flint in his other, and struck, his practiced scrape shooting a constellation of sparks outward, where dozens landed on the soaked wool. It flared instantly.

Swiftly she nocked the arrow, aimed for the mass of casks, and let loose. It dropped short and burned lazily five yards from the casks.

They lit the second and she drew harder, running the flaming tip almost to her bow hand, and let loose. This one struck between two barrels, and for a moment it looked as though nothing would ignite. But then curls of blue flame crawled in two directions, and suddenly scaled two casks.

They watched, transfixed, as the flames captured two barrels and then a third.

Then she pulled the bow over her shoulder and they began the long retreat to the woods, even as the mounting flame began to throw light.

The naked limbs of the cottonwoods hid them. Skye turned, and saw men boil out of the tents, stare at the flame, and study the darkness. He heard Skittles shouting orders. The men returned to their tents for arms, bloomed into the firelight, and deployed to either side, away from the blinding light.

Skye and Victoria reached the horses, grabbed lead lines, and tugged them hard. The ponies, laden with packs, snorted and clopped through a couple inches of snow, gaining speed, putting distance between them and the great blaze.

But then revolvers cracked. A bullet sang through limbs, clipping wood. The traders had seen something through the trees and were firing, perhaps blindly, but with a soldier's discipline. A ball raked past Skye.

Victoria tugged the ponies, hastening them, pulling them until she was running beside them.

The fire retreated as more and more trees blocked its light from Skye and Victoria. But now the moonlight from the Snowies caught them, and Skye felt naked.

The throaty crack of the Sharps rifles spoke, and he knew some of those murderous bullets were probing clear through the woods.

He glanced at his party: Victoria first, tugging the lines of two ponies. He was second, tugging two more ponies. Jawbone was somewhere near Victoria. The mare was somewhere behind. He could see them all, vaguely, ghostly shapes racing toward safety.

A Sharps cracked, and Skye heard something he dreaded, the thump of a slug smacking horseflesh. But nothing changed. They continued to escape. Rifles cracked. No one followed. But one of his horses was wheezing, its breath labored. The sound was loud and agonizing in the night.

"Victoria, slow," he said.

She slowed. They were out of effective range, and the traders had their hands full with the fire.

Now they would just keep on walking, never stop, walk and walk toward the Musselshell.

Then the laboring horse stumbled, and walked another twenty yards, and slowly capsized. Skye raced to it, and knew at once it was the old mare, the very horse that had carried Victoria, sick and wounded, to safety. The horse that had borne Jawbone.

They halted. Skye ran back, found the mare lying in the light snow, her old head on the ground, her neck stretched backward. There was a hole in her chest, seeping blackness into the pale snow.

Skye fell to his knees, drew his thick hand over her neck, under her mane, even as she died, one last cough and a shudder convulsing her.

Jawbone squealed. He danced around her, nudged her, smelled her nostrils, from which no moist breath emerged.

Skye studied the back trail sharply but saw no one. For the moment the traders had enough to keep them busy. But this light snow left a perfect trace of Skye's passage, and it would not be long before experienced soldiers were after them.

They could not wait.

Skye nodded to Victoria, and they moved ahead, leaving the old mare sprawled in the snow. Jawbone wailed. He stood solidly over the mare, unbudging, loyal, his fierce soul guarding his mother.

Skye could not bear to watch. If Jawbone stayed, that was his right. He and Victoria tugged their ponies into action again and raced southward, wishing for the cloud cover that would shroud them once again. He stared at dark shadows,

at anything that moved or seemed to move. Once they got
their ponies moving, he found his old Hawken, untied it
from the packsaddle, pulled his powder horn over his shoulder, hunted for the small vault of caps and wads, slipped a
cap over the nipple of the Hawken, but still didn't know if
the weapon was charged. It had lain in the traders' wagon
for many days and kept from him.

It was all he had to answer those Sharps rifles carried by
the traders.

They worked over naked slopes, hour after hour, open
country, buffalo country, its dried grasses good fodder even
in winter.

He could not stop. Skittles would follow, on horse, on
foot, whatever it took, so long as there was a trail to follow,
and there was. Skye could do nothing at all about those
prints in the snow, his prints, Victoria's moccasin prints.

At least the cloud cover thickened again, and the Snowy
Mountains slipped from view. A blackness lowered over
them that matched the blackness of his heart.

And then he heard a squeal, the patter of hooves, and Jawbone was walking beside him.

47

With the dawn came spring. As the golden light quickened, so did the warmth. By the time the sun was a finger's width above the horizon, a tender joy was spreading over the northern lands, wiping away snow as if it hadn't existed.

The whole world seemed ready for the warmth, and the chastened snow retreated into small heaps where there were shadows to protect it, and then sank into the pungent earth.

Skye and Victoria plunged southward, tired but dogged after a sleepless night. Something about this day was touching them both. Skye paused, shed his blanket capote, and tied it to one of the packs. He lifted his top hat and let the tendrils of warm air eddy through his hair.

No one followed, and with each passing minute it would be harder to follow, the trail less visible, especially to traders, former army men not well versed in the lore of the wild.

Below stretched the sleepy valley of the Musselshell, basking in the morning. The whole world was quiet. The lightest zephyrs curled over the dried grasses. Skye glanced back again, not wanting surprises, and saw only the peace of a morning on the high plains. Not even a crow soared, not even a hawk hunted.

He led his entourage down a long grade to the river, where

ice jams lined the banks but green grasses were poking up next to the rippling water. Jawbone nipped the grasses, then caught up in little rushes.

A little way east there would be sandstone bluffs, and he welcomed a chance to curl up in one of the innumerable caves wrought in them by wind and rain and frost and sunlight. Victoria was worn, though her step had quickened with the golden light, and he saw joy in her face. Their eyes caught and he knew she was thinking about a rest. It had been a long and perilous night.

They hiked east along the river bottoms until they struck the sandstone bluffs, and Skye pushed them onward a little way more. He saw a good hollow in the south-facing cliff, with green grass below it and a good view in most directions.

He pointed, she nodded, and they struck toward the bluff, climbing slowly, crossing over some talus. The little hollow was like a throne, perched above a wild kingdom. Skye swiftly unloaded the packhorses, turned them loose on grass, picketed one for swift use if needed, and then plucked up his bedroll and stretched it in the warm hollow. He stood there a moment, Victoria beside him, feeling as if he were the lord of all he could see; that this was his dominion and hers, and his kingdom was the most beautiful kingdom ever known.

He was ready for a nap. And when he awoke, he wanted to come to decisions. Victoria lay down on her old robe beside him, curled up, and fell asleep. He sat motionless, feeling the sun heat his buckskins, feeling the warmth caught in the stubble on his cheeks, feeling the sunlight ride his chafed flesh and cleanse it of hurt.

He had his outfit back now: a rifle, a bedroll, some horses, the various tools he needed to survive. It was a poor man's outfit but he believed he was rich. What began in the fall with a surprise Blackfoot raid on a Crow hunting camp had come clear around to this.

He eased back until he was supported by the rear wall of the shallow cave, and he could sit and wait. That struck him as an odd thing, sitting and waiting. Waiting for what? For Mister Skittles and a vengeful pack of traders?

It was quite possible Mister Skittles didn't even know who or what struck him. He and his traders would have seen arrows poking from the whiskey casks, and might well have supposed they had been raided by Indians.

Mister Skittles was a mystery that Skye could not fathom. He and his colleagues had expended enormous energies upon their whiskey trading trip. They had organized and trained a company of men to pillage the plains villages. They had invested heavily in wagons and draft horses, in a uniform of sorts, in weapons, tents, and all the rest. They had welded a deal with the licensed fur and robe companies, the ones more or less abiding by the flat Yank prohibition against the whiskey trade.

Why? So much effort and capital could have won Skittles rewards in any legitimate business. Why this? Skye almost wished the man would show up and submit to questions. Why, sir, have you come a thousand miles from your borders to do this? Why, sir, do you treat the tribes worse than you would treat a mad dog? Why, sir, do you clothe it all in the cloak of civility, courtesy, and your Yank republican virtues, even as you engage in a patently illegal and cruel enterprise?

Skye thought he would never know. That whiskey that burned last night probably cost the company twenty thousand dollars of profit, and meant that their entire enterprise was a failure. They would straggle east, not even covering expenses from the few loads of robes and pelts they had acquired.

Yes, he would like to talk to the Honorable Mister Skittles, for this man had risen out of a young new nation that Skye didn't entirely grasp, and which in some ways repelled him as much as it attracted him. And that reminded him that even now, as his hair was turning gray, he remained a man without a country. More, a man without a people. He felt that old stab of separateness that had tormented him ever since he escaped his virtual imprisonment in the Royal Navy. For he was a man alone and had been alone ever since he set foot in North America.

His mind floated and drifted as he dozed through the middle of the day, his sleep-starved body making what it could of a brief respite halfway up a sandstone bluff.

Then he was awakened. His name was floating upward from below, down in the bottoms of the Musselshell River. Victoria had come alert also, her gaze outward. And yet nothing very threatening loomed. The horses grazed, or stood yawning.

"Mister Skye, sir. May I have a word?"

Skye dared not lift his head for fear that a ball from a rifle trained on him would tear into his skull. But it was clear someone knew he was there, and that someone sounded very like Skittles.

He turned to Victoria. "What can you see?"

"Not a damn thing."

"We're trapped."

"Maybe I can sneak out and get a better look."

Skye shook his head. He found his top hat, stuck it over the barrel of his Hawken, and slowly lifted it until the sun shone plainly on it. He wiggled it a bit. Nothing happened. The half-dozen shots he had anticipated and feared, knowing what a ricochet could do in that cavity, didn't happen.

"Who is it?" Skye asked, making his rifle ready.

"It is Joshua Skittles, sir."

"And what do you want?"

"I wish to talk to you."

"Alone?"

"Entirely alone, Mister Skye. I came alone."

"How did you find us?"

"The horses, sir. They left prints in the mud."

"Why are you here?"

"I'm not sure I know, Mister Skye."

Skye could hardly imagine a conversation with Skittles along these lines, but it was happening.

Skittles picked up where he had left off. "At first we thought Indians had set the whiskey on fire, sir. Arrows. I thought it was Indians until we started out in the melting snow and found your dead mare. So it wasn't Indians, it was Skye. Now this'll surprise you, sir. I sent the men back to camp to wait for help and salvage what they could, and see about getting at least one wagon free. They went back reluctantly and I took our remaining saddle horse and followed you here."

Skye could not imagine it.

"May I come up there and talk? Will you grant me safe passage?"

"While your men do what, Mister Skittles?"

"I am alone, and you have my word and pledge."

Oddly, Skye believed him, and cursed himself for playing the fool.

"Come up with your hands above your head. Leave your horse below."

Victoria found her bow. It was not an easy task to arm a powerful bow while lying down, but soon she achieved her goal, found an arrow, nocked it, and waited.

If ever there was a mystery, Skittles's appearance alone and in a pacific mood was one.

The distance was only fifty yards or so. Skye, lying on his belly, watched Skittles move slowly over talus, his hands held above his head, then up a grassy slope past the horses, and finally large and close.

"Stop," said Skye. "Turn around. Show me your back."

Skittles slowly revolved. There was no weapon, nothing but the back of his shirt. He wore no coat.

"All right, Mister Skittles."

Victoria slid to one side. The trader would have an arrow in him if he tried anything.

But Skittles, his bare hands before him, stepped to the lip of the sandstone cliff cave, and Skye nodded him in.

Skye could not imagine what this was about. "Talk," he barked.

Skittles sat down, carefully staying several feet from Skye, and studied Victoria, who eyed him fiercely.

For a moment the man seemed unable to say anything. He blinked, stared at Skye, and was plainly trying to organize his thoughts, or at least find some way to begin.

"I wish to start my life over," he said.

48

O f all the things that Skittles might have said, that was the least expected. Skye stared at the man.

Skittles said nothing for a moment, plainly struggling for words. Then he startled Skye again.

"It was the dead mare that did it. You were attached to the mare. I don't know why. A wreck of a horse. But there was some sort of bond, and a bullet destroyed it."

Skye nodded. The loss of the mare was an open wound. Skittles had been unwise to bring it up.

"I'm ruined, you know," Skittles said. "You delivered the coup de grace, but I was ruined before you burned the spirits. The mired wagons, the dead teams. Worse, we got word from a courier that one of our wagons loaded with hides tipped over when they were fording a creek, Flat Willow Creek, I believe, and we lost the whole load. I can't pay my men. I can't pay my creditors. We thought to make at least ten dollars on the dollar, and now I'm in debt."

Skye sat, annoyed. He didn't want to hear of the man's troubles. Skittles was a scoundrel, ruining villages with illegal whiskey, demoralizing a whole tribe.

"If I wish to change my life, Mister Skye, it's because you've inspired me." He turned to Victoria. "And you also, madam."

She muttered something under her breath that was an Absaroka version of "Off with his head." Skye smiled slightly.

Skye settled down for an ordeal. It was plain that Skittles would be a bore and the glorious spring day would waste away in a drone of words. He noticed a great disturbance of ravens up the valley a bit, and watched it closely. Something, or someone, was approaching. Victoria noticed it and glanced sharply at Skye.

But Skittles didn't seem to notice. He was caught in his own world. "I started after you at dawn. Of course I had no idea who it was. Arrows stuck from every burning cask. Indians, of course. Indians, burning my spirits. It was a bonfire, all right, Mister Skye. Flames climbed maybe twenty feet at the worst of it, and we couldn't get anywhere near. I told my men to pull our tents back, and pull our supplies away. That was after I ordered them to shoot at any faint movement. I told them not to blind themselves looking at the fire, but to run out to the darkness and then study the world. They did, and they shot your mare."

"You're a military man," Skye said.

"I was. A lieutenant. But there is no future in it."

The horses were alert to whatever was coming down the Musselshell Valley. They all stared, ears forward. Skye was less interested in Skittles than he was in the invader.

"There was no saving those barrels, sir. I ordered my horse saddled. But it was too dark; I couldn't pick up a trace, so I waited until first light, and I started with three men, leaving the rest behind to guard what was left of my outfit."

Skittles had at last settled into a narrative, and was droning along.

Skye saw the cinnamon bear as it worked along the bottoms; no, not cinnamon, but brown, and with the massive hump at its shoulders. A grizzly.

The ravens followed, making a fuss.

Skye pointed. "He's fresh out of his den, hungry, and

mean as a man with a sore tooth. There's not much to eat now."

Skittles stared. "I have not seen one," he said.

The bear was pawing at stumps and deadwood, sniffing the earth, paying attention to nothing but himself. The horses were tugging at their pickets. But Skye thought nothing much would happen. The bear was far below, in the bottoms.

Skittles drew a breath and plunged in. "We found your mare a mile from camp. I knew at once who had come. And I knew why. You were destroying something evil. Something that endangered your, ah, lady's people."

"And other native people," Skye said. Suddenly Skittles was more interesting than the grizzly.

"Yes," Skittles said. "Mister Skye, I saw that mare and I realized you had taken great risks, put yourself in harm's way, to destroy a stock of Indian whiskey. I wondered why. Why would a white man do that? You see, it's all about race. You planned an assault on my camp. Was it vengeance? Hardly. You were doing it for your friends the Crows. I had my men inventory my supplies and found that nothing was stolen. You could have made off with all sorts of valuables.

"So, again, I asked myself, what is this man up to? And again it came to me that you were protecting your Crow friends. And that surprised me. Why would any man, any Englishman, do that? And it came to me that you were acting entirely from altruistic motives. Because spirits are evil, or at least evil to people who have no experience with them and know no restraint. And I realized the Crows were more than your friends; they had become your people and you were defending them against . . . predators. At risk of your life. We are well armed and we are all formerly in the services, and we are well trained to deal with trouble. And I was the predator. Like that bear there, working along the river."

Skye could think of nothing to say to this man.

"So, sir, I stared at your dead mare, and I put it all together, what was taken, what was still in our camp, what your assault had accomplished. It stopped us cold, sir. As long as I had the stock of pure grain spirits, I might yet recoup our losses, but once that burned, I had nothing and the whole trading expedition was a disaster."

The grizzly was now directly below the bluff, and the horses were watching itchily, their withers and flanks twitching as if they were being attacked by horseflies. But the big, hump-shouldered beast paid no heed. It was hunting for anything that lived under rocks and deadwood.

"I stopped at the dead mare, and knew you had suffered. I had the measure of you then, Mister Skye. But that wasn't all. I had the measure of myself. I told my men I would go ahead alone on horse; they were to return and put the camp in order, put up the tents, and wait for further instruction. I came along alone and I found you. I came to tell you, sir, that by your example you have set me upon a new chart."

The grizzly paused, raised up on his hind legs, studied the nervous horses, and dropped to fours again. He shuffled upriver, past Skye's aerie, a menace slowly receding.

"So I came here to tell you that you have changed a life, sir. I will never be the same. I'll have to go back and see to my men. It's my obligation to get them back East unharmed. I can offer them nothing more. The few hides we've gotten to the fur posts won't even cover our expenses, wagons, teams, supplies, all that. But I'm done with this."

Skye listened, a thousand questions whirling through his mind. Who was this man? How did he get involved in a scheme to debauch the Indians of the northern plains? Why was he quitting? Traders routinely suffer disasters; most try again.

"You hungry, Mister Skittles? We have a little pemmican."

"I've been too hungry all my life, sir, so I will decline, with gratitude."

Skye couldn't puzzle that one out, either.

"I'm West Point, 'forty-five. Saw some action in Mexico, stagnated ever since, and resigned my commission last year. There were things afoot. The Indian Bureau's under the army, you know. Some officers, they see the tribes as barriers to western expansion. Some thought that if the buffalo were killed off, the tribes would collapse. They live on buffalo. They need to be turned into farmers. But there's a much simpler way, faster, crueler but more effective, and it fell to me to attempt it on behalf of men who preferred not to be involved, at least openly. But they are not averse to profit.

"It was all for white civilization, sir. Europeans will own the whole world."

Skye sighed. It was coming to this, then. He wondered how Victoria was coping with this.

"Absaroka say we are in the best place in the world," she said. "Not too hot, not too cold. Mountains and lakes for us in the summer, grasslands with lots of buffalo in the winter. But there's too many Piegans and too many Lakota! We have to fight for our place on the breast of the earth."

Skye thought Victoria and Skittles could understand one another.

Skittles smiled thinly. "Madam, perhaps you are right."

Skye wanted to know more. "Who financed this? Who expected a profit?"

"I am not at liberty to say, sir. I am honor bound to keep silent. But I can say this much: this rose out of the army, and required that no active-duty soldier or officer be involved."

Skye hardly knew what to say. "What are your plans, Mister Skittles?"

"I am going east to tell people in power that the Indian Bureau should not be run by the army. I am going to remember your example. You risked your lives, not for any private gain, but for your wife's people. I will bear you in mind as I find my way."

He paused. "Mister Skye. I don't quite know what I'll do. But I have met a man of honor here, a man who sees what must be done for his people, his people of another race but his people, and then he does it at great cost to himself. I don't know how to say that to you. I'll go back to my camp, get my men back East, and then see what I can do to salvage my life. I'm the one who has to look at myself in the looking glass each day. I hope someday I will like what I see. You must like what you see in your glass, sir."

"What I see, Mister Skittles, is a man in need of a shave and improvement."

Skittles stood, eyed the peaceful valley. "I came to tell you this." He turned to Victoria. "I hurt your people. I am sorry. I have no way to repair what was broken, but please convey to Chief Robber my regrets."

Skittles fled.

49

Victoria was grouchy. She was squinting at Skye as if he were an evil spirit. She was stomping around among the horses, making a hash of a beautiful spring day, yanking girths tight, mauling the animals until they laid back their ears. One tried to kick her.

Skye had a guaranteed cure for Victoria's moods. He slipped up beside her and patted her on the rear.

"Go to hell," she retorted.

This was getting serious.

"What is it?" he asked.

She faced him, hands on her hips. "When a bunch of white men talk I don't understand a damned word."

"When a bunch of redskins talk I don't either," he retorted.

"Skye, dammit, what was that all about?"

He found a sun-warmed yellow rock, dug into a parfleche, and extracted some pemmican wrapped in greasy leather. He cut off a slice and handed the piece to her.

"Skittles was doing something he knew, at bottom, he shouldn't be doing. And we inspired him to quit."

She nibbled at the pemmican, squinting at him as if he were on trial.

"The Yanks back East, you've seen them, think they own

the whole world. This land, anyway, from one sea to the other. It belongs to them, not to native people. They keep pushing west. Settlement, they call it. They start farms, plant crops, drive off the Indians, and take over."

"Well, Skye, I'd like to drive the Lakota into the ocean. So I got that, all right."

"It's not the same. The white men, sort of cousins of my English people, think they own this land. And think they're smart and wise and the world belongs to them. But the tribes stand in the way. Especially these tribes, living off buffalo, well armed, with more fighting men than two or three of their bluecoat armies put together. So the officers, the chiefs, have ideas. How can they get rid of the Indians? They could maybe kill the buffalo and make the tribes start planting crops. They talk about that. But there's an easier way. Bring spirits out here, ruin your people, and get rich ruining them, by getting their robes and hides for almost nothing. You following me?"

"Sonsofbitches," she said.

"It's illegal. The Fathers in the capital, Washington, say they can't do that. Treat the tribes right, at least in theory. Give them credit for that."

"Theory?"

"The laws are intended to protect the native people. But they can be evaded."

"Protect us? Why the hell would they do that? Give me a Blackfoot and I'll make a slave out of her. In fact, Skye, I'm tired of doing all your work."

"How about another wife?"

"Hell yes. Three wives. You're a lot of work. Chief Robber, he's got four."

Victoria smiled, her first smile of the hour. She nibbled the fatty pemmican and stared at the serene valley. "I will hold you to it," she said.

"Their army checks the steamboats coming up the river for spirits. No spirits are allowed. They are quite strict about it. But they can't control spirits going out the trails, the Santa Fe Trail, and now the Oregon Trail. That was Skittles's chance. He resigned from the army, made an agreement with the fur companies, and took spirits into the villages. You know the rest."

She stared at him stonily, and he knew she wasn't liking this at all.

"Why did he come here, then?"

Skye knew he had to try. "To thank me. He saw me trying my best to defend the Absarokas, to keep them from destroying themselves."

"Why did he talk like that? Mister this, Mister that?"

"His way of being civilized. His way of saying to the Indians, you're savages."

"Well, sonofabitch! I should put a savage arrow into his civilized ass. I should tie him up and peel a little flesh off him."

"I want to go back to your village and tell The Robber that we burnt the barrels of spirits. And that Skittles won't be back."

"Yeah? Why won't he?"

"He had a change of heart. Here's the thing about that man. He is a man of honor. And he couldn't stand what he was doing."

"You white people are crazy, Skye."

"Let's get going. It's a good day."

She walked in circles, round and round. He had never seen her circle around like that.

"You're one hell of a chief, Skye. You sent them back to where they came from with new ideas."

"Skittles has very old ideas, but now he is listening to them."

She homed in on him, stood before him. "You're one hell of a chief, Skye. You help the Absaroka people. You make Skittles different.

"Let's go back to my people. You don't talk. Maybe they

need to listen to me. I'm going to talk. You just stand there and let me tell them."

"I think that is a good idea," he said.

They bounded through a glorious spring afternoon, with the moist earth scenting the air, and a warm sun pummeling their buckskins. They plunged down the valley of the Musselshell, and Skye kept a sharp eye out for Old Ephraim, but the grizzly had vanished, probably for a siesta in the benevolent sunlight.

Jawbone alternated between leading the caravan and sliding to the rear, the tug of his dead mother sometimes capturing his brave heart. But he was doing more; he was acting as a vedette, prowling the country fore and aft and to both sides. The colt was made for war.

Late that day Skye and Victoria approached The Robber's winter camp, but something wasn't right. No one was outside the village. No village police were prowling. No women were collecting firewood. The village stood defenseless. Skye walked uneasily, fearful that some new disaster had befallen Victoria's people. But when they at last rounded a river bend and discovered the village in place, wisps of smoke rising from lodge fires, and people huddled about, there seemed to be some shred of normalcy. Maybe the men were out hunting.

"Damn," Victoria said.

She trotted ahead, dragging her packhorses, heading for her brother's lodge. Skye followed, his eye sharp upon the half-empty village. Victoria reached Two Dogs' lodge and scratched politely. In a moment Parts Her Hair opened. She had a bloody bandage wrapped about her hand, and Skye knew at once what had happened. She had cut off a finger.

He got the whole story later. Two Dogs was dead and buried, along with three others of the village. Chief Robber still lay abed, deathly sick. Something evil in the traders' whiskey had felled them. Instead of getting up the next day, they lay quiet and sweated and cold and sick, and gradually slipped into the spirit place where they might walk the path to the stars.

The village was sick. Its leaders were sick or dead. It lay helpless. No one did the daily work. No village police patrolled the area. In some cottonwoods close to the river, there were four burial scaffolds, each with a blanket-wrapped victim of the traders' whiskey.

Bug powder.

Skye knew of it. Experienced traders added a pinch just to make the Indians crazy. These inexperienced soldier-traders added more than a pinch. And the result was murder. A horrible death. For strychnine produces convulsions, nausea, paroxysms, inability to breathe, wave after wave until the victim gives up and dies. One more crime laid at Skittles's feet. The man might repent, but could never redeem himself.

Victoria fell into the arms of her sisters-in-law and wailed. Skye stood helplessly just inside the lodge door, and finally slipped out into the warm twilight. Knots of people stared. Maybe they were blaming him, or his medicine colt, or all white men for this. He could only stand and wait for what was to come, a stranger in a strange land.

He heard his name, turned, and found Walks to the Top, wrapped in an ancient blanket, summoning him. He followed the proud old Tobacco Planter to the seer's small lodge, and entered, swiftly sitting cross-legged before the dour old man.

"All this I saw," Walks to the Top said. "All this evil. And I saw the rest."

Skye wondered what that might be.

"The whiskey traders are leaving and will not come back. And this is because you destroyed the whiskey. And you did it for my people."

"Yes, sir, that is so."

"Then you will lead us. This I saw too."

50

Lead this band? Skye recoiled from that. "I am not one of your people," he said to the elder, hoping his limited Crow tongue sufficed to make his views known.

"You must lead us. I have seen it."

"I do not know your customs."

"There is no one else."

Walks to the Top stood before him, flinty, adamant, determined, his gaze boring into Skye.

Skye hesitated. This thing was not unknown. His friend from the trapper days, Jim Beckwourth, had been a subchief. Others had lived with the Crows. Still, it didn't seem right. And he had no honors at war. There were men in this village, the headman Otter, for instance, who had counted many coups, won much praise.

"Many in this band would oppose it," he said.

"What band?" The old seer swept his gnarled hand imperiously. "What do you see? Nothing but ruin."

Skye saw a village that looked half dead. On a vibrant spring day this village should be teeming with life and joy.

But the task of restoring it should not be Skye's.

"I must be with Many Quill Woman now," he said. "She grieves her brother, and so do I."

"And let my people be naked before the world?"

Skye retreated a bit. "I will help put things in good order," he said.

Walks to the Top nodded curtly and walked away.

Skye beheld a mournful place, deep in grief, rudderless, in peril. There were always Blackfeet prowling, especially now that one could move over the land.

He glanced at Two Dogs' lodge, and saw no one. Victoria was within, and so were Two Dogs' wives and family, and the flap was closed to the world.

Many of the lodges were closed to the world. No one hunted. No one patrolled. No one gathered wood. Old people did not sit in the sun and smile.

It could not be right, he becoming a subchief. It was not real. To be sure, he had been adopted long ago by Rotten Belly, and that made him a Crow after a fashion.

He stood in the quiet, and decided the first step was to visit The Robber. He was silently welcomed and invited in by one of the chief's wives, and found the chief sitting in a reed backrest, a blanket about his legs. The chief looked unwell, a grayness just beneath his coppery flesh. Two of his wives lay quietly in their robes, staring at him. Two others were ministering to them all, and seemed well enough.

"The Seer said you would come, Mister Skye. Have a seat beside me. Smoke the pipe if you wish. There's the pouch."

That was bad. The chief was not preparing the tobacco himself.

Skye slowly filled a pipe and lit it with coals. "How can I help you?" he asked, after sucking the fragrant smoke and exhaling it.

"I do not wish to do anything. When the sun is warm, I will sit in front of my lodge and greet the world."

"Are you unwell?"

The chief pursed his lips, and nodded.

"Was it the traders' whiskey?"

"It ate the heart out of me, with little teeth like a mink's that devoured my flesh."

"You'll get better," Skye said. "It will pass."

"I want only to sit in front of my lodge on a warm day and watch the People."

"Who will lead them?"

"You will. The Seer has seen it."

"I am not a warrior. I don't know your ways."

"It is done," the chief said, sharply.

Skye finished his pipe in silence, thanked the chief for his hospitality, and left that unhappy lodge. There was one other thing he must do.

He found Otter, the headman who had suffered so much loss on the hunting trip. Otter was unsmiling. "I knew you would come. The Seer told me."

"Then I need say only one thing: you should lead the band now. It is yours."

"It is not my medicine, Mister Skye."

Skye saw how this would go. "It will be soon. I will try to help this band but only for a little time. Then you will be its chief."

Otter smiled. "You are the right one. I will help. I will hunt. It is in me that we will have a great hunt and soon there will be more robes and plenty of meat."

So it was done.

Skye said, "Come with me. I want the young men to police the village and protect it. I want a night herder to watch over the horses. I want young men out, watching, the eyes and ears of this band."

"They will hear you," Otter said.

"I have one more thing to do. Many Quill Woman must decide."

"Her?"

"She is one of you."

"It is so," Otter said.

Skye found her sitting quietly within her brother's lodge,

and beckoned her. She stepped outside, into a somber spring evening.

"They want me to lead them," he said. "Is that right?"

"Goddammit, Skye, if you don't kick them in the ass, no one will!"

and beckoned him. She stepped outside into a sudden spring evening.

"They want me to lead them," he said. "Is that right?"

"You thought so or you don't know I am in the ... no one will."